WITHOUT FAIL

Also by Lee Child

KILLING FLOOR
DIE TRYING
TRIPWIRE
THE VISITOR
ECHO BURNING

WITHOUT FAIL

LEE CHILD

LONDON NEW YORK SYDNEY TORONTO

This edition published 2002
by BCA
by arrangement with Bantam Press
a division of Transworld Publishers

The Random House Group Ltd

CN 104626

First reprint 2002

Typeset in Century Old Style by
Kestrel Data, Exeter, Devon.

Printed and bound in Germany by
GGP Media, Pössneck

This one is for my brother Richard in Gloucester, England; my brother David in Brecon, Wales; my brother Andrew in Sheffield, England; and my friend Jack Hutcheson in Penicuik, Scotland.

WITHOUT FAIL

ONE

THEY FOUND OUT ABOUT HIM IN JULY AND STAYED ANGRY ALL through August. They tried to kill him in September. It was way too soon. They weren't ready. The attempt was a failure. It could have been a disaster, but it was actually a miracle. *Because nobody noticed.*

They used their usual method to get past security and set up a hundred feet from where he was speaking. They used a silencer and missed him by an inch. The bullet must have passed right over his head. Maybe even *through his hair*, because he immediately raised his hand and patted it back into place as if a gust of wind had disturbed it. They saw it over and over again, afterwards, on television. He raised his hand and patted his hair. He did nothing else. He just kept on with his speech, unaware, because by definition a silenced bullet is too fast to see and too quiet to hear. So it missed him and flew on. It missed everybody standing behind him. It struck no obstacles, hit no buildings. It flew on straight and true until its energy was spent and gravity hauled it to earth in the far distance where there was nothing except empty grassland. There was no response. No reaction. *Nobody noticed.* It was like the bullet had never been fired at all. They didn't fire again. They were too shaken up.

So, a failure, but a miracle. And a lesson. They spent October acting like the professionals they were, starting over, calming down, thinking, learning, preparing for their second attempt. It would be a better attempt, carefully planned and properly executed, built around technique and nuance and sophistication, and enhanced by unholy fear. A worthy attempt. A *creative* attempt. Above all, an attempt that wouldn't fail.

Then November came, and the rules changed completely.

Reacher's cup was empty but still warm. He lifted it off the saucer and tilted it and watched the sludge in the bottom flow towards him, slow and brown, like river silt.

'When does it need to be done?' he asked.

'As soon as possible,' she said.

He nodded. Slid out of the booth and stood up.

'I'll call you in ten days,' he said.

'With a decision?'

He shook his head. 'To tell you how it went.'

'I'll *know* how it went.'

'OK, to tell you where to send my money.'

She closed her eyes and smiled. He glanced down at her.

'You thought I'd refuse?' he said.

She opened her eyes. 'I thought you might be a little harder to persuade.'

He shrugged. 'Like Joe told you, I'm a sucker for a challenge. Joe was usually right about things like that. He was usually right about a lot of things.'

'Now I don't know what to say, except thank you.'

He didn't reply. Just started to move away, but she stood up right next to him and kept him where he was. There was an awkward pause. They stood for a second face to face, trapped by the table. She put out her hand and he shook it. She held on a fraction too long, and then she stretched up tall and kissed him on the cheek. Her lips were soft. Their touch burned him like a tiny voltage.

'A handshake isn't enough,' she said. 'You're going to do it for us.' Then she paused. 'And you were nearly my brother-in-law.'

He said nothing. Just nodded and shuffled out from behind the table and glanced back once. Then he headed up the stairs and out to the street. Her perfume was on his hand. He walked around to the cabaret lounge and left a note for his friends in their dressing room. Then he headed out to the highway, with ten whole days to find a way to kill the fourth-best-protected person on the planet.

It had started eight hours earlier, like this: team leader M. E. Froelich came to work on that Monday morning, thirteen days after the election, an hour before the second strategy meeting, seven days after the word *assassination* had first been used, and made her final decision. She set off in search of her immediate superior and found him in the secretarial pen outside his office, clearly on his way to somewhere else, clearly in a hurry. He had a file under his arm and a definite *stay back* expression on his face. But she took a deep breath and made it clear that she needed to talk right then. Urgently. And off the record and in private, obviously. So he paused a moment and turned abruptly and went back inside his office. He let her step in after him and closed the door behind her, softly enough to make the unscheduled meeting feel a little conspiratorial, but firmly enough to leave her in no doubt he was annoyed about the interruption to his routine. It was just the click of a door latch, but it was also an unmistakable message, parsed exactly in the language of office hierarchies everywhere: *you better not be wasting my time with this.*

He was a twenty-five-year veteran well into his final lap before retirement, well into his middle fifties, the last echo of the old days. He was still tall, still fairly lean and athletic, but greying fast and softening in some of the wrong places. His name was Stuyvesant. Like the last Director-General of New Amsterdam, he would say when the spelling was questioned. Then, acknowledging the modern world, he would say: like the cigarette. He wore Brooks Brothers every day of his life without exception, but he was considered capable of flexibility in his tactics. Best of all, he had never failed. Not ever, and he had been around a long time, with more than his fair share of difficulties. But there had been no failures, and no bad luck, either. Therefore, in the merciless calculus of organizations everywhere, he was considered a good guy to work for.

'You look a little nervous,' he said.

'I am, a little,' Froelich said back.

His office was small, and quiet, and sparsely furnished, and very clean. The walls were painted bright white and lit with halogen. There was a window, with white vertical blinds half closed against grey weather outside.

'Why are you nervous?' he asked.

'I need to ask your permission.'

'For what?'

'For something I want to try,' she said. She was twenty years younger than Stuyvesant, exactly thirty-five. Tall rather than short, but not excessively. Maybe only an inch or two over the average for American women of her generation, but the kind of intelligence and energy and vitality she radiated took the word *medium* right out of the equation. She was halfway between lithe and muscular, with a bright glow in her skin and her eyes that made her look like an athlete. Her hair was short and fair and casually unkempt. She gave the impression of having hurriedly stepped into her street clothes after showering quickly after winning a gold medal at the Olympics by playing a crucial role in some kind of team sport. Like it was no big deal, like she wanted to get out of the stadium before the television interviewers got through with her team mates and started in on her. She looked like a very competent person, but a very modest one.

'What kind of something?' Stuyvesant asked. He turned and placed the file he was carrying on his desk. His desk was large, topped with a slab of grey composite. High-end modern office furniture, obsessively cleaned and polished like an antique. He was famous for always keeping his desktop clear of paperwork and completely empty. The habit created an air of extreme efficiency.

'I want an outsider to do it,' Froelich said.

Stuyvesant squared the file on the desk corner and ran his fingers along the spine and the adjacent edge, like he was checking the angle was exact.

'You think that's a good idea?' he asked.

Froelich said nothing.

'I suppose you've got somebody in mind?' he asked.

'An excellent prospect.'

'Who?'

Froelich shook her head. 'You should stay outside the loop,' she said. 'Better that way.'

'Was he recommended?'

'Or she.'

Stuyvesant nodded. *The modern world.* 'Was the person you have in mind recommended?'

'Yes, by an excellent source.'

'In-house?'

'Yes,' Froelich said again.

'So we're already in the loop.'

'No, the source isn't in-house any more.'

Stuyvesant turned again and moved his file parallel to the long edge of the desk. Then back again parallel with the short edge.

'Let me play devil's advocate,' he said. 'I promoted you four months ago. Four months is a long time. Choosing to bring in an outsider *now* might be seen to betray a certain lack of self-confidence, mightn't it? Wouldn't you say?'

'I can't worry about that.'

'Maybe you should,' Stuyvesant said. 'This could hurt you. There were six guys who wanted your job. So if you do this and it leaks, then you've got real problems. You've got half a dozen vultures muttering *told you so* the whole rest of your career. Because you started second-guessing your own abilities.'

'Thing like this, I *need* to second-guess myself. I think.'

'You think?'

'No, I know. I don't see an alternative.'

Stuyvesant said nothing.

'I'm not happy about it,' Froelich said. 'Believe me. But I think it's got to be done. And that's my judgement call.'

The office went quiet. Stuyvesant said nothing.

'So will you authorize it?' Froelich asked.

Stuyvesant shrugged. 'You shouldn't be asking. You should have just gone ahead and done it regardless.'

'Not my way,' Froelich said.

'So don't tell anybody else. And don't put anything on paper.'

'I wouldn't anyway. It would compromise effectiveness.'

Stuyvesant nodded vaguely. Then, like the good bureaucrat he had become, he arrived at the most important question of all.

'How much would this person cost?' he asked.

'Not much,' Froelich said. 'Maybe nothing at all. Maybe expenses only. We've got some history together. Theoretically. Of a sort.'

'This could stall your career. No more promotions.'

'The alternative would *finish* my career.'

'You were my choice,' Stuyvesant said. 'I picked you. Therefore anything that damages you damages me, too.'

'I understand that, sir.'

'So take a deep breath and count to ten. Then tell me that it's really necessary.'

Froelich nodded, and took a breath and kept quiet, ten or eleven seconds.

'It's really necessary,' she said.

Stuyvesant picked up his file.

'OK, do it,' he said.

She started immediately after the strategy meeting, suddenly aware that *doing it* was the hard part. Asking for permission had seemed like such a hurdle that she had characterized it in her mind as the most difficult stage of the whole project. But now it felt like nothing at all compared with actually hunting down her target. All she had was a last name and a sketchy biography that might or might not have been accurate and up to date eight years ago. If she even remembered the details correctly. They had been mentioned casually, playfully, late one night, by her lover, part of some drowsy pillow talk. She couldn't even be sure she had been paying full attention. So she decided not to rely on the details. She would rely solely on the name itself.

She wrote it in large capital letters at the top of a sheet of yellow paper. It brought back a lot of memories. Some bad, most good. She stared at it for a long moment, and then she crossed it out and wrote *UNSUB* instead. That would help her concentration, because it made the whole thing impersonal. It put her mind in a groove, took her right back to basic training. An *unknown subject* was somebody to be identified and located. That was all, nothing more and nothing less.

Her main operational advantage was computer power. She had more access to more databases than the average citizen gets. *UNSUB* was military, she knew that for sure, so she went to the National Personnel Records Center's database. It was compiled in St Louis, Missouri, and listed literally every man or woman who had served in a U.S. military uniform, anywhere, ever. She typed in the last name and waited and the enquiry software came back with just three short responses. One she eliminated immediately, by given name. *I know for sure it's not him, don't I?* Another she eliminated by date of birth. *A whole generation too old.* So the third had to be *UNSUB*. No other possibility. She stared at the full name for a second and copied the date of birth and the Social Security number onto her yellow paper. Then she hit the icon for *details* and entered her password. The screen redrew and came up with an abbreviated career summary.

Bad news. UNSUB wasn't military any more. The career summary dead-ended five whole years ago with an honourable discharge after thirteen years of service. Final rank was major. There were medals listed, including a Silver Star and a Purple Heart. She read the citations and wrote down the details and drew a line across the yellow paper to signify the end of one era and the start of another. Then she ploughed on.

Next logical step was to look at Social Security's Master Death Index. *Basic training.* No point trying to chase down somebody who was already dead. She entered the number and realized she was holding her breath. But the enquiry came back blank. *UNSUB* was still alive, as far as the government knew. Next step was to check in with the National Crime Information Center. *Basic training again.* No point trying to sign up somebody who was serving time in prison, for instance, not that she thought it was remotely likely, not in *UNSUB*'s case. But you never knew. There was a fine line, with some personality types. The NCIC database was always slow, so she shoved drifts of accumulated paperwork into drawers and then left her desk and refilled her coffee cup. Strolled back to find a negative arrest-or-conviction record waiting on her screen. Plus a short note to say *UNSUB* had an FBI file somewhere in their records. *Interesting.* She closed NCIC and went straight to the FBI's database. She found the file and couldn't open it. But she knew enough about the Bureau's classification system to be able to decode the header flags. It was a simple narrative file, inactive. Nothing more. *UNSUB* wasn't a fugitive, wasn't wanted for anything, wasn't currently in trouble.

She wrote it all down, and then clicked her way into the nationwide DMV database. *Bad news again. UNSUB* didn't have a driving licence. *Which was very weird. And which was a very big pain in the butt.* Because no driving licence meant no current photograph and no current address listing. She clicked her way into the Veterans' Administration computer in Chicago. Searched by name, rank, and number. The enquiries came up blank. *UNSUB* wasn't receiving federal benefits and hadn't offered a forwarding address. *Why not? Where the hell are you?* She went back into Social Security and asked for contributions records. There weren't any. *UNSUB* hadn't been employed since leaving the military, at least not legally. She tried the IRS for confirmation. Same story. *UNSUB* hadn't paid taxes in five years. Hadn't even filed.

OK, so let's get serious. She hitched straighter in her chair and quit the government sites and fired up some illicit software that took her straight into the banking industry's private world. Strictly speaking she shouldn't be using it for this purpose. Or for any purpose. It was an obvious breach of official protocol. But she didn't expect to get any comeback. And she did expect to get a result. If *UNSUB* had even a single bank account anywhere in the fifty states, it would show up. Even a humble little current account. Even an empty or abandoned account. Plenty of people got by without bank accounts, she knew that, but she felt in her gut *UNSUB* wouldn't be one of them. Not somebody who had been a U.S. Army major. With medals.

She entered the Social Security number twice, once in the SSN field and once in the taxpayer ID field. She entered the name. She hit *search*.

One hundred and eighty miles away, Jack Reacher shivered. Atlantic City in the middle of November wasn't the warmest spot on earth. Not by any measure. The wind came in off the ocean carrying enough salt to keep everything permanently damp and clammy. It whipped and gusted and blew trash around and flattened his pants against his legs. Five days ago he had been in Los Angeles, and he was pretty sure he should have stayed there. Now he was pretty sure he should go back. Southern California was a very attractive place in November. The air was warm down there, and the ocean breezes were soft balmy caresses instead of endless lashing fusillades of stinging salt cold. He should go back there. He should go *somewhere*, that was for damn sure.

Or maybe he should stick around like he'd been asked to, and buy a coat.

He had come back east with an old black woman and her brother. He had been hitching rides east out of L.A. in order to take a one-day look at the Mojave desert. The old couple had picked him up in an ancient Buick Roadmaster. He saw a microphone and a primitive PA system and a boxed Yamaha keyboard among the suitcases in the load space and the old lady told him she was a singer heading for a short residency all the way over in Atlantic City. Told him her brother accompanied her on the keyboard and drove the car, but he wasn't much of a talker any more, and he wasn't much of a driver any more, and the Roadmaster wasn't much of a car any more. It was all true. The old guy was completely silent and they were all in mortal danger several times inside the first five miles. The old lady started singing to calm herself. She gave it a few bars of Dawn Penn's *You Don't Love Me* and Reacher immediately decided to go all the way east with her just to hear more. He offered to take over the driving chores. She kept on singing. She had the kind of sweet smoky voice that should have made her a blues superstar long ago, except she was probably in the wrong place too many times and it had never happened for her. The old car had failed power steering to wrestle with and all kinds of ticks and rattles and whines under the hammer-heavy V-8 beat and at about fifty miles an hour the noises all came together and sounded like a backing track. The radio was weak and picked up an endless succession of local AM stations for about twenty minutes each. The old woman sang along with them and the old guy kept completely quiet and slept most of the way on the back seat. Reacher drove eighteen hours a day for three solid days, and arrived in New Jersey feeling like he'd been on vacation.

The residency was at a fifth-rate lounge eight blocks from the boardwalk, and the manager wasn't the kind of guy you would necessarily trust to respect a contract. So Reacher made it his business to count the customers and keep a running total of the cash that should show up in the pay envelope at the end of the week. He made it very obvious and watched the manager grow more and more resentful about it. The guy took to making short cryptic phone calls with his hand shielding the receiver and his eyes locked on Reacher's face. Reacher looked straight back at him with a wintry smile and an unblinking gaze and stayed put. He sat through all three sets two weekend nights running, but then he started to get restless. And cold. So on the Monday morning he was about to change his mind and get back on the road when the old keyboard player walked him back from breakfast and finally broke his silence.

'I want to ask you to stick around,' he said. He pronounced it *wanna ax*, and there was some kind of hope in the rheumy old eyes. Reacher didn't answer.

'You don't stick around, that manager's going to stiff us for sure,' the old guy said, like getting stiffed for money was something that just happened to musicians, like flat tyres and head colds. 'But we get paid, we got gas money to head up to New York, maybe get us a gig from B. B. King in Times Square, resurrect our careers. Guy like you could make a big difference in that department, count on it.'

Reacher said nothing.

'Of course, I can see you being worried,' the old guy said. 'Management like that, bound to be some unsavoury characters lurking in the background.'

Reacher smiled at the subtlety.

'What are you, anyway?' the old guy asked. 'Some kind of a boxer?'

'No,' Reacher said. 'No kind of a boxer.'

'Wrestler?' the old guy asked. He said it *wrassler*. 'Like on cable television?'

'No.'

'You're big enough, that's for damn sure,' the old guy said. 'Plenty big enough to help us out, if you wanted to.'

He said it *he'p*. No front teeth. Reacher said nothing.

'What are you, anyway?' the old guy asked again.

'I was a military cop,' Reacher said. 'In the army, thirteen years.'

'You quit?'

'As near as makes no difference.'

'No jobs for you folks afterwards?'

'None that I want,' Reacher said.

'You live in L.A.?'

'I don't live anywhere,' Reacher said. 'I move around.'

'So road folk should stick together,' the old guy said. 'Simple as that. Help each other. Keep it a mutual thing.'

He'p each other.

'It's very cold here,' Reacher said.

'That's for damn sure,' the old guy said. 'But you could buy a coat.'

So he was on a windswept corner with the sea gale flattening his pants against his legs, making a final decision. *The highway, or a coat store?* He ran a brief fantasy through his head, La Jolla maybe, a cheap room, warm nights, bright stars, cold beer. Then: the old woman at B. B. King's new club in New York, some retro-obsessed young A&R man stops by, gives her a contract, she makes a CD, she gets a national tour, a sidebar in *Rolling Stone*, fame, money, a new house. *A new car.* He turned his back on the highway and hunched against the wind and walked east in search of a clothing store.

On that particular Monday there were nearly twelve thousand FDIC-insured banking organizations licensed and operating inside the United States and between them they carried over a thousand million separate accounts, but only one of them was listed against *UNSUB*'s name and Social Security number. It was a simple current account held at a branch of a regional bank in Arlington, Virginia. M. E. Froelich stared at the branch's business address in surprise. *That's less than four miles from where I'm sitting right now.* She copied the details onto her yellow paper. Picked up her phone and called a senior colleague on the other side of the organization and asked him to contact the bank in question for all the details he could get. Especially a home address. She asked him to be absolutely as fast as possible, but discreet, too. And completely off the record. Then she hung up and waited, anxious and frustrated about being temporarily hands-off. Problem was, the other side of the organization could ask banks discreet questions quite easily, whereas for Froelich to do so herself would be regarded as very odd indeed.

Reacher found a discount store three blocks nearer the ocean and ducked inside. It was narrow but ran back into the building a couple of hundred feet. There were fluorescent tubes all over the ceiling and racks of garments stretching as far as the eye could see. Seemed to be women's stuff on the left, children's in the centre, and men's on the right. He started in the far back corner and worked forward.

There were all kinds of coats commercially available, that was for damn sure. The first two rails had short padded jackets. *No good.* He went by something an old army buddy had told him: *a good coat is like a good lawyer. It covers your ass.* The third rail was more promising. It had neutral-coloured thigh-length canvas coats made bulky by thick flannel linings. Maybe there was some wool in there. Maybe some other stuff, too. They certainly felt heavy enough.

'Can I help you?'

He turned round and saw a young woman standing right behind him.

'Are these coats good for the weather up here?' he asked.

'They're perfect,' the woman said. She was very animated. She told him all about some kind of special stuff sprayed on the canvas to repel moisture. She told him all about the insulation inside. She promised it would keep him warm right down to a sub-zero temperature. He ran his hand down the rail and pulled out a dark olive XXL.

'OK, I'll take this one,' he said.

'You don't want to try it on?'

He paused and then shrugged into it. It fitted pretty well.

Nearly. Maybe it was a little tight across the shoulders. The sleeves were maybe an inch too short.

'You need the 3XLT,' the woman said. 'What are you, a fifty?'

'A fifty what?'

'Chest.'

'No idea. I never measured it.'

'Height about six-five?'

'I guess,' he said.

'Weight?'

'Two-forty,' he said. 'Maybe two-fifty.'

'So you definitely need the big-and-tall fitting,' she said. 'Try the 3XLT.'

The 3XLT she handed him was the same dull colour as the XXL he had picked. It fitted much better. A little roomy, which he liked. And the sleeves were right.

'You OK for pants?' the woman called. She had ducked away to another rail and was flicking through heavy canvas work pants, glancing at his waist and the length of his legs. She came out with a pair that matched one of the colours in the flannel lining inside the coat. 'And try these shirts,' she said. She jumped over to another rail and showed him a rainbow of flannel shirts. 'Put a T-shirt underneath it and you're all set. Which colour do you like?'

'Something dull,' he said.

She laid everything out on top of one of the rails. The coat, the pants, the shirt, a T-shirt. They looked pretty good together, muddy olives and khakis.

'OK?' she said brightly.

'OK,' he said. 'You got underwear too?'

'Over here,' she said.

He rooted through a bin of reject-quality boxers and selected a pair in white. Then a pair of socks, mostly cotton, flecked with all kinds of organic colours.

'OK?' the woman said again. He nodded and she led him to the register at the front of the store and bleeped all the tags under the little red light.

'One hundred and eighty-nine dollars even,' she said.

He stared at the red figures on the register's display. 'I thought this was a discount store,' he said.

'That's incredibly reasonable, really,' she said. He shook his head and dug into his pocket and came out with a wad of crumpled bills. Counted out a hundred and ninety. The dollar change she gave him left him with four bucks in his hand.

The senior colleague from the other side of the organization called Froelich back within twenty-five minutes.

'You get a home address?' she asked him.

'One hundred Washington Boulevard,' the guy said. 'Arlington, Virginia. Zip code is 20310-1500.'

Froelich wrote it down. 'OK, thanks. I guess that's all I need.'

'I think you might need a little more.'

'Why?'

'You know Washington Boulevard?'

Froelich paused. 'Runs up to the Memorial Bridge, right?'

'It's just a highway.'

'No buildings? Got to be buildings.'

'There is *one* building. Pretty big one. Couple hundred yards off the east shoulder.'

'What?'

'The Pentagon,' the guy said. 'This is a phony address, Froelich. One side of Washington Boulevard is Arlington Cemetery and the other side is the Pentagon. That's it. Nothing else. There's no number one hundred. There are no private mailing addresses at all. I checked with the Postal Service. And that zip code is the Department of the Army, inside the Pentagon.'

'Great,' Froelich said. 'You tell the bank?'

'Of course not. You told me to be discreet.'

'Thanks. But I'm back at square one.'

'Maybe not. This is a bizarre set-up, Froelich. Six-figure balance, but it's all just stuck in a current account, earning nothing. And the customer accesses it via Western Union only. Never comes in. It's a phone arrangement. Customer calls in with a password, the bank wires cash through Western Union, wherever.'

'No ATM card?'

'No cards at all. No cheque book was ever issued, either.'

'Western Union *only*? I never heard of that before. Are there any records?'

'Geographically, all over the place, literally. Forty states and counting in five years. Occasional deposits and plenty of nickel-and-dime withdrawals, all of them to Western Union offices in the boonies, in the cities, everywhere.'

'Bizarre.'

'Like I said.'

'Anything you can do?'

'Already done it. They're going to call me next time the customer calls them.'

'And then you're going to call me?'

'I might.'

'Is there a frequency pattern?'

'It varies. Maximum interval recently has been a few weeks. Sometimes it's every few days. Mondays are popular. Banks are closed on the weekend.'

'So I could get lucky today.'

'Sure you could,' the guy said. 'Question is, am I going to get lucky too?'

'Not that lucky,' Froelich said.

The lounge manager watched Reacher step into his motel lobby. Then he ducked back into a windy side street and fired up his cell phone. Cupped his hand round it and spoke low and urgently, and convincingly, but respectfully, as was required.

'Because he's dissing me,' he said, in answer to a question.

'Today would be good,' he said, in answer to another.

'Two at least,' he said, in answer to the final question. 'This is a big guy.'

Reacher changed one of his four dollars for quarters at the motel desk and headed for the pay phone. Dialled his bank from memory and gave his password and arranged for five hundred bucks to be wired to Western Union in Atlantic City by close of business. Then he went to his room and bit off all the tags and put his new clothes on. Transferred all his pocket junk across and threw his summer gear in the trash and looked himself over in the long mirror behind the closet door. *Grow a beard and get some sunglasses and I could walk all the way to the North Pole*, he thought.

* * *

Froelich heard about the proposed wire transfer eleven minutes later. Closed her eyes for a second and clenched her hands in triumph and then reached behind her and pulled a map of the eastern seaboard off a shelf. *Maybe three hours if the traffic co-operates. I might just make it.* She grabbed her jacket and her purse and ran down to the garage.

Reacher wasted an hour in his room and then went out to test the insulating properties of his new coat. *Field trial*, they used to call it, way back when. He headed east towards the ocean, into the wind. Felt rather than saw somebody behind him. Just a characteristic little burr down in the small of his back. He slowed up and used a store window for a mirror. Caught a glimpse of movement fifty yards back. Too far away for details.

He walked on. The coat was pretty good, but he should have bought a hat to go with it. That was clear. The same buddy with the opinion on coats used to claim that half of total heat loss was through the top of the head, and that was certainly how it felt. The cold was blowing through his hair and making his eyes water. A military-issue watch cap would have been valuable, in November on the Jersey shore. He made a mental note to keep an eye out for surplus stores on his way back from the Western Union office. In his experience they often inhabited the same neighbourhoods.

He reached the boardwalk and walked south, with the same itch still there in the small of his back. He turned suddenly and saw nothing. Walked back north to where he had started. The boards under his feet were in good shape. There was a notice claiming they were made from some special hardwood, the hardest timber the world's forests had to offer. The feeling was still there in the small of his back. He turned and led his invisible shadows out onto the Central Pier. It was the original structure, preserved. It looked like he guessed it must have way back when it was built. It was deserted, which was no surprise considering the weather, and added to the feeling of unreality. It was like an architectural photograph from a history book. But some of the little antique booths were open and selling things, including one selling modern coffee in Styrofoam cups. He bought a twenty-ounce black regular, which took all his remaining cash, but warmed him through. He walked to the end of the pier as he drank it. Dropped the cup in the trash and stood and watched the grey ocean for a spell. Then he turned back and headed for the shore and saw two men walking towards him.

They were useful-sized guys, short but wide, dressed pretty much alike in blue pea coats and grey denim pants. They both had hats. Little knitted watch caps made from grey wool, jammed down over meaty heads. Clearly they knew how to dress for the climate. They had their hands in their pockets, so he couldn't tell whether they had gloves to match. Their pockets were high on their coats, so their elbows were forced outward. They both wore heavy boots, the sort of things a steelworker or a stevedore might choose. They were both a little bow-legged, or maybe they were just attempting an intimidating swagger. They both had a little scar tissue around their brows. They looked like fairground scufflers or dockyard bruisers from fifty years ago. Reacher glanced back and saw nobody behind him, all the way to Ireland. So he just stopped walking. Didn't worry about putting his back against the rail.

The two men walked on and stopped eight feet in front of him and faced him head on. Reacher flexed his fingers by his side, to test how cold they were. Eight feet was an interesting choice of distance. It meant they were going to talk before they tangled. He flexed his toes and ran some muscle tension up through his calves, his thighs, his back, his shoulders. Moved his head side to side and then back a little, to loosen his neck. He breathed in through his nose. The wind was on his back. The guy on the left took his hands out of his pockets. No gloves. And either he had bad arthritis or he was holding rolls of quarters in both palms.

'We got a message for you,' he said.

Reacher glanced at the pier rail and the ocean beyond. The sea was grey and roiled. Probably freezing. Throwing them in would be close to homicide.

'From that club manager?' he asked.

'From his people, yeah.'

'He's got people?'

'This is Atlantic City,' the guy said. 'Stands to reason he's got people.'

Reacher nodded. 'So let me guess. I'm supposed to get out of town, skedaddle, beat it, get lost, never come back, never darken your door again, forget I was ever here.'

'You're on the ball today.'

'I can read minds,' Reacher said. 'I used to work a fairground booth. Right next to the bearded lady. Weren't you guys there too? Three booths along? The World's Ugliest Twins?'

The guy on the right took his hands out of his pockets. He had the same neuralgic pain in his knuckles, or else a couple more rolls of quarters. Reacher smiled. He liked rolls of quarters. Good old-fashioned technology. And they implied the absence of firearms. Nobody clutches rolls of coins if they've got a gun in their pocket.

'We don't want to hurt you,' the guy on the right said.

'But you got to go,' the guy on the left said. 'We don't need people interfering in this town's economic procedures.'

'So take the easy way out,' the guy on the right said. 'Let us walk you to the bus depot. Or the old folk could wind up getting hurt, too. And not just financially.'

Reacher heard an absurd voice in his head: straight from his childhood, his mother saying *please don't fight when you're wearing new clothes*. Then he heard a boot-camp unarmed-combat instructor saying *hit them fast, hit them hard, and hit them a lot*. He flexed his shoulders inside his coat. Suddenly felt very grateful to the woman in the store for making him take the bigger size. He gazed at the two guys, exactly nothing in his eyes except a little amusement and a lot of absolute self-confidence. He moved a little to his left, and they rotated with him. He moved a little closer to them, tightening the triangle. He raised his hand and smoothed his hair where the wind was disturbing it.

'Better just to walk away now,' he said.

They didn't, like he knew they wouldn't. They responded to the challenge by crowding in towards him, imperceptibly, just a fractional muscle movement that eased their body weight forward rather than backward. *They need to be laid up for a week*, he thought. *Cheekbones, probably. A sharp blow, depressed fractures, maybe temporary loss of consciousness, bad headaches. Nothing too severe.* He waited until the wind gusted again and raised his right hand and swept his hair back behind his left ear. Then he kept his hand there, with his elbow poised high, like a thought had just struck him.

'Can you guys swim?' he asked.

It would have taken superhuman self-control not to glance at the ocean. They weren't superhuman. They turned their heads like robots. He clubbed the right-hand guy in the face with his raised elbow and cocked it again and hit the left-hand guy as his head snapped back towards the sound of his buddy's bones breaking. They went down on the boards together and their rolls of quarters split open and coins rolled everywhere and pirouetted small silver circles and collided and fell over, heads and tails. Reacher coughed in the bitter cold and stood still and replayed it in his head: two guys, two seconds, two blows, game over. *You've still got the good stuff.* He breathed hard and wiped cold sweat from his forehead. Then he walked away. Stepped off the pier onto the boardwalk and went in search of Western Union.

He had looked at the address in the motel phone book, but he didn't need it. You could find a Western Union office by feel. By intuition. It was a simple algorithm: stand on a street corner and ask yourself, is it more likely to be left or right now? Then you turned left or right as appropriate, and pretty soon you were in the right neighbourhood, and pretty soon you found it. This one had a two-year-old Chevy Suburban parked on a fireplug right outside the door. The truck was black with smoked windows, and it was immaculately clean and shiny. It had three short UHF antennae on the roof. There was a woman alone in the driver's seat. He glanced at her once, and then again. She was fair-haired and looked relaxed and alert all at the same time. Something about the way her arm was resting against the window. And she was cute, no doubt about that. Some kind of magnetism about her. He glanced away and went inside the office and claimed his cash. Folded it into his pocket and came back out and found the woman on the sidewalk, standing right in front of him, looking straight at him. At his face, like she was checking off similarities and differences against a mental image. It was a process he recognized. He had been looked at like that once or twice before.

'Jack Reacher?' she said.

He double-checked his memory, because he didn't want to be wrong, although he didn't think he was. Short fair hair, great eyes looking right at him, some kind of quiet confidence in the way she held herself. She had qualities he would remember. He was sure of that. But he didn't remember them. Therefore he had never seen her before.

'You knew my brother,' he said.

She looked surprised, and a little gratified. And temporarily lost for words.

'I could tell,' he said. 'People look at me like that, they're thinking about how we look a lot alike, but also a lot different.'

She said nothing.

'Been nice meeting you,' he said, and moved away.

'Wait,' she called.

He turned back.

'Can we talk?' she said. 'I've been looking for you.'

He nodded. 'We could talk in the car. I'm freezing my ass off out here.'

She was still for a second longer, with her eyes locked on his face. Then she moved suddenly and opened the passenger door.

'Please,' she said. He climbed in and she walked round the hood and climbed in on her side. Started the engine to run the heater, but didn't go anywhere.

'I knew your brother very well,' she said. 'We dated, Joe and I. More than dated, really. We were pretty serious for a time. Before he died.'

Reacher said nothing. The woman flushed.

'Well, obviously before he died,' she said. 'Stupid thing to say.'

She went quiet.

'When?' Reacher asked.

'We were together two years. We broke up a year before it happened.'

Reacher nodded.

'I'm M. E. Froelich,' she said.

She left an unspoken question hanging in the air: *did he ever mention me?* Reacher nodded again, trying to make it like the name meant something. But it didn't. *Never heard of you*, he thought. *But maybe I wish I had.*

'Emmy?' he said. 'Like the television thing?'

'M. E.,' she said. 'I go by my initials.'

'What are they for?'

'I won't tell you that.'

He paused a beat. 'What did Joe call you?'

'He called me Froelich,' she said.

He nodded. 'Yes, he would.'

'I still miss him,' she said.

'Me too, I guess,' Reacher said. 'So is this about Joe, or is it about something else?'

She was still again, for another beat. Then she shook herself, a tiny subliminal quiver, and came back all business.

'Both,' she said. 'Well, mainly something else, really.'

'Want to tell me what?'

'I want to hire you for something,' she said. 'On a kind of posthumous recommendation from Joe. Because of what he used to say about you. He talked about you, time to time.'

Reacher nodded. 'Hire me for what?'

Froelich paused again and came up with a tentative smile. 'I've rehearsed this line,' she said. 'Couple of times.'

'So let me hear it.'

'I want to hire you to assassinate the Vice President of the United States.'

TWO

'GOOD LINE,' REACHER SAID. 'INTERESTING PROPOSITION.'

'What's your answer?' Froelich asked.

'No,' he said. 'Right now I think that's probably the safest all-around response.'

She smiled the tentative smile again and picked up her purse. 'Let me show you some ID,' she said.

He shook his head. 'Don't need it,' he said. 'You're United States Secret Service.'

She looked at him. 'You're pretty quick.'

'It's pretty clear,' he said.

'Is it?'

He nodded. Touched his right elbow. It was bruised.

'Joe worked for them,' he said. 'And knowing the way he was he probably worked pretty hard, and he was a little shy, so anybody he dated was probably in the office, otherwise he would never have met them. Plus, who else except the government keeps two-year-old Suburbans this shiny? And parks next to hydrants? And who else but the Secret Service could track me this efficiently through my banking arrangements?'

'You're pretty quick,' she said again.

'Thank you,' he said back. 'But Joe didn't have anything to do with Vice Presidents. He was in Financial Crimes, not the White House protection detail.'

She nodded. 'We all start out in Financial Crimes. We pay our dues as anti-counterfeiting grunts. And he ran anti-counterfeiting. And you're right, we met in the office. But he wouldn't date me then. He said it wasn't appropriate. But I was planning on transferring across to the protection detail as soon as I could anyway, and as soon as I did, we started going out.'

Then she went a little quiet again. Looked down at her purse.

'And?' Reacher said.

She looked up. 'Something he said one night. I was kind of keen and ambitious back then, you know, starting a new job and all, and I was always trying to figure out if we were doing the best we could, and Joe and I were goofing around, and he said the only real way for us to test ourselves would be to hire some outsider to try to get to the target. To see if it was possible, you know. A security audit, he called it. I asked him, like who? And he said, my little brother would be the one. If anybody could do it, he could. He made you sound pretty scary.'

Reacher smiled. 'That sounds like Joe. A typical hare-brained scheme.'

'You think?'

'For a smart guy, Joe could be very dumb sometimes.'

'Why is it dumb?'

'Because if you hire some outsider, all you need to do is watch for him coming. Makes it way too easy.'

'No, his idea was the person would come in anonymously and unannounced. Like now, absolutely nobody knows about you except me.'

Reacher nodded. 'OK, maybe he wasn't so dumb.'

'He felt it was the only way. You know, however hard we work, we're always thinking inside the box. He felt we should be prepared to test ourselves against some random challenge from the outside.'

'And he nominated me?'

'He said you'd be ideal.'

'So why wait so long to try it? Whenever this conversation was, it has to be at least six years ago. Didn't take you six years to find me.'

'It was eight years ago,' Froelich said. 'Right at the start of our relationship, just after I got the transfer. And it only took me one day to find you.'

'So you're pretty quick, too,' Reacher said. 'But why wait eight years?'

'Because now I'm in charge. I was promoted head of the Vice President's detail four months ago. And I'm still keen and ambitious, and I still want to know that we're doing it right. So I decided to follow Joe's advice, now that it's my call. I decided to try a security audit. And you were recommended, so to speak. All those years ago, by somebody I trusted very much. So I'm here to ask you if you'll do it.'

'You want to get a cup of coffee?'

She looked surprised, like coffee wasn't on the agenda. 'This is urgent business,' she said.

'Nothing's too urgent for coffee,' he said. 'That's been my experience. Drive me back to my motel and I'll take you to the downstairs lounge. Coffee's OK, and it's a very dark room. Just right for a conversation like this.'

The government Suburban had a DVD-based navigation system built into the dash, and Reacher watched her fire it up and pick the motel's street address off a long list of potential Atlantic City destinations.

'I could have told you where it is,' he said.

'I'm used to this thing,' she said. 'It talks to me.'

'I wasn't going to use hand signals,' he said.

She smiled again and pulled out into the traffic. There wasn't much. Evening gloom was falling. The wind was still blowing. The casinos might do OK, but the boardwalk and the piers and the beaches weren't going to see much business for the next six months. He sat still next to her in the warmth from the heater and thought about her with his dead brother for a moment. Then he just watched her drive. She was pretty good at it. She parked outside the motel door and he led her inside and down a half-flight of stairs to the lounge. It smelled stale and sticky, but it was warm and there was a flask of coffee on the machine behind the bar. He pointed at it, and then at himself and Froelich, and the barman got busy. Then he walked to a corner booth and slid in across the vinyl with his back to the wall and the whole room in sight. *Old habits.* Froelich clearly had the same habits because she did the same thing, so they ended up close together and side by side. Their shoulders were almost touching.

'You're very similar to him,' she said.

'In some ways,' he said. 'Not in others. Like, I'm still alive.'

'You weren't at his funeral.'

'It came at an inopportune time.'

'You sound just the same.'

'Brothers often do.'

The barman brought the coffee, on a beer-stained cork tray. Two cups, black, little plastic pots of fake milk, little paper packets of sugar. Two cheap little spoons, pressed out of stainless steel.

'People liked him,' Froelich said.

'He was OK, I guess.'

'Is that all?'

'That's a compliment, one brother to another.'

He lifted his cup and tipped the milk and the sugar and the spoon off his saucer.

'You drink it black,' Froelich said. 'Just like Joe.'

Reacher nodded. 'Thing I can't get my head around is I was always the kid brother, but now I'm three years older than he ever got to be.'

Froelich looked away. 'I know. He just stopped being there, but the world carried on anyway. It should have changed, just a little bit.'

She sipped her coffee. Black, no sugar. *Just like Joe.*

'Nobody ever think of doing it, apart from him?' Reacher asked. 'Using an outsider for a security audit?'

'Nobody.'

'Secret Service is a relatively old organization.'

'So?'

'So I'm going to ask you an obvious question.'

She nodded. 'President Lincoln signed us into existence just after lunch on April the fourteenth, 1865. Then he went to the theatre that same night and got assassinated.'

'Ironic.'

'From our perspective, now. But back then we were only supposed to protect the currency. Then McKinley was assassinated in 1901 and they figured they should have somebody looking out for the President full time, and we got the job.'

'Because there was no FBI until the 1930s.'

She shook her head. 'Actually there was an early incarnation called the Office of the Chief Examiner, founded in 1908. It became the FBI in 1935.'

'That sounds like the sort of pedantic stuff Joe would know.'

'I think it was him who told me.'

'He would. He loved all that historical stuff.'

He saw her make an effort not to go quiet again.

'So what was your obvious question?' she said.

'You use an outsider for the very first time in a hundred and one years, got to be because of something more than you're a perfectionist.'

She started to answer, and then she stopped. She paused a beat. He saw her decide to lie. He could sense it, in the angle of her shoulder.

'I'm under big pressure,' she said. 'You know, professionally. There are a lot of people waiting for me to screw up. I need to be sure.'

He said nothing. Waited for the embellishments. Liars always embellish.

'I wasn't an easy choice,' she said. 'It's still rare for a woman to head up a team. There's a gender thing going on, same as anywhere else, I guess, same as always. Some of my colleagues are a little Neanderthal.'

He nodded. Said nothing.

'It's always on my mind,' she said. 'I've got to slam-dunk the whole thing.'

'Which vice president?' he asked. 'The new one or the old one?'

'The new one,' she said. 'Brook Armstrong. The Vice President-elect, strictly speaking. I was assigned to lead his team back when he joined the ticket, and we want continuity, so it's a little bit like an election for us, too. If our guy wins, we stay on the job. If our guy loses, we're back to being foot soldiers.'

Reacher smiled. 'So did you vote for him?'

She didn't answer.

'What did Joe say about me?' he asked.

'He said you'd relish the challenge. You'd beat your brains out to find a way of getting it done. He said you had a lot of ingenuity and you'd find three or four ways of doing it and we'd learn a lot from you.'

'And you said?'

'This was eight years ago, don't forget. I was kind of full of myself, I guess. I said no way would you even get close.'

'And he said?'

'He said plenty of people had made that same mistake.'

Reacher shrugged. 'I was in the army eight years ago. I was probably ten thousand miles away, up to my eyes in bullshit.'

She nodded. 'Joe knew that. It was kind of theoretical.'

He looked at her. 'But now it's not theoretical, apparently. Eight years later you're going ahead with it. And I'm still wondering why.'

'Like I said, now it's my call. And I'm under big-time pressure to perform well.'

He said nothing.

'Would you consider doing it?' Froelich asked.

'I don't know a lot about Armstrong. Never heard much about him before.'

She nodded. 'Nobody has. He was a surprise choice. Junior senator from North Dakota, standard-issue family man, wife, grown-up daughter, cares long-distance for his sick old mother, never made any kind of national impact. But he's an OK guy, for a politician. Better than most. I like him a lot, so far.'

Reacher nodded. Said nothing.

'We would pay you, obviously,' Froelich said. 'That's not a problem. You know, a professional fee, as long as it's reasonable.'

'I'm not very interested in money,' Reacher said. 'I don't need a job.'

'You could volunteer.'

'I was a soldier. Soldiers never volunteer for anything.'

'That's not what Joe said about you. He said you did all kinds of stuff.'

'I don't like to be employed.'

'Well, if you want to do it for free we certainly wouldn't object.'

He was quiet for a beat. 'There would be expenses, probably, if a person did this sort of a thing properly.'

'We'd reimburse them, naturally. Whatever the person needed. All official and above board, afterwards.'

He looked down at the table. 'Exactly what would you want the person to do?'

'I want you, not a person. Just to act the part of an assassin. To scrutinize things from an outside perspective. Find the holes. Prove to me if he's vulnerable, with times, dates, places. I could start you off with some schedule information, if you want.'

'You offer that to all assassins? If you're going to do this you should do it for real, don't you think?'

'OK,' she said.

'You still think nobody could get close?'

She considered her answer carefully, maybe ten seconds. 'On balance, yes, I do. We work very hard. I think we've got everything covered.'

'So you think Joe was wrong back then?'

She didn't answer.

'Why did you break up?' he asked.

She glanced away for a second and shook her head. 'That's private.'

'How old are you?'

'Thirty-five.'

'So eight years ago you were twenty-seven.'

She smiled. 'Joe was nearly thirty-six. An older man. I celebrated his birthday with him. And his thirty-seventh.'

Reacher moved sideways a little and looked at her again. *Joe had good taste*, he thought. Close up, she looked good. Smelled good. Perfect skin, great eyes, long lashes. Good cheekbones, a small straight nose. She looked lithe and strong. She was attractive, no doubt about it. He wondered what it would be like to hold her, kiss her. Go to bed with her. He pictured Joe wondering the same thing, first time she walked into the office he ran. And he eventually found out. *Way to go, Joe.*

'I guess I forgot to send a birthday card,' he said. 'Either time.'

'I don't think he minded.'

'We weren't very close,' he said. 'I don't really understand why not.'

'He liked you,' she said. 'He made that clear. Talked about you, time to time. I think he was quite proud of you, in his own way.'

Reacher said nothing.

'So will you help me out?' she asked.

'What was he like? As a boss?'

'He was terrific. He was a superstar, professionally.'

'What about as a boyfriend?'

'He was pretty good at that, too.'

There was a long silence.

'Where have you been since you left the service?' Froelich asked. 'You haven't left much of a paper trail.'

'That was the plan,' Reacher said. 'I keep myself to myself.'

Questions in her eyes.

'Don't worry,' he said. 'I'm not radioactive.'

'I know,' she said. 'Because I checked. But I'm kind of curious, now that I've met you. You were just a name before.'

He glanced down at the table, trying to look at himself as a third party, described second-hand in occasional bits and pieces by a brother. It was an interesting perspective.

'Will you help me out?' she asked again.

She unbuttoned her coat, because of the warmth of the room. She was wearing a pure white blouse under the coat. She moved a little closer, and half turned to face him. They were as close as lovers on a lazy afternoon.

'I don't know,' he said.

'It'll be dangerous,' she said. 'I have to warn you that nobody will know you're out there except me. That's a big problem if you're spotted anywhere. Maybe it's a bad idea. Maybe I shouldn't be asking.'

'I wouldn't be spotted anywhere,' Reacher said.

She smiled. 'That's exactly what Joe told me you'd say, eight years ago.'

He said nothing.

'It's very important,' she said. 'And urgent.'

'You want to tell me why it's important?'

'I've already told you why.'

'Want to tell me why it's urgent?'

She said nothing.

'I don't think this is theoretical at all,' he said.

She said nothing.

'I think you've got a situation,' he said.

She said nothing.

'I think you know somebody is out there,' he said. 'An active threat.'

She looked away. 'I can't comment on that.'

'I was in the army,' he said. 'I've heard answers like that before.'

'It's just a security audit,' she said. 'Will you do it for me?'

He was quiet for a long time.

'There would be two conditions,' he said.

She turned back and looked at him. 'Which are?'

'One, I get to work somewhere cold.'

'Why?'

'Because I just spent a hundred and eighty-nine dollars on warm clothes.'

She smiled, briefly. 'Everywhere he's going should be cold enough for you in the middle of November.'

'OK,' he said. He dug in his pocket and slid her a matchbook and pointed to the name and address printed on it. 'And there's an old couple working a week in this particular club and they're worried about getting ripped off for their wages. Musicians. They should be OK, but I need to be sure. I want you to talk to the cops here.'

'Friends of yours?'

'Recent.'

'When's payday supposed to be?'

'Friday night, after the last set. Midnight, maybe. They need to pick up their money and get their stuff to their car. They'll be heading to New York.'

'I'll ask one of our agents to check in with them every day. Better than the cops, I think. We've got a field office here.

Big-time money laundering in Atlantic City. It's the casinos. So you'll do it?'

Reacher went quiet again and thought about his brother. *He's back to haunt me,* he thought. *I knew he would be, one day.* His coffee cup was empty but still warm. He lifted it off the saucer and tilted it and watched the sludge in the bottom flow towards him, slow and brown, like river silt.

'When does it need to be done?' he asked.

At that exact moment less than a hundred and thirty miles away in a warehouse behind Baltimore's Inner Harbor cash was finally exchanged for two weapons and matching ammunition. A lot of cash. Good weapons. Special ammunition. The planning for the second attempt had started with an objective analysis of the first attempt's failure. As realistic professionals they were reluctant to blame the whole debacle on inadequate hardware, but they agreed that better firepower couldn't hurt. So they had researched their needs and located a supplier. He had what they wanted. The price was right. They negotiated a guarantee. It was their usual type of arrangement. They told the guy that if there was a problem with the merchandise they would come back and shoot him through the spinal cord, low down, put him in a wheelchair.

Getting their hands on the guns was the last preparatory step. Now they were ready to go fully operational.

Vice President-elect Brook Armstrong had six main tasks in the ten weeks between election and inauguration. Sixth and least important was the continuation of his duties as junior senator from North Dakota until his term officially ended. There were nearly six hundred and fifty thousand people in the state and any one of them might want attention at any time, but Armstrong assumed they all understood they were in limbo until his successor took over. Equally, Congress wasn't doing much of anything until January. So his senatorial duties didn't occupy much of his attention.

Fifth task was to ease his successor into place back home. He had scheduled two rallies in the state so he could hand the new guy on to his own tame media contacts. It had to be a visual thing, shoulder to shoulder, plenty of grip-and-grin for the cameras, Armstrong taking a metaphoric step backward, the new guy taking a metaphoric step forward. The first rally was planned for the twentieth of November, the other four days later. Both would be irksome, but party loyalty demanded it.

Fourth task was to learn some things. He would be a member of the National Security Council, for instance. He would be exposed to stuff a junior senator from North Dakota couldn't be expected to know. A CIA staffer had been assigned as his personal tutor, and there were Pentagon people coming in, and Foreign Service people. It was all kept as fluid as possible, but there was a lot of work to be fitted around everything else.

And everything else was increasingly urgent. The third task was where it started to get important. There were some tens of thousands of contributors who had supported the campaign nationally. The really big donors would be taken care of in other ways, but the individual thousand-dollar-and-up supporters needed to share the success, too. So the party had scheduled a number of big receptions in D.C. where they could all mill around and feel important and at the centre of things. Their local committees would invite them to fly in and dress up and rub shoulders. They would be told it wasn't officially certain yet whether it would be the new President or the new Vice President hosting them. In practice three-quarters of the duty was already scheduled to fall to Armstrong.

The second task was where it started to get *really* important. Second task was to stroke Wall Street. A change of administration was a sensitive thing, financially. No real reason why there should be anything but smooth continuity, but temporary nerves and jitters could snowball fast, and market instability could cripple a new presidency from the get-go. So a lot of effort went into investor reassurance. The President-elect handled most of it himself, with the crucial players getting extensive personal face-time in D.C., but Armstrong was slated to handle the second-division people up in New York. There were five separate trips planned during the ten-week period.

But Armstrong's first and most important task of all was to run the transition team. A new administration needs a roster of nearly eight thousand people, and about eight hundred of them need confirmation by the Senate, of which about eighty are really key players. Armstrong's job was to participate in their selection, and then use his Senate connections to grease their way through the upcoming confirmation process. The transition operation was based in the official space on G Street, but it made sense for Armstrong to lead it from his old Senate office. All in all, it wasn't fun. It was grunt work, but that's the difference between being first and second on the ticket.

So the third week after the election went like this: Armstrong spent the Tuesday, Wednesday and Thursday inside the Beltway, working with the transition team. His wife was taking a well-earned post-election break at home in North Dakota, so he was temporarily living alone in his Georgetown row house. Froelich packed his protection detail with her best agents and kept them all on high alert.

He had four agents camping out with him in the house and four Metro cops permanently stationed outside in cars, two in front and two in the alley behind. A Secret Service limo picked him up every morning and drove him to the Senate offices, with a second car following. The gun car, it was called. There was the usual efficient transfer across the sidewalks at both ends. Then three agents stayed with him throughout the day. His personal detail, three tall men, dark suits, white shirts, quiet ties, sunglasses even in November. They kept him inside a tight unobtrusive triangle of protection, always unsmiling, eyes always roving, physical placement always subtly adjusting. Sometimes he could hear faint sounds from their radio earpieces. They wore microphones on their wrists and carried automatic weapons under their jackets. He thought the whole experience was impressive, but he knew he was in no real danger inside the office building. There were D.C. cops outside, the Hill's own security inside, permanent metal detectors on all the street doors, and all the people he saw were either elected members or their staffers, who had been security-cleared many times over.

But Froelich wasn't as sanguine as he was. She watched for Reacher in Georgetown and on the Hill, and saw no sign of him. He wasn't there. Neither was anybody else worth worrying about. It should have relaxed her, but it didn't.

The first scheduled reception for mid-level donors was held on the Thursday evening, in the ballroom of a big chain hotel. The whole building was swept by dogs during the afternoon, and key interior positions were occupied by Metro cops who would stay put until Armstrong finally left many hours later. Froelich put two Secret Service agents on the door, six in the lobby, and eight in the ballroom itself. Another four secured the loading dock, which was where Armstrong would enter. Discreet video cameras covered the whole of the lobby and the whole of the ballroom and each was connected to its own recorder. The recorders were all slaved to a master timecode generator, so there would be a permanent real-time record of the whole event.

The guest list was a thousand people long. November weather meant they couldn't line up on the sidewalk and the tenor of the event meant security had to be pleasantly unobtrusive, so the standard winter protocol applied, which was to get the guests in off the street and into the lobby immediately through a temporary metal detector placed inside the frame of the entrance door. Then they milled around inside the lobby and eventually made their way to the ballroom door. Once there, their printed invitations were checked and they were asked for photo-ID. The invitations were laid face down on a glass sheet for a moment, and then handed back as souvenirs. Under the glass sheet was a video camera working to the same timecode as the others, so names and faces were permanently tied together in the visual record. Finally, they passed through a second metal detector and onward into the ballroom. Froelich's crew were serious but good-humoured, and made it seem as if they were protecting the guests themselves from some thrilling unspecified danger, rather than protecting Armstrong from *them*.

Froelich spent her time staring at the video monitors, looking for faces that didn't fit. She saw none, but she kept on worrying anyway. She saw no sign of Reacher. She wasn't sure whether to be relieved or annoyed about that. *Was he doing it or not?* She thought about cheating and issuing his description to her team. Then she thought better of it. *Win or lose, I need to know*, she thought.

Armstrong's two-car convoy entered the loading dock a half-hour later, by which time the guests had drunk a couple of glasses of cheap sparkling wine and eaten as many soggy canapés as they wanted. His personal three-man detail brought him in through a rear passageway and kept to a ten-foot radius for the duration. His appearance was timed to last two hours, which gave him an average of a little over seven seconds per guest. On a rope line seven seconds would be an eternity, but this situation was different, primarily in the handshaking method. A campaigning politician learns very quickly to fumble a handshake and grip the *back* of the recipient's hand, not the palm. It creates a breathless *so-much-support-here-I've-got-to-be-quick* type of drama, and better still it means it's strictly the pol's choice when he lets go, not the supporter's. But in an event of this nature, Armstrong couldn't use that tactic. So he had to shake properly and work fast to keep to seven seconds each. Some guests were content with brevity and others hung on a little longer, gushing their congratulations as if maybe he hadn't experienced any before. There were some men who went for the two-handed forearm grip. Some put their arms round his shoulders for private photographs. Some were disappointed that his wife wasn't there. Some weren't. There was one woman in particular who took his hand in a firm grip and held on for ten or twelve seconds, even pulling him nice and close and whispering something in his ear. She was surprisingly strong and nearly pulled him off balance. He didn't really hear what she whispered. Maybe her room number. But she was slim and pretty, with dark hair and a great smile, so he wasn't too upset about it. He just smiled back gratefully and moved on. His Secret Service detail didn't bat an eye.

He worked a complete circle round the room, eating nothing, drinking nothing, and made it back out of the rear door after two hours and eleven minutes. His personal detail put him back in his car and drove him home. The sidewalk crossing was completely uneventful and another eight minutes later his house was locked down for the night and secure. Back at the hotel the rest of the security detail withdrew unnoticed and the thousand guests left over the next hour or so.

* * *

Froelich drove straight back to her office and called Stuyvesant at home just before midnight. He answered right away and sounded like he had been holding his breath and waiting for the phone to ring.

'Secure,' she said.

'OK,' he replied. 'Any problems?'

'None that I saw.'

'You should review the video anyway. Look for faces.'

'I plan to.'

'Happy about tomorrow?'

'I'm not happy about anything.'

'Your outsider working yet?'

'Waste of time. Three full days and he's nowhere to be seen.'

'What did I tell you? It wasn't necessary.'

There was nothing to accomplish in D.C. on the Friday morning so Armstrong stayed home and had his CIA guy come in for two hours' teaching. Then his detail rehearsed the full motorcade exfiltration. They used an armoured Cadillac with two escort Suburbans flanked by two cop cars and a motorcycle escort. They drove him to Andrews Air Force Base for a midday flight to New York City. As a courtesy the defeated incumbents had allowed him the use of Air Force Two, although technically it couldn't use that call sign until it had a real inaugurated Vice President in it, so for the moment it was just a comfortable private aeroplane. It flew into La Guardia and three cars from the Secret Service's New York field office picked the party up and drove them south to Wall Street, with an NYPD motorcycle escort riding ahead of them.

Froelich was already in position inside the Stock Exchange. The New York field office had plenty of experience working with the NYPD and she was comfortable that the building was adequately secure. Armstrong's reassurance meetings were held in a back office and lasted two hours, so she relaxed until the photo call. The transition team's media handlers wanted news pictures on the sidewalk in front of the building's pillars, sometime after the closing bell. She had no chance whatever of persuading them otherwise, because they desperately needed the positive exposure. But she was profoundly unhappy about her guy standing still in the open air for any period of time. She had agents video the photographers for the record and check their press credentials twice and search every camera bag and every pocket of every vest. She checked in by radio with the local NYPD lieutenant and confirmed that the perimeter was definitively secured to a thousand feet on the ground and five hundred vertically. Then she allowed Armstrong out with the assorted brokers and bankers and they posed for five whole agonizing minutes. The photographers crouched on the sidewalk right at Armstrong's feet so they could get group head-and-shoulders shots with the *New York Stock Exchange* lintel inscription floating overhead. *Too much proximity*, Froelich thought. Armstrong and the financial guys stared optimistically and resolutely into the middle distance, endlessly. Then, mercifully, it was over. Armstrong gave his patented *I'd-love-to-stay* wave and backed away into the building. The financiers followed him and the photographers dispersed. Froelich relaxed again. Next up was a routine road trip back to Air Force Two and a flight to North Dakota for the first of Armstrong's handover rallies the next day, which meant she had maybe fourteen hours without major pressure.

Her cell phone rang in the car as they got close to La Guardia. It was her senior colleague from the Treasury side of the organization, at his desk in D.C.

'That bank account we're tracking?' he said. 'The customer just called in again. He's wiring twenty grand to Western Union in Chicago.'

'In cash?'

'No, cashier's cheque.'

'A Western Union cashier's cheque? For twenty grand? He's paying somebody for something. Goods or services. Got to be.'

Her colleague made no reply, and she clicked her phone off and just held it in her hand for a second. *Chicago?* Armstrong wasn't going anywhere near Chicago.

Air Force Two landed in Bismarck and Armstrong went home to join his wife and spend the night in his own bed in the family house in the lake country south of the city. It was a big old place with an apartment above the garage block that the Secret Service took over as its own. Froelich withdrew Mrs Armstrong's personal detail to give the couple some privacy. She gave all the personal agents the rest of the night off and tasked four more to stake out the house, two in front, two behind. State troopers made up the numbers, parked in cars on a three-hundred-yard radius. She walked the whole area herself as a final check, and her cell phone rang as she came back into the driveway.

'Froelich?' Reacher said.

'How did you get this number?'

'I was a military cop. I can get numbers.'

'Where are you?'

'Don't forget those musicians, OK? In Atlantic City? Tonight's the night.'

Then the phone went dead. She walked up to the apartment above the garage and idled some time away. She called the Atlantic City office at one in the morning and was told that the old couple had been paid the right money at the right time and escorted to their car and all the way out to I-95, where they had turned north. She clicked off her phone and sat for a spell in a window seat, just thinking. It was a quiet night, very dark. Very lonely. Cold. Distant dogs barked occasionally. No moon, no stars. She hated nights like this. The family-house situations were always the trickiest. Eventually anybody got thoroughly sick of being guarded, and even though Armstrong was still amused by the novelty she could tell he was ready for some down time. And certainly his wife was. So she had nobody at all in the interior and was relying exclusively on perimeter defence. She knew she should be doing more, but she had no real option, at least not until they explained the extent of the present danger to Armstrong himself, which they hadn't yet done, because the Secret Service never does.

Saturday dawned bright and cold in North Dakota, and preparations began immediately after breakfast. The rally was scheduled for one o'clock in the grounds of a church community centre on the south side of the city. Froelich had been surprised that it was an outdoor event, but Armstrong had told her that it would be heavy overcoat weather, nothing more. He told her that North Dakotans usually didn't retreat indoors until well after Thanksgiving. At which point she was almost overcome by an irrational desire to cancel the whole event. But she knew the transition team would oppose her, and she didn't want to fight losing battles this early. So she said nothing. Then she almost proposed Armstrong wear a Kevlar vest under his heavy overcoat, but eventually she decided against it. *Poor guy's got four years of this, maybe eight,* she thought. *He's not even inaugurated yet. Too early.* Later, she wished she'd gone with her first instinct.

The church community centre's grounds were about the size of a soccer field and were bordered to the north by the church itself, which was a handsome white clapboard structure traditional in every way. The other three sides were well fenced and two of them backed onto established housing subdivisions, with the third fronting onto the street. There was a wide gateway that opened into a small parking lot. Froelich banned parking for the day and put two agents and a local cop car on the gate, with twelve more cops on foot on the grass just inside the perimeter. She put two cop cars in each of the surrounding streets and had the church itself searched by the local police canine unit and then closed and locked. She doubled the personal detail to six agents, because Armstrong's wife was accompanying him. She told the detail to stick close to the couple at all times. Armstrong didn't argue with that. Being seen in the centre of a prowling pack of six tough guys looked very high-level. His successor-designate would be happy about it, too. Some of that D.C. power-elite status might rub off on him.

The Armstrongs made it a rule never to eat at public events. It was too easy to look like idiots, greasy fingers, trying to talk while chewing. So they had an early lunch at home and drove up in convoy and got right to the business at hand. It was easy enough. Even relaxing, in a way. Local politics was not Armstrong's problem any more. Wouldn't be much of a problem for his successor either, to be truthful. He had a handsome newly minted majority and was basking in a lot of reflected glow. So the afternoon turned out to be not much more than a pleasant stroll around a pleasant piece of real estate. His wife was beautiful, his successor stayed at his side throughout, there were no awkward questions from the press, all four network affiliates and CNN were there, all the local papers had sent photographers, and stringers from the *Washington Post* and the *New York Times* showed up, too. All in all it went so well he began to wish they hadn't bothered to schedule the follow-up event. It really wasn't necessary.

Froelich watched the faces. She watched the perimeters. She watched the crowd, straining to sense any alteration in the herd behaviour that might indicate tension or uneasiness or sudden panic. She saw nothing. Saw no sign of Reacher, either.

Armstrong stayed thirty minutes longer than anticipated, because the weak fall sun bathed the field in gold, and there was no breeze, and he was having a good time, and there was nothing scheduled for the evening except a quiet dinner with key members of the state legislature. So his wife was escorted home and his personal detail herded him back towards the cars and drove him north into the city of Bismarck itself. There was a hotel adjacent to the restaurant and Froelich had arranged rooms for the dead time before the meal. Armstrong napped for an hour and then showered and dressed. The meal was going well when his chief of staff fielded a call. The outgoing President and Vice President were formally summoning the President-elect and the Vice President-elect to a one-day transition conference at the Naval Support Facility in Thurmont, starting early the next morning. It was a conventional invitation, because inevitably there was business to discuss. And it was delivered in the traditional way, last-minute and pompous, because the lame ducks wanted to push the world around one last time. But Froelich was delighted, because the unofficial name for the Naval Support Facility in Thurmont is Camp David, and there is no safer place in the world than that particular wooded clearing in the Maryland mountains. She decided they should all fly back to Andrews immediately and take Marine helicopters straight out to the compound. If they spent all night and all day there she would be able to relax completely for twenty-four hours.

* * *

But late on the Sunday morning a navy steward found her at breakfast in the mess hall and plugged a telephone into a baseboard socket near her chair. Nobody uses cordless or cellular phones at Camp David. Too vulnerable to electronic eavesdropping.

'Call transferred from your main office, ma'am,' the steward said.

There was empty silence for a second, and then a voice.

'We should get together,' Reacher said.

'Why?'

'Can't tell you on the phone.'

'Where have you been?'

'Here and there.'

'Where are you now?'

'In a room at the hotel you used for the reception Thursday.'

'You got something urgent for me?'

'A conclusion.'

'Already? It's only been five days. You said ten.'

'Five was enough.'

Froelich cupped the phone. 'What's the conclusion?' Then she found herself holding her breath.

'It's impossible,' Reacher said.

She breathed out and smiled. 'Told you so.'

'No, your job is impossible. You need to talk to me urgently. You should get over here, right now.'

THREE

SHE DROVE BACK TO D.C. IN HER SUBURBAN AND ARGUED WITH herself the whole way. *If the news is really bad, when do I involve Stuyvesant? Now? Later?* In the end she pulled over on Dupont Circle and called him at home and asked him the question direct.

'I'll get involved when I need to,' he said. 'Who did you use?'

'Joe Reacher's brother.'

'*Our* Joe Reacher? I didn't know he had a brother.'

'Well, he did.'

'What's he like?'

'Just like Joe, maybe a little rougher.'

'Older or younger?'

'Both,' Froelich said. 'He started out younger, and now he's older.'

Stuyvesant went quiet for a moment.

'Is he as smart as Joe?' he asked.

'I don't know yet,' Froelich said.

Stuyvesant went quiet again. 'So call me when you need to. But sooner rather than later, OK? And don't say anything to anybody else.'

She ended the call and threaded back into the Sunday traffic and drove the last mile and parked outside the hotel. The desk was expecting her and sent her straight up to 1201, twelfth floor. She followed a waiter through the door. He was carrying a tray with a pot of coffee and two upside-down cups on saucers. No milk, no sugar, no spoons, and a single pink rose in a narrow china vase. The room was standard-issue city hotel. Two queen beds, flowery prints at the window, bland lithographs on the walls, a table, two chairs, a desk with a complicated phone, a credenza with a television, a connecting door to the next room. Reacher was sitting on the nearer bed. He was wearing a black nylon warm-up jacket with a black T-shirt and black jeans and black shoes. He had an earpiece in his ear and a pretty good fake Secret Service pin in the collar of the jacket. He was clean shaven and his hair had been cut very short and was neatly combed.

'What have you got for me?' she asked.

'Later,' he said.

The waiter put the tray on the table and backed silently out of the room. Froelich watched the door click shut behind him and turned back to Reacher. Paused.

'You look just like one of us,' she said.

'You owe me lots of money,' he said.

'Twenty grand?'

He smiled. 'Most of that. They told you about it?'

She nodded. 'But why a cashier's cheque? That puzzled me.'

'It won't, soon.'

He stood up and stepped across to the table. Righted the cups and picked up the pot and poured the coffee.

'You timed the room service well,' she said.

He smiled again. 'I knew where you were, I knew you'd be driving back. It's Sunday, no traffic. Easy enough to derive an ETA.'

'So what have you got to tell me?'

'That you're good,' he said. 'That you're really, really good. That I don't think anybody else could do this better than you.'

She went quiet. 'But?'

'But you're not good enough. You need to face that whoever it is out there could walk right in and get the job done.'

'I never said there's anybody out there.'

He said nothing.

'Just give me the information, Reacher.'

'Three and a half,' he said.

'Three and a half what? Out of ten?'

'No, Armstrong's dead, three and a half times over.'

She stared at him. 'Already?'

'That's how I score it,' he said.

'What do you mean, a half?'

'Three definites and one possible.'

She stopped halfway to the table and just stood there, bewildered.

'In five *days*?' she said. 'How? What aren't we doing?'

'Have some coffee,' he said.

She moved towards the table like an automaton. He handed her a cup. She took it and backed away to the bed. The cup rattled in the saucer.

'Two main approaches,' Reacher said. 'Like in the movies, John Malkovich or Edward Fox. You've seen those movies?'

She nodded blankly. 'We have a guy monitoring the movies. In the Office of Protection Research. He analyses all the assassination movies. John Malkovich made *In the Line of Fire* with Clint Eastwood.'

'And Rene Russo,' Reacher said. 'She was pretty good.'

'Edward Fox was in *The Day of the Jackal*, way back.'

Reacher nodded. 'John Malkovich was looking to take out the President of the United States, and Edward Fox was looking to take out the President of France. Two competent assassins, working solo. But there was a fundamental difference between them. John Malkovich knew all along he wasn't going to survive the mission. He knew he'd die a second after the President. But Edward Fox aimed to get away with it.'

'He didn't, though.'

'It was a movie, Froelich. Had to end that way. He could have gotten away with it, easy as anything.'

'So?'

'It gives us two strategies to consider. A close-up suicide mission, or a clean long-distance job.'

'We know all that. I told you, we have a person working on it. We get transcripts, analysis, memos, position papers. We talk to the screenwriters sometimes, if there's new stuff. We want to know where they get their ideas from.'

'Learn anything?'

She shrugged and sipped her coffee and he saw her trawl back through her memory, like she had all the transcripts and all the memos and all the position papers stashed away in a mental filing cabinet.

'*The Day of the Jackal* impressed us, I think,' she said. 'Edward Fox played a pro shooter who had a rifle built so it could be disguised as a crutch for a handicapped veteran. He used the disguise to get into a nearby building some hours before a public appearance and planned a long-range head shot from a high-floor window. He was using a silencer, so he could get away afterwards. Could have worked, in theory. But the story was set a long time ago. Before I was born. Early Sixties, I think. General de Gaulle, after the Algerian crisis, wasn't it? We enforce far wider perimeters now. The movie was a factor in that, I guess. Plus our own problems in the early Sixties, of course.'

'And *In the Line of Fire*?' Reacher asked.

'John Malkovich played a renegade CIA operative,' she said. 'He manufactured a plastic pistol in his basement so he could beat the metal detectors and conned his way into a campaign rally and intended to shoot the President from very close range. Whereupon, as you say, we would have taken him down immediately.'

'But old Clint jumped into the path of the bullet,' Reacher said. 'Good movie, I thought.'

'Implausible, we thought,' Froelich answered. 'Two main faults. First, the idea that you can build a working pistol from hobbyist material is absurd. We look at stuff like that all the time. His gun would have exploded, blown his hand off at the wrist. The bullet would have just fallen out of the wreckage onto the floor. And second, he spent about a hundred thousand dollars along the way. Lots and lots of travel, phony offices for mail-drops, plus a fifty-thousand-dollar donation to the party that got him into the campaign rally in the first place. Our assessment was a maniac personality like that wouldn't have big bucks to spend. We dismissed it.'

'It was only a movie,' Reacher said. 'But it was illustrative.'

'Of what?'

'Of the idea of getting into a rally and attacking the target from close quarters, as opposed to the old idea of going for long-distance safety.'

Froelich paused. Then she smiled, a little warily at first, like a grave danger might be receding into the distance.

'Is this all you've got?' she said. 'Ideas? You had me worried.'

'Like the rally here on Thursday night,' Reacher said. 'A thousand guests. Time and place announced in advance. Advertised, even.'

'You found the transition's web site?'

Reacher nodded. 'It was very useful. Lots of information.'

'We vet it all.'

'But it still told me everyplace Armstrong's going to be,' Reacher said. 'And when. And in what kind of a context. Like the rally right here, Thursday night. With the thousand guests.'

'What about them?'

'One of them was a dark-haired woman who got hold of Armstrong's hand and pulled him a little off-balance.'

She stared at him. 'You were there?'

He shook his head. 'No, but I heard about it.'

'How?'

He ignored the question. 'Did you see it?'

'Only on video,' she said. 'Afterwards.'

'That woman could have killed Armstrong. That was the first opportunity. Up to that point you were doing real well. You were scoring A-plus during the government stuff around the Capitol.'

She smiled again, a little dismissively. 'Could have? You're wasting my time, Reacher. I wanted better than *could have*. I mean, anything *could* happen. A bolt of lightning could hit the building. A meteorite, even. The universe could stop expanding and time could reverse. That woman was an invited guest. She was a party contributor, she passed through two metal detectors and she was ID-checked at the door.'

'Like John Malkovich.'

'We've been through that.'

'Suppose she was a martial-arts expert. Maybe military-trained in black ops. She could have broken Armstrong's neck like you could break a pencil.'

'Suppose, suppose.'

'Suppose she was armed.'

'She wasn't. She passed through two metal detectors.'

Reacher put his hand in the pocket of his jacket and came out with a slim brown object.

'Ever seen one of these?' he asked.

It looked like a penknife, maybe three and a half inches long. A curved handle. He clicked a button and a speckled brown blade snapped outward.

'This is entirely ceramic,' he said. 'Same basic stuff as a bathroom tile. Harder than anything except a diamond. Certainly harder than steel, and sharper than steel. And it doesn't trigger a metal detector. That woman could have been carrying this thing. She could have slit Armstrong open from his belly button to his chin with it. Or cut his throat. Or stuck it in his eye.'

He passed the weapon over. Froelich took it and studied it.

'Made by a firm called Böker,' Reacher said. 'In Solingen, Germany. They're expensive, but they're relatively available.'

Froelich shrugged. 'OK, so you bought a knife. Doesn't prove anything.'

'That knife was in the ballroom Thursday night. It was clutched in that woman's left hand, in her pocket, with the blade open, all the time she was shaking Armstrong's hand and pulling him close. She got his belly within three inches of it.'

Froelich stared at him. 'Are you serious? Who was she?'

'She was a party supporter called Elizabeth Wright, from Elizabeth, New Jersey, as it happens. She gave the campaign four thousand bucks, a grand each in her name, her husband's, and her two kids'. She stuffed envelopes for a month, put a big sign in her front yard and operated a phone tree on election day.'

'So why would she carry a knife?'

'Well, actually, she didn't.'

He stood up and walked to the connecting door. Pulled his half open and knocked hard on the inner half.

'OK, Neagley,' he called.

The inner door opened and a woman walked in from the next room. She was somewhere in her late thirties, medium height and slim, dressed in blue jeans and a soft grey sweatshirt. She had dark hair. Dark eyes. A great smile. The way she moved and the tendons in her wrists spoke of serious gym time.

'You're the woman on the video,' Froelich said.

Reacher smiled. 'Frances Neagley, meet M. E. Froelich. M. E. Froelich, meet Frances Neagley.'

'Emmy?' Frances Neagley said. 'Like the television thing?'

'Initials,' Reacher said.

Froelich stared at him. 'Who is she?'

'The best master sergeant I ever worked with. Beyond expert-qualified on every kind of close-quarters combat you can think of. Scares the hell out of me, certainly. She got cut loose around the same time I did. Works as a security consultant in Chicago.'

'Chicago,' Froelich repeated. 'That's why the cheque went there.'

Reacher nodded. 'She funded everything, because I don't have a credit card or a cheque book. As you already know, probably.'

'So what happened to Elizabeth Wright from New Jersey?'

'I bought these clothes,' Reacher said. 'Or rather, you bought them for me. And the shoes. Sunglasses, too. My version of Secret Service fatigues. I went to the barber. Shaved every day. I wanted to look plausible. Then I wanted a lone woman from New Jersey, so I met a couple of Newark flights at the airport here on Thursday. Watched the crowd and latched onto Ms Wright and told her I was a Secret Service agent and there was a big security snafu going on and she should come with me.'

'How did you know she was headed to the rally?'

'I didn't. I just looked at all the women coming out of baggage claim and tried to judge by how they looked and what they were carrying. Wasn't easy. Elizabeth Wright was the sixth woman I approached.'

'And she believed you?'

'I had impressive ID. I bought this radio earpiece from Radio Shack, two bucks. Little electrical cord disappearing down the back of my neck, see? I had a rented Town Car, black. I looked the part, believe me. *She* believed me. She was quite excited about the whole thing, really. I brought her back to this room and guarded her all evening while Neagley took over. I kept listening to my earpiece and talking into my watch.'

Froelich switched her gaze across to Neagley.

'We wanted New Jersey for a reason,' Neagley said. 'Their driving licences are the easiest to forge, you know that? I had a laptop and a colour printer with me. I'd just gotten through making Reacher's Secret Service ID for him. No idea if it was anything like the real thing, but it sure looked good. So I made up a Jersey licence with my picture and her name and address on it, printed it out, laminated it with a thing we bought from Staples for sixty bucks, sandpapered the edges clean, scuffed it around a little bit and shoved it in my bag. Then I dressed up some and took Ms Wright's party invitation with me and headed downstairs. I got into the ballroom OK. With the knife in my pocket.'

'And?'

'I hung around, then I got hold of your guy. Held on for a spell.'

Froelich looked straight at her. 'How would you have done it?'

'I had hold of his right hand in my right. I pulled him close, he rotated slightly, I had a clear shot at the right side of his neck. Three-and-a-half-inch blade, I'd have stuck it through his carotid artery. Then jerked it around some. He'd have bled to death inside thirty seconds. I was one arm movement away from doing it. Your guys were ten feet away. They'd have plugged me afterward for sure, but they couldn't have stopped me from getting it done.'

Froelich was pale and silent. Neagley looked away.

'Without the knife would have been harder,' she said. 'But not impossible. Breaking his neck would have been tricky because he's got some muscle up there. I'd have had to do a quick two-step to get his weight moving, and if your guys were fast enough they might have stopped me halfway. So I guess I'd have gone with a blow to his larynx, hard enough to crush it. A jab with my left elbow would have done the trick. I'd have been dead before him, probably, but he'd have suffocated right afterwards, unless you've got people who could do an emergency tracheotomy on the ballroom floor within a minute or so, which I guess you don't have.'

'No,' Froelich said. 'We don't have.' Then she fell silent again.

'Sorry to ruin your day,' Neagley said. 'But hey, you wanted to know this stuff, right? No point doing a security audit and not telling you the outcome.'

Froelich nodded. 'What did you whisper to him?'

'I said, I've got a knife. Just for the hell of it. But very quietly. If anybody had challenged me I was going to claim I'd said, where's your wife? Like I was coming on to him. I imagine that happens, time to time.'

Froelich nodded again. 'It does,' she said. 'Time to time. What else?'

'Well, he's safe in his house,' Neagley said.

'You checked?'

'Every day,' Reacher said. 'We've been on the ground in Georgetown since Tuesday night.'

'I didn't see you.'

'That was the plan.'

'How did you know where he lives?'

'We followed your limos.'

Froelich said nothing.

'Good limos,' Reacher said. 'Slick tactics.'

'Friday morning was especially good,' Neagley said.

'But the rest of Friday was pretty bad,' Reacher said. 'Lack of co-ordination produced a major communications error.'

'Where?'

'Your D.C. people had video of the ballroom but clearly your New York people never saw it, because as well as being the woman in the party dress Thursday night Neagley was also one of the photographers outside the Stock Exchange.'

'Some North Dakota paper has a web site,' Neagley said. 'Like all of them, with a graphic of their masthead. I downloaded it and modified it into a press pass. Laminated it and put brass eyelets in it and slung it around my neck with a nylon cord. Trawled the secondhand stores in lower Manhattan for battered old photo gear. Kept a camera up in front of my face the whole time so Armstrong wouldn't recognize me.'

'You should operate an access list,' Reacher said. 'Control it, somehow.'

'We can't,' Froelich said. 'It's a constitutional thing. The First Amendment guarantees journalistic access, any old time they want it. But they were all searched.'

'I wasn't carrying,' Neagley said. 'I was just breaching your security for the hell of it. But I *could* have been carrying, that's for damn sure. I could have gotten a bazooka past that kind of a search.'

Reacher stood up and stepped to the credenza. Pulled open a drawer and took out a stack of photographs. They were commercial one-hour six-by-four colour prints. He held up the first picture. It was a low-angle shot of Armstrong standing outside the Stock Exchange with the carved lintel inscription floating like a halo over his head.

'Neagley's,' Reacher said. 'Good picture, I thought. Maybe we should sell it to a magazine, defray some of the twenty grand.'

He stepped back to the bed and sat down and passed the photograph to Froelich. She took it and stared at it.

'Point is I was four feet away,' Neagley said. 'I could have gotten to him if I'd wanted to. A John Malkovich situation again, but what the hell.'

Froelich nodded blankly. Reacher dealt the next print, like a playing card. It was a grainy telephoto picture clearly taken from a great distance, looking down from way above street level. It showed Armstrong outside the Stock Exchange, tiny in the centre of the frame. There was a crude gunsight drawn round his head with a ballpoint pen.

'This is the half,' Reacher said. 'I was on the sixtieth floor of an office building three hundred yards away. Inside the police perimeter, but higher than they were checking.'

'With a rifle?'

He shook his head. 'With a piece of wood the same size and shape as a rifle. And another camera, obviously. And a big lens. But I played it out for real. I wanted to see if it was possible. I figured people wouldn't like to see a rifle-shaped package, so I got a big square box from a computer monitor and put the wood in diagonally, top corner to bottom corner. Then I just wheeled it into the elevator on a hand truck, pretended it was real heavy. I saw a few cops. I was wearing these clothes without the fake pin or the earpiece. I guess they thought I was a delivery driver or something. Friday after the closing bell, the district's getting quiet enough to be convenient. I found a window in an empty conference room. It wouldn't open, so I guess I'd have had to cut out a circle of glass. But I could have taken a shot, just like I took the picture. And I'd have been Edward Fox. I could have gotten clean away.'

Froelich nodded, reluctantly. 'Why only a half?' she asked. 'Looks like you had him fair and square.'

'Not in Manhattan,' Reacher said. 'I was about nine hundred feet away and six hundred feet up. That's an eleven-hundred-foot shot, give or take. Not a problem for me ordinarily, but the wind currents and the thermals around those towers turn it into a lottery. They're always changing, second to second. Swirling, up and down and side to side. They make it so you can't guarantee a hit. That's the good news, really. No competent rifleman would try a distance shot in Manhattan. Only an idiot would, and an idiot's going to miss anyway.'

Froelich nodded again, a little relieved. 'OK,' she said.

So she's not worried about an idiot, Reacher thought. *Must be a professional.*

'So,' he said. 'Call it a total score of three, if you want, and forget the half. Don't worry about New York at all. It was tenuous.'

'But Bismarck wasn't tenuous,' Neagley said. 'We got there about midnight. Commercial flights, through Chicago.'

'I called you from a mile away,' Reacher said. 'About the musicians.'

He dealt the next two photographs.

'Infrared film,' he said. 'In the dark.'

The first picture showed the back of the Armstrong family house. The colours were washed out and distorted, because of the infrared photography. But it was a fairly close shot. Every detail was clearly visible. Doors, windows. Froelich could even see one of her agents, standing in the yard.

'Where were you?' she asked.

'On the neighbour's property,' Reacher said. 'Maybe fifty feet away. Simple night manoeuvre, infiltration in the dark. Standard infantry techniques, quiet and stealthy. Couple of dogs barked some, but we got around them. The State troopers in the cars didn't see a thing.'

Neagley pointed to the second picture. It showed the front of the house. Same colours, same detail, same distance.

'I was across the street, at the front,' she said. 'Behind somebody's garage.'

Reacher sat forward on the bed. 'Plan would have been to have an M16 each, with the grenade launcher on it. Plus some other full-auto long guns. Maybe even M60 machine-guns on tripods. We certainly had enough time to set them up. We'd have put phosphorus grenades into the building with the M16s, simultaneously front and back, one each, ground floor, and either Armstrong would burn up in bed or we'd shoot him down as he ran out the door or jumped out the window. We'd have timed it for maybe four in the morning. Shock would have been total. Confusion would have been tremendous. We could have taken your agents out in the mêlée, easy as anything. We could have chewed the whole house to splinters. We'd have probably exfiltrated OK too, and then it would have boiled down to a standard manhunt situation, which wouldn't have been ideal out there in the boonies, but we'd probably have made it, with a bit of luck. Edward Fox again.'

There was silence.

'I don't believe it,' Froelich said. She stared at the pictures. 'This can't be Friday night. This was some other night. You weren't really there.'

Reacher said nothing.

'Were you?' she asked.

'Well, check this out,' Reacher said. He handed her another photograph. It was a telephoto shot. It showed her sitting in the apartment window above the garage, staring out into the darkness, holding her cell phone. Her heat signature was picked up in strange reds and oranges and purples. But it was her. No doubt about it. Like she was close enough to touch.

'I was calling New Jersey,' she said, quietly. 'Your musician friends got away OK.'

'Good,' Reacher said. 'Thanks for arranging it.'

She stared at the three infrared pictures, one after the other, and said nothing.

'So the ballroom and the family house were definites,' Reacher said. 'Two-zip for the bad guys. But the next day was the real clincher. Yesterday. That rally at the church.'

He passed the last photo across. It was regular daylight film, taken from a high angle. It showed Armstrong in his heavy overcoat walking across the community centre lawns. The late golden sun threw a long shadow out behind him. He was surrounded by a loose knot of people, but his head was clearly visible. It had another crude gunsight inked round it.

'I was in the church tower,' Reacher said.

'The church was locked.'

'At eight o'clock in the morning. I'd been in there since five.'

'It was searched.'

'I was up where the bells were. At the top of a wooden ladder, behind a trapdoor. I put pepper on the ladder. Your dogs lost interest and stayed on the ground floor.'

'It was a local unit.'

'They were sloppy.'

'I thought about cancelling the event.'

'You should have.'

'Then I thought about asking him to wear a vest.'

'Wouldn't have mattered. I would have aimed at his head. It was a beautiful day, Froelich. Clear sky, sunny, no wind at all. Cool, dense air. *True* air. I was a couple hundred feet away. I could have shot his eyes out.'

She went quiet.

'John Malkovich or Edward Fox?' she asked.

'I'd have hit Armstrong and then as many other people as I could, three or four seconds. Cops mostly, I guess, but women and children too. I'd have aimed to wound them, not kill them. In the stomach, probably. More effective that way. People flopping around and bleeding all over the place, it would have created mass panic. Enough to get away, probably. I'd have busted out of the church within ten seconds and gotten away into the surrounding subdivision fast enough. Neagley was standing by in a car. She'd have been rolling soon as she heard the shots. So I'd probably have been Edward Fox.'

Froelich stood up and walked to the window. Put her hands palms down on the sill and stared out at the weather.

'This is a disaster,' she said.

Reacher said nothing.

'I guess I didn't anticipate your level of focus,' she said. 'I didn't know it was going to be all-out guerrilla warfare.'

Reacher shrugged. 'Assassins aren't necessarily going to be the gentlest people you'll ever meet. And they're the ones who make the rules here.'

Froelich nodded. 'And I didn't know you were going to get help, especially not from a woman.'

'I kind of warned you,' Reacher said. 'I told you it couldn't work if you were watching for me coming. You can't expect assassins to call ahead with their plans.'

'I know,' she said. 'But I was imagining a lone man, is all.'

'It's always going to be a team,' Reacher said. 'There are no lone men.'

He saw an ironic half-smile reflected in the glass.

'So you don't believe the Warren Report?' she asked.

He shook his head. 'Neither do you,' he said. 'No professional ever will.'

'I don't feel like much of a professional today,' she said.

Neagley stood up and stepped over and perched on the sill, next to Froelich, her back against the glass.

'Context,' she said. 'That's what you've got to think about. It's not so bad. Reacher and I were United States Army Criminal Investigation Division specialists. We were trained in all kinds of ways. Trained to think, mostly. Trained to be inventive. And to be ruthless, for sure, and self-confident. And tougher than the people we were responsible for, and some of *them* were plenty tough. So we're very unusual. People as specialized as us, there's not more than maybe ten thousand in the whole country.'

'Ten thousand is a lot,' Froelich said.

'Out of two hundred and eighty-one million? And how many of them are currently the right age and available and motivated? It's a statistically irrelevant fraction. So don't sweat it. Because you've got an impossible job, anyway. You're *required* to leave him vulnerable. Because he's a politician. He's got to do all this visible stuff. We would never have *dreamed* of letting anybody do what Armstrong does. Never in a million years. It would have been completely out of the question.'

Froelich turned round and faced the room. Swallowed once and nodded vaguely into the middle distance.

'Thanks,' she said. 'For trying to make me feel better. But I've got some thinking to do, haven't I?'

'Perimeters,' Reacher said. 'Keep the perimeters to a half-mile all round, keep the public away from him, and keep at least four agents literally within touching distance at all times. That's all you can do.'

Froelich shook her head. 'Can't do it,' she said. 'It would be considered unreasonable. Undemocratic, even. And there are going to be hundreds of weeks like this one over the next three years. *After* three years it'll start to get worse because they'll be in their final year and they'll be trying to get re-elected and everything will have to be looser still. And about seven years from now Armstrong will start looking for the nomination in his own right. Seen how they do that? Crowd scenes all over the place from New Hampshire onward? Town meetings in shirtsleeves? Fund-raisers? It's a complete nightmare.'

The room went quiet. Neagley peeled off the window sill and walked across the room to the credenza. Took two thin files out of the drawer the photographs had been in. She held up the first.

'A written report,' she said. 'Salient points and recommendations, from a professional perspective.'

'OK,' Froelich said.

Neagley held up the second file.

'And our expenses,' she said. 'They're all accounted for. Receipts and all. You should make the cheque payable to Reacher. It was his money.'

'OK,' Froelich said again. She took the files and clasped them to her chest, as if they offered her protection from something.

'And there's Elizabeth Wright from New Jersey,' Reacher said. 'Don't forget her. She needs to be taken care of. I told her to make up for missing the reception you'd probably invite her to the Inauguration Ball.'

'OK,' Froelich said for the third time. 'The Ball, whatever. I'll speak to somebody about it.'

Then she just stood still.

'This is a disaster,' she said again.

'You've got an impossible job,' Reacher said. 'Don't beat up on yourself.'

She nodded. 'Joe used to tell me the same thing. He said, in the circumstances, we should consider a ninety-five per cent success rate a triumph.'

'Ninety-four per cent,' Reacher said. 'You've lost one president out of eighteen since you guys took over. Six per cent failure rate. That's not too bad.'

'Ninety-four, ninety-five,' she said. 'Whatever, I guess he was right.'

'Joe was right about a lot of things, the way I recall it.'

'But we've never lost a vice president,' she said. 'Not yet.'

She put the files under one arm and stacked the photographs on the credenza and butted them around with her fingertips until they were neatly piled. Picked them up and put them in her bag. Then she glanced at each of the four walls in turn, as if she was memorizing their exact details. A distracted little gesture. She nodded at nothing in particular and headed for the door.

'Got to go,' she said.

She walked out of the room and the door sucked shut behind her. There was silence for a spell. Then Neagley stood up straight at the end of one of the beds and clamped the cuffs of her sweatshirt in her palms and stretched her arms high above her head. She tilted her head back and yawned. Her hair cascaded over her shoulders. The hem of her shirt rode up and Reacher saw hard muscle above the waistband of her jeans. It was ridged like a turtle's back.

'You still look good,' he said.

'So do you, in black.'

'Feels like a uniform,' he said. 'Five years since I last wore one.'

Neagley finished stretching. Smoothed her hair and pulled the hem of her shirt back down into place.

'Are we done here?' she asked.

'Tired?'

'Exhausted. We worked our butts off, ruining that poor woman's day.'

'What did you think of her?'

'I liked her. And like I told her, I think she's got an impossible job. And all in all, I think she's pretty good at it. I doubt if anybody else could do it better. And I think she kind of knows that too, but it's burning her up that she's forced to settle for ninety-five per cent instead of a hundred.'

'I agree.'

'Who's this guy Joe she was talking about?'

'An old boyfriend.'

'You knew him?'

'My brother. She dated him.'

'When?'

'They broke up six years ago.'

'What's he like?'

Reacher glanced at the floor. Didn't correct the *is* to a *was*.

'Like a civilized version of me,' he said.

'So maybe she'll want to date you, too. Civilized can be an overrated virtue. And collecting the complete set is always fun for a girl.'

Reacher said nothing. The room went quiet.

'I guess I'll head home,' Neagley said. 'Back to Chicago. Back to the real world. But I got to say, it was a pleasure working with you again.'

'Liar.'

'No, really, I mean it.'

'So stick around. A buck gets ten she'll be back inside an hour.'

Neagley smiled. 'What, to ask you out?'

Reacher shook his head. 'No, to tell us what her real problem is.'

FOUR

FROELICH WALKED ACROSS THE SIDEWALK TO HER SUBURBAN. Spilled the files onto the passenger seat. Started the engine and kept her foot hard on the brake. Pulled her phone from her bag and flipped it open. Entered Stuyvesant's home number digit by digit and then paused with her finger resting on the call button. The phone waited patiently with the number displayed on the tiny green screen. She looked ahead through the windshield, fighting with herself. She looked down at the phone. Back out at the street. Her finger rested on the button. Then she flipped the phone shut and dropped it on top of the files. Pulled the transmission lever into drive and took off from the kerb with a loud chirp from all four tyres. Hung a left and a right and headed for her office.

The room service guy came back to collect the coffee tray. Reacher took his jacket off and hung it in the closet. Pulled the T-shirt out of the waistband of his jeans.

'Did you vote in the election?' Neagley asked him.

He shook his head. 'I'm not registered anywhere. Did you?'

'Sure,' she said. 'I always vote.'

'Did you vote for Armstrong?'

'Nobody votes for vice president. Except his family, maybe.'
'But did you vote for that ticket?'
She nodded. 'Yes, I did. Would you have?'
'I guess so,' he said. 'You ever hear anything about Armstrong before?'
'Not really,' she said. 'I mean, I'm interested in politics, but I'm not one of those people who can name all hundred senators.'
'Would you run for office?'
'Not in a million years. I like a low profile, Reacher. I was a sergeant, and I always will be, inside. Never wanted to be an officer.'
'You had the potential.'
She shrugged and smiled, all at the same time. 'Maybe I did. But what I didn't have was the desire. And you know what? Sergeants have plenty of power. More than you guys ever realized.'
'Hey, I realized,' he said. 'Believe me, I realized.'
'She's not coming back, you know. We're sitting here talking and wasting time and I'm missing all kinds of flights home, and she's not coming back.'
'She's coming back.'

Froelich parked in the garage and headed upstairs. Presidential protection was a non-stop operation, but Sundays still felt different. People dressed differently, the air was quieter, phone traffic was down. Some people spent the day at home. *Like Stuyvesant, for instance.* She closed her office door and sat at her desk and opened a drawer. Took out the things she needed and slipped them into a large brown envelope. Then she opened Reacher's expenses file and copied the figure on the bottom line onto the top sheet of her yellow pad and switched her shredder on. Fed the whole file into it, sheet by sheet, and then followed it with the file of recommendations and all the six-by-four photographs, one by one. She fed the file folders themselves in and stirred the long curling shreds around in the output bin until they were hopelessly tangled. Then she switched the machine off again and picked up the envelope and headed back down to the garage.

* * *

Reacher saw her car from the hotel room window. It came round the corner and slowed. There was no traffic on the street. Late in the afternoon, on a November Sunday in D.C. The tourists were in their hotels, showering, getting ready for dinner. The natives were home, reading their newspapers, watching the NFL on television, paying bills, doing chores. The air was fogging with evening. Streetlights were sputtering to life. The black Suburban had its headlights on. It pulled a wide U across both lanes and slid into an area reserved for waiting taxis.

'She's back,' Reacher said.

Neagley joined him at the window. 'We can't help her.'

'Maybe she isn't looking for help.'

'Then why would she come back?'

'I don't know,' he said. 'A second opinion? Validation? Maybe she just wants to talk. You know, a problem shared is a problem halved.'

'Why talk to us?'

'Because we didn't hire her and we can't fire her. And we weren't rivals for her position. You know how these organizations work.'

'Is she *allowed* to talk to us?'

'Didn't you ever talk to somebody you shouldn't have?'

Neagley made a face. 'Occasionally. Like, I talked to you.'

'And I talked to you, which was worse, because you weren't an officer.'

'But I had the potential.'

'That's for damn sure,' he said, looking down. 'Now she's just sitting there.'

'She's on the phone. She's calling somebody.'

The room phone rang.

'Us, evidently,' Reacher said.

He picked up the phone.

'We're still here,' he said.

Then he listened for a moment.

'OK,' he said, and put the phone down.

'She coming up?' Neagley asked. He nodded and went back to the window in time to see Froelich climbing out of the car.

She was holding an envelope. She skipped across the sidewalk and disappeared from sight. Two minutes later they heard the distant chime of the elevator arriving on their floor. Twenty seconds after that, a knock on the door. Reacher stepped over and opened up and Froelich walked in and stopped in the middle of the room. Glanced first at Neagley, and then at Reacher.

'Can we have a minute in private?' she asked him.

'Don't need one,' he said. 'The answer is yes.'

'You don't know the question yet.'

'You trust me, because you trusted Joe and Joe trusted me, therefore that loop is closed. Now you want to know if I trust Neagley, so you can close *that* loop also, and the answer is yes, I trust her absolutely, therefore you can too.'

'OK,' Froelich said. 'I guess that was the question.'

'So take your jacket off and make yourself at home. You want more coffee?'

Froelich slipped out of her jacket and dumped it on the bed. Stepped over to the table and laid the envelope down.

'More coffee would be fine,' she said.

Reacher dialled room service and asked for a large pot and three cups, three saucers, and absolutely nothing else.

'I only told you half the truth before,' Froelich said.

'I guessed,' Reacher said.

Froelich nodded apologetically and picked up the envelope. Opened the flap and pulled out a clear vinyl page protector. There was something in it.

'This is a copy of something that came in the mail,' she said.

She dropped it on the table and Reacher and Neagley inched their chairs closer to take a look. The page protector was a standard office product. The thing inside it was an eight-by-ten colour photograph of a single sheet of white paper. It was shown lying on a wooden surface and had a wooden office ruler laid alongside it to indicate scale. It looked like a normal letter-sized sheet. Centred left-to-right on it, an inch or so above the middle, were five words: *You are going to die*. The words were crisp and bold, obviously printed from a computer.

The room stayed quiet.

'When did it come?' Reacher asked.

'The Monday after the election,' Froelich said. 'First class mail.'

'Addressed to Armstrong?'

Froelich nodded. 'At the Senate. But he hasn't seen it yet. We open all public mail addressed to protectees. We pass on whatever is appropriate. We didn't think this was appropriate. What do you think of it?'

'Two things, I guess. Firstly, it's true.'

'Not if I can help it.'

'You discovered the secret of immortality? Everybody's going to die, Froelich. I am, you are. Maybe when we're a hundred, but we aren't going to live for ever. So technically it's a statement of fact. An accurate prediction, as much as a threat.'

'Which raises a question,' Neagley said. 'Is the sender smart enough to have phrased it that way on purpose?'

'What would be the purpose?'

'To avoid prosecution if you find him? Or her? To be able to say, hey, it wasn't a threat, it was a statement of fact? Anything we can infer from the forensics about the sender's intelligence?'

Froelich looked at her in surprise. And with a measure of respect.

'We'll get to that,' she said. 'And we're pretty sure it's a him, not a her.'

'Why?'

'We'll get to that,' Froelich said again.

'But why are you worrying about it?' Reacher asked. 'That's my second reaction. Surely those guys get sackloads of threats in the mail.'

Froelich nodded. 'Several thousand a year, typically. But most of them are sent to the President. It's fairly unusual to get one directed specifically at the Vice President. And most of them are on old scraps of paper, written in crayon, bad spelling, crossings out. Defective, in some way. And this one isn't defective. This one stood out from the start. So we looked at it pretty hard.'

'Where was it mailed?'

'Las Vegas,' Froelich said. 'Which doesn't really help us. In terms of Americans travelling inside America, Vegas has the biggest transient population there is.'

'You're sure an American sent it?'

'It's a percentage game. We've never had a written threat from a foreigner.'

'And you don't think he's a Vegas resident?'

'Very unlikely. We think he travelled there to mail it.'

'Because?' Neagley asked.

'Because of the forensics,' Froelich said. 'They're spectacular. They indicate a very careful and cautious guy.'

'Details?'

'Were you a specialist? In the military police?'

'She was a specialist in breaking people's necks,' Reacher said. 'But I guess she took an intelligent interest in the other stuff.'

'Ignore him,' Neagley said. 'I spent six months training in the FBI labs.'

Froelich nodded. 'We sent this to the FBI. Their facilities are better than ours.'

There was a knock at the door. Reacher stood up and walked over and put his eye to the peephole. The room service guy, with the coffee. Reacher opened the door and took the tray from him. A large pot, three upside-down cups, three saucers, no milk or sugar or spoons, and a single pink rose in a thin china vase. He carried the tray back to the table and Froelich moved the photograph to give him room to put it down. Neagley righted the cups and started to pour.

'What did the FBI find?' she asked.

'The envelope was clean,' Froelich said. 'Standard brown letter-size, gummed flap, metal butterfly closure. The address was printed on a self-adhesive label, presumably by the same computer that printed the message. The message was inserted unfolded. The flap gum was wetted with faucet water. No saliva, no DNA. No fingerprints on the metal closure. There were five sets of prints on the envelope itself. Three of them were postal workers. Their prints are on file as government workers. It's a condition of their employment. The fourth was the Senate mail handler who passed it on to us. And the fifth was our agent, who opened it.'

Neagley nodded. 'So forget the envelope. Except in as much as the faucet water was pretty thoughtful. This guy's a reader, keeps up with the times.'

'What about the letter itself?' Reacher asked.

Froelich picked up the photograph and tilted it towards the room light.

'Very weird,' she said. 'The FBI lab says the paper was made by the Georgia-Pacific company, their high-bright, twenty-four-pound heavyweight, smooth finish, acid-free laser stock, standard eight-and-a-half by eleven-inch letter-size. Georgia-Pacific is the third largest supplier into the office market. They sell hundreds of tons a week. So a single sheet is completely untraceable. But it's a buck or two more expensive per ream than basic paper, so that might mean something. Or it might not.'

'What about the printing?'

'It's a Hewlett-Packard laser. They can tell by the toner chemistry. Can't tell which model, because all their black-and-white lasers use the same basic toner powder. The typeface is Times New Roman, from Microsoft Works 4.5 for Windows 95, fourteen point, printed bold.'

'They can narrow it down to a single computer program?'

Froelich nodded. 'They've got a guy who specializes in that. Typefaces tend to change very subtly between different word processors. The software writers fiddle with the kerning, which is the spacing between individual letters, as opposed to the spacing between words. If you look long enough, you can kind of sense it. Then you can measure it and identify the program. But it doesn't help us much. There must be a million zillion PCs out there with Works 4.5 bundled in.'

'No prints, I guess,' Neagley said.

'Well, this is where it gets weird,' Froelich answered. She moved the coffee tray an inch and laid the photograph flat. Pointed to the top edge. 'Right here on the actual edge we've got microscopic traces of talcum dust.' Then she pointed to a spot an inch below the top edge. 'And here we've got two definite smudges of talcum dust, one on the back, one on the front.'

'Latex gloves,' Neagley said.

'Exactly,' Froelich said. 'Disposable latex gloves, like a doctor's or a dentist's. They come in boxes of fifty or a hundred pairs. Talcum powder inside the gloves, to help them slip on.

But there's always some loose talcum in the box, so it transfers from the outside of the glove, too. The dust on the top edge is baked, but the smudges aren't.'

'OK,' Neagley said. 'So the guy puts on his gloves, breaks open a new ream of paper, fans it out so it won't jam, which puts talcum dust on the top edge where he flips it, then he loads the printer, prints out his message, whereby he bakes the dust.'

'Because a laser printer uses heat,' Froelich said. 'The toner powder is attracted to the paper by an electrostatic charge in the shape of the required letters, and then a heater bakes it permanently into place. Somewhere around two hundred degrees, I think, momentarily.'

Neagley leaned close. 'Then he lifts the paper out of the output tray by clamping it between his finger and thumb, which accounts for the smudges front and back near the top, which aren't baked because it's after the heat treatment. And you know what? This is a home office, not a work office.'

'Why?'

'The front and back finger-clamping thing means the paper is coming out of the printer vertically. Popping up, like a toaster. If it was feeding out flat the marks would be different. There would be a smear on the front where he slides it. Less of a mark on the back. And the only Hewlett-Packard lasers that feed the paper vertically are the little ones. Home office things. I've got one myself. It's too slow to use high-volume. And the toner cartridge only lasts twenty-five hundred pages. Strictly amateur. So this guy did this in his den at home.'

Froelich nodded. 'Stands to reason, I guess. He's going to look a little strange using latex gloves in front of other people in an office.'

Neagley smiled, like she was making progress. 'OK, he's in his den, he lifts the message out of his printer and slides it straight into the envelope and seals it with faucet water while he's still got his gloves on. Hence none of his prints.'

Froelich's face changed. 'No, this is where it gets *very* weird.' She pointed to the photograph. Laid her fingernail on a spot an inch below the printed message, and a little right of centre. 'What might we expect to find here, if this were a regular letter, for instance?'

'A signature,' Reacher said.

'Exactly,' Froelich said. She kept her fingernail on the spot. 'And what we've *got* here is a thumbprint. A big, clear, definite thumbprint. Obviously deliberate. Bold as anything, exactly vertical, clear as a bell. Way too big to be a woman's. He's signed the message with his thumb.'

Reacher pulled the photograph out from under Froelich's finger and studied it.

'You're tracing the print, obviously,' Neagley said.

'They won't find anything,' Reacher said. 'The guy must be completely confident his prints aren't on file anywhere.'

'We've come up blank so far,' Froelich said.

'Which *is* very weird,' Reacher said. 'He signs the note with his thumbprint, which he's happy to do because his prints aren't on file anywhere, but he goes to extraordinary lengths to make sure his prints don't appear anywhere else on the letter or the envelope. Why?'

'Effect?' Neagley said. 'Drama? Neatness?'

'But it explains the expensive paper,' Reacher said. 'The smooth coating holds the print. Cheap paper would be too porous.'

'What did they use at the lab?' Neagley asked. 'Iodine fuming? Ninhydrin?'

Froelich shook her head. 'It came right up on the fluoroscope.'

Reacher was quiet for a spell, just looking at the photograph. Full dark had fallen outside the window. Shiny, damp, city dark.

'What else?' he said to Froelich. 'Why are you so uptight?'

'Should she need something else?' Neagley asked him.

He nodded. *You know how these organizations work*, he had told her.

'There has to be something else,' he said. 'I mean, OK, this is scary and challenging and intriguing, I guess, but she's really panicking here.'

Froelich sighed and picked up her envelope and slid out a second item. It was identical to the first in almost every respect. A plastic page protector, with an eight-by-ten colour photograph inside it. The photograph showed a sheet of white paper. There were eight words printed on it: *Vice-President-elect Armstrong is going to die.* The paper was lying on a different surface, and it had a different ruler next to it. The surface was grey laminate, and the ruler was clear plastic.

'It's virtually identical,' Froelich said. 'The forensics are the same, and it's got the same thumbprint for a signature.'

'And?'

'It showed up on my boss's desk,' Froelich said. 'One morning, it was just *there*. No envelope, no nothing. And absolutely no way of telling how it got there.'

Reacher stood up and moved to the window. Found the track cord and pulled the drapes closed. No real reason. It just felt like the appropriate thing to do.

'When did it show up?' he asked.

'Three days after the first one came in the mail,' Froelich said.

'Aimed at you,' Neagley said. 'Rather than Armstrong himself. Why? To make sure you take the first one seriously?'

'We were already taking it seriously,' Froelich said.

'When does Armstrong leave Camp David?' Reacher asked.

'They'll have dinner there tonight,' Froelich said. 'Probably shoot the breeze for a spell. They'll fly back after midnight, I guess.'

'Who's your boss?'

'Guy called Stuyvesant,' Froelich said. 'Like the cigarette.'

'You tell him about the last five days?'

Froelich shook her head. 'I decided not to.'

'Wise,' Reacher said. 'Exactly what do you want us to do?'

Froelich was quiet for a spell.

'I don't really know,' she said. 'I've asked myself that for six days, ever since I decided to find you. I asked myself, in a situation like this, what do I really want? And you know what? I really want to talk to somebody. Specifically, I really want to talk to Joe. Because there are complexities here, aren't there? You can see that, right? And Joe would find a way through them. He was smart like that.'

'You want me to be Joe?' Reacher said.

'No, I want Joe to be still alive.'

Reacher nodded. 'You and me both. But he ain't.'

'So maybe you could be the next best thing.'

Then she was quiet again.

'I'm sorry,' she said. 'That didn't come out very well.'

'Tell me about the Neanderthals,' Reacher said. 'In your office.'

She nodded. 'That was my first thought too.'

'It's a definite possibility,' he said. 'Some guy gets all jealous and resentful, lays all this stuff on you and hopes you'll crack up and look stupid.'

'My first thought,' she said again.

'Any likely candidates in particular?'

She shrugged. 'On the surface, none of them. Below the surface, any of them. There are six guys on my old pay grade who got passed over when I got the promotion. Each one of them has got friends and allies and supporters in the grades below. Like networks inside networks. Could be anybody.'

'Gut feeling?'

She shook her head. 'I can't come up with a favourite. And all their prints are on file. Condition of employment for us too. And this period between the election and the inauguration is very busy. We're stretched. Nobody's had time for a weekend in Vegas.'

'Didn't have to be a weekend. Could have been in and out in a single day.'

Froelich said nothing.

'What about discipline problems?' Reacher asked. 'Anybody resent the *way* you're leading the team? You had to yell at anybody yet? Anybody underperforming?'

She shook her head. 'I've changed a few things. Spoken to a couple of people. But I've been tactful. And the thumbprint doesn't match anybody anyway, whether I've spoken to them or not. So I think it's a genuine threat from out there in the world.'

'Me too,' Neagley said. 'But there's *some* insider involvement, right? Like, who else could wander around your building and leave something on your boss's desk?'

Froelich nodded. 'I need you to come see the office,' she said. 'Will you do that?'

* * *

They rode the short distance in the government Suburban. Reacher sprawled in the back and Neagley rode with Froelich in the front. The night air was damp, suspended somewhere between drizzle and evening mist. The roads were glossy with water and orange light. The tyres hissed and the windshield wipers thumped back and forth. Reacher glimpsed the White House railings and the front of the Treasury Building before Froelich turned a corner and drove into a narrow alley and headed for a garage entrance straight ahead. There was a steep ramp and a guard in a glass booth and a bright wash of white light. There were low ceilings and thick concrete pillars. She parked the Suburban on the end of a row of six identical models. There were Lincoln Town Cars here and there, and Cadillacs of various vintages and sizes with awkward rebuilt frames around the windows where bulletproof glass had been installed. Every vehicle was black and shiny and the whole garage was painted gloss white, walls and ceiling and floor alike. The place looked like a monochrome photograph. There was a door with a small porthole of wired glass. Froelich led them through it and up a narrow mahogany staircase into a small first-floor lobby. There were marble pilasters and a single elevator door.

'You two shouldn't really be here,' Froelich said. 'So say nothing, stick close to me and walk fast, OK?'

Then she paused a beat. 'But come look at something first.'

She led them through another inconspicuous door and round a corner into a vast dark hall that felt the size of a football field.

'The building's main lobby,' she said. Her voice echoed in the marble emptiness. The light was dim. White stone looked grey in the gloom.

'Here,' she said.

The walls had giant raised panels carved out of marble, reeded at the edges in the classical style. The one they were standing under was engraved at the top: *The United States Department of the Treasury*. The inscription ran laterally for eight or nine feet. Underneath it was another inscription: *Roll of Honor*. Then starting in the top left corner of the panel was an engraved list of dates and names. Maybe three or four dozen of them. The last but one place on the list was *J. Reacher, 1997*.

Last was *M. B. Gordon, 1997.* Then there was plenty of empty space. Maybe a column and a half.

'That's Joe,' Froelich said. 'Our tribute.'

Reacher looked up at his brother's name. It was neatly chiselled. Each letter was maybe two inches high and inlaid with gold leaf. The marble looked cold, and it was veined and flecked like marble everywhere. Then he caught a glimpse in his mind of Joe's face, maybe twelve years old, maybe at the dinner table or the breakfast table, always a millisecond faster than anyone else to see a joke, always a millisecond slower to start a smile. Then a glimpse of him leaving home, which at that time was a service bungalow somewhere hot, his shirt wet with sweat, his kitbag on his shoulder, heading out to the flight-line and a ten-thousand-mile journey to West Point. Then at the graveside at their mother's funeral, which was the last time he had seen him alive. He'd met Molly Beth Gordon, too. About fifteen seconds before she died. She had been a bright, vivacious blonde woman. Not so very different from Froelich herself.

'No, that's not Joe,' he said. 'Or Molly Beth. Those are just names.'

Neagley glanced at him and Froelich said nothing and led them back to the small lobby with the single elevator. They went up three floors to a different world. It was full of narrow corridors and low ceilings and businesslike adaptations. Acoustic tile overhead, halogen light, white linoleum and grey carpet on the floors, offices divided into cubicles with shoulder-high padded fabric panels on adjustable feet. Banks of phones, fax machines, piles of paper, computers everywhere. There was a literal hum of activity built from the whine of hard drives and cooling fans and the muted screech of modems and the soft ringing of phones. Inside the main door was a reception counter with a man in a suit sitting behind it. He had a phone cradled in his shoulder and was writing something on a message log and couldn't manage more than a puzzled glance and a distracted nod of greeting.

'Duty officer,' Froelich said. 'They work a three-shift system round the clock. This desk is always manned.'

'Is this the only way in?' Reacher asked.

'There are fire stairs way in back,' Froelich said. 'But don't get ahead of yourself. See the cameras?'

She pointed to the ceiling. There were miniature surveillance cameras everywhere there needed to be to cover every corridor.

'Take them into account,' she said.

She led them deeper into the complex, turning left and right until they ended up at what must have been the back of the floor. There was a long narrow corridor that opened out into a windowless square space. Against the side wall of the square was a secretarial station with room for one person, with a desk and filing cabinets and shelves loaded with three-ring binders and piles of loose memos. There was a portrait of the current President on the wall and a furled Stars and Stripes in a corner. A coat rack next to the flag. Nothing else. Everything was tidy. Nothing was out of place. Behind the secretary's desk was the fire exit. It was a stout door with an acetate plaque showing a green man running. Above the exit was a surveillance camera. It stared forward like an unblinking glass eye. Opposite the secretarial station was a single blank door. It was closed.

'Stuyvesant's office,' Froelich said.

She opened the door and led them inside. Flicked a switch and bright halogen light filled the room. It was a reasonably small office. Smaller than the square anteroom outside it. There was a window, with white fabric blinds closed against the night.

'Does the window open?' Neagley asked.

'No,' Froelich said. 'And it faces Pennsylvania Avenue, anyway. Some burglar climbs up three floors on a rope, somebody's going to notice, believe me.'

The office was dominated by a huge desk with a grey composite top. It was completely empty. There was a leather chair pushed exactly square against it.

'Doesn't he use a phone?' Reacher asked.

'Keeps it in the drawer,' Froelich said. 'He likes the desktop clear.'

There were tall cabinets against the wall, faced with the same grey laminate as the desk. There were two visitor chairs made of leather. Apart from that, nothing. It was a serene space. It spoke of a tidy mind.

'OK,' Froelich said. 'The mail threat came on the Monday in

the week after the election. Then, on the Wednesday evening, Stuyvesant went home about seven thirty. Left his desk clear. His secretary left a half-hour later. Popped her head in the door just before she went, like she always does. She confirms that the desk was clear. And she'd notice, right? If there was a sheet of paper on the desk, it would stand out.'

Reacher nodded. The desktop looked like the foredeck of a battleship made ready for inspection by an admiral. A speck of dust would have stood out.

'Eight o'clock Thursday morning, the secretary comes in again,' Froelich said. 'She walks straight to her own desk and starts work. Doesn't open Stuyvesant's door at all. Ten after eight, Stuyvesant himself shows up. He's carrying a briefcase and wearing a raincoat. He takes off the raincoat and hangs it up on the coat rack. His secretary speaks to him and he sets his briefcase upright on her desk and confers with her about something. Then he opens his door and walks into his office. He's not carrying anything. He's left his briefcase on the secretary's desk. About four or five seconds later he comes back out. Calls his secretary in. They both confirm that at that point, the sheet of paper was there on the desk.'

Neagley glanced around the office, at the door, at the desk, at the distance between the door and the desk.

'Is this just their testimony?' she asked. 'Or do the surveillance cameras record to videotape?'

'Both,' Froelich said. 'All the cameras record to separate tapes. I've looked at this one, and everything happens exactly as they describe it, coming and going.'

'So unless they're in it together, neither of them put the paper there.'

Froelich nodded. 'That's the way I see it.'

'So who did?' Reacher asked. 'What else does the tape show?'

'The cleaning crew,' Froelich said.

She led them back to her own office and took three videocassettes out of her desk drawer. Stepped over to a bank of shelves, where a small Sony television with a built-in video nestled between a printer and a fax machine.

'These are copies,' she said. 'The originals are locked away.

The recorders work on timers, six hours on each tape. Six in the morning until noon, noon until six, six until midnight, midnight until six, and start again.'

She found the remote in a drawer and switched the television on. Put the first tape in the mechanism. It clicked and whirred and a dim picture settled on the screen.

'This is the Wednesday evening,' she said. 'Six p.m. onward.'

The picture was grey and milky and the detail definition was soft, but the clarity was completely adequate. The camera showed the whole square area from behind the secretary's head. She was at her desk, on the phone. She looked old. She had white hair. Stuyvesant's door was on the right of the picture. It was closed. There was a date and time burned into the picture at the bottom left. Froelich hit fast wind and the motion sped up. The secretary's white head moved with comical jerkiness. Her hand batted up and down as she finished calls and fielded new ones. Some person bustled into shot and delivered a stack of internal mail and turned and bustled away. The secretary sorted the mail with the speed of a machine. She opened every envelope and piled the contents neatly and took out a stamp and ink pad and stamped every new letter at the top.

'What's she doing?' Reacher asked.

'Date of receipt,' Froelich said. 'This whole operation runs on accurate paperwork. Always has.'

The secretary was using her left hand to curl each sheet back and her right to stamp the date. The tape's fast motion made her look frantic. In the bottom corner of the picture the date held steady and the time unspooled just about fast enough to read. Reacher turned away from the screen and looked around Froelich's office. It was a typical government space, pretty much the civilian equivalent of the offices he'd spent his time in, aggressively plain and expensively shoehorned into a fine old building. Tough grey nylon carpet, laminate furniture, IT wiring routed carefully in white plastic conduit. Foot-high piles of paper everywhere, reports and memoranda tacked to the walls. There was a glass-fronted cabinet with a yard of procedure manuals inside. There was no window in the room. But she still had a plant. It was in a plastic pot on the desk, pale and dry and struggling to survive. There were no photographs. No mementoes. Nothing personal at all except a faint trace of her perfume in the air and the fabric of her chair.

'OK, this is where Stuyvesant goes home,' she said.

Reacher looked back at the screen and saw the time counter race through seven thirty, and then seven thirty-one. Stuyvesant stepped out of his office at triple speed. He was a tall man, wide across the shoulders, slightly stooped, greying at the temples. He was carrying a slim briefcase. The video made him move with absurd energy. He raced across to the coat rack and took down a black raincoat. Hurled it onto his shoulders and raced back to the secretary's desk. Bent abruptly and said something and raced away again out of sight. Froelich pressed the fast wind button harder and the speed redoubled again. The secretary jerked and swayed in her seat. The time counter blurred. As the seven turned to an eight the secretary jumped up and Froelich slowed the tape back to triple speed in time to catch her opening Stuyvesant's door for a second. She held on to the handle and leaned inside with one foot off the ground and turned immediately and closed the door. Rushed around the square space and collected her purse and an umbrella and a coat and disappeared into the gloom at the far end of the corridor. Froelich doubled the playback speed once again and the time counter unspooled faster but the picture remained entirely static. The stillness of a deserted office descended and held steady as time rushed by.

'When do the cleaners come in?' Reacher asked.

'Just before midnight,' Froelich said.

'That late?'

'They're night workers. This is a round-the-clock operation.'

'And there's nothing else visible before then?'

'Nothing at all.'

'So spool ahead. We get the picture.'

Froelich operated the buttons and shuttled between fast-forward with snow on the screen and regular-speed playback with a picture to check the timecode. At eleven fifty p.m. she let the tape run. The counter clicked ahead, a second at a time. At eleven fifty-two there was motion at the far end of the corridor. A team of three people emerged from the gloom. There were two women and a man, all of them wearing dark overalls. They looked Hispanic. They were all short and compact, dark-haired, stoic. The man was pushing a cart. It had a black garbage bag locked into a hoop at the front, and trays stacked with cloths and spray bottles on shelves at the rear. One of the women was carrying a vacuum cleaner. It rode on her back like a pack. It had a long hose with a broad nozzle. The other woman was carrying a bucket in one hand and a mop in the other. The mop had a square foam pad on the head and a complicated hinge halfway up the handle, for squeezing excess water away. All three of them were wearing rubber gloves. The gloves looked pale on their hands. Maybe clear plastic, maybe light yellow. All three of them looked tired. Like night workers. But they looked neat and clean and professional. They had tidy haircuts and their expressions said: *we know this ain't the world's most exciting job, but we're going to do it properly.* Froelich paused the tape and froze them as they approached Stuyvesant's door.

'Who are they?' Reacher asked.

'Direct government employees,' Froelich said. 'Most office cleaners in this city are contract people, minimum wage, no benefits, high turnover nobodies. Same in any city. But we hire our own. The FBI, too. We need a high degree of reliability, obviously. We keep two crews at all times. They're properly interviewed, they're background-checked, and they don't get in the door unless they're good people. Then we pay them real well, and give them full health plans, and dental, and paid vacations, the whole nine yards. They're department members, same as anybody else.'

'And they respond?'

She nodded. 'They're terrific, generally.'

'But you think this crew smuggled the letter in.'

'No other conclusion to come to.'

Reacher pointed at the screen. 'So where is it now?'

'Could be in the garbage bag, in a stiff envelope. Could be in a page protector, taped underneath one of the trays or the shelves. Could be taped to the guy's back, under his overalls.'

She hit play and the cleaners continued onward into Stuyvesant's office. The door swung shut behind them. The camera stared forward blankly. The time counter ticked on, five minutes, seven, eight. Then the tape ran out.

'Midnight,' Froelich said.

She ejected the cassette and put the second tape in. Pressed play and the date changed to Thursday and the timer restarted at midnight exactly. It crawled onward, two minutes, four, six.

'They certainly do a thorough job,' Neagley said. 'Our office cleaners would have done the whole building by now. A lick and a promise.'

'Stuyvesant likes a clean working environment,' Froelich said.

At seven minutes past midnight the door opened and the crew filed out.

'So now you figure the letter is there on the desk,' Reacher said.

Froelich nodded. The video showed the cleaners starting work around the secretarial station. They missed nothing. Everything was energetically dusted and wiped and polished. Every inch of carpet was vacuumed. Garbage was emptied into the black bag. It had bellied out to twice its size. The man looked a little dishevelled by his efforts. He pushed the cart backward foot by foot and the women retreated with him. Sixteen minutes past midnight, they backed away into the gloom and left the picture still and quiet, as it had been before they came.

'That's it,' Froelich said. 'Nothing more for the next five hours and forty-four minutes. Then we change tapes again and find nothing at all from six a.m. until eight, when the secretary comes in, and then it goes down exactly as she and Stuyvesant claimed it did.'

'As one might expect,' said a voice from the door. 'I think our word can be trusted. After all, I've been in government service for twenty-five years, and my secretary even longer than that, I believe.'

FIVE

THE GUY AT THE DOOR WAS STUYVESANT, NO DOUBT ABOUT THAT. Reacher recognized him from his appearance on the tape. He was tall, broad-shouldered, over fifty, still in reasonable shape. A handsome face, tired eyes. He was wearing a suit and a tie, on a Sunday. Froelich was looking at him, worried. But he in turn was staring straight at Neagley.

'You're the woman on the video,' he said. 'In the ballroom, Thursday night.'

He was clearly thinking hard. Running conclusions through his head and then nodding imperceptibly to himself whenever they made sense. After a moment he moved his gaze from Neagley to Reacher and stepped right into the room.

'And you're Joe Reacher's brother,' he said. 'You look just like him.'

Reacher nodded. 'Jack Reacher,' he said, and offered his hand.

Stuyvesant took it. 'I'm sorry for your loss,' he said. 'Five years late, I know, but the Treasury Department still remembers your brother with affection.'

Reacher nodded again. 'This is Frances Neagley,' he said.

'Reacher brought her in to help with the audit,' Froelich said.

Stuyvesant smiled a brief smile. 'I gathered that,' he said. 'Smart move. What were the results?'

The office went quiet.

'I apologize if I offended you, sir,' Froelich said. 'You know, before. Talking about the tape like that. I was just explaining the situation.'

'What were the audit results?' Stuyvesant asked again.

She said nothing back.

'That bad?' Stuyvesant said to her. 'Well, I certainly hope so. I knew Joe Reacher, too. Not as well as you did, but we came into contact, time to time. He was impressive. I'm assuming his brother is at least half as smart. Ms Neagley, probably smarter still. In which case they must have found ways through. Am I right?'

'Three definites,' Froelich said.

Stuyvesant nodded. 'The ballroom, obviously,' he said. 'Probably the family house and that damn outdoors event in Bismarck, too. Am I right?'

'Yes,' Froelich said.

'Extreme levels of performance,' Neagley said. 'Unlikely to be duplicated.'

Stuyvesant held up his hand and cut her off. 'Let's go to the conference room,' he said. 'I want to talk about baseball.'

He led them through narrow winding corridors to a relatively spacious room in the heart of the complex. It had a long table in it with ten chairs, five to a side. No windows. The same grey synthetic carpet underfoot and the same white acoustic tile overhead. The same bright halogen light. There was a low cabinet against one wall. It had closed doors and three telephones on it. Two were white and one was red. Stuyvesant sat down and waved to the chairs on the other side of the table. Reacher glanced at a huge notice board full of memos labelled *confidential.*

'I'm going to be uncharacteristically frank,' Stuyvesant said. 'Just temporarily, you understand, because I think we owe you an explanation, and because Froelich involved you with my initial approval, and because Joe Reacher's brother is family, so to speak, and therefore his colleague is too.'

'We worked together in the military,' Neagley said.

Stuyvesant nodded, like that was an inference he had drawn long ago. 'Let's talk about baseball,' he said. 'You follow the game?'

They all waited.

'The Washington Senators had already gone when I hit town,' he said. 'So I've had to make do with the Baltimore Orioles, which has been a mixed bag in terms of fun. But do you understand what's unique about the game?'

'The length of the season,' Reacher said. 'The win percentages.'

Stuyvesant smiled, like he was conferring praise.

'Maybe you're better than half as smart,' he said. 'The thing about baseball is that the regular season is one hundred and sixty-two games long. Way, way longer than any other sport. Any other sport has fifteen or twenty or thirty-some games. Basketball, hockey, football, soccer, anything. Any other sport, the players can start out thinking they can win every single game all season long. It's just about a realistic motivational goal. It's even been achieved, here and there, now and then. But it's impossible in baseball. The very best teams, the greatest champions, they all lose around a third of their games. They lose fifty or sixty times a year, at least. Imagine what that feels like, from a psychological perspective. You're a superb athlete, you're fanatically competitive, but you know for sure you're going to lose repeatedly. You have to make mental adjustments, or you couldn't cope with it. And presidential protection is exactly the same thing. That's my point. We can't win every day. So we get used to it.'

'You only lost once,' Neagley said. 'Back in 1963.'

'No,' Stuyvesant said. 'We lose repeatedly. But not every loss is significant. Just like baseball. Not every hit they get produces a run against you, not every defeat they inflict loses you the World Series. And with us, not every mistake kills our guy.'

'So what are you saying?' Neagley asked.

Stuyvesant sat forward. 'I'm saying that despite what your audit might have revealed you should still have considerable faith in us. Not every error costs us a run. Now, I completely understand that kind of so-what self-confidence must seem very offhand to an outsider. But *you* must understand we're forced to think that way. Your audit showed up a few holes, and what we have to do now is judge whether it's possible to fill them. Whether it's *reasonable.* I'm going to leave that to Froelich's own judgement. It's her show. But what I'm suggesting is that you get rid of any sense of doubt you're feeling about us. As private citizens. Any sense of our failure. Because we're not failing. There are always going to be holes. Part of the job. This is a democracy. Get used to it.'

Then he sat back, like he was finished.

'What about this specific threat?' Reacher asked him.

He paused, and then he shook his head. His face had changed. The mood in the whole room had changed.

'That's precisely where I stop being frank,' he said. 'I told you it was a temporary indulgence. And it was a very serious lapse on Froelich's part to reveal the existence of any threat at all. All I'm prepared to say is we intercept a lot of threats. Then we deal with them. *How* we deal with them is entirely confidential. Therefore I would ask you to understand you are now under an absolute obligation never to mention this situation to anybody after you leave here tonight. Or any aspect of our procedures. That obligation is rooted in federal statute. There are sanctions available to me.'

There was silence. Reacher said nothing. Neagley sat quiet. Froelich looked upset. Stuyvesant ignored her completely and gazed at Reacher and Neagley, at first hostile, and then suddenly pensive. He started thinking hard again. He stood up and walked over to the low cabinet with the telephones on it. Squatted down in front of it. Opened the doors and took out two yellow legal pads and two ballpoint pens. Walked back and dropped one of each in front of Reacher and one of each in front of Neagley. Circled round the head of the table again and sat back down in his chair.

'Write your full names,' he said. 'All and any aliases, dates of birth, social security numbers, military ID numbers, and current addresses.'

'What for?' Reacher asked.

'Just do it,' Stuyvesant said.

Reacher paused and picked up his pen. Froelich looked at

him, anxiously. Neagley glanced at him and shrugged and started writing on her pad. Reacher waited a second and then followed her example. He was finished well before her. He had no middle name and no current address. Stuyvesant walked around behind them and scooped the pads off the table. Said nothing and carried on walking straight out of the room with the pads held tight under his arm. The door slammed loudly behind him.

'I'm in trouble,' Froelich said. 'And I've made trouble for you guys, too.'

'Don't worry about it,' Reacher said. 'He's going to make us sign some kind of confidentiality agreement, is all. He's gone to get them typed up, I guess.'

'But what's he going to do to me?'

'Nothing, probably.'

'Demote me? Fire me?'

'He authorized the audit. The audit was necessary because of the threats. The two things were connected. We'll tell him we pushed you with questions.'

'He'll demote me,' Froelich said. 'He wasn't happy about me running the audit in the first place. Told me it indicated a lack of self-confidence.'

'Bullshit,' Reacher said. 'We did stuff like that all the time.'

'Audits *build* self-confidence,' Neagley said. 'That was our experience. Better to know something for sure than just hope for the best.'

Froelich looked away. Didn't reply. The room went quiet. They all waited, five minutes, then ten, then fifteen. Reacher stood up and stretched. Stepped over to the low cabinet and looked at the red phone. He picked it up and held it to his ear. There was no dial tone. He put it back and scanned the confidential memos on the notice board. The ceiling was low and he could feel heat on his head from the halogen lights. He sat down again and turned his chair and tilted it back and put his feet on the next one in line. Glanced at his watch. Stuyvesant had been gone twenty minutes.

'Hell is he doing?' he said. 'Typing them himself?'

'Maybe he's calling his agents,' Neagley said. 'Maybe we're all going to jail, to guarantee our everlasting silence for ever.'

Reacher yawned and smiled. 'We'll give him ten more minutes. Then we're leaving. We'll all go out and get some dinner.'

Stuyvesant came back after five more. He walked into the room and closed the door. He was carrying no papers. He stepped over and sat down in his original seat and placed his hands flat on the table. Drummed a staccato little rhythm with his fingertips.

'OK,' he said. 'Where were we? Reacher had a question, I think.'

Reacher took his feet off the chair and turned to face front.

'Did I?' he said.

Stuyvesant nodded. 'You asked about this specific threat. Well, it's either an inside job or it's an outside job. It's got to be one or the other, obviously.'

'We're discussing this now?'

'Yes, we are,' Stuyvesant said.

'Why? What changed?'

Stuyvesant ignored the question. 'If it's an outside job, should we necessarily worry? Perhaps not, because that's like baseball, too. If the Yankees come to town saying they're going to beat the Orioles, does that mean it's true? Boasting about it is not the same thing as actually doing it.'

Nobody spoke.

'I'm asking for your input here,' Stuyvesant said.

Reacher shrugged. 'OK,' he said. 'You think it *is* an outside threat?'

'No, I think it's inside intimidation intended to damage Froelich's career. Now ask me what I'm going to do about it.'

Reacher glanced at him. Glanced at his watch. Glanced at the wall. *Twenty-five minutes, a Sunday evening, deep inside the D.C.-Maryland-Virginia triangle.*

'I know what you're going to do about it,' he said.

'Do you?'

'You're going to hire me and Neagley for an internal investigation.'

'Am I?'

Reacher nodded. 'If you're worried about inside intimidation then you need an internal investigation. That's clear. And you can't use one of your own people, because you might hit on the bad guy by chance. And you don't want to bring the FBI in, because that's not how Washington works. Nobody washes their dirty linen in public. So you need some other outsider. And you've got two of them sitting right in front of you. They're already involved, because Froelich just involved them. So either you terminate that involvement, or you choose to expand on it. You'd prefer to expand on it, because that way you don't have to find fault with an excellent agent you just promoted. So can you use us? Of course you can. Who better than Joe Reacher's little brother? Inside Treasury, Joe Reacher is practically a saint. So your ass is covered. And mine is too. Because of Joe I'll get automatic credibility from the start. And I was a good investigator in the military. So was Neagley. You know that, because you just checked. My guess is you just spent twenty-five minutes talking to the Pentagon and the National Security Agency. That's why you wanted those details. They ran us through their computers and we came out clean. More than clean, probably, because I'm sure our security clearances are still on file, and I'm sure they're still way higher than you actually need them to be.'

Stuyvesant nodded. He looked satisfied.

'An excellent analysis,' he said. 'You get the job, just as soon as I get hard copies of those clearances. They should be here in an hour or two.'

'You can do this?' Neagley said.

'I can do what I want,' Stuyvesant said. 'Presidents tend to give a lot of authority to the people they hope will keep them alive.'

Silence in the room.

'Will I be a suspect?' Stuyvesant asked.

'No,' Reacher said.

'Maybe I should be. Maybe I should be your number-one suspect. Perhaps I felt forced to promote a woman because of contemporary pressures to do so, but I secretly resent it, so I'm working behind her back to panic her and thereby discredit her.'

Reacher said nothing.

'I could have found a friend or a relative who had never been fingerprinted. I could have placed the paper on my desk at seven thirty Wednesday evening and instructed my secretary not to notice it. She'd have followed my orders. Or I could have instructed the cleaners to smuggle it in that night. They'd have followed my orders, too. But they'd have followed Froelich's orders equally. She should be your number-two suspect, probably. Maybe she has a friend or a relative with no prints on file either, and maybe she's setting this whole thing up in order to deal with it spectacularly and earn some enhanced credibility.'

'Except I'm not setting it up,' Froelich said.

'Neither of you is a suspect,' Reacher said.

'Why not?' Stuyvesant asked.

'Because Froelich came to me voluntarily, and she knew something about me from my brother. You hired us directly after seeing our military records. Neither of you would have done those things if you had something to hide. Too much risk.'

'Maybe we think we're smarter than you are. An internal investigation that missed us would be the best cover there is.'

Reacher shook his head. 'Neither of you is that dumb.'

'Good,' Stuyvesant replied. He looked satisfied. 'So let's agree it's a jealous rival elsewhere in the department. Let's assume he conspired with the cleaners.'

'Or she,' Froelich said.

'Where are the cleaners now?' Reacher asked.

'Suspended,' Stuyvesant said. 'At home, on full pay. They live together. One of the women is the man's wife and the other woman is his sister-in-law. The other crew is working overtime to make up, and costing me a fortune.'

'What's their story?'

'They know nothing about anything. They didn't bring in any sheet of paper, they never saw it, it wasn't there when they were there.'

'But you don't believe them.'

Stuyvesant was quiet for a long moment. He fiddled with his shirt cuffs and then laid his hands flat on the table again.

'They're trusted employees,' he said. 'They're very nervous about being under suspicion. Very upset. Frightened, even. But they're also *calm*. Like we won't be able to prove anything, because they didn't do anything. They're a little puzzled. They passed a lie-detector test. All three of them.'

'So you do believe them.'

Stuyvesant shook his head. 'I can't believe them. How can I? You saw the tapes. Who else put the damn thing there? A ghost?'

'So what's your opinion?'

'I think somebody they knew inside the building asked them to do it, and explained it away as a routine test procedure, like a war game or a secret mission, said there was no harm in it, and coached them through what would happen afterwards in terms of the video and the questioning and the lie-detector. I think that might give a person enough composure to pass the polygraph. If they were convinced they weren't in the wrong and there would be no adverse consequences. If they were convinced they were really helping the department somehow.'

'Have you pursued that with them yet?'

Stuyvesant shook his head. 'That'll be your job,' he said. 'I'm not good at interrogation.'

He left as suddenly as he had arrived. Just upped and walked out of the room. The door swung shut behind him and left Reacher and Neagley and Froelich sitting together at the table in the bright light and the silence.

'You won't be popular,' Froelich said. 'Internal investigators never are.'

'I'm not interested in being popular,' Reacher said.

'I've already got a job,' Neagley said.

'Take some vacation time,' Reacher said. 'Stick around, be unpopular with me.'

'Will I get paid?'

'I'm sure there'll be a fee,' Froelich said.

Neagley shrugged. 'OK. I guess my partners could see this as a prestige thing. You know, government work? I could go back to the hotel, make some calls, see if they can cope without me for a spell.'

'You want to get that dinner first?' Froelich asked.

Neagley shook her head. 'No, I'll eat in my room. You two get dinner.'

They wound their way back through the corridors to Froelich's office and she called a driver for Neagley. Then she escorted her down to the garage and came back upstairs to find Reacher sitting quiet at her desk.

'Are you two having a relationship?' she asked.

'Who?'

'You and Neagley.'

'What kind of a question is that?'

'She was weird about dinner.'

He shook his head. 'No, we're not having a relationship.'

'Did you ever? You seem awful close.'

'Do we?'

'She obviously likes you, and you obviously like her. And she's cute.'

He nodded. 'I do like her. And she is cute. But we never had a relationship.'

'Why not?'

'Why not? It just never happened. You know what I mean?'

'I guess.'

'I'm not sure what it's got to do with you, anyway. You're my brother's ex, not mine. I don't even know your name.'

'M. E.,' she said.

'Martha Enid?' he said. 'Mildred Eliza?'

'Let's go,' she said. 'Dinner, my place.'

'Your place?'

'Restaurants are impossible here on Sunday night. And I can't afford them anyway. And I've still got some of Joe's things. Maybe you should have them.'

She lived in a small warm row house in an unglamorous neighbourhood across the Anacostia river near Bolling Air Force Base. It was one of those city homes where you close the drapes and concentrate on the inside only. There was street parking and a wooden front door with a small foyer behind it that led directly into a living room. It was a comfortable space. Wood floors, a rug, old-fashioned furniture. A small television set with a big cable box wired to it. Some books on a shelf, a small music system with a yard of CDs propped against it. The heaters were turned up high so Reacher peeled off his black jacket and dumped it on the back of a chair.

'I don't want it to be an insider,' Froelich said.

'Better that than a real outside threat.'

She nodded and moved towards the back of the room where an arch opened into an eat-in kitchen. She looked around, a little vague, like she was wondering what all the machines and cabinets were for.

'We could send out for Chinese food,' Reacher called.

She took off her jacket and folded it in half and laid it on a stool.

'Maybe we should,' she said.

She had a white blouse on and without the jacket it looked softer and more feminine. The kitchen was lit with regular bulbs turned low and they were kinder to her skin than the bright office halogen had been. He looked at her and saw what Joe must have seen, eight years previously. She found a take-away menu in a drawer and dialled a number and called in an order. Hot and sour soup and General Tso's chicken, times two.

'That OK?' she asked.

'Don't tell me,' he said. 'It's what Joe liked.'

'I've still got some of his things,' she said. 'You should come see them.'

She walked ahead of him back to the foyer and up the stairs. There was a guest room at the front of the house. It had a deep closet with a single door. A light bulb came on automatically when she opened it. The closet was full of miscellaneous junk, but the hanging rail had a long line of suits and shirts still wrapped in the dry cleaner's plastic. The plastic had turned a little yellow and brittle with age.

'These are his,' Froelich said.

'He left them here?' Reacher asked.

She touched the shoulder of one of the suits through the plastic.

'I figured he'd come back for them,' she said. 'But he didn't, the whole year. I guess he didn't need them.'

'He must have had a lot of suits.'

'Couple of dozen, I guess,' she said.

‘How can a person have twenty-four suits?’

‘He was a dresser,’ she said. ‘You must remember that.’

He stood still. The way he remembered it, Joe had lived in one pair of shorts and one T-shirt. In the winters he wore khakis. When it was very cold he added a worn-out leather pilot’s jacket. That was it. At their mother’s funeral he wore a very formal black suit, which Reacher had assumed was rented. But maybe it wasn’t. Maybe working in Washington had changed his approach.

‘You should have them,’ Froelich said. ‘They’re your property, anyway. You were his next of kin, I guess.’

‘I guess I was,’ he said.

‘There’s a box, too,’ she said. ‘Stuff he left around and never came back for.’

He followed her gaze to the closet floor and saw a cardboard box sitting underneath the hanging rail. The flaps were folded over each other.

‘Tell me about Molly Beth Gordon,’ he said.

‘What about her?’

‘After they died I kind of inferred they’d had a thing going.’

She shook her head. ‘They were close. No doubt about that. But they worked together. She was his assistant. He wouldn’t date people in the office.’

‘Why did you break up?’ he asked.

The doorbell rang downstairs. It sounded loud in the Sunday hush.

‘The food,’ Froelich said.

They went down and ate together at the kitchen table, silently. It felt curiously intimate, but also distant. Like sitting next to a stranger on a long plane ride. You feel connected, but also not connected.

‘You can stay here tonight,’ she said. ‘If you like.’

‘I didn’t check out of the hotel.’

She nodded. ‘So check out tomorrow. Then base yourself here.’

‘What about Neagley?’

Silence for a second.

‘Her, too, if she wants. There’s another bedroom on the third floor.’

'OK,' he said.

They finished the meal and he put the containers in the trash and rinsed the plates. She set the dishwasher going. Then her phone rang. She stepped through to the living room to answer it. Talked for a long moment and then hung up and came back.

'That was Stuyvesant,' she said. 'He's giving you the formal go-ahead.'

He nodded. 'So call Neagley and tell her to get her ass in gear.'

'Now?'

'Get a problem, solve a problem,' he said. 'That's my way. Tell her to be out front of the hotel in thirty minutes.'

'Where are you going to start?'

'With the video,' he said. 'I want to watch the tapes again. And I want to meet with the guy who runs that part of the operation.'

Thirty minutes later they scooped Neagley off the sidewalk in front of the hotel. She had changed into a black suit with a short jacket. The pants were cut tight. They looked pretty good from the back, in Reacher's opinion. He saw Froelich arrive at the same conclusion. But she said nothing. Just drove, five minutes, and then they were back in the Secret Service offices. Froelich headed straight for her desk and left Reacher and Neagley with the agent who ran the video surveillance. He was a small thin nervous guy in Sunday clothes who had come in at short notice to meet with them. He looked a little dazed about it. He led them to a closet-sized equipment room full of racks of recorders. One wall was a floor-to-ceiling shelving unit with hundreds of VHS tapes stacked neatly in black plastic boxes. The recorders themselves were plain grey industrial units. The whole tiny space was full of neat wiring and procedural memos tacked to the walls and soft noise from small motors turning and the smell of warm circuit boards and the green glow of LED numbers ticking over relentlessly.

'System really looks after itself,' the guy said. 'There are four recorders slaved to each camera, six hours to a tape, so we change all the tapes once a day, file them away, keep them three months and then reuse them.'

'Where are the originals from the night in question?' Reacher asked.

'Right here,' the guy said. He fiddled in his pocket and came out with a bunch of small brass keys on a ring. Squatted down in the limited space and opened a low cupboard. Took out three boxes.

'These are the three I copied for Froelich,' he said, on his knees.

'Some place where we can look at them?'

'They're no different than the copies.'

'Copying causes detail loss,' Reacher said. 'First rule, start with the originals.'

'OK,' the guy said. 'You can look at them right here, I guess.'

He stood up awkwardly and pushed and pulled some equipment around on a bench and angled a small monitor outward and switched on a standalone player. A blank grey square appeared on the screen.

'No remotes on these things,' he said. 'You have to use the buttons.'

He stacked the three tape boxes in the correct time sequence.

'Got chairs?' Reacher asked.

The guy ducked out and came back dragging two typist's chairs. They tangled in the doorway and he had trouble fitting them both in front of the narrow bench. Then he glanced around like he was unhappy about leaving strangers alone in his little domain.

'I guess I'll wait in the foyer,' he said. 'Call me when you're through.'

'What's your name?' Neagley asked.

'Nendick,' the guy said, shyly.

'OK, Nendick,' she said. 'We'll be sure to call you.'

He left the room and Reacher put the third tape in the machine.

'You know what?' Neagley said. 'That guy didn't sneak a peek at my ass.'

'Didn't he?'

'Guys usually do when I'm wearing these pants.'

'Do they?'

'Usually.'

Reacher kept his gaze firmly on the blank video screen. 'Maybe he's gay,' he said.

'He was wearing a wedding band.'

'Then maybe he tries hard to avoid inappropriate feelings. Or maybe he's tired.'

'Or maybe I'm getting old,' she said.

He hit fast rewind. The motor whirred.

'Third tape,' he said. 'Thursday morning. We'll do this backward.'

The player spooled fast. He watched the counter and hit play and the picture came up with an empty office with the timecode burned in over it showing the relevant Thursday's date and the time at seven fifty-five a.m. He hit forward scan and then froze the picture when the secretary entered the frame at exactly eight o'clock in the morning. He settled in his chair and hit play and the secretary walked into the square area and took off her coat and hung it on the rack. Walked within three feet of Stuyvesant's door and bent down behind her desk.

'Stowing her purse,' Neagley said. 'On the floor in the footwell.'

The secretary was a woman of maybe sixty. For a moment she was face on to the camera. She was a matronly figure. Stern, but kindly. She sat down heavily and hitched her chair in and opened a book on the desk.

'Checking the diary,' Neagley said.

The secretary stayed firmly in her chair, busy with the diary. Then she started in on a tall stack of memos. She filed some of them in a drawer and used her rubber stamp on others and moved them right to left across her desk.

'You ever see so much paperwork?' Reacher said. 'Worse than the army.'

The secretary broke off from her memo stack twice, to answer the phone. But she didn't move from her chair. Reacher fast-forwarded until Stuyvesant himself swept into view at ten past eight. He was wearing a dark raincoat, maybe black or charcoal. He was carrying a slim briefcase. He took off his coat and hung it on the rack. Advanced into the square area and the secretary's head moved as if she was speaking to him. He set his briefcase on her desk at an exact angle and adjusted its position. Bent to confer with her. Nodded once and straightened up and stepped to his door without his briefcase and disappeared into his office. The timer ticked off four seconds. Then he was back out in the doorway, calling to his secretary.

'He found it,' Reacher said.

'The briefcase thing is weird,' Neagley said. 'Why would he leave it?'

'Maybe he had an early meeting,' Reacher said. 'Maybe he left it out there because he knew he was leaving again right away.'

He fast-forwarded through the next hour. People ducked in and out of the office. Froelich made two trips. Then a forensic team arrived and left twenty minutes later with the letter in a plastic evidence bag. He hit reverse scan. The whole morning's activity unfolded again, backward. The forensic team left and then arrived, Froelich came out and in twice, Stuyvesant arrived and left, and then his secretary did the same.

'Now for the boring part,' Reacher said. 'Hours and hours of nothing.'

The picture settled to a steady shot of an empty area with the timer rushing backward. Absolutely nothing happened. The level of detail coming off the original tape was better than the copy, but there wasn't much in it. It was grey and milky. OK for a surveillance situation, but it wouldn't have won any technical awards.

'You know what?' Reacher said. 'I was a cop for thirteen years, and I never found anything significant on a surveillance tape. Not even once.'

'Me neither,' Neagley said. 'The hours I spent like this.'

At six a.m. the tape jammed to a stop and Reacher ejected it and fast wound the second tape to the far end and started the patient backward search again. The timer sped through five o'clock and headed fast toward four. Nothing happened. The office just sat there, still and grey and empty.

'Why are we doing this tonight?' Neagley asked.

'Because I'm an impatient guy,' Reacher said.

'You want to score one for the military, don't you? You want to show these civilians how the real pros work.'

'Nothing left to prove,' Reacher said. 'We already scored three and a half.'

He bent closer to the screen. Fought to keep his eyes focused. Four o'clock in the morning. Nothing was happening. Nobody was delivering any letters.

'Or maybe there's another reason we're doing this tonight,' Neagley said. 'Maybe you're trying to outpoint your brother.'

'Don't need to. I know exactly how we compared. And it doesn't matter to me what anybody else thinks about it.'

'What happened to him?'

'He died.'

'I gathered that, belatedly. But how?'

'He was killed. In the line of duty. Just after I left the army. Down in Georgia, south of Atlanta. Clandestine rendezvous with an informer from a counterfeiting operation. They were ambushed. He was shot in the head, twice.'

'They get the guys who did it?'

'No.'

'That's awful.'

'Not really. I got them instead.'

'What did you do?'

'What do you think?'

'OK, how?'

'It was a father and son team. I drowned the son in a swimming pool. I burned the father to death in a fire. After shooting him in the chest with a hollow-point .44.'

'That ought to do it.'

'Moral of the story, don't mess with me or mine. I just wish they'd known that ahead of time.'

'Any comeback?'

'I exfiltrated fast. Stayed out of circulation. Had to miss the funeral.'

'Bad business.'

'The guy he was meeting with got it, too. Bled to death under a highway ramp. There was a woman, as well. From Joe's office. His assistant, Molly Beth Gordon. They knifed her at the Atlanta airport.'

'I saw her name. On the roll of honour.'

Reacher was quiet. The video sped backward. Three in the

morning, then two fifty-something. Then two forty. Nothing happening.

'The whole thing was a can of worms,' he said. 'It was his own fault, really.'

'That's harsh.'

'It was a stretch for him. I mean, would you get ambushed at a rendezvous?'

'No.'

'Me neither.'

'I'd do all the usual stuff,' Neagley said. 'You know, arrive three hours early, stake it out, surveil, block the approaches.'

'But Joe didn't do any of that. He was out of his depth. Thing about Joe, he looked tough. He was six-six, two-fifty, built like a brick outhouse. Hands like shovels, face like a catcher's mitt. We were clones, physically, the two of us. But we had different brains. Deep down, he was a cerebral guy. Kind of *pure*. Naive, even. He never thought dirty. Everything was a game of chess with him. He gets a call, he sets up a meet, he drives down there. Like he's moving his knight or his bishop around. He just didn't expect somebody to come along and blow the whole chessboard away.'

Neagley said nothing. The tape sped on backward. Nothing was happening on it. The square office area just sat there, dim and steady.

'Afterwards I was angry he was so careless,' Reacher said. 'But then I figured I couldn't blame him for that. To be careless, first of all you've got to know what you're supposed to be careful about. And he just didn't. He didn't know. He didn't see stuff like that. Didn't think that way.'

'So?'

'So I guess I was angry I didn't do it for him.'

'Could you have?'

He shook his head. 'I hadn't seen him for seven years. I had no idea where he was. He had no idea where I was. But somebody *like* me should have done it for him. He should have asked for help.'

'Too proud?'

'No, too naive. That's the bottom line.'

'Could he have reacted? At the scene?'

Reacher made a face. 'They were pretty good, I guess. Semi-proficient, by our standards. There must have been some chance. But it would have been a split-second thing, purely instinctive. And Joe's instincts were all buried under the cerebral stuff. He probably stopped to think. He always did. Just enough to make him come out timid.'

'Naive and timid,' Neagley said. 'They don't share that opinion around here.'

'Around here he must have looked like a wild man. Everything's comparative.'

Neagley shifted in her chair and watched the screen.

'Stand by,' she said. 'The witching hour approaches.'

The timer spun back through half past midnight. The office was undisturbed. Then at sixteen minutes past midnight the cleaning crew rushed backward out of the gloom of the exit corridor. Reacher watched them at high speed until they reversed into Stuyvesant's office at seven minutes past. Then he ran the tape forward at normal speed and watched them come out again and clean the secretarial station.

'What do you think?' he asked.

'They look pretty normal,' Neagley said.

'If they'd just left the letter in there, would they look so composed?'

They weren't hurrying. They weren't furtive or anxious or stressed or excited. They weren't glancing back at Stuyvesant's door. They were just cleaning, efficiently and speedily. He reversed the tape again and sped back through seven minutes past midnight and onward until it jammed to a stop at midnight exactly. He ejected it and inserted the first tape. Wound to the far end and scanned backward until they first entered the picture just before eleven fifty-two. Ran the tape forward and watched them walk into shot and froze the tape when they were all clearly visible.

'So where would it be?' he asked.

'Like Froelich speculated,' Neagley said. 'Could be anywhere.'

He nodded. She was right. Between the three of them and the cleaning cart, they could have concealed a dozen letters.

'Do they look worried?' he asked.

She shrugged. 'Run the tape. See how they move.'

He let them walk onward. They headed straight for Stuyvesant's door and disappeared from view inside, eleven fifty-two exactly.

'Show me again,' Neagley said.

He ran the segment again. Neagley leaned back and half closed her eyes.

'Their energy level is a little different than when they came out,' she said.

'You think?'

She nodded. 'A little slower? Like they're hesitant?'

'Or like they're dreading having to do something bad in there?'

He ran it again.

'I don't know,' she said. 'Kind of hard to interpret. And it's no kind of evidence, that's for sure. Just a subjective feeling.'

He ran it again. There was no real overt difference. Maybe they looked a little less wired going in than coming out. Or more tired. But then, they spent fifteen minutes in there. And it was a relatively small office. Already quite clean and neat. Maybe it was their habit to take a ten-minute rest in there, out of sight of the camera. Cleaners weren't dumb. Maybe they put their feet on the desk, not a letter.

'I don't know,' Neagley said again.

'Inconclusive?' Reacher said.

'Naturally. But who else have we got?'

'Nobody at all.'

He hit fast rewind and stared at nothing until he found eight o'clock in the evening. The secretary got up from her desk, put her head round Stuyvesant's door, and went home. He wound back to seven thirty-one and watched Stuyvesant himself leave.

'OK,' he said. 'The cleaners did it. On their own initiative?'

'I seriously doubt it.'

'So who told them to?'

They stopped in the foyer and found Nendick and sent him back to tidy up his equipment room. Then they went in search of Froelich and found her deep in a stack of paperwork at her desk, on the phone, co-ordinating Brook Armstrong's return from Camp David.

'We need to speak with the cleaners,' Reacher said.

'Now?' Froelich said.

'No better time. Late-night interrogation always works best.'

She looked blank. 'OK. I'll drive you, I guess.'

'Better that you're not there,' Neagley said.

'Why not?'

'We're military. We'll probably want to slap them around some.'

Froelich stared at her. 'You can't do that. They're department members, no different than me.'

'She's kidding,' Reacher said. 'But they're going to feel better talking to us if there's nobody else from the department around.'

'OK, I'll wait outside. But I'm going with you.'

She finished up her phone calls and tidied up her paperwork and then led them back to the elevator and down to the garage. They climbed into the Suburban and Reacher closed his eyes for twenty minutes as she drove. He was tired. He had been working hard for six days straight. Then the car came to a stop and he opened his eyes again in a mean neighbourhood full of ten-year-old sedans and hurricane fencing. There was an orange glow from streetlights here and there. Patched blacktop and scrawny weeds in the sidewalks. The thump of a loud car stereo blocks away.

'This is it,' Froelich said. 'Number 2301.'

2301 was the left-hand half of a two-family house. It was a low clapboard structure with paired front doors in the centre and symmetrical windows left and right. There was a low wire fence defining a front yard. The yard had a lawn that was partly dead. No bushes or flowers or shrubs. But it was neat enough. No trash. The steps up to the door were swept clean.

'I'll wait right here,' Froelich said.

Reacher and Neagley climbed out of the car. The night air was cold and the distant stereo was louder. They went in through the gate. Up a cracked concrete walk to the door. Reacher pressed the bell and heard it sound inside the house. They waited. Heard the slap of footsteps on what sounded like a bare floor, and then something metal being hauled out of the way. The door opened and a man stood there, holding the handle. He was the cleaner from the video, no doubt about it. They had looked at him forward and backward for hours. He was not young, not old. Not short, not tall. Just a completely average guy. He was wearing cotton pants and a Redskins sweatshirt. His skin was dark and his cheekbones were high and flat. His hair was black and glossy, with an old-fashioned cut still crisp and neat around the edges.

'Yes?' he said.

'We need to talk about the thing at the office,' Reacher said.

The guy didn't ask any questions. Didn't ask for ID. Just glanced at Reacher's face and stepped backward and over the thing he had moved to get the door open. It was a children's seesaw made out of brightly coloured curved metal tubes. It had little seats at each end, like you might see on a children's tricycle, and plastic horses' heads with little handlebars coming out of the sides below the ears.

'Can't leave it outside at night,' the guy said. 'It would be stolen.'

Neagley and Reacher climbed over it into a narrow hallway. There were more toys neatly packed onto shelves. Bright grade-school paintings visible on the front of the refrigerator in the kitchen. The smell of cooking. There was a living room off the hallway with two silent, scared women in it. They were wearing Sunday dresses, which were very different from their work overalls.

'We need to know your names,' Neagley said.

Her voice was halfway between warm friendliness and the cold knell of doom. Reacher smiled to himself. That was Neagley's way. He remembered it well. Nobody ever argued with her. It was one of her strengths.

'Julio,' the man said.

'Anita,' the first woman said. Reacher assumed she was Julio's wife, by the way she glanced at him before answering.

'Maria,' the second woman said. 'I'm Anita's sister.'

There was a small sofa and two armchairs. Anita and Maria squeezed up to let Julio sit with them on the sofa. Reacher took that as an invitation and sat down in one of the armchairs.

Neagley took the other. It put the two of them at a symmetrical angle, like the sofa was a television screen and they were sitting down to watch it.

'We think you guys put the letter in the office,' Neagley said.

There was no reply. No reaction at all. No expression on the three faces. Just some kind of silent blank stoicism.

'Did you?' Neagley asked.

No reply.

'The kids in bed?' Reacher asked.

'They're not here,' Anita said.

'Are they yours or Maria's?'

'They're mine.'

'Boys or girls?'

'Both girls.'

'Where are they?'

She paused. 'With cousins.'

'Why?'

'Because we work nights.'

'Not for much longer,' Neagley said. 'You won't be working at all, unless you tell somebody something.'

No response.

'No more health insurance, no more benefits.'

No response.

'You might even go to jail.'

Silence in the room.

'Whatever happens to us will happen,' Julio said.

'Did somebody ask you to put it there? Somebody you know in the office?'

Absolutely no response.

'Somebody you know outside the office?'

'We didn't do anything with any letter.'

'So what *did* you do?' Reacher asked.

'We cleaned. That's what we're there for.'

'You were in there an awful long time.'

Julio looked at his wife, like he was puzzled.

'We saw the tape,' Reacher said.

'We know about the cameras,' Julio said.

'You follow the same routine every night?'

'We have to.'

'Spend that long in there every night?'

Julio shrugged. 'I guess so.'

'You rest up in there?'

'No, we clean.'

'Same every night?'

'Everything's the same every night. Unless somebody's spilled some coffee or left a lot of trash around or something. That might slow us up some.'

'Was there something like that in Stuyvesant's office that night?'

'No,' Julio said. 'Stuyvesant is a clean guy.'

'You spent some big amount of time in there.'

'No more than usual.'

'You got an exact routine?'

'I guess so. We vacuum, wipe things off, empty the trash, put things neat, move on to the next office.'

Silence in the room. Just the faint thump of the far-off car stereo, much attenuated by the walls and the windows.

'OK,' Neagley said. 'Listen up, guys. The tape shows you going in there. Afterwards, there was a letter on the desk. We think you put it there because somebody asked you to. Maybe they told you it was a joke or a trick. Maybe they told you it was OK to do it. And it was OK. There's no harm done. But we need to know who asked you. Because this is part of the game, too, us trying to find out. And now you've got to tell us, otherwise the game is over and we have to figure you put it there off of your own bat. And that's not OK. That's real bad. That's making a threat against the Vice President-elect of the United States. And you can go to prison for that.'

No reaction. Another long silence.

'Are we going to get fired?' Maria asked.

'Aren't you listening?' Neagley said. 'You're going to jail, unless you tell us who it was.'

Maria's face went still, like a stone. And Anita's, and Julio's. Still faces, blank eyes, stoic miserable expressions straight from a thousand years of peasant experience: *sooner or later, the harvest always fails.*

'Let's go,' Reacher said.

They stood up and stepped through to the hallway. Climbed

over the seesaw and let themselves out into the night. Made it back to the Suburban in time to see Froelich snapping her cell phone shut. There was panic in her eyes.

'What?' Reacher asked.

'We got another one,' she said. 'Ten minutes ago. And it's worse.'

SIX

IT WAS WAITING FOR THEM IN THE CENTRE OF THE LONG TABLE IN THE conference room. A small crowd of people had gathered around it. The halogen spots in the ceiling lit it perfectly. There was a brown nine-by-twelve envelope with a metal closure and a torn flap. And a single sheet of white letter-size paper. On it were printed ten words: *The day upon which Armstrong will die is fast approaching.* The message was split into two lines, exactly centred between the margins and set slightly above the middle of the paper. There was nothing else visible. People stared at it in silence. The guy in the suit from the reception desk pushed backward through the crowd and spoke to Froelich.

'I handled the envelope,' he said. 'I didn't touch the letter. Just spilled it out.'

'How did it arrive?' she asked.

'The garage guard took a bathroom break. Came back and found it on the ledge inside his booth. He brought it straight up to me. So I guess his prints are on the envelope too.'

'When, exactly?'

'Half-hour ago.'

'How does the garage guard work his breaks?' Reacher asked.

The room went quiet. People turned towards the new voice. The desk guy started in with a fierce *who-the-hell-are-you* look. But then he saw Froelich's face and shrugged and answered obediently.

'He locks the barrier down,' he said. 'That's how. Runs to the bathroom, runs back. Maybe two or three times a shift. He's down there eight hours at a stretch.'

Froelich nodded. 'Nobody's blaming him. Anybody call a forensic team yet?'

'We waited for you.'

'OK, leave it on the table, nobody touch it, and seal this room tight.'

'Is there a camera in the garage?' Reacher asked.

'Yes, there is.'

'So get Nendick to bring us tonight's tape, right now.'

Neagley craned over the table. 'Rather florid wording, don't you think? And "fast" definitely takes the prediction defence away, I would say. Turns the whole thing into an overt threat.'

Froelich nodded. 'You got that right,' she said slowly. 'If this is somebody's idea of a game or a joke, it just turned very serious very suddenly.'

She said it loud and clear and Reacher caught her purpose fast enough to watch the faces in the room. There was absolutely no reaction on any of them. Froelich checked her watch.

'Armstrong's in the air,' she said. 'On his way home.'

Then she was quiet for a beat.

'Call out an extra team,' she said. 'Half to Andrews, half to Armstrong's house. And put an extra vehicle in the convoy. And take an indirect route back.'

There was a split second of hesitation and then people started moving with the practised efficiency of an elite team readying itself for action. Reacher watched them carefully, and he liked what he saw. Then he and Neagley followed Froelich back to her office. She called an FBI number and asked for a forensics team, urgent. Listened to the reply and hung up.

'Not that there's much doubt about what they'll find,' she

said, to nobody in particular. Then Nendick knocked and came in, carrying two video tapes.

'Two cameras,' he said. 'One is inside the booth, high up, looking down and sideways, supposed to ID individual drivers in their cars. The other is outside, looking straight up the alley, supposed to pick up approaching vehicles.'

He put both cassettes on the desk and went back out. Froelich picked up the first tape and scooted her chair over to her television set. Put the tape in and pressed play. It was the sideways view from inside the booth. The angle was high, but it was about right to catch a driver framed in a car window. She wound back thirty-five minutes. Pressed play again. The guard was shown sitting on his stool with the back of his left shoulder in shot. Doing nothing. She fast-wound forward until he stood up. He touched a couple of buttons and disappeared. Nothing happened for thirty seconds. Then an arm snaked into view from the extreme right edge of the picture. Just an arm, in a heavy soft sleeve. A tweed overcoat, maybe. The hand on the end of it was gloved in leather. There was an envelope in the hand. It was pushed through the half-closed sliding window and dropped onto the ledge. Then the arm disappeared.

'He knew about the camera,' Froelich said.

'Clearly,' Neagley said. 'He was a yard shy of the booth, stretching out.'

'But did he know about the other camera?' Reacher asked.

Froelich ejected the first tape and inserted the second. Wound backward thirty-five minutes. Pressed play. The view was straight up the alley. The quality was poor. There were pools of light from outdoor spotlights and the contrast with areas of darkness was vivid. The shadows lacked detail. The angle was high and tight. The top of the picture cut off well before the street end of the alley. The bottom of the shot stopped maybe six feet in front of the booth. But the width was good. Very good. Both walls of the alley were clearly in view. There was no way of approaching the garage entrance without passing through the camera's field of vision.

The tape ran. Nothing happened. They watched the timecode counter until it reached a point twenty seconds before the arm had appeared. Then they watched the screen. A figure appeared at the top. Definitely male. No doubt about it. There was no mistaking the shoulders or the walk. He was wearing a heavy tweed overcoat, maybe grey or dark brown. Dark pants, heavy shoes, a muffler round his neck. And a hat on his head. A wide-brimmed hat, dark in colour, tilted way down in front. He walked with his chin tucked down. The video picked up a perfect view of the crown of his hat, all the way down the alley.

'He knew about the second camera,' Reacher said.

The tape ran on. The guy walked fast, but purposefully, not hurrying, not running, not out of control. He had the envelope in his right hand, holding it flat against his body. He disappeared out of the bottom of the shot and reappeared three seconds later. Without the envelope. He walked at the same purposeful pace all the way back up the alley and out of shot at the top of the screen.

Froelich froze the tape. 'Description?'

'Impossible,' Neagley said. 'Male, a little short and squat. Right-handed, probably. No visible limp. Apart from that we don't know diddly. We saw nothing.'

'Maybe not too squat,' Reacher said. 'The angle foreshortens things a little.'

'He had inside knowledge,' Froelich said. 'He knew about the cameras and the bathroom breaks. So he's one of us.'

'Not necessarily,' Reacher said. 'He could be an outsider who staked you out. The exterior camera must be visible if you're looking for it. And he could assume the interior camera. Most places have them. And a couple of nights' surveillance would teach him the bathroom break procedure. But you know what? Insider or outsider, we drove right past him. We must have. When we went out to see the cleaners. Because even if he's an insider, he needed to time the bathroom break exactly right. So he needed to be watching. He must have been across the street for a couple of hours, looking down the alley. Maybe with binoculars.'

The office went quiet.

'I didn't see anybody,' Froelich said.

'Me neither,' Neagley said.

'I had my eyes closed,' Reacher said.

'We wouldn't have seen him,' Froelich said. 'He hears a vehicle coming up the ramp, he ducks out of sight, surely.'

'I guess so,' Reacher said. 'But we were real close to him, temporarily.'

'Shit,' Froelich said.

'Yeah, shit,' Neagley echoed.

'So what do we do?' Froelich asked.

'Nothing,' Reacher said. 'Nothing we can do. This was more than forty minutes ago. If he's an insider, he's back home by now. Maybe tucked up in bed. If he's an outsider, he's already on I-95 or something, west or north or south, maybe thirty miles away. We can't call the troopers in four states and ask them to look for a right-handed man in a car who doesn't limp, no better description than that.'

'They could look for an overcoat and a hat on the back seat or in the trunk.'

'It's November, Froelich. Everybody's got a hat and a coat with them.'

'So what do we do?' she asked again.

'Hope for the best, plan for the worst. Concentrate on Armstrong, just in case this whole thing is for real. Keep him wrapped up tight. Like Stuyvesant said, threatening isn't necessarily the same thing as succeeding.'

'What's his schedule?' Neagley asked.

'Home tonight, the Hill tomorrow,' Froelich said.

'So you'll be OK. You scored perfect around the Capitol. If Reacher and I couldn't get to him there, no squat guy in an overcoat is going to. Assuming a squat guy in an overcoat *wants* to, instead of just shaking you up for the fun of it.'

'You think?'

'Like Stuyvesant said, take a deep breath and tough it out. Be confident.'

'Doesn't feel good. I need to know who this guy is.'

'We'll find out who he is, sooner or later. Until then, if you can't attack at one end you have to defend at the other.'

'She's right,' Reacher said. 'Concentrate on Armstrong, just in case.'

Froelich nodded vaguely and took the tape out of the machine and put the first one back in. Restarted it and stared at the screen until the garage guard came back from his bathroom break and noticed the envelope and picked it up and hurried out of shot with it.

'Doesn't feel good,' she said again.

An FBI forensics crew came by an hour later and photographed the sheet of paper on the conference room table. They used an office ruler for a scale reference and then used a pair of sterile plastic tweezers to lift the paper and the envelope into separate evidence bags. Froelich signed a form to keep the chain of evidence intact and they took both items away for examination. Then she got on the phone for twenty minutes and tracked Armstrong out of the Marine helicopter at Andrews and all the way home.

'OK, we're secure,' she said. 'For now.'

Neagley yawned and stretched. 'So take a break. Be ready for a hard week.'

'I feel stupid,' Froelich said. 'I don't know if this is a game or for real.'

'You feel too much,' Neagley said.

Froelich looked at the ceiling. 'What would Joe do now?'

Reacher paused and smiled. 'Go to the store and buy a suit, probably.'

'No, seriously.'

'He'd close his eyes for a minute and work it all out like it was a chess puzzle. He read Karl Marx, you know that? He said Marx had this trick of explaining everything with one single question, which was, who benefits?'

'So?'

'Let's say it *is* an insider doing this. Karl Marx would say, OK, the insider plans to benefit from it. Joe would ask, OK, *how* does he plan to benefit from it?'

'By making me look bad in front of Stuyvesant.'

'And getting you demoted or fired or whatever, because that rewards him in some way. That would be his aim. But that would be his *only* aim. Situation like that, there's no serious threat against Armstrong. That's an important point. And then Joe would say, OK, suppose it's not an insider, suppose it's an outsider. How does *he* plan to benefit?'

'By assassinating Armstrong.'

'Which gratifies him in some other way. So Joe would say what you've got to do is proceed *as if* it's an outsider, and proceed very calmly and without panicking, and above all successfully. That's two birds with one stone. If you're calm, you deny the insider his benefit. If you're successful, you deny the outsider *his* benefit.'

Froelich nodded, frustrated. 'But which is it? What did the cleaners tell you?'

'Nothing,' Reacher said. 'My read is somebody they know persuaded them to smuggle it in, but they aren't admitting to anything.'

'I'll tell Armstrong to stay home tomorrow.'

Reacher shook his head. 'You can't. You do that, you'll be seeing shadows every day and he'll be in hiding for the next four years. Just stay calm and tough it out.'

'Easy to say.'

'Easy to do. Just take a deep breath.'

Froelich was still and silent for a spell. Then she nodded.

'OK,' she said. 'I'll get you a driver. Be back here at nine in the morning. There'll be another strategy meeting. Exactly a week after the last one.'

The morning was damp and very cold, as if nature wanted to be done with fall and get started with winter. Exhaust fumes drifted down the streets in low white clouds and pedestrians hurried by on the sidewalks with their faces ducked deep into scarves. Neagley and Reacher met at eight forty at the cab line outside the hotel and found a Secret Service Town Car waiting for them. It was double-parked with the engine running and the driver standing next to it. He was maybe thirty years old, dressed in a dark overcoat and gloves, and he was up on his toes, scanning the crowd anxiously. He was breathing hard and his breath was pluming in the air.

'He looks worried,' Neagley said.

The inside of the car was hot. The driver didn't speak once during the journey. Didn't even say his name. Just bulled through the morning traffic and squealed into the underground garage. Led them at a fast walk into the interior lobby and into the elevator. Up three floors and across to the reception desk. It was manned by a different guy. He pointed down the corridor towards the conference room.

'Started without you,' he said. 'You better hurry.'

The conference room was empty apart from Froelich and Stuyvesant sitting face to face across the width of the table. They were both still and silent. Both pale. On the polished wood between them lay two photographs. One was the official FBI crime scene eight-by-ten of yesterday's ten-word message: *The day upon which Armstrong will die is fast approaching.* The other was a hasty Polaroid of another sheet of paper. Reacher stepped close and bent to look.

'Shit,' he said.

The Polaroid showed a single sheet of letter-sized paper, exactly like the first three in every detail. It followed the same format, a printed two-line message neatly centred near the middle of the page. Nine words: *A demonstration of your vulnerability will be staged today.*

'When did it come?' he asked.

'This morning,' Froelich said. 'In the mail. Addressed to Armstrong at his office. But we're bringing all his mail through here now.'

'Where is it from?'

'Orlando, Florida, postmarked Friday.'

'Another popular tourist destination,' Stuyvesant said.

Reacher nodded. 'Forensics on yesterday's?'

'Just got a heads-up by phone,' Froelich said. 'Everything's identical, thumbprint and all. I'm sure this one will be the same. They're working on it now.'

Reacher stared at the pictures. The thumbprints were completely invisible, but he felt he could just about see them there, like they were glowing in the dark.

'I had the cleaners arrested,' Stuyvesant said.

Nobody spoke.

'Gut call?' Stuyvesant said. 'Joke or real?'

'Real,' Neagley said. 'I think.'

'Doesn't matter yet,' Reacher said. 'Because nothing's happened yet. But we act like it's for real until we know otherwise.'

Stuyvesant nodded. 'That was Froelich's recommendation. She quoted Karl Marx at me. *The Communist Manifesto*.'

'*Das Kapital*, actually,' Reacher said. He picked up the Polaroid and looked at it again. The focus was a little soft and the paper was very white from the strobe, but there was no mistaking what the message meant.

'Two questions,' he said. 'First, how secure are his movements today?'

'As good as it gets,' Froelich said. 'I've doubled his detail. He's scheduled to leave home at eleven. I'm using the armoured stretch again instead of the Town Car. Full motorcade. We're using awnings across the sidewalks at both ends. He won't see open air at any point. We'll tell him it's another rehearsal procedure.'

'He still doesn't know about this yet?'

'No,' Froelich said.

'Standard practice,' Stuyvesant said. 'We don't tell them.'

'Thousands of threats a year,' Neagley said.

Stuyvesant nodded. 'Exactly. Most of them are background noise. We wait until we're absolutely sure. And even then, we don't always make a big point out of it. They've got better things to do. It's our job to worry.'

'OK, second question,' Reacher said. 'Where's his wife? And he has a grown-up kid, right? We have to assume that messing with his family would be a pretty good demonstration of his vulnerability.'

Froelich nodded. 'His wife is back here in D.C. She came in from North Dakota yesterday. As long as she stays in or near the house she's OK. His daughter is doing graduate work in Antarctica. Meteorology, or something. She's in a hut surrounded by a hundred thousand square miles of ice. Better protection than we could give her.'

Reacher put the Polaroid back down on the table.

'Are you confident?' he asked. 'About today?'

'I'm nervous as hell.'

'But?'

'I'm as confident as I can be.'

'I want Neagley and me on the ground, observing.'

'Think we're going to screw up?'

'No, but I think you're going to have your hands full. If the guy's in the neighbourhood, you might be too busy to spot him. And he'll have to be in the neighbourhood if he's for real and he wants to stage a demonstration of something.'

'OK,' Stuyvesant said. 'You and Ms Neagley, on the ground, observing.'

Froelich drove them to Georgetown in her Suburban. They arrived just before ten o'clock. They got out three blocks short of Armstrong's house and Froelich drove on. It was a cold day, but a watery sun was trying its best. Neagley stood still and glanced around, all four directions.

'Deployment?' she asked.

'Circles, on a three-block radius. You go clockwise and I'll go counterclockwise. Then you stay south and I'll stay north. Meet back at the house after he's gone.'

Neagley nodded and walked away west. Reacher went east into the weak morning sun. He wasn't especially familiar with Georgetown. Apart from short periods during the previous week spent watching Armstrong's house he had explored it only once, briefly, just after he left the service. He was familiar with the college feel and the coffee shops and the smart houses. But he didn't know it the way a cop knows his beat. A cop depends on a sense of *inappropriateness*. What doesn't fit? What's out of the ordinary? What's the wrong type of face or the wrong type of car for the neighbourhood? Impossible to answer those questions without long habituation to the place. And maybe impossible to answer them at all in a place like Georgetown. Everybody who lives there comes from somewhere else. They're there for a reason, to study at the university or to work in the government. It's a transient place. It has a temporary, shifting population. You graduate, you leave. You get voted out, you go someplace else. You get rich, you move to Chevy Chase. You go broke, you go sleep in a park.

So just about everybody he saw was suspicious. He could have made a case against any of them. Who belonged? An old Porsche with a blown exhaust rumbled past him. Oklahoma plates. An unshaven driver. Who was he? A brand new Mercury Sable was parked nose to tail with a rusted-out Rabbit. The

Sable was red and almost certainly a rental. Who was using it? Some guy just in for the day for a special purpose? He detoured next to it and glanced in through the windows at the rear seat. No overcoat, no hat. No open ream of Georgia-Pacific office paper. No box of latex medical gloves. And who owned the Rabbit? A graduate student? Or some backwoods anarchist with a Hewlett-Packard printer at home?

There were people on the sidewalks. Maybe four or five of them visible at any one time in any one direction. Young, old, white, black, brown. Men, women, young people carrying backpacks full of books. Some of them hurrying, some of them strolling. Some of them obviously on their way to the market, some of them obviously on their way back. Some of them looking like they had no particular place to go. He watched them all in the corner of his eye, but nothing special jumped out at him.

Time to time he checked upper-storey windows as he walked. There were a lot of them. It was good rifle territory. A warren of houses, back gates, narrow alleys. But a rifle would be no good against an armoured stretch limo. The guy would need an anti-tank missile for that. Of which there were plenty to choose from. The AT-4 would be favourite. It was a three-foot disposable fibreglass tube that fired a six-and-a-half-pound projectile through eleven inches of armour. Then the *BASE* principle took over. *Behind Armour Secondary Effect.* The entrance hole stayed small and tight, so the explosive event stayed confined to the interior of the vehicle. Armstrong would be reduced to little floating carbon pieces not much bigger than charred wedding confetti. Reacher glanced up at the windows. He doubted that a limo would have much armour plate in the roof, anyway. He made a mental note to ask Froelich about it. And to ask if she often rode in the same car as her charge.

He turned a corner and came out at the top of Armstrong's street. Looked up at the high windows again. A mere demonstration wouldn't require an actual missile. A rifle would be functionally ineffective, but it would make a point. A couple of chips in the limo's bulletproof glass would serve some kind of notice. A paintball gun would do the trick. A couple of red splatters on the rear window would be a message. But the upper-floor windows were quiet as far as the eye could see. They were clean and neat and draped and closed against the cold. The houses themselves were quiet and calm, serene and prosperous.

There was a small crowd of onlookers watching the Secret Service team erect an awning between Armstrong's house and the kerb. It was like a long narrow white tent. Heavy white canvas, completely opaque. The house end fitted flat against the brick around Armstrong's front door. The kerb end had a radius like a jetway at an airport. It would hug the profile of the limo. The limo's door would open right inside it. Armstrong would pass from the safety of his house straight into the armoured car without ever being visible to an observer.

Reacher walked a circle round the group of curious people. They looked unthreatening. Neighbours, mostly, he guessed. Dressed like they weren't going far. He moved back up the street and continued the search for open upper-storey windows. That would be inappropriate, because of the weather. But there weren't any. He looked for people loitering. There were plenty of those. There was a block where every second storefront was a coffee shop, and there were people passing time in every one of them. Sipping espresso, reading papers, talking on cell phones, writing in cramped notebooks, playing with electronic organizers.

He picked a coffee shop that gave him a good view south down the street and a marginal view east and west and bought a tall regular, black, and took a table. Sat down to wait and watch. At ten fifty-five a black Suburban came up the street and parked tight against the kerb just north of the tent. It was followed by a black Cadillac stretch that parked tight against the tent's opening. Behind that was a black Town Car. All three vehicles looked very heavy. All three had reinforced window frames and one-way glass. Four agents spilled out of the lead Suburban and took up station on the sidewalk, two of them north of the house and two of them south. Two Metro Police cruisers snuffled up the street and the first stopped right in the centre of the road well ahead of the Secret Service convoy and the second hung back well behind it. They lit up their light bars to hold the traffic. There wasn't much. A blue Chevy Malibu and a gold

Lexus SUV waited to get by. Reacher had seen neither vehicle before. Neither had been out cruising the area. He looked at the tent and tried to guess when Armstrong was passing through it. Impossible. He was still gazing at the house end when he heard the faint thump of an armoured door closing and the four agents stepped back to their Suburban and the whole convoy took off. The lead cop car leapt forward and the Suburban and the Cadillac and the Town Car fell in behind it and moved fast up the street. The second police cruiser brought up the rear. All five vehicles turned east right in front of Reacher's coffee shop. Tyres squealed on the blacktop. The cars accelerated. He watched them disappear. Then he turned back and watched the small crowd in the street disperse. The whole neighbourhood went quiet and still.

They watched the motorcade drive away from a vantage point about eighty yards from where Reacher was sitting. Their surveillance confirmed what they already knew. Professional pride prevented them from writing off his commute to work as actually *impossible*, but as a viable opportunity it was going to be way down on their list. Way, way down. Right there at the bottom. Which made it all the more fortunate that the transition web site offered so many other tempting choices.

They walked a circuitous route through the streets and made it back to their rented red Sable without incident.

Reacher finished his last mouthful of coffee and walked down towards Armstrong's house. He stepped off the sidewalk where the tent blocked it. It was a white canvas tunnel leading directly to Armstrong's front door. The door was closed. He walked on and stepped back on the sidewalk and met Neagley coming up from the opposite direction.

'OK?' he asked her.

'Opportunities,' she said. 'Didn't see anybody about to exploit any of them.'

'Me neither.'

'I like the tent and the armoured car.'

Reacher nodded. 'Takes rifles out of the equation.'

'Not entirely,' Neagley said. 'A .50 sniper rifle would get

through the armour. With the Browning AP round, or the API.'

He made a face. Either bullet was a formidable proposition. The standard armour-piercing item just blasted through steel plate, and the alternative armour-piercing incendiary burned its way through. But in the end he shook his head.

'No chance to aim,' he said. 'First you'd have to wait until the car was rolling, to be sure he was in it. Then you're putting a bullet into a large moving vehicle with dark windows. Hundred to one you'd hit Armstrong himself inside.'

'So you'd need an AT-4.'

'What I thought.'

'Either with the high-explosive against the car, or else you could use it to put a phosphorus bomb into the house.'

'From where?'

'I'd use an upper-floor window in a house behind Armstrong's. Across the alley. Their defence is mostly concentrated on the front.'

'How would you get in?'

'Phony utility guy, water company, electric company. Anybody who could get in carrying a big tool box.'

Reacher nodded. Said nothing.

'It's going to be a hell of a four years,' Neagley said.

'Or eight.'

Then there was the hiss of tyres and the sound of a big engine behind them and they turned to see Froelich easing up in her Suburban. She stopped alongside them, twenty yards short of Armstrong's house. Gestured them into the vehicle. Neagley got in the front and Reacher sprawled in the back.

'See anybody?' Froelich asked.

'Lots of people,' Reacher said. 'Wouldn't buy a cheap watch from any of them.'

Froelich took her foot off the brake and let the engine's idle speed crawl the car along the road. She kept it tight in the gutter and stopped it again when the nearside rear door was exactly level with the end of the tent. Lifted her hand from the wheel and spoke into the microphone wired to her wrist.

'One, ready,' she said.

Reacher looked to his right down the length of the canvas

tunnel and saw the front door open and a man step out. It was Brook Armstrong. No doubt about it. His photograph had been all over the papers for five solid months and Reacher had spent four whole days watching his every move. He was wearing a khaki raincoat and carrying a leather briefcase. He walked through the tent, not fast, not slow. An agent in a suit watched him from the door.

'The convoy was a decoy,' Froelich said. 'We do it that way, time to time.'

'Fooled me,' Reacher said.

'Don't tell him this isn't a rehearsal,' Froelich said. 'Remember he's not aware of anything yet.'

Reacher sat up straight and moved over to make room. Armstrong opened the door and climbed in beside him.

'Morning, M. E.,' he said.

'Morning, sir,' she replied. 'These are associates of mine, Jack Reacher and Frances Neagley.'

Neagley half turned and Armstrong threaded a long arm over the seat to shake her hand.

'I know you,' he said. 'I met you at the party on Thursday evening. You're a contributor, aren't you?'

'She's a security person, actually,' Froelich said. 'We had a little cloak-and-dagger stuff going there. An efficiency analysis.'

'I was impressed,' Neagley said.

'Excellent,' Armstrong said to her. 'Believe me, ma'am, I'm very grateful for the care everybody takes of me. Way more than I deserve. Really.'

He was magnificent, Reacher thought. His voice and his face and his eyes spoke of nothing but boundless fascination with Neagley alone. Like he would rather talk to her than do anything else in the whole world. And he had one hell of a visual memory, to place one face in a thousand from four days ago. That was clear. A born politician. He turned and shook Reacher's hand and lit up the car with a smile of genuine pleasure.

'Pleased to meet you, Mr Reacher,' he said.

'Pleasure's all mine,' Reacher said. Then he found himself smiling back. He liked the guy, immediately. He had charm to burn. There was charisma coming off him like heat. And even if you discounted ninety-nine per cent of it as political bullshit you could still like the fragment that was left. You could like it a lot.

'You in security too?' Armstrong asked him.

'Adviser,' Reacher said.

'Well, you guys do a hell of a great job. Glad to have you aboard.'

There was a tiny sound from Froelich's earpiece and she took off down the street and made her way towards Wisconsin Avenue. Merged into the traffic stream and headed south and east for the centre of town. The sun had disappeared again and the city looked grey through the deep tint in the windows. Armstrong made a little sound like a happy sigh and looked out at it, like he was still thrilled with it. Under the raincoat he was immaculate in a suit and a broadcloth shirt and a silk tie. He looked larger than life. Reacher had five years and three inches and fifty pounds on him but felt small and dull and shabby in comparison. But the guy also looked *real*. Very genuine. You could forget the suit and the tie and picture him in a torn old plaid jacket, out there splitting logs in his yard. He looked like a very serious politician, but a fun guy, too. He was tall and wired with energy. Blue eyes, plain features, unruly hair flecked with gold. He looked fit. Not with the kind of polish a gym gives you, but like he was just born strong. He had good hands. A slim gold wedding ring and no others. Cracked, untidy nails.

'Ex-military, am I right?' he asked.

'Me?' Neagley said.

'Both of you, I should think. You're both a little wary. He's checking me out and you're checking the windows, especially at the lights. I recognize the signs. My dad was military.'

'Career guy?'

Armstrong smiled. 'You didn't read my campaign bios? He planned on a career, but he was invalided out before I was born and started a lumber business. Never lost the look, though. He always walked the walk, that's for sure.'

Froelich came off M Street and headed parallel with Pennsylvania Avenue, past the Executive Office Building, past the front of the White House. Armstrong craned to look out at it. Smiled, with the laugh lines deepening around his eyes.

'Unbelievable, isn't it?' he said. 'Out of everybody who's

surprised I'm going to be a part of that, I'm the *most* surprised of all, believe me.'

Froelich drove straight past her own office in the Treasury Building and headed for the Capitol dome in the distance.

'Wasn't there a Reacher at Treasury?' Armstrong asked.

Hell of a memory for names too, Reacher thought.

'My elder brother,' he said.

'Small world,' Armstrong said.

Froelich made it onto Constitution Avenue and drove past the side of the Capitol. Made a left onto First Street and headed for a white tent leading to a side door in the Senate Offices. There were two Secret Service Town Cars flanking the tent. Four agents out on the sidewalks, looking cautious and cold. Froelich drove straight for the tent and eased to a stop tight against the kerb. Checked her position and rolled forward a foot to put Armstrong's door right inside the canvas shelter. Reacher saw a group of three agents waiting inside the tunnel. One of them stepped forward and opened the Suburban's door. Armstrong raised his eyebrows, like he was bemused by all the attention.

'Good meeting you both,' he said. 'And thanks, M. E.'

Then he stepped out into the canvas gloom and shut the door and the agents surrounded him and walked him down the length of the tent towards the building. Reacher glimpsed uniformed Capitol security people waiting inside. Armstrong stepped through the door and it closed solidly behind him. Froelich pulled away from the kerb and eased round the parked cars and headed north in the direction of Union Station.

'OK,' she said, like she was very relieved. 'So far so good.'

'You took a chance there,' Reacher said.

'Two in two hundred and eighty-one million,' Neagley said.

'What are you talking about?'

'Could have been one of us who sent the letters.'

Froelich smiled. 'My guess is it wasn't. What did you think of him?'

'I liked him,' Reacher said. 'I really did.'

'Me too,' Neagley said. 'I've liked him since Thursday. So now what?'

'He's in there all day for meetings. Lunch in the dining room.

We'll take him home around seven o'clock. His wife is home. So we'll rent them a video or something. Keep them locked up tight all evening.'

'We need intelligence,' Reacher said. 'We don't know what exact form this demonstration might take. Or where it will be. Could be anything from graffiti upward. We don't want to let it pass us by without noticing. If it happens at all.'

Froelich nodded. 'We'll check at midnight. Assuming we get to midnight.'

'And I want Neagley to interview the cleaners again. We get what we need from them, we can put our minds at rest.'

'I'd like to do that,' Froelich said.

They dropped Neagley at the Federal lock-up and then drove back to Froelich's office. Written FBI forensics reports were in on the latest two messages. They were identical to the first two in every respect. But there was a supplementary report from a Bureau chemist. He had detected something unusual about the thumbprints.

'Squalene,' Froelich said. 'You ever heard of that?'

Reacher shook his head.

'It's an acyclic hydrocarbon. A type of oil. There are traces of it present in the thumbprints. Slightly more on the third and fourth than the first and second.'

'Prints always have oils. That's how they get made.'

'But usually it's regular human finger oil. This stuff is different. C-thirty-H-fifty. It's a fish oil. Shark-liver oil, basically.'

She passed the paper across her desk. It was all covered in complicated stuff about organic chemistry. Squalene was a natural oil used as an old-fashioned lubricant for delicate machinery, like clockwork watches. There was an addendum at the bottom which said that when hydrogenated, squalene with an *e* becomes squalane with an *a*.

'What's hydrogenated?' Reacher asked.

'You add water?' Froelich said. 'Like hydroelectric power?'

He shrugged and she pulled a dictionary off the shelf and flicked through to *H*.

'No,' she said. 'It means you add extra hydrogen atoms to the molecule.'

'Well, that makes everything clear as mud. I scored pretty low in chemistry.'

'It means this guy could be a shark fisherman.'

'Or he guts fish for a living,' Reacher said. 'Or he works in a fish store. Or he's an antique watchmaker with his hands dirty from lubricating something.'

Froelich opened a drawer and flipped through a file and pulled a single sheet. Passed it across. It was a life-size fluoroscope photograph of a thumbprint.

'This our guy?' Reacher asked.

Froelich nodded. It was a very clear print. Maybe the clearest print Reacher had ever seen. All the ridges and whorls were exactly delineated. It was bold and astonishingly provocative. And it was big. Very big. The pad of the thumb measured nearly an inch and a half across. Reacher pressed his own thumb alongside it. His thumb was smaller, and he didn't have the most delicate hands in the world.

'That's not a watchmaker's thumb,' Froelich said.

Reacher nodded slowly. The guy must have hands like bunches of bananas. And rough skin, to print with that degree of clarity.

'Manual worker,' he said.

'Shark fisherman,' Froelich said. 'Where do they catch a lot of sharks?'

'Florida, maybe.'

'Orlando's in Florida.'

Her phone rang. She picked it up and her face fell. She looked up at the ceiling and pressed the phone into her shoulder.

'Armstrong needs to go over to the Department of Labor,' she said. 'And he wants to walk.'

SEVEN

IT WAS EXACTLY TWO MILES FROM THE TREASURY BUILDING TO THE Senate Offices and Froelich drove the whole way one-handed while she talked on her phone. The weather was grey and the traffic was heavy and the trip was slow. She parked at the mouth of the white tent on First Street and killed the motor and snapped her phone closed all at the same time.

'Can't the Labor guys come over here?' Reacher asked.

She shook her head. 'It's a political thing. There are going to be changes over there and it's more polite if Armstrong makes the effort himself.'

'Why does he want to walk?'

'Because he's an outdoors type. He likes fresh air. And he's stubborn.'

'Where does he have to go, exactly?'

She pointed due west. 'Less than half a mile that way. Call it six or seven hundred yards across Capitol Plaza.'

'Did he call them or did they call him?'

'He called them. It's going to leak so he's trying to pre-empt the bad news.'

'Can you stop him going?'

'Theoretically,' she said. 'But I really don't want to. That's not the sort of argument I want to have right now.'

Reacher turned and looked down the street behind them. Nothing there except grey weather and speeding cars on Constitution Avenue.

'So let him do it,' he said. 'He called them. Nobody's luring him out into the open. It's not a trick.'

She glanced ahead through the windshield. Then she turned and stared past him, through his side window, down the length of the tent. Flipped her phone open and spoke to people in her office again. She used abbreviations and a torrent of jargon he couldn't follow. Finished the call and closed her phone.

'We'll bring a Metro traffic chopper in,' she said. 'Keep it low enough to be obvious. He'll have to pass the Armenian Embassy, so we'll put some extra cops there. They'll blend in. I'll follow him in the car on D Street fifty yards behind. I want you out ahead of him with your eyes wide open.'

'When are we doing this?'

'Within ten minutes. Go up the street and left.'

'OK,' he said. She restarted the car and rolled forward so he could step onto the sidewalk clear of the tent. He got out and zipped his jacket and walked away into the cold. Up First Street and left onto C Street. There was traffic on Delaware Avenue ahead of him and beyond it he could see Capitol Plaza. There were low bare trees and open brown lawns. Paths made from crushed sandstone. A fountain in the centre. A pool to the right. To the left and farther on, some kind of an obelisk memorial to somebody.

He dodged cars and ran across Delaware. Walked on into the plaza. Grit crunched under his shoes. It was very cold. His soles were thin. It felt like there were ice crystals mixed in with the crushed stone underfoot. He stopped just short of the fountain. Looked around. Perimeters were good. To the north was open ground and then a semicircle of state flags and some other monument and the bulk of Union Station. To the south was nothing except for the Capitol Building itself far away across Constitution Avenue. Ahead to the west was a building he assumed was the Department of Labor. He looped around the fountain with his eyes focused on the middle distance and saw nothing that worried him. Poor cover, no close windows. There were people in the park, but no assassin hangs around all day just in case somebody's schedule changes unexpectedly.

He walked on. C Street restarted on the far side of the plaza, just about opposite the obelisk. It was more of an upright slab, really. There was a sign pointing towards it: *Taft Memorial*. C Street crossed New Jersey Avenue and then Louisiana Avenue. There were crosswalks. Fast traffic. Armstrong was going to spend some time standing still waiting for lights. The Armenian Embassy was ahead on the left. A police cruiser was pulling up in front of it. It parked on the kerb and four cops got out. He heard a distant helicopter. Turned round and saw it low in the north and west, skirting the prohibited airspace around the White House. The Department of Labor was dead ahead. There were plenty of convenient side doors.

He crossed C Street to the north sidewalk. Strolled back fifty yards to where he could see into the plaza. Waited. The helicopter was stationary in the air, low enough to be obvious, high enough not to be deafening. He saw Froelich's Suburban come round the corner, tiny in the distance. It pulled over and waited at the kerb. He watched people. Most of them were hurrying. It was too cold for loitering. He saw a group of men way on the far side of the fountain. Six guys in dark overcoats surrounded a seventh in a khaki raincoat. They walked in the centre of the sandstone path. The two agents on point were alert. The others crowded tight, like a moving huddle. They passed the fountain and headed for New Jersey Avenue. Waited at the light. Armstrong was bareheaded. The wind blew his hair. Cars streamed past. Nobody paid attention. Drivers and pedestrians occupied different worlds, based on relative time and space. Froelich kept her distance. Her Suburban idled along in the gutter fifty yards back. The light changed and Armstrong and his team walked on. So far, so good. The operation was working well.

Then it wasn't.

First the wind pushed the police helicopter slightly off station. Then Armstrong and his team were halfway across the narrow triangular spit of land between New Jersey Avenue and Louisiana Avenue when a lone pedestrian did a perfect double-take from ten yards away. He was a middle-aged guy, lean from neglect, bearded, long-haired, unkempt. He was wearing a belted raincoat greasy with age. He stood completely still for a split second and then launched himself towards Armstrong with his legs taking long bouncing strides and his arms windmilling uselessly and his mouth wide open in a snarl. The two nearest agents jumped forward to intercept him and the other four pulled back and crowded round Armstrong himself. They jostled and manoeuvred until they had all six bodies between the crazy guy and Armstrong. Which left Armstrong totally vulnerable from the opposite direction.

Reacher thought *decoy* and spun round. Nothing there. Nothing anywhere. Just the cityscape, still and cold and indifferent. He checked windows for movement. He looked for the flash of sun on glass. Nothing. Nothing at all. He looked at cars on the avenues. All of them oblivious and moving fast. None of them slowing. He turned back and saw the crazy guy on the ground with two agents holding him down and two more with guns covering him. He saw Froelich's Suburban speeding up and taking the corner fast. She stopped hard on the kerb and two agents bundled Armstrong straight across the sidewalk and into the back seat.

But the Suburban didn't go anywhere. It just sat there with traffic spilling around it. The helicopter drifted back on station and lost a little altitude and came down for a closer look. Its noise beat the air. Nothing happened. Then Armstrong got back out of the car. The two agents got out with him and walked him over to the crazy guy on the ground. Armstrong squatted down. Rested his elbows on his knees. It looked like he was talking. Froelich left her motor running and joined him on the sidewalk. Raised her hand and spoke into her wrist microphone. After a long moment a Metro cruiser came round the corner and pulled up behind the Suburban. Armstrong stood up straight and watched the two agents with the guns put the guy in the back of the cop car. The cop car drove away and Froelich went back to her Suburban and Armstrong re-grouped with his escort and walked on towards the Department of Labor. The helicopter drifted above them. As they finally crossed Louisiana Avenue one way Reacher crossed it the other and jogged down to Froelich in her car. She was sitting in the driver's seat with her head turned to watch Armstrong walk away. Reacher tapped on the window and she whirled round in surprise. Saw who it was and buzzed the glass down.

'You OK?' he asked her.

She turned back again to watch Armstrong. 'I must be nuts.'

'Who was the guy?'

'Just some street person. We'll follow it up, but I can tell you right now it's not connected. No way. If that guy had sent the messages we'd still be smelling the bourbon on the paper. Armstrong wanted to *talk* to him. Said he felt sorry for him. And then he insisted on sticking with the walkabout. He's nuts. And I'm nuts for allowing it.'

'Is he going to walk back?'

'Probably. I need it to rain, Reacher. Why doesn't it ever rain when you want it to? A real downpour an hour from now would help me out.'

He glanced up at the sky. It was grey and cold, but all the cloud was high and unthreatening. It wasn't going to rain.

'You should tell him,' he said.

She shook her head and turned to face front. 'We just don't do that.'

'Then you should get one of his staff to call him back in a hurry. Like something's real urgent. Then he'd have to ride.'

She shook her head again. 'He's running the transition. He sets the pace. Nothing's urgent unless he says it is.'

'So tell him it's another rehearsal. A new tactic or something.'

Froelich glanced across at him. 'I guess I could do that. It's still the pre-game period. We're entitled to rehearse with him. Maybe.'

'Try it,' he said. 'The walk back is more dangerous than the walk there. There'll be a couple of hours for somebody to find out he's going to do it.'

'Get in,' she said. 'You look cold.'

He walked round the Suburban's hood and climbed in on the passenger side. Unzipped his jacket and held it open to allow the warm air from the heater to funnel up inside it. They sat and watched until Armstrong and his minders disappeared inside the Labor building. Froelich immediately called her office. Left instructions that she was to be informed before Armstrong moved again. Then she put the car in gear and took off south and west towards the East Wing of the National Gallery. She made a left and drove past the Capitol Building's reflecting pool. Then a right onto Independence Avenue.

'Where are we going?' Reacher asked.

'Nowhere in particular,' she said. 'I'm just killing time. And trying to decide if I should resign today or keep on beating my brains out.'

She drove past all the museums and made a left onto 14th Street. The Bureau of Engraving and Printing rose up on their right, between them and the Tidal Basin. It was a big grey building. She pulled up at the kerb opposite its main entrance. Kept the engine running and her foot on the brake. Gazed up at one of the high office windows.

'Joe spent time in there,' she said. 'Back when they were designing the new hundred-dollar bill. He figured if he was going to have to protect it, he should have some input on it. A long time ago, now.'

Her head was tilted up. Reacher could see the curve of her throat. He could see the way it met the opening of her shirt. He said nothing.

'I used to meet him here sometimes,' she said. 'Or on the steps of the Jefferson Memorial. We'd walk around the Basin, late in the evening. In spring or summer.'

Reacher looked ahead to his right. The Memorial crouched low among the bare trees and was reflected perfectly in the still water.

'I loved him, you know,' Froelich said.

Reacher said nothing. Just looked at her hand resting on the wheel. And her wrist. It was slim. The skin was perfect. There was a trace of a faded summer tan.

'And you're very like him,' she said.

'Where did he live?'

She glanced at him. 'Don't you know?'

'I don't think he ever told me.'

Silence in the idling car.

'He had an apartment in the Watergate,' she said.

'Rented?'

She nodded. 'It was very bare. Like it was only temporary.'

'It would be. Reachers don't own property. I don't think we ever have.'

'Your mother's family did. They had estates in France.'

'Did they?'

'You don't know that either?'

He shrugged. 'I know they were French, obviously. Not sure I ever heard about their real-estate situation.'

Froelich eased her foot off the brake and glanced in the mirror and gunned the motor and rejoined the traffic stream.

'You guys had a weird idea of family,' she said. 'That's for damn sure.'

'Seemed normal at the time,' he said. 'We thought every family was like that.'

Her cell phone rang. A low electronic trill in the quiet of the car. She flipped it open. Listened for a moment and said, 'OK,' and closed it up.

'Neagley,' she said. 'She's finished with the cleaners.'

'She get anything?'

'Didn't say. She's meeting us back at the office.'

She looped round south of the Mall and drove north on 14th Street. Her phone rang again. She fumbled it open one-handed and listened as she drove. Said nothing and snapped it shut. Glanced at the traffic ahead on the street.

'Armstrong's ready to get back,' she said. 'I'm going to go try and make him ride with me. I'll drop you in the garage.'

She drove down the ramp and stopped long enough for Reacher to jump out. Then she turned round in the crowded space and headed back up to the street. Reacher found the door with the wired-glass porthole and walked up the stairs to the lobby with the single elevator. Rode it to the third floor and found Neagley waiting in the reception area. She was sitting upright on a leather chair.

'Stuyvesant around?' Reacher asked her.

She shook her head. 'He went next door. To the White House.'

'I want to go look at that camera.'

They walked together past the counter towards the rear of the floor and came out in the square area outside Stuyvesant's office. His secretary was at her desk with her purse open. She had a tiny tortoiseshell mirror and a stick of lip gloss in her hands. The pose made her look human. Efficient, for sure, but like an amiable old soul, too. She saw them coming and put her cosmetic equipment away fast, like she was embarrassed to be caught with it. Reacher looked over her head at the surveillance camera. Neagley looked at Stuyvesant's door. Then she glanced at the secretary.

'Do you remember the morning the message showed up in there?' she asked.

'Of course I do,' the secretary said.

'Why did Mr Stuyvesant leave his briefcase out here?'

The secretary thought for a moment. 'Because it was a Thursday.'

'What happens on a Thursday? Does he have an early meeting?'

'No, his wife goes to Baltimore, Tuesdays and Thursdays.'

'How is that connected?'

'She volunteers at a hospital there.'

Neagley looked straight at her. 'How does that affect her husband's briefcase?'

'She drives,' the secretary said. 'She takes their car. They only have one. No department vehicle either, because Mr Stuyvesant isn't operational any more. So he has to come to work on the Metro.'

Neagley looked blank. 'The subway?'

The secretary nodded. 'He has a special briefcase for Tuesdays and Thursdays because he's forced to place it on the floor of the subway car. He won't do that with his regular briefcase, because he thinks it gets dirty.'

Neagley stood still. Reacher thought back to the video tapes, Stuyvesant leaving late on Wednesday evening, returning early on Thursday morning.

'I didn't notice a difference,' he said. 'Looked like the same case to me.'

The secretary nodded in agreement.

'They're identical items,' she said. 'Same make, same vintage. He doesn't like people to realize. But one is for his automobile and the other is for the subway car.'

'Why?'

'He hates dirt. I think he's afraid of it. Tuesdays and Thursdays, he won't take his subway-car briefcase into his office at all. He leaves it out here all day and I have to bring him things from it. If it's been raining he leaves his shoes out here too. Like his office was a Japanese temple.'

Neagley glanced at Reacher. Made a face.

'It's a harmless eccentricity,' the secretary said. Then she lowered her voice, as if she might be overheard all the way from the White House. 'And absolutely unnecessary, in my opinion. The D.C. Metro is famous for being the cleanest subway in the world.'

'OK,' Neagley said. 'But weird.'

'It's harmless,' the secretary said again.

Reacher lost interest and stepped behind her and looked at the fire door. It had a brushed-steel push bar at waist height, like the city construction codes no doubt required it to have. He put his fingers on it and it clicked back with silky precision. He pushed a little harder and it folded up against the painted wood and the door swung back. It was a heavy fireproof item and there were three large steel hinges carrying its weight. He stepped through to a small square stairwell. The stairs were concrete and newer than the stone fabric of the building. They ran up to the higher floors and down towards street level. They had steel handrails. There were dim emergency lights behind glass in wire cages. Clearly a narrow space had been appropriated in the back of the building during the modernization and dedicated to a full-bore fire escape system.

There was a regular knob on the back of the door that operated the same latch as the push bar. It had a keyhole, but it wasn't locked. It turned easily. *Makes sense*, he thought. The building was secure as a whole. There was no need for every floor to be isolated as well. He let the door close behind him and waited in the gloom on the stairwell for a second. Turned the knob again and reopened the door and stepped back into the brightness of the secretarial area, one pace. Twisted and looked up at the surveillance camera. It was right there above his head, set so it would pick him up some time during his second step. He inched forward and let the door close behind him. Checked the camera again. It would be seeing him by now. And he still had more than eight feet to go before he reached Stuyvesant's door.

'The cleaners put the message there,' the secretary said. 'There's no other possible explanation.'

Then her phone rang and she excused herself politely and answered it. Reacher and Neagley walked back through the maze of corridors and found Froelich's office. It was quiet and dark and empty. Neagley flicked the halogen lights on and sat down at the desk. There was no other chair, so Reacher sat on the floor with his legs straight out and his back propped against the side of a filing cabinet.

'Tell me about the cleaners,' he said.

Neagley drummed a rhythm on the desk with her fingers. The click of her nails alternated with little papery thumps from the pads of her fingers.

'They're all lawyered up,' she said. 'The department sent them attorneys, one each. They're all Mirandized, too. Their human rights are fully protected. Wonderful, isn't it? The civilian world?'

'Terrific. What did they say?'

'Nothing much. They clammed up tight. Stubborn as hell. But worried as hell, too. They're looking at a rock and a hard place. Obviously very frightened about revealing who told them to put the paper there, and equally frightened about losing their jobs and maybe going to jail. They can't win. It wasn't attractive.'

'You mention Stuyvesant's name?'

'Loud and clear. They know his name, obviously, but I'm not sure they know who he *is*, specifically. They're night workers. All they see is a bunch of offices. They don't see people. They didn't react to his name at all. They didn't really react to anything. Just sat there, scared to death, looking at their lawyers, saying nothing.'

'You're slipping. People used to eat out of your hand, the way I recall it.'

She nodded. 'I told you, I'm getting old. I couldn't get a handle on them anywhere. The lawyers wouldn't let me, really. The civilian justice system is very off-putting. I never felt so disconnected.'

Reacher said nothing. Checked his watch.

'So what now?' Neagley asked.

'We wait,' he said.

The wait went slowly. Froelich came back after an hour and a half and reported that Armstrong was safely back in his own office. She had persuaded him to come with her in the car. She told him she understood that he preferred to walk, but she made the point that her team needed operational fine-tuning and there was no better time to do it than right now. She pushed it to the point where a refusal would have seemed like a prima-donna pain in the ass, and Armstrong wasn't like that, so he climbed into the Suburban quite happily. The transfer through the tent at the Senate Offices had worked without incident.

'Now make some calls,' Reacher said. 'See if anything's happened that we need to know about.'

She checked with the D.C. cops first. There was the usual list of urban crimes and misdemeanours, but it would have been a stretch to categorize any of them as a demonstration of Armstrong's vulnerability. She transferred to the precinct holding the crazy guy and took a long verbal report on his status. Hung up and shook her head.

'Not connected,' she said. 'They know him. IQ below eighty, alcoholic, sleeps on the street, barely literate, and his prints don't match. He's got a record a yard long for jumping on anybody he's ever seen in the newspapers he sleeps under. Some kind of a bipolar problem. I suggest we forget all about him.'

'OK,' Reacher said.

Then she opened up the National Crime Information Center database and looked at recent entries. They were flooding in from all over the country at a rate faster than one every second. Faster than she could read them.

'Hopeless,' she said. 'We'll have to wait until midnight.'

'Or one o'clock,' Neagley said. 'It might happen on central time, out there in Bismarck. They might shoot up his house. Or throw a rock through the window.'

So Froelich called the cops in Bismarck and asked for

immediate notification of anything that could be even remotely connected to an interest in Armstrong. Then she made the same request to the North Dakota State Police and the FBI nationwide.

'Maybe it won't happen,' she said.

Reacher looked away. *You better hope it does*, he thought.

Around seven o'clock in the evening the office complex began to quiet down. Most of the people visible in the corridors were drifting one way only, towards the front exit. They were wearing raincoats and carrying bags and briefcases.

'Did you check out of the hotel?' Froelich asked.

'Yes,' Reacher said.

'No,' Neagley said. 'I make a terrible house guest.'

Froelich paused, a little taken aback. But Reacher wasn't surprised. Neagley was a very solitary person. Always had been. She kept herself to herself. He didn't know why.

'OK,' Froelich said. 'But we should take some time out. Rest up and regroup later. I'll drop you guys off and then go try to get Armstrong home safely.'

They rode together down to the garage and Froelich fired up her Suburban and drove Neagley to the hotel. Reacher walked with her as far as the bell captain's stand and reclaimed his Atlantic City clothes. They were packed with his old shoes and his toothbrush and his razor, folded up inside a black garbage bag he had taken from a maid's cart. It didn't impress the bellboy. But he carried it out to the Suburban anyway and Reacher took it from him and gave him a dollar. Then he climbed back in alongside Froelich and she drove on. It was cold and dark and damp and the traffic was bad. There was congestion everywhere. Long lines of red brake lights streamed ahead of them, long lines of bright white headlights streamed towards them. They drove south across the 11th Street Bridge and fought through a maze of streets to Froelich's house. She double-parked with the motor running and fiddled behind the steering wheel and took her door key off its ring. Handed it to him.

'I'll be back in a couple of hours,' she said. 'Make yourself at home.'

He took his bag and got out and watched her drive off. She made a right to loop back north over a different bridge and disappeared from sight. He crossed the sidewalk and unlocked her front door. The house was dark and warm. It had her perfume in it. He closed the door behind him and fumbled for a light switch. A low-wattage bulb came on inside a yellow shade on a lamp on a small chest of drawers. It gave a soft, muted light. He put the key down next to it and dropped his bag at the foot of the stairs and stepped into the living room. Switched on the light. Walked on into the kitchen. Looked around.

There were basement stairs in there, behind a door. He stood still for a second with his ritual curiosity nagging at him. It was an ingrained reflex, like breathing. But was it polite to search your host's house? Just out of habit? *Of course not.* But he couldn't resist. He walked down the stairs, switching lights on as he went. The basement itself was a dark space walled with smooth old concrete. It had a furnace and a water softener in it. A washing machine and an electric dryer. Shelving units. Old suitcases. Plenty of miscellaneous junk stacked all around, but nothing of any great significance. He walked back up. Turned off the lights. Opposite the head of the stairs was an enclosed space right next to the kitchen. It was larger than a closet, smaller than a room. Maybe a pantry, originally. It had been fitted out as a tiny home office. There was a rolling chair and a desk and shelves, all of them a few years old. They looked like chain store versions of real office furniture, with plenty of wear and tear on them. Maybe they were secondhand. There was a computer, fairly old. An inkjet printer connected to it with a fat cable. He moved back into the kitchen.

He looked at all the usual places women hide things in kitchens and found five hundred dollars in mixed bills inside an earthenware casserole on a high shelf inside a cupboard. Emergency cash. Maybe an old Y2K precaution that she decided to stick with afterwards. He found an M9 Beretta nine-millimetre sidearm in a drawer, carefully hidden under a stack of place mats. It was old and scratched and stained with dried oil in random patches. Probably army surplus, redistributed to another government department. Last-generation Secret Service issue, without a doubt. It was unloaded. The magazine was missing. He opened the next drawer to the left and put his hand on four spares laid out in a line under an oven glove. They were all loaded with standard jacketed cartridges. Good news and bad news. The layout was smart. Pick up the gun with your right hand, access the magazines with your left. Sound ergonomics. But storing magazines full of bullets was a bad idea. Leave them long enough, the spring in the magazine learns its compressed shape and won't function right. More jams are caused by tired magazine springs than any other single reason. Better to keep the gun with a single shell locked in the chamber and all the other bullets loose. You can fire once right-handed while you thumb loose shells into an empty magazine with your left. Slower than the ideal, but a lot better than pulling the trigger and hearing nothing at all except a dull click.

He closed the kitchen drawers and moved back into the living room. Nothing there, except a hollowed-out book on the shelves, and it was empty. He turned on the TV, and it worked. He had once known a guy who hid things inside a gutted TV set. The guy's quarters had been searched eight times before anybody thought to check that everything was exactly as it seemed.

There was nothing in the hallway. Nothing taped under the drawers in the little chest. Nothing in the bathrooms. Nothing of significance in the bedrooms except a shoe box under Froelich's bed. It was full of letters addressed in Joe's handwriting. He put them back without reading them. Went back downstairs and carried his garbage bag up to the guest room. Decided to wait an hour and then eat alone if she wasn't back. He would send for the hot and sour and the General Tso's again. It had been pretty good. He put his bathroom items next to the sink. Hung his Atlantic City clothes in the closet next to Joe's abandoned suits. He looked at them and stood still for a long moment and then selected one at random and pulled it off the rail.

The plastic wrap tore as he stripped it away. It was stiff and brittle. The label inside the suit coat had a single Italian word embroidered in fancy script. Not a brand he recognized. The material was some kind of fine wool. It was very dark grey and had a faint sheen to it. The lining was acetate made to look like dark red silk. Maybe it *was* silk. It had a watermark. There was no vent in the back. He laid it on the bed and put the pants next to it. They were very plain. No pleats, no cuffs.

He went back to the closet and took out a shirt. Lifted the plastic off it. It was pure white broadcloth. No buttons on the collar. A small label inside the neckband with two names in copperplate script, too obscure to read. *Somebody & Somebody.* Either an exclusive London shirtmaker, or some sweatshop faking it. The fabric was hefty. Not thick like fatigues, but there was some weight to it.

He unlaced his shoes. Took off his jacket and jeans and folded them over a chair. Followed them with his T-shirt and his underwear. Stepped into the bathroom and set the shower running. Stepped into the stall. There was soap and shampoo in there. The soap was dried rock-hard and the shampoo bottle was stuck shut with old suds. Clearly Froelich didn't have frequent house guests. He soaked the bottle under the stream of hot water and forced it open. Washed his hair and soaped his body. Leaned out and grabbed his razor and shaved carefully. Rinsed all over and got out and dripped on the floor and searched for a towel. He found one in a cupboard. It was thick and new. Too new to be any good at drying. It just slid the water around on his skin. He did his best with it and then wrapped it round his waist and combed his hair with his fingers.

He stepped back into the bedroom and picked up Joe's shirt. Hesitated a second, and then put it on. Flipped the collar up and buttoned it at the neck. Buttoned it down the front. Opened the closet door and checked the fit in the mirror. It was perfect, more or less. Could have been tailored for him. He buttoned the cuffs. Sleeve length was excellent. He twisted left and right. Caught sight of a shelf behind the rail. The space where the suit and the shirt had been let him see it. There were neckties neatly rolled and placed side by side. Tissue-paper packages from a laundry, sealed with sticky labels. He opened one and found a pile of clean white boxers. Opened another and found black socks folded together in pairs.

He moved back to the bed and dressed in his brother's clothes. Selected a dark maroon tie with a discreet pattern.

British, like it represented a regimental association or one of those expensive high schools. He put it on and cracked the shirt collar down over it. Put on a pair of boxers and a pair of socks. Stepped into the suit pants. Shrugged into the jacket. He put his new shoes on and used the discarded tissue paper to scrub the scuffs off them. Stood up straight and walked back to the mirror. The suit fitted very well. It was maybe a fraction long in the arms and legs, because he was a fraction shorter than Joe had been. And it was maybe a fraction tight, because he was a little heavier. But overall he looked very impressive in it. Like a completely different person. Older. More authoritative. More serious. More like Joe.

He bent down and picked up the cardboard box from the closet floor. It was heavy. Then he heard a sound down in the hallway. Somebody out on the step, knocking on the front door. He put the box back under the hanging rail and headed down the stairs. Opened up. It was Froelich. She was standing in the evening mist with her hand raised ready to knock again. Light from the street behind her put her face in shadow.

'I gave you my key,' she said.

He stepped back and she stepped in. Looked up and froze. She fumbled behind her back and pushed the door shut and leaned hard up against it. Just stared at him. Something in her eyes. Shock, fear, panic, loss, he didn't know.

'What?' he said.

'I thought you were Joe,' she said. 'Just for a second.'

Her eyes filled with tears and she laid her head back against the wood of the door. She blinked against the tears and looked at him again and started crying hard. He stood still for a second and then stepped forward and took her in his arms. She dropped her purse and burrowed into his chest.

'I'm sorry,' he said. 'I tried on his suit.'

She said nothing. Just cried.

'Stupid, I guess,' he said.

She moved her head, but he couldn't tell if she was saying *yes, it was* or *no, it wasn't*. She locked her arms around his body and just held on. He put one hand low on her back and used the other to smooth her hair. He held her like that for minutes. She fought the tears and then gulped twice and pulled away. Swiped at her eyes with the back of her hand.

'Not your fault,' she said.

He said nothing.

'You looked so real. I bought him that tie.'

'I should have thought,' Reacher said.

She ducked down to her purse and came back with a tissue. Blew her nose and smoothed her hair.

'Oh, God,' she said.

'I'm sorry,' he said again.

'Don't worry,' she said. 'I'll be OK.'

He said nothing.

'You looked so good, is all,' she said. 'Just standing there.'

She was staring at him quite openly. Then she reached out and straightened his tie. Touched a spot on his shirt where her tears had dampened it. Ran her fingers behind the lapels of his jacket. Stepped forward on tiptoe and locked her hands behind his neck and kissed him on the mouth.

'So good,' she said, and kissed him again, hard.

He held still for a second and then kissed her back. Hard. Her mouth was cool. Her tongue was swift. She tasted faintly of lipstick. Her teeth were small and smooth. He could smell perfume on her skin and in her hair. He put one hand low on her side and the other behind her head. He could feel her breasts against his chest. Her ribs, yielding slightly under his hand. Her hair, between his fingers. Her hand was cold and urgent on the back of his neck. Her fingers were raking upward into the stubble from his haircut. He could feel her nails on his skin. He slid his hand up her back. Then she stopped moving. Held still. Pulled away. She was breathing heavily. Her eyes were closed. She touched the back of her hand to her mouth.

'We shouldn't do this,' she said.

He looked at her. 'Probably not,' he said.

She opened her eyes. Said nothing.

'So what should we do?' he asked.

She moved sideways and stepped into her living room. 'I don't know,' she said. 'Eat dinner, I guess. Did you wait?'

He followed her into the room. 'Yes,' he said. 'I waited.'

'You're very like him,' she said.

'I know,' he said.

'Do you understand what I mean?'

He nodded. 'What you saw in him you see in me, a little bit.'

'But *are* you like him?'

He knew exactly what she was asking. *Did you see things the same? Did you share tastes? Were you attracted to the same women?*

'Like I told you,' he said. 'There are similarities. And there are differences.'

'That's no answer.'

'He's dead,' Reacher said. 'That's an answer.'

'And if he wasn't?'

'Then a lot of things would be different.'

'Suppose I'd never known him. Suppose I'd gotten your name some other way.'

'Then I might not be here at all.'

'Suppose you were anyway.'

He looked at her. Took a deep breath, and held it, and let it out.

'Then I doubt if we'd be standing here talking about dinner,' he said.

'Maybe you wouldn't be a substitute,' she said. 'Maybe you'd be the real thing and Joe was the substitute.'

He said nothing.

'This is too weird,' she said. 'We can't do this.'

'No,' he said. 'We can't.'

'It was a long time ago,' she said. 'Six years.'

'Is Armstrong OK?'

'Yes,' she said. 'He's OK.'

Reacher said nothing.

'We broke up, remember,' she said. 'A year before he died. It's not like I'm his tragic widow or something.'

Reacher said nothing.

'And it's not like you're really his grieving brother either,' she said. 'You hardly knew him.'

'Mad at me about that?'

She nodded. 'He was a lonely man. He needed somebody. So I'm a little mad about it.'

'Not half as much as I am.'

She said nothing in reply. Just moved her wrist and checked her watch. It was a strange gesture, so he checked his, too. The second hand hit nine thirty exactly. Her cell phone rang inside her open purse out in the hallway. It was loud in the silence.

'My people checking in,' she said. 'From Armstrong's house.'

She stepped back to the hallway and bent down and answered the call. Hung up without comment.

'All quiet,' she said. 'I told them to call every hour.'

He nodded. She looked anywhere but straight at him. The moment was gone.

'Chinese again?' she asked.

'Suits me,' he said. 'Same order.'

She called it in from the kitchen phone and disappeared upstairs to take a shower. He waited in the living room and took the food from the delivery guy when he eventually showed up with it. She came down again and they ate across from each other at the kitchen table. She brewed coffee and they drank two cups each, slowly, not talking. Her cell phone rang again at exactly ten thirty. She had it next to her at the table and answered it immediately. Just a short message.

'All quiet,' she said. 'So far so good.'

'Stop worrying,' he said. 'It would take an air strike to get him in his house.'

She smiled suddenly. 'Remember Harry Truman?'

'My favourite president,' Reacher said. 'From what I know about him.'

'Ours, too,' she said. 'From what *we* know about him. One time around 1950 the White House residence was being renovated and he was living in Blair House across Pennsylvania Avenue. Two men came to kill him. One was taken out by the cops on the street, but the other made it to the door. Our people had to pull *Truman* off the assassin. He said he was going to take his gun away and stick it up his ass.'

'Truman was like that.'

'You bet he was. You should hear some of the old stories.'

'Would Armstrong be like that?'

'Maybe. Depends how the moment struck him, I guess. He's pretty gentle physically, but he's not a coward. And I've seen him very angry.'

'And he looks tough enough.'

Froelich nodded. Checked her watch. 'We should get back to the office now. See if anything's happened anywhere else. You call Neagley while I clear up here. Tell her to be ready to roll in twenty minutes.'

They were back in the office before eleven fifteen. The message logs were blank. Nothing of significance from the D.C. police department. Nothing from North Dakota, nothing from the FBI. Updates were still streaming into the National Crime Information Center's database. Froelich started combing through the day's reports. She found nothing of interest. Her cell phone rang at eleven thirty. All was quiet and peaceful in Georgetown. She turned back to the computer. Nothing doing. Time ticked around to midnight. Monday finished and Tuesday started. Stuyvesant showed up again. He just appeared in the doorway like he had before. Said nothing. The only chair in the room was Froelich's own. Stuyvesant leaned against the door frame. Reacher sat on the floor. Neagley perched on a file cabinet.

Froelich waited ten minutes and called the D.C. cops. They had nothing to report. She called the Hoover Building and the FBI told her nothing significant had happened before midnight in the east. She turned back to the computer screen. Called out occasional incoming stories but neither Stuyvesant nor Reacher nor Neagley could twist them into any kind of a connection with a potential threat to Armstrong. The clock moved on to one in the morning. Midnight, central time. She called the police department in Bismarck. They had nothing for her. She called the North Dakota State Police. Nothing at all. She tried the FBI again. Nothing reported from their field offices in the last sixty minutes. She put the phone down and scooted her chair back from her desk. Breathed out.

'Well, that's it,' she said. 'Nothing happened.'

'Excellent,' Stuyvesant said.

'No,' Reacher said. 'Not excellent. Not excellent at all. It's the worst possible news we could have gotten.'

EIGHT

STUYVESANT LED THEM STRAIGHT BACK TOWARDS THE CONference room. Neagley walked next to Reacher, close by his shoulder in the narrow corridors.

'Great suit,' she whispered.

'First one I ever wore,' he whispered back. 'We on the same page with this?'

'On the same page and out of a job, probably,' she said. 'That is, if you're thinking what I'm thinking.'

They turned a corner. Walked on. Stuyvesant stopped and shepherded them into the conference room and came in after them and hit the lights and closed the door. Reacher and Neagley sat together on one side of the long table and Stuyvesant sat next to Froelich on the other, like he foresaw an adversarial element to the conversation.

'Explain,' he said.

Silence for a second.

'This is definitely *not* an inside job,' Neagley said.

Reacher nodded. 'Although we were fooling ourselves by ever thinking it was entirely one thing or the other. It was always both. But it was useful shorthand. The real question was where the balance lay. Was it fundamentally an inside job with trivial help from the outside? Or was it basically an outside job with trivial help from the inside?'

'The trivial help being what?' Stuyvesant asked.

'A potential insider needed a thumbprint that wasn't his. A potential outsider needed a way to get the second message inside this building.'

'And you've concluded that it's the outsider?'

Reacher nodded again. 'Which is absolutely the worst news we could have gotten. Because whereas an insider messing around is merely a pain in the ass, an outsider is truly dangerous.'

Stuyvesant looked away. 'Who?'

'No idea,' Reacher said. 'Just some outsider with a loose one-time connection to an insider, sufficient to get the message in and nothing more.'

'The insider being one of the cleaners.'

'Or all of them,' Froelich said.

'I assume so, yes,' Reacher said.

'You sure about this?'

'Completely.'

'How?' Stuyvesant asked.

Reacher shrugged. 'Lots of reasons,' he said. 'Some of them small, one of them big.'

'Explain,' Stuyvesant said again.

'I look for simplicity,' Reacher said.

Stuyvesant nodded. 'So do I. I hear hoof beats, I think horses, not zebras. But the simple explanation here is an insider trying to get under Froelich's skin.'

'Not really,' Reacher said. 'The chosen method is way too complex for that. They'd be doing all the usual stuff instead. The easy stuff. I'm sure we've all seen it before. Mysterious communications failures, computer crashes, bogus alarm calls to non-existent addresses in the bad part of town, she arrives, calls in for back-up, nobody shows, she gets scared, she panics on the radio, a recording gets made and starts to circulate. Any law enforcement department has got a stack of examples a yard high.'

'Including the military police?'

'Sure. Especially with women officers.'

Stuyvesant shook his head.

'No,' he said. 'That's conjecture. I'm asking how you *know*.'

'I know because nothing happened today.'

'Explain,' Stuyvesant said for the third time.

'This is a smart opponent,' Reacher said. 'He's bright and he's confident. He's in *command*. But he threatened something and he didn't deliver.'

'So? He failed, is all.'

'No,' Reacher said. 'He didn't even *try*. Because he didn't know he had to. Because he didn't know his letter arrived today.'

Silence in the room.

'He expected it to arrive tomorrow,' Reacher said. 'It was mailed on Friday. Friday to Monday is pretty fast for the U.S. mail. It was a fluke. He banked on Friday to Tuesday.'

Nobody spoke.

'He's an outsider,' Reacher said. 'He's got no direct connection to the department and therefore he's unaware his threat showed up a day early, or he'd have delivered today *for sure*. Because he's an arrogant son of a bitch, and he wouldn't have wanted to let himself down. Count on it. So he's out there somewhere, waiting to deliver on his threat tomorrow, which is exactly when he expected he'd have to all along.'

'Great,' Froelich said. 'There's another contributor reception tomorrow.'

Stuyvesant was quiet for a beat.

'So what do you suggest?' he asked.

'We have to cancel,' Froelich said.

'No, I meant long-term strategy,' Stuyvesant said. 'And we can't cancel *anything*. We can't just give up and say we can't protect our principal.'

'You have to tough it out,' Reacher said. 'It'll only be a demonstration. Designed to torment you. My guess is it'll specifically avoid Armstrong altogether. It'll penetrate somewhere he has been or will be some other time.'

'Like where?' Froelich asked.

'His house, maybe,' Reacher said. 'Either here or in Bismarck. His office. Somewhere. It'll be theatrical, like these damn messages. It'll be some spectacular thing in a place

Armstrong just was or is heading for next. Because right now this whole thing is a *contest*, and the guy promised a demonstration, and I think he'll keep his word, but I'm betting the next move will be parallel somehow. Otherwise why phrase the message the way he did? Why talk about a demonstration? Why not just go ahead and say Armstrong, you're going to die today?'

Froelich made no reply.

'We have to identify this guy,' Stuyvesant said. 'What do we know about him?'

Silence.

'Well, we know we're fooling ourselves again,' Reacher said. 'Or else still speaking in shorthand. Because it's not a *him*. It's *them*. It's a team. It always is. It's two people.'

'That's a guess,' Stuyvesant said.

'You wish,' Reacher said back. 'It's provable.'

'How?'

'It bothered me way back that there was the thumbprint on the letter along with clear evidence of latex gloves. Why would he swing both ways? Either his prints are on file or they aren't. But it's two people. The thumbprint guy has never been printed. The gloves guy has been. It's two people, working together.'

Stuyvesant looked very tired. It was nearly two o'clock in the morning.

'You don't really need us any more,' Neagley said. 'This isn't an internal investigation now. This is out there in the world.'

'No,' Stuyvesant said. 'It's still internal as long as there's something to get from the cleaners. They must have met with these people. They must know who they are.'

Neagley shrugged. 'You gave them lawyers. You made it very difficult.'

'They had to have counsel, for God's sake,' Stuyvesant said. 'They were arrested. That's the law. It's their Sixth Amendment right.'

'I guess it is,' Neagley said. 'So tell me, is there a law for when the Vice President gets killed before his inauguration?'

'Yes, there is,' Froelich said quietly. 'The Twentieth Amendment. Congress chooses another one.'

Neagley nodded. 'Well, I sure hope they've got their shortlist ready.'

Silence in the room.

'You should bring in the FBI,' Reacher said.

'I will,' Stuyvesant replied. 'When we've got names. Not before.'

'They've already seen the letters.'

'Only in the labs. Their left hand doesn't know what their right hand is doing.'

'You need their help.'

'And I'll ask for it. Soon as we've gotten names I'm going to give them to the Bureau on a silver platter. But I'm not going to tell them where they came from. I'm not going to tell them we were internally compromised. And I'm sure as hell not bringing them in while we still *are* internally compromised.'

'Is it that big a deal?'

'Are you kidding? CIA had a problem with that Ames guy, remember? The Bureau got hold of it and they laughed up their sleeves for years. Then they had their own problems with Hanssen, and they didn't look so smart after all. This is the big leagues, Reacher. Right now the Secret Service is number one, by a very healthy margin. We've only recorded one defeat in our entire history, and that was almost forty years ago. So we're not about to take a dive down the league table just for the fun of it.'

Reacher said nothing.

'And don't get all superior with me,' Stuyvesant said. 'Don't tell me the army reacted any different. I don't recall you guys running to the Bureau for assistance. I don't recall your embarrassing little secrets all over the *Washington Post*.'

Reacher nodded. Most of the army's embarrassments were cremated. Or six feet under. Or sitting in a stockade somewhere, too scared even to open their mouths. Or back home, too scared to tell their own mothers why. He had arranged some of those circumstances himself.

'So we'll take it a step at a time,' Stuyvesant said. 'Prove these guys are outsiders. Get their names from the cleaners. Lawyers or no lawyers.'

Froelich shook her head. 'First priority is getting Armstrong to midnight alive.'

'It's only going to be a demonstration,' Reacher said.

'I heard you before,' she said. 'But it's my call. And you're just guessing. All we've got is nine words on a piece of paper. And your interpretation might be plain wrong. I mean, what better demonstration would there be than actually *doing* it? Really getting to him would demonstrate his vulnerability, wouldn't it? I mean, what better way *is* there of demonstrating it?'

Neagley nodded. 'And it would be a way of hedging their bets, also. An attempt that fails could be passed off as a demonstration, maybe. You know, to save face.'

'If you're right to begin with,' Stuyvesant said.

Reacher said nothing. The meeting came to an end a couple of minutes later. Stuyvesant made Froelich run through Armstrong's schedule for the day. It was an amalgam of familiar parts. First, intelligence briefings from the CIA at home, like on Friday morning. Then afternoon transition meetings on the Hill, the same as most days. Then the evening reception at the same hotel as Thursday. Stuyvesant noted it all down and went home just before two thirty in the morning. Left Froelich on her own at the long table in the bright light and the silence, opposite Reacher and Neagley.

'Advice?' she said.

'Go home and sleep,' Reacher said.

'Great.'

'And then do exactly what you've been doing,' Neagley said. 'He's OK in his house. He's OK in his office. Keep the tents in place and the transfers are OK too.'

'What about the hotel reception?'

'Keep it short and take a lot of care.'

Froelich nodded. 'All I can do, I guess.'

'Are you good at your job?' Neagley asked.

Froelich paused.

'Yes,' she said. 'I'm pretty good.'

'No, you're not,' Reacher said. 'You're the best. The absolute best there has ever been. You're so damn good it's unbelievable.'

'That's how you've got to think,' Neagley said. 'Pump yourself up. Get to the point where it's impossible to imagine that these jerky guys with their silly notes are going to get within a million miles of you.'

Froelich smiled, briefly. 'Is this military-style training?'

'For me it was,' Neagley said. 'Reacher was born thinking that way.'

Froelich smiled again.

'OK,' she said. 'Home and sleep. Big day tomorrow.'

Washington D.C. is quiet and empty in the middle of the night and it took just two minutes to reach Neagley's hotel and only another ten to get back to Froelich's house. Her street was crowded with parked cars. They looked like they were asleep, dark and still and inert and heavily dewed with cold mist. The Suburban was more than eighteen feet long and they had to go two whole blocks before they found a space big enough for it. They locked it up and walked back together in the chill. Made it to the house and opened the door and stepped inside. The lights were still on. The heating was still running hard. Froelich paused in the hallway.

'Are we OK?' she asked. 'About earlier?'

'We're fine,' he said.

'I just don't want us to get our signals mixed.'

'I don't think they're mixed.'

'I'm sorry I disagreed with you,' she said. 'About the demonstration.'

'It's your call,' he said. 'Only you can make it.'

'I had other boyfriends,' she said. 'You know, after.'

He said nothing.

'And Joe had other girlfriends,' she said. 'He wasn't all that shy, really.'

'But he left his stuff here.'

'Does that matter?'

'I don't know,' he said. 'Got to mean something.'

'He's dead, Reacher. Nothing can affect him now.'

'I know.'

She was quiet for a second.

'I'm going to make tea,' she said. 'You want some?'

He shook his head. 'I'm going to bed.'

She stepped into the living room on her way to the kitchen

and he walked upstairs. Closed the guest room door quietly behind him and opened up the closet. Stripped off Joe's suit and put it back on the wire dry cleaner's hanger. Hung it on the rail. Took off the tie and rolled it and put it back on the shelf. Took off the shirt and dropped it on the closet floor. He didn't need to save it. There were four more on the rail, and he didn't expect to be around longer than four more days. He peeled off the socks and dropped them on top of the shirt. Walked into the bathroom wearing only his boxers.

He took his time in there and when he came out Froelich was standing in the guest room doorway. Wearing a nightgown. It was white cotton. Longer than a T-shirt, but not a whole lot longer. The hallway light behind her made it transparent. Her hair was tousled. Without shoes she looked smaller. Without makeup she looked younger. She had great legs. A wonderful shape. She looked soft and firm, all at the same time.

'He broke up with me,' she said. 'It was his choice, not mine.'

'Why?'

'He met somebody he preferred.'

'Who?'

'Doesn't matter who. Nobody you ever heard of. Just somebody.'

'Why didn't you say so?'

'Denial, I guess,' she said. 'Trying to protect myself, maybe. And trying to protect his memory in front of his brother.'

'He wasn't nice about it?'

'Not very.'

'How did it happen?'

'He just told me one day.'

'And walked out?'

'We weren't really living together. He spent time here, I spent time there, but we always kept separate places. His stuff is still here because I wouldn't let him come back to get it. I wouldn't let him in the door. I was hurt and angry with him.'

'I guess you would be.'

She shrugged. The hem of her nightgown rode up an inch on her thigh.

'No, it was silly of me,' she said. 'I mean, it's not like things like that never happen, is it? It was just a relationship that started and then finished. Hardly unique in human history. Hardly unique in *my* history. And half the times it was me who did the walking away.'

'Why are you telling me?'

'You know why,' she said.

He nodded. Didn't speak.

'So you can start with a blank slate,' she said. 'How you react to me can be about you and me, not about you and me and Joe. He took himself out of the picture. It was his choice. So it's none of his business, even if he was still around.'

He nodded again.

'But how blank is your slate?' he asked.

'He was a great guy,' she said. 'I loved him once. But you're not him. You're a separate person. I know that. I'm not looking to get him back. I don't want a ghost.'

She took one step into the room.

'That's good,' he said. 'Because I'm not like him. Hardly at all. You need to be real clear about that from the start.'

'I'm clear about it,' she said. 'The start of what?' She took another step into the room and then stood still.

'The start of whatever,' he said. 'But the end will turn out the same, you know. You need to be real clear about that, too. I'll leave, just like he did. I always do.'

She came closer. They were a yard apart.

'Soon?' she asked.

'Maybe,' he said. 'Maybe not.'

'I'll take my chances,' she said. 'Nothing lasts for ever.'

'Doesn't feel right,' he said.

She glanced at his face. 'What doesn't?'

'I'm standing here wearing your ex-lover's clothes.'

'Not many of them,' she said. 'And it's a situation that can be easily remedied.'

He paused.

'Is it?' he said. 'Want to show me how?'

He stepped forward again and she put her hands on his waist. Slipped her fingers under the elastic waistband of his boxers and remedied the situation. Stepped back a little and raised her arms above her head. Her nightgown slipped off very easily. Fell to the floor. They barely made it to the bed.

* * *

They got three hours' sleep and woke up at seven when her alarm started ringing in her own room. It sounded faraway and faint through the guest room wall. He was on his back and she was curled under his arm. Her thigh was hooked over his. Her head was resting against his shoulder. Her hair touched his face. He felt comfortable in that position. And warm. Warm and comfortable. And tired. Warm and comfortable and tired enough to want to ignore the noise and stay put. But she struggled free and sat up in the bed, dazed and sleepy.

'Good morning,' he said.

There was grey light from the window. She smiled and yawned and pulled her elbows back and stretched. The clock in the next room kept on making noise. Then it went into a new mode and got louder. He slid his hand flat against her stomach. Moved it up to her breasts. She yawned again and smiled again and twisted round and ducked her head and nuzzled into his neck.

'Good morning to you too,' she said.

The alarm blared on through the wall. It clearly had a feature that made it get more and more urgent if it was ignored. He pulled her down on top of him. Smoothed her hair away from her face and kissed her. The distant clock started chirping and howling like a cop car. He was glad he wasn't in the same room with it.

'Got to get up,' she said.

'We will,' he said. 'Soon.'

He held her. She stopped struggling. They made love breathlessly, like the alarm clock was spurring them on. It sounded like they were in a nuclear bunker with missile sirens ticking off the last moments of their lives. They finished, panting, and she heaved herself out of bed and ran through to her own room and shut the noise off. The silence was deafening. He lay back on the pillow and looked up at the ceiling. An oblique bar of grey light from the window showed some imperfections in the plaster. She came back, naked, walking slowly.

'Come back to bed,' he said.

'Can't,' she said. 'Got to go to work.'

'He'll be OK for a spell. And if he isn't, they can always get another one. That Twentieth Amendment thing. They'll be lining up around the block.'

'And I'll be lining up for a new job. Maybe flipping burgers.'

'You ever done that?'

'What, flipped burgers?'

'Been out of work.'

She shook her head. 'Never.'

He smiled. 'I haven't really worked for five years.'

She smiled back. 'I know. I checked the computers. But you're working today. So get your ass out of bed.'

She gave him a fine view of her own ass as she walked away to her own bathroom. He lay still for a second longer with Dawn Penn's old song coming back at him. You don't love me, yes I know now. He shook it out of his head and threw back the covers and stood up and stretched. One arm up to the ceiling, then the other. He arched his back. Pointed his toes and stretched his legs. That was the whole of his fitness routine. He walked to the guest bathroom and went for the full twenty-two-minute ablution sequence. Teeth, shave, hair, shower. He dressed in another of Joe's old suits. This one was pure black, same brand, same tailoring details. He paired it with another fresh shirt, same *Somebody & Somebody* label, same pure white cotton. Clean boxers, clean socks. A dark blue silk tie with tiny silver parachutes all over it. There was a British manufacturer's label on it. Maybe it was from the Royal Air Force. He checked himself in the mirror and then ruined the look by putting his new Atlantic City coat over the suit. It was coarse and clumsy in comparison and the colours didn't match, but he figured to be spending some time out in the cold today, and it didn't seem that Joe had left any overcoats behind. He must have skipped out in summer.

He met Froelich at the bottom of the stairs. She was in a feminine version of his own outfit, a black trouser suit with an open-necked white blouse. But her coat was better. It was dark grey wool, very formal. She was putting her earpiece in. It had a curly wire that straightened after six inches to run down her back.

'Want to help?' she said. She pulled her elbows back in the same gesture she had used when she woke up. It pushed her jacket collar off the back of her neck. He dropped the wire down between her jacket and her blouse. The tiny plug on the end acted like a counterweight and took it all the way to her waist. She pulled her coat and her jacket aside and he found a black radio unit clipped to her belt in the small of her back. The microphone lead was already plugged in and threaded up her back and down her left sleeve. He plugged the earpiece in. She let her jacket and her coat fall back into place and he saw her gun in a holster clipped to her belt near her left hip, butt forward for easy access by her right hand. It was a big boxy SIG-Sauer P226, which he was happy about. Altogether a better proposition than the previous-issue Beretta in her kitchen drawer.

'OK,' she said. Then she took a deep breath. Checked her watch. Reacher did the same thing. It was nearly a quarter to eight.

'Sixteen hours and sixteen minutes to go,' she said. 'Call Neagley and tell her we're on our way.'

He used her mobile as they walked back to her Suburban. The morning was damp and cold, exactly the same as the night had been except now there was some grudging grey light in the sky. The Suburban's windows were all misted over with dew. But it started on the first turn of the key and the heater worked fast and the interior was warm and comfortable by the time Neagley climbed on board outside the hotel.

Armstrong slipped a leather jacket over his sweater and stepped out of his back door. The wind caught his hair and he zipped the coat as he walked to his gate. Two paces before he got there he was picked up in the scope. The scope was a Hensoldt 1.5-6x42 BL originally supplied with a SIG SSG3000 sniper rifle, but it had been adapted by the Baltimore gunsmith to fit its new home, which was on top of a Vaime Mk2. *Vaime* was a word registered by *Oy Vaimennin Metalli Ab*, which was a Finnish weapons specialist that correctly figured it needed a simplified name if it was going to sell its excellent products in the West. And the Mk2 *was* an excellent product. It was a silenced sniper rifle that used a low-powered version of the standard 7.62 millimetre NATO round. Low-powered, because the bullet had to fly at subsonic speeds to preserve the silence that the built-in suppressor created. And because of the low power and the suppressor's complex exhaust gas management scheme there was very little recoil. Almost none at all. Just the gentlest little kick imaginable. It was a fine rifle. With a good scope like the Hensoldt it was a guaranteed killer at any range up to two hundred yards. And the man with his eye to the scope was only a hundred and twenty-six yards from Armstrong's back gate. He knew that for an exact fact, because he had just checked the distance with a laser range finder. He was exposed to the weather, but he was adequately prepared. He knew how to do this. He was wearing a dark green down coat and a black hat made of synthetic fleece. He had gloves made from the same material, with the right-hand fingertips cut off for control. He was lying down out of the wind, which kept his eyes clear of tears. He anticipated absolutely no problems at all.

The way a man goes through a gate works like this: he stops walking momentarily. He stands still. He has to, whichever way the gate hinges. If it hinges towards him, he reaches out for the latch and flips it open and pulls the gate and kind of stands on tiptoe and arches his legs so the gate can swing past them. If it hinges away from him, he stands still while he finds the latch and pushes it open. That's faster, but there's still a moment where there's no real forward motion at all. And this particular gate opened towards the house. That fact was clearly visible through the Hensoldt. There was going to be a two-second window of perfect opportunity.

Armstrong reached the gate. Stopped walking. One hundred and twenty-six yards away the man with his eye to the scope nudged the rifle a fraction left until the target was exactly centred. Held his breath. Eased his finger back. Took up the slack in the trigger. Then he squeezed it all the way. The rifle coughed loudly and kicked gently. The bullet took a hair over four-tenths of a second to travel the hundred and twenty-six yards. It hit Armstrong with a wet *thump* high on the forehead. It penetrated his skull and followed a downward angle through his frontal lobe, through his central ventricles, through his cerebellum. It shattered his first vertebra and exited at the base of his neck through soft tissue near the top of his spinal cord. It flew on and struck the ground eleven feet farther back and buried itself deep in the earth.

Armstrong was clinically dead before he hit the ground. The bullet's path caused massive brain trauma and its kinetic energy pulsed outward through brain tissue and was reflected back by the inside of the skull bones like a big wave in a small swimming pool. The resulting damage was catastrophic. All brain function ceased before gravity dropped the body.

One hundred and twenty-six yards away the man with his eye to the scope lay perfectly still for a second. Then he cradled the rifle flat against his torso and rolled away until it was safe to stand. He racked the rifle's bolt and caught the hot shell case in his gloved hand and dropped it into his pocket. Moved backward into cover and then walked away, completely shielded from view.

Neagley was uncharacteristically quiet in the car. Maybe she was worried about the day ahead. Maybe she could sense the altered chemistry. Reacher didn't know, and either way he wasn't in a hurry to find out. He just sat quiet while Froelich battled the traffic. She looped northwest and used the Whitney Young bridge across the river and drove past the RFK football stadium. Then she took Massachusetts Avenue and stayed away from the congestion around the government part of town. But Mass Ave was slow itself, and it was nearly nine o'clock before they arrived in Armstrong's Georgetown street. She parked behind another Suburban near the mouth of the tent. An agent stepped off the sidewalk and rounded the hood to talk to her.

'The spook just got here,' he said. 'They'll be into Spying 101 by now.'

'Should be 201 by now, surely,' Froelich said. 'He's been doing it long enough.'

'No, CIA stuff is awful complicated,' the guy said. 'For plain folks, anyway.'

Froelich smiled and the guy walked away. Took up station again on the sidewalk. Froelich buzzed her window up and half turned to face Reacher and Neagley equally.

'Foot patrol?' she said.

'Why I wore my coat,' Reacher said.

'Four eyes are better than two,' Neagley said.

They got out together and left Froelich in the warmth of the car. The street side of the house was quiet and well covered so they walked north and turned right to get a view of the back. There were cop cars top and bottom of the alley. Nothing was happening. Everything was buttoned up tight against the cold. They walked onward to the next street. There were cop cars there, too.

'Waste of time,' Neagley said. 'Nobody's going to get him in his house. I assume the police would notice somebody hauling in an artillery piece.'

'So let's get breakfast,' Reacher said. They walked back to the cross street and found a doughnut shop. Bought coffee and crullers and perched on stools in front of a long counter built inside the store window. The window was misted with condensation. Neagley used a napkin and wiped crescent shapes to see through.

'Different tie,' she said.

He glanced down at it.

'Different suit,' she said.

'You like it?'

'I would if we still lived in the 1990s,' she said.

He said nothing. She smiled.

'So,' she said.

'What?'

'Ms Froelich collected the set.'

'You could tell?'

'Unmistakable.'

'Free will on my part,' Reacher said.

Neagley smiled again. 'I didn't think she raped you.'

'You going to be all judgemental now?'

'Hey, your call. She's a nice lady. But so am I. And you never come on to *me*.'

'You ever wanted me to?'

'No.'

'That's the point. I like my interest to be welcome.'

'Which must limit your options some.'

'Some,' he said. 'But not completely.'

'Apparently not,' Neagley said.

'You disapprove?'

'Hell no. Be my guest. Why do you think I stayed on in the hotel? I didn't want to get in her way, is all.'

'*Her* way? Was it that obvious?'

'Oh please,' Neagley said.

Reacher sipped his coffee. Ate a cruller. He was hungry and it tasted great. Iced hard on the outside, light in the middle. He ate another and sucked his fingertips clean. Felt the caffeine and the sugar hit his bloodstream.

'So who are these guys?' Neagley asked. 'You got any feelings?'

'Some,' Reacher said. 'I'd have to concentrate hard to line them up. Not worth starting with that until we know if we're staying on the job.'

'We won't be,' Neagley said. 'Our job ends with the cleaners. And that's a waste of time in itself. No way will they have a *name* for us. Or if they do, it'll be phony. Best we'll get is a description. Which is bound to be useless.'

Reacher nodded. Finished his coffee.

'Let's go,' he said. 'Once round the block for form's sake.'

They walked as slowly as they could bear to in the cold. Nothing was happening. Everything was quiet. There were cop cars or Secret Service vehicles on every street. Their exhaust fumes clouded white and drifted in the still air. Apart from that absolutely nothing was moving. They turned corners and came up on Armstrong's street from the south. The white tent was ahead of them on the right. Froelich was out of her car, waving to them urgently. They hurried up the sidewalk to meet her.

'Change of plan,' she said. 'There was a problem on the Hill. He cut the CIA thing short and headed up there.'

'He left already?' Reacher asked.

Froelich nodded. 'He's rolling now.'

Then she paused and listened to a voice in her earpiece.

'He's arriving,' she said.

She lifted her wrist and spoke into her microphone.

'Situation report, over,' she said, and listened again.

There was a wait. Thirty seconds. Forty.

'OK, he's inside,' she said. 'Secure.'

'So what now?' Reacher said.

Froelich shrugged. 'Now we wait. That's what this job is. It's about waiting.'

They drove back to the office and waited the rest of the morning and most of the afternoon. Froelich received regular situation reports. Reacher built up a pretty good picture of how things were organized. Metro cops were stationed outside the Senate Office buildings in cars. Secret Service agents held the sidewalk. Inside the street doors were members of the Capitol's own police force, one officer manning each metal detector, plenty more patrolling the hallways. Mingled in with them were more Secret Service. The transition business itself took place in upstairs offices with pairs of agents outside every door. Armstrong's personal detail stayed with him at all times. The radio reports spoke of a fairly static day. There was a lot of sitting around and talking going on. Plenty of deals being made. That was clear. Reacher recalled the phrase *smoke-filled rooms*, except he guessed nobody was allowed to smoke any more.

At four o'clock they drove over to Neagley's hotel, which was being used again for the contributor function. Start time was scheduled for seven in the evening, which gave them three hours to secure the building. Froelich had a pre-planned protocol that involved a squeeze search starting in the kitchen loading bay and the penthouse suites simultaneously. Metro cops with dogs were accompanied by Secret Service people and worked patiently, floor by floor. As each floor was cleared three cops took up permanent station, one at each end of the bedroom corridor and one covering the elevator bank and the fire stairs. The two search teams met on the ninth floor at six o'clock, by which time temporary metal detectors were in place inside the lobby and at the ballroom door. The cameras were set up and recording.

'Ask for two forms of ID this time,' Neagley said. 'Driving licence and a credit card, maybe.'

'Don't worry,' Froelich said. 'I plan to.'

Reacher stood in the ballroom doorway and glanced around the room. It was a vast space, but a thousand people were going to crowd it out to the point of discomfort.

* * *

Armstrong took the elevator down from his office and turned a tight left in the lobby. Pushed through an unmarked door that led to a rear exit. He was wearing a raincoat and carrying a briefcase. The corridor behind the unmarked door was a plain narrow space that smelled of janitorial supplies. Some kind of strong detergent cleaner. He had to squeeze past two stacks of cartons. One of the stacks was neat and new, made up from recent deliveries. The other was unsteady and ragged, made up of empty boxes waiting for the trash collector. He turned his body sideways to get past the second pile. Held his briefcase out behind him and led with his right forearm. He pushed open the exit door and stepped out into the cold.

There was a small square internal courtyard, partly open on the north side. It was an unglamorous space. Tin trunking for the building's ventilation system was clipped to the walls above head height. There were red-painted pipes and brass-collared valves at shin level, feeding the fire sprinklers. There was a line of three trash containers painted dark blue. They were large steel boxes the size of automobiles. Armstrong had to walk past them to get to the back street. He got past the first one. He got past the second one. Then a quiet voice called to him.

'Hey,' it said. He turned and saw a man cramped into the small space between the second and the third container. He registered a dark coat and a hat and some kind of brutal weapon. It was short and fat and black. It came up and coughed.

It was a Heckler & Koch MP5SD6 silenced sub-machine gun, set to fire three-round bursts. It used standard nine-millimetre Parabellums. No need for low-powered versions, because the SD6's barrel has thirty holes in it to bleed gas and reduce muzzle velocity to subsonic speeds. It fires at a cyclic rate of eight hundred rounds per minute, so that each three-round burst was complete in a fraction over a fifth of a second. The first burst hit Armstrong in the centre of his chest. The second hit him in the centre of his face.

The basic H&K MP5 has a lot of advantages, including extreme reliability and extreme accuracy. The silenced version works even better because the weight of the integral suppressor mitigates the natural tendency that any sub-machine gun has towards muzzle climb during operation. Its sole drawback is the vigour with which it spits out its empty cartridge cases. They come out of the side almost as fast as the bullets come out of the front. They travel a long way. Not really a problem in its intended arenas of operation, which are confined to the necessary operations of the world's elite military and paramilitary units. But it was a problem in this situation. It meant the shooter had to leave six empty shell cases behind as he stuffed the gun under his coat and stepped over Armstrong's body and walked out of the small courtyard and away to his vehicle.

By six forty there were almost seven hundred guests in the hotel lobby. They formed a long loose line from the street door to the coat check to the ballroom entrance. There was loud excited conversation in the air, and the heady stink of mingling perfumes. There were new dresses and white tuxedos and dark suits and bright ties. There were clutch purses and small cameras in leather cases. Patent shoes and high heels and the flash of diamonds. Fresh perms and bare shoulders and a lot of animation.

Reacher watched it all, leaning on a pillar near the elevators. He could see three agents through the glass on the street. Two at the door, operating a metal detector. They had its sensitivity set high, because it was beeping at every fourth or fifth guest. The agents were searching purses and patting down pockets. They were smiling conspiratorially as they did so. Nobody minded. There were eight agents roaming the lobby, faces straight, eyes always moving. There were three agents at the ballroom door. They were checking ID and inspecting invitations. Their metal detector was just as sensitive. Some people were searched for a second time. There was already music in the ballroom, audible in waves as the crowd noise peaked and died.

Neagley was triangulated across the lobby on the second step of the mezzanine staircase. Her gaze moved like radar, back and forth across the sea of people. Every third sweep she would lock eyes with Reacher and give a tiny shake of her head. Reacher could see Froelich moving randomly. She looked good. Her black suit was elegant enough for evening, but she wouldn't be mistaken for a guest. She was full of authority. Time to time she would talk to one of her agents face to face. Other times she would talk to her wrist. He got to the point where he could tell exactly when she was hearing messages in her earpiece. Her movements lost a little focus as she concentrated on what she was being told.

By seven o'clock most of the guests were safely in the ballroom. There was a small gaggle of latecomers lining up for the first metal detector and a corresponding number waiting at the ballroom door. Guests who had bought an overnight package at the hotel were drifting out of the elevators in couples or foursomes. Neagley was now isolated on the mezzanine staircase. Froelich had sent her agents into the ballroom one by one as the lobby crowd thinned out. They joined the eight already in there. She wanted all sixteen prowling around by the time the action started. Plus the three on the personal detail, and three on the ballroom door, and two on the street door. Plus cops in the kitchen, cops in the loading bay, cops on all seventeen floors, cops on the street.

'How much is all this costing?' Reacher asked her.

'You don't want to know,' she said. 'You really don't.'

Neagley came down off the staircase and joined them by the pillar. 'Is he here yet?' she asked.

Froelich shook her head. 'We're compressing his exposure time. He's arriving late and leaving early.'

Then she stiffened and listened to her earpiece. Put her finger on it to cut out the background noise. She raised her other wrist and spoke into the microphone.

'Copy, out,' she said. She was pale.

'What?' Reacher asked.

She ignored him. Spun round and called to the last remaining agent free in the lobby. Told him he was acting on-site team leader for the rest of the night. Spoke into her microphone and repeated that information to all the agents on the local net. Told them to double their vigilance, halve their perimeters, and further compress exposure time wherever possible.

'What?' Reacher asked again.

'Back to base,' Froelich said. 'Now. That was Stuyvesant. Seems like we've got a real big problem.'

NINE

SHE USED THE RED STROBES BEHIND THE SUBURBAN'S GRILLE AND barged through the evening traffic like it was life and death. She lit up the siren at every light. Pushed through and accelerated hard into gaps. Didn't talk at all. Reacher sat completely still in the front passenger seat and Neagley leaned forward from the back with her eyes locked on the road ahead. The three-ton vehicle bucked and swayed. The tyres fought for grip on the slick tarmac. They made it back to the garage inside four minutes. They were in the elevator thirty seconds later. In Stuyvesant's office less than one minute after that. He was sitting motionless behind his immaculate desk. Slumped in his chair like he had taken a punch to the stomach. He was holding a sheaf of papers. The light shone through them and showed the kind of random coded headings you get by printing from a database. There were two blocks of dense text under the headings. His secretary was standing next to him, handing him more paper, sheet by sheet. She was white in the face. She left the room without saying a single word. Closed the door, which intensified the silence.

'What?' Reacher said.

Stuyvesant glanced up at him. 'Now *I* know.'

'Know what?'

'That this is an outside job. For sure. Without any possible doubt.'

'How?'

'You predicted theatrical,' Stuyvesant said. 'Or spectacular. Those were your predictions. To which we might add dramatic, or incredible, or whatever.'

'What was it?'

'Do you know what the homicide rate is, nationally?'

Reacher shrugged. 'High, I guess.'

'Almost twenty thousand every year.'

'OK.'

'That's about fifty-four homicides every day.'

Reacher did the arithmetic in his head. 'Nearer fifty-five,' he said. 'Except in leap years.'

'Want to hear about two of today's?' Stuyvesant asked.

'Who?' Froelich asked.

'Small sugar beet farm in Minnesota,' Stuyvesant said. 'The farmer walks out his back gate this morning and gets shot in the head. For no apparent reason. Then this afternoon there's a small strip mall outside Boulder, Colorado. A CPA's office in one of the upstairs rooms. The guy comes down and walks out of the rear entrance and gets killed with a machine gun in the service yard. Again, no apparent reason.'

'So?'

'The farmer's name was Bruce Armstrong. The accountant's was Brian Armstrong. Both of them were white men about Brook Armstrong's age, about his height, about his weight, similar appearance, same colour eyes and hair.'

'Are they family? Are they related?'

'No,' Stuyvesant said. 'Not in any way. Not to each other, not to the VP. So therefore I'm asking myself, what are the odds? That two random men whose last name is Armstrong and whose first names both begin with BR are going to get senselessly killed the same day we're facing a serious threat against our guy? And I'm thinking, the answer is about a trillion billion to one.'

Silence in the office.

'The demonstration,' Reacher said.

'Yes,' Stuyvesant said. 'That was the demonstration. Cold-blooded murder. Two innocent men. So I agree with you. These are not insiders having a joke.'

Neagley and Froelich made it to Stuyvesant's visitor chairs and just sat down without being asked. Reacher leaned on a tall filing cabinet and stared out of the window. The blinds were still open, but it was full dark outside. Washington's orange night-time glow was the only thing he could see.

'How were you notified?' he asked. 'Did they call in and claim responsibility?'

Stuyvesant shook his head. 'FBI alerted us. They've got software that scans the NCIC reports. Armstrong is one of the names that they flag up.'

'So now they're involved anyway.'

Stuyvesant shook his head again. 'They passed on some information, is all. They don't understand its significance.'

The room stayed quiet. Just four people breathing, lost in sombre thoughts.

'We got any details from the scenes?' Neagley asked.

'Some,' Stuyvesant said. 'The first guy was a single shot to the head. Killed him instantly. They can't find the bullet. The guy's wife didn't hear anything.'

'Where was she?'

'About twenty feet away in the kitchen. Doors and windows shut because of the weather. But you'd expect her to hear something. She hears hunters all the time.'

'How big was the hole in his head?' Reacher asked.

'Bigger than a .22,' Stuyvesant said. 'If that's what you're thinking.'

Reacher nodded. The only handgun inaudible from twenty feet would be a silenced .22. Anything bigger than that, you'd probably hear something, suppressor or no suppressor, windows or no windows.

'So it was a rifle,' he said.

'Trajectory looks like it,' Stuyvesant said. 'Medical examiner figures the bullet was travelling downward. It went through his head front to back, high to low.'

'Hilly country?'

'All around.'

'So it was either a very distant rifle or a silenced rifle. And I don't like either one. Distant rifle means somebody's a great shooter, silenced rifle means somebody owns a bunch of exotic weapons.'

'What about the second guy?' Neagley asked.

'It was less than eight hours later,' Stuyvesant said. 'But more than eight hundred miles away. So most likely the team split up for the day.'

'Details?'

'Coming through in bits and pieces. First impression from the locals is the weapon was some kind of machine gun. But again, nobody heard anything.'

'A silenced machine gun?' Reacher said. 'Are they sure?'

'No question it was a machine gun,' Stuyvesant said. 'The corpse was all chewed up. Two bursts, head and chest. Hell of a mess.'

'Hell of a demonstration,' Froelich said.

Reacher stared through the window. There was light fog in the air.

'But what exactly does it demonstrate?' he said.

'That these are not very nice people.'

He nodded. 'But not very much more than that, does it? It doesn't really demonstrate Armstrong's vulnerability as such, not if they weren't connected to him in any way. Are we *sure* they weren't related? Like very distant cousins or something? At least the farmer? Minnesota is next to North Dakota, right?'

Stuyvesant shook his head.

'My first thought, obviously,' he said. 'But I double checked. First, the VP isn't from North Dakota originally. He moved in from Oregon. Plus we have the complete text of his FBI background check from when he was nominated. It's pretty exhaustive. And he doesn't have any living relatives that anybody's aware of except an elder sister who lives in California. His wife has got a bunch of cousins but none of them are called Armstrong and most of them are younger. Kids, basically.'

'OK,' Reacher said. *Kids.* He had a flash in his mind of a seesaw, and stuffed toys and lurid paintings stuck to a refrigerator with magnets. *Cousins.*

'It's weird,' he said. 'Killing two random unconnected lookalikes called Armstrong is dramatic enough, I guess, but it doesn't show any great ingenuity. Doesn't prove anything. Doesn't make us worried about our security here.'

'Makes us sad for them,' Froelich said. 'And their families.'

'No doubt,' Reacher said. 'But two hicks in the sticks going down doesn't really make us *sweat*, does it? It's not like we were protecting them as well. Doesn't make us doubt ourselves. I really thought it would be something more personal. More intriguing. Like some equivalent of the letter showing up on your desk.'

'You sound disappointed,' Stuyvesant said.

'I am disappointed. I thought they might come close enough to give us a chance at them. But they stayed away. They're cowards.'

Nobody spoke.

'Cowards are bullies,' Reacher said. 'Bullies are cowards.'

Neagley glanced at him. Knew him well enough to sense when to push.

'So?' she asked.

'So we need to go back and rethink a couple of things. Information is stacking up fast and we're not processing it. Like, now we know these guys are outsiders. Now we know this is not a genteel inside game.'

'So?' Neagley asked again.

'And what happened in Minnesota and Colorado shows us these guys are prepared to do just about anything at all.'

'So?'

'The cleaners. What do we know about them?'

'That they're involved. That they're scared. That they're not saying anything.'

'Correct,' Reacher said. 'But why are they scared? Why aren't they saying anything? Way back we thought they might be playing some cute game with an insider. But they're not doing that. Because these guys aren't insiders. And they're not cute people. And this isn't a game.'

'So?'

'So they're being coerced in some serious way. They're being scared and silenced. By some serious people.'

'OK, how?'

'You tell me. How do you scare somebody without leaving a mark on them?'

'You threaten something plausible. Serious harm in the future, maybe.'

Reacher nodded. 'To them, or to somebody they care about. To the point where they're paralysed with terror.'

'OK.'

'Where have you heard the word *cousins* before?'

'All over the place. I've got cousins.'

'No, recently.'

Neagley glanced at the window. 'The cleaners,' she said. 'Their kids are with cousins. They told us.'

'But they were a little hesitant about telling us, remember?'

'Were they?'

Reacher nodded. 'They paused a second and looked at each other first.'

'So?'

'Maybe their kids *aren't* with cousins.'

'Why would they lie?'

Reacher looked at her. 'Is there a better way to coerce somebody than taking their kids away as insurance?'

They moved fast, but Stuyvesant made sure they moved properly. He called the cleaners' lawyers and told them he needed the answer to just one question: the name and address of the children's babysitters. He told them a quick answer would be much better than a delay. He got the quick answer. The lawyers called back within a quarter of an hour. The name was Gálvez and the address was a house a mile from the cleaners' own.

Then Froelich motioned for quiet and got on the radio net and asked for a complete situation update from the hotel. She spoke to her acting on-site leader and four other key positions. There were no problems. Everything was calm. Armstrong was working the room. Perimeters were tight. She instructed that all agents should accompany Armstrong through the loading bay at the function's conclusion. She asked for a human wall, all the way to the limo.

'And make it soon,' she said. 'Compress the exposure.'

Then they squeezed into the single elevator and rode down to the garage. Climbed into Froelich's Suburban for the drive Reacher had slept through first time around. This time he stayed awake as Froelich raced through traffic to the cheap part of town. They passed right by the cleaners' house. Threaded another mile through dark streets made narrow by parked cars and came to a stop outside a tall thin two-family house. It was ringed by a wire fence and had trash cans chained to the gatepost. It was boxed in on one side by a package store and on the other by a long line of identical houses. There was a sagging twenty-year-old Cadillac parked at the kerb. Yellow sodium lighting was cutting through the fog.

'So what do we do?' Stuyvesant said.

Reacher looked through the window. 'We go talk with these people. But we don't want a mob scene. They're scared already. We don't want to panic them. They might think the bad guys are back. So Neagley should go first.'

Stuyvesant was about to offer an objection but Neagley slid straight out of the car and headed for the gate. Reacher watched her turn a fast circle on the sidewalk before going in, to read the surroundings. Watched her glance left and right as she walked up the path. Nobody was around. Too cold. She reached the door. Searched for a bell. Couldn't find one, so she rapped on the wood with her knuckles.

There was a one-minute wait and then the door opened and was stopped short by a chain. A bar of warm light flooded out. There was a one-minute conversation. The door eased forward to release the chain. The bar of light narrowed and widened again. Neagley turned and waved. Froelich and Stuyvesant and Reacher climbed out of the Suburban and walked up the path. There was a small dark guy standing in the doorway, waiting for them, smiling shyly.

'This is Mr Gálvez,' Neagley said. They introduced themselves and Gálvez backed into the hallway and made a *follow-me* gesture with the whole of his arm, like a butler. He was a small guy dressed in suit pants and a patterned sweater. He had a fresh haircut and an open expression. They followed him inside. The house was small and clearly overcrowded, but it was very clean. There was a line of seven children's coats hung neatly on a row of pegs inside the door. Some of them were small, some of them were a little bigger. There were seven school backpacks lined up on the floor underneath them. Seven pairs of shoes. There were toys neatly piled here and there. Three women visible in the kitchen. Shy children peering out from behind their skirts. More easing their heads round the living room door. They kept moving. Kept appearing and disappearing in random sequences. They all looked the same. Reacher couldn't get an accurate count. There were dark eyes everywhere, open wide.

Stuyvesant seemed a little out of his depth, like he didn't know how to broach the subject. Reacher squeezed past him and moved ahead towards the kitchen. Stopped in the doorway. There were seven school lunch boxes lined up on a counter. The lids were up, like they were ready for assembly-line loading first thing in the morning. He moved back to the hallway. Squeezed past Neagley and looked at the little coats. They were all colourful nylon items, like small versions of the things he had browsed in the Atlantic City store. He lifted one off its peg. It had a white patch inside the collar. Somebody had used a laundry marker and written *J. Gálvez* on it in careful script. He put it back and checked the other six. Each was labelled with a surname and a single initial. Total of five *Gálvez* and two *Alvárez.*

Nobody was speaking. Stuyvesant looked awkward. Reacher caught Mr Gálvez's eye and nodded him through to the living room. Two children scuttled out as they stepped in.

'You got five kids?' Reacher asked.

Gálvez nodded. 'I'm a lucky man.'

'So who do the two Alvárez coats belong to?'

'My wife's cousin Julio's children.'

'Julio and Anita's?'

Gálvez nodded. Said nothing.

'I need to see them,' Reacher said.

'They're not here.'

Reacher glanced away. 'Where are they?' he asked quietly.

'I don't know,' Gálvez said. 'At work, I guess. They work nights. For the federal government.'

Reacher glanced back. 'No, I mean their kids. Not them. I need to see their kids.'

Gálvez looked at him, puzzled. 'See their kids?'

'To check they're OK.'

'You just saw them. In the kitchen.'

'I need to see which ones they are exactly.'

'We're not taking money,' Gálvez said. 'Except for their food.'

Reacher nodded. 'This isn't about licences or anything. We don't care about that stuff. We just need to see their kids are OK.'

Gálvez still looked puzzled. But he called out a long rapid sentence in Spanish and two small children separated themselves from the group in the kitchen and threaded between Stuyvesant and Froelich and trotted into the room. They stopped near the doorway and stood perfectly still, side by side. Two little girls, very beautiful, huge dark eyes, soft black hair, serious expressions. Maybe five and seven years old. Maybe four and six. Maybe three and five. Reacher had no idea.

'Hey, kids,' he said. 'Show me your coats.'

They did exactly what they were told, the way kids sometimes do. He followed them out to the hallway and watched as they stood up on tiptoe and touched the two little jackets he knew were marked *Alvárez*.

'OK,' he said. 'Now go get a cookie or something.'

They scuttled back to the kitchen. He watched them go. Stood still and quiet for a second and then stepped back to the living room. Got close to Gálvez and lowered his voice again.

'Anybody else been enquiring about them?' he asked.

Gálvez just shook his head.

'You sure?' Reacher asked. 'Nobody watching them, no strangers around?'

Gálvez shook his head again.

'We can fix it,' Reacher said. 'If you're worried about anything, you should go ahead and tell us right now. We'll take care of it.'

Gálvez just looked blank. Reacher watched his eyes. He had spent his career watching eyes, and these two were innocent. A little disconcerted, a little puzzled, but the guy wasn't hiding anything. He had no secrets.

'OK,' he said. 'We're sorry to have interrupted your evening.'

He kept very quiet on the drive back to the office.

* * *

They used the conference room again. It seemed to be the only facility with seating for more than three. Neagley let Froelich put herself next to Reacher. She sat with Stuyvesant on the opposite side of the table. Froelich got on the radio net and heard that Armstrong was about to leave the hotel. He was cutting the evening short. Nobody seemed to mind. It worked both ways. Spend a lot of time with them, and they're naturally thrilled about it. Rush it through, and they're equally delighted such a busy and important guy found any time for them at all. Froelich listened to her earpiece and tracked him all the way out of the ballroom, through the kitchens, into the loading bay, into the limo. Then she relaxed. All that was left was a high-speed convoy out to Georgetown and a transfer through the tent in the darkness. She fiddled behind her back and turned the earpiece volume down a little. Sat back and glanced at the others, questions in her eyes.

'Makes no sense to me,' Neagley said. 'It implies there's something they're *more* worried about than their children.'

'Which would be what?' Froelich asked.

'Green cards? Are they legal?'

Stuyvesant nodded. 'Of course they are. They're United States Secret Service employees, same as anybody else in this building. Background-checked from here to hell and back. We snoop on their financial situation and everything. They were clean, far as we knew.'

Reacher let the talk drift into the background. He rubbed the back of his neck with the palm of his hand. The stubble from his haircut was growing out. It felt softer. He glanced at Neagley. Stared down at the carpet. It was grey nylon, ribbed, somewhere between fine and coarse. He could see individual hairy strands glittering in the halogen light. It was an immaculately clean carpet. He closed his eyes. Thought hard. Ran the surveillance video in his head all over again. Watched it like there was a screen inside his eyelids. It went like this: eight minutes before midnight, the cleaners enter the picture. They walk into Stuyvesant's office. Seven minutes past midnight, they come out. They spend nine minutes cleaning the secretarial station. They shuffle off the way they had come at sixteen minutes past midnight. He ran it again, forward and then backward. Concentrated on every frame. Every movement. Then he opened his eyes. Everybody was staring at him like he had been ignoring their questions. He glanced at his watch. It was almost nine o'clock. He smiled. A wide, happy grin.

'I liked Mr Gálvez,' he said. 'He seemed really happy to be a father, didn't he? All those lunch boxes lined up? I bet they get wholewheat bread. Fruit, too, probably. All kinds of good nutrition.'

They all looked at him.

'I was an army kid,' he said. 'I had a lunch box. Mine was an old ammunition case. We all had them. It was considered the thing back then, on the bases. I stencilled my name on it, with a real army stencil. My mother hated it. Thought it was way too militaristic, for a kid. But she gave me good stuff to eat anyway.'

Neagley stared at him. 'Reacher, we've got big problems here, two people are dead, and you're talking about lunch boxes?'

He nodded. 'Talking about lunch boxes, and thinking about haircuts. Mr Gálvez had just been to the barber, you notice that?'

'So?'

'And with the greatest possible respect, Neagley, I'm thinking about your ass.'

Froelich stared at him. Neagley blushed.

'Your point being?' she said.

'My point being, I don't think there *is* anything more important to Julio and Anita than their children.'

'So why are they still clamming up?'

Froelich sat forward and pressed her finger on her earpiece. Listened for a second and raised her wrist.

'Copy,' she said. 'Good work, everybody, out.'

Then she smiled.

'Armstrong's home,' she said. 'Secure.'

Reacher looked at his watch again. Nine o'clock exactly. He glanced across at Stuyvesant. 'Can I see your office again? Right now?'

Stuyvesant looked blank, but he stood up and led the way out of the room. They followed the corridors and arrived at the rear of the floor. The secretarial station was quiet and deserted. Stuyvesant's door was closed. He pushed it open and hit the lights.

There was a sheet of paper on the desk.

They all saw it. Stuyvesant stood completely still for a second and then walked across the floor and stared down at it. Swallowed. Breathed out. Picked it up.

'Fax from Boulder PD,' he said. 'Preliminary ballistics. My secretary must have left it.' He smiled with relief.

'Now check,' Reacher said. 'Concentrate. Is this how your office usually looks?'

Stuyvesant held the fax and glanced around the room.

'Exactly,' he said.

'So this is how the cleaners see it every night?'

'Well, the desk is usually clear,' Stuyvesant said. 'But otherwise, yes.'

'OK,' Reacher said. 'Let's go.'

They walked back to the conference room. Stuyvesant read the fax.

'They found six shell cases,' he said. 'Nine-millimetre Parabellums. Strange impact marks on the sides. They've sent a drawing.'

He slid the paper to Neagley. She read it through. Made a face. Slid it across to Reacher. He looked at the drawing and nodded.

'Heckler & Koch MP5,' he said. 'It punches the empty brass out like nobody's business. The guy had it set to bursts of three. Two bursts, six cases. They probably ended up twenty yards away.'

'Probably the SD6 version,' Neagley said. 'If it was silenced. That's a nice weapon. Quality sub-machine gun. Expensive. Rare, too.'

'Why did you want to see my office?' Stuyvesant asked.

'We're wrong about the cleaners,' Reacher said.

The room went quiet.

'In what way?' Neagley asked.

'In every way,' Reacher said. 'Every possible way we could be. What happened when we talked to them?'

'They stonewalled like crazy.'

He nodded. 'That's what I thought too. They went into some kind of a stoic silence. All of them. Almost like a trance. I interpreted that as a response to some kind of danger. Like they were really digging deep and defending against whatever hold somebody had over them. Like it was vitally important. Like they knew they couldn't afford to say a single word. But you know what?'

'What?'

'They just didn't have a clue what we were talking about. Not the first idea. We were two crazy white people asking them impossible questions, is all. They were too polite and too inhibited to tell us to get lost. They just sat there patiently while we rambled on.'

'So what are you saying?'

'Think about what else we know. There's a weird sequence of facts on the tape. They look a little tired going into Stuyvesant's office, and a little less tired coming out. They look fairly neat going in, and a little dishevelled coming out. They spend fifteen minutes in there, and only nine in the secretarial area.'

'So?' Stuyvesant asked.

Reacher smiled. 'Your office is probably the world's cleanest room. You could do surgery in there. You keep it that way deliberately. We know about the thing with the briefcase and the wet shoes, by the way.'

Froelich looked blank. Stuyvesant's turn to blush.

'It's tidy to the point of obsession,' Reacher said. 'And yet the cleaners spent fifteen minutes in there. Why?'

'They were unpacking the letter,' Stuyvesant said. 'Placing it in position.'

'No, they weren't.'

'Was it just Maria on her own? Did Julio and Anita come out first?'

'No.'

'So who put it there? My secretary?'

'No.'

The room went quiet.

'Are you saying I did?' Stuyvesant asked.

Reacher shook his head. 'All I'm doing is asking why the

cleaners spent fifteen minutes in an office that was already very clean.'

'They were resting?' Neagley said.

Reacher shook his head again. Froelich smiled suddenly.

'Doing something to make themselves dishevelled?' she said.

Reacher smiled back. 'Like what?'

'Like having sex?'

Stuyvesant went pale. 'I sincerely hope not,' he said. 'And there were three of them, anyway.'

'Threesomes aren't unheard of,' Neagley said.

'They live together,' Stuyvesant said. 'They want to do that, they can do it at home, can't they?'

'It can be an erotic adventure,' Froelich said. 'You know, making out at work.'

'Forget the sex,' Reacher said. 'Think about the dishevelment. What exactly created that impression for us?'

Everybody shrugged. Stuyvesant was still pale. Reacher smiled.

'Something else on the tape,' he said. 'Going in, the garbage bag is reasonably empty. Coming out, it's much fuller. So was there a lot of trash in the office?'

'No,' Stuyvesant said, like he was offended. 'I never leave trash in there.'

Froelich sat forward. 'So what was in the bag?'

'Trash,' Reacher said.

'I don't understand,' Froelich said.

'Fifteen minutes is a long time, people,' Reacher said. 'They worked efficiently and thoroughly in the secretarial area and had it done in nine minutes. That's a slightly bigger and slightly more cluttered area. Things all over the place. So compare the two areas, compare the complexity, assume they work just as hard everywhere, and tell me how long they *should* have spent in the office.'

Froelich shrugged. 'Seven minutes? Eight? About that long?'

Neagley nodded. 'I'd say nine minutes, tops.'

'I like it clean,' Stuyvesant said. 'I leave instructions to that effect. I'd want them in there for ten minutes, at least.'

'But not fifteen,' Reacher said. 'That's excessive. And we

asked them about it. We asked them, why so long in there? And what did they say?'

'They didn't answer,' Neagley said. 'Just looked puzzled.'

'Then we asked them whether they spent the same amount of time in there every night. And they said yes, they did.'

Stuyvesant looked to Neagley for confirmation. She nodded.

'OK,' Reacher said. 'We've boiled it down. We're looking at fifteen particular minutes. You've all seen the tapes. Now tell me how they spent that time.'

Nobody spoke.

'Two possibilities,' Reacher said. 'Either they didn't, or they spent the time growing their hair.'

'What?' Froelich said.

'That's what makes them look dishevelled. Julio especially. His hair is a little longer coming out than going in.'

'How is that possible?'

'It's possible because we weren't looking at one night's activities. We were looking at two separate nights spliced together. Two halves of two different nights.'

Silence in the room.

'Two tapes,' Reacher said. 'The tape change at midnight is the key. The first tape is kosher. Has to be, because early on it shows Stuyvesant and his secretary going home. That was the real thing. The real Wednesday. The cleaners show up at eleven fifty-two. They look tired, because maybe that's the first night in their shift pattern. Maybe they've been up all day doing normal daytime things. But it's been a routine night at work so far. They're on time. No spilled coffee anywhere, no huge amount of trash anywhere. The garbage bag is reasonably empty. My guess is they had the office finished in about nine minutes. Which is probably their normal speed. Which is reasonably fast. Which is why they were puzzled when we claimed it was slow. My guess is in reality they came out at maybe one minute past midnight and spent another nine minutes on the secretarial station and left the area at ten past midnight.'

'But?' Froelich asked.

'But after midnight we were looking at a different night altogether. Maybe from a couple of weeks ago, before the guy got his latest haircut. A night when they arrived in the area later, and therefore left the area later. Because of some earlier snafu in some other office. Maybe some big pile of trash that filled up their bag. They looked more energetic coming out because they were hurrying to catch up. And maybe it was a night in the middle of their work week and they'd adjusted to their pattern and slept properly. So we saw them go in on Wednesday and come out on a completely different night.'

'But the date was correct,' Froelich said. 'It was definitely Thursday's date.'

Reacher nodded. 'Nendick planned it ahead of time.'

'Nendick?'

'Your tape guy,' Reacher said. 'My guess is for a whole week he had that particular camera's midnight-to-six tape set up to show that particular Thursday's date. Maybe two whole weeks. Because he needed three options. Either the cleaners would be in *and* out before midnight, or in before midnight and out after midnight, or in and out *after* midnight. He had to wait to match his options. If they'd been in and out before midnight, he'd have given you a matching tape showing nothing at all between midnight and six. If they'd been in and out after midnight, that's what you'd have seen. But the way it happened, he had to use one that showed them leaving only.'

'Nendick left the letter?' Stuyvesant asked.

Reacher nodded. 'Nendick is the insider. Not the cleaners. What that particular camera *really* recorded that night was the cleaners leaving just after midnight and then sometime before six in the morning Nendick himself stepping in through the fire door with gloves on and the letter in his hand. Probably around five thirty, I would guess, so he wouldn't have to wait long before trashing the real tape and choosing his substitute.'

'But it showed me arriving in the morning. My secretary, too.'

'That was the third tape. There was another change at six a.m., back to the real thing. Only the middle tape was swapped.'

Silence in the room.

'He probably described the garage cameras for them too,' Reacher said. 'For the Sunday night delivery.'

'How did you spot it?' Stuyvesant asked. 'The hair?'

'Partly. It was Neagley's ass, really. Nendick was so nervous around the tapes he didn't pay attention to Neagley's ass. She noticed. She told me that's very unusual.'

Stuyvesant blushed again, like maybe he was able to vouch for that fact personally.

'So we should let the cleaners go,' Reacher said. 'Then we should talk to Nendick. He's the one who's met with these guys.'

Stuyvesant nodded. 'And been threatened by them, presumably.'

'I hope so,' Reacher said. 'I hope he's not involved of his own free will.'

Stuyvesant used his master key and entered the video recording room with the duty officer as a witness. They found that ten consecutive midnight-to-six tapes were missing prior to the Thursday in question. Nendick had entered them in a technical log as faulty recordings. Then they picked a dozen random tapes from the last three months and watched parts of them. They confirmed that the cleaners never spent more than nine minutes in his office. So Stuyvesant made a call and secured their immediate release.

Then there were three options: call Nendick in on a pretext, or send agents out to arrest him, or drive themselves over to his house and get some questioning started before the Sixth Amendment kicked in and began to complicate things.

'We should go right now,' Reacher said. 'Exploit the element of surprise.'

He was expecting resistance, but Stuyvesant just nodded blankly. He looked pale and tired. He looked like a man with problems. Like a man juggling a sense of betrayal and righteous anger against the standard Beltway instinct for concealment. And the instinct for concealment was going to be much stronger with a guy like Nendick than with the cleaners. Cleaners would be regarded as mere ciphers. Sooner or later somebody could spin it *hey, cleaners, what can you do*. But a guy like Nendick was different. A guy like that was a main component in an organization that should know better. So Stuyvesant booted up his secretary's computer and found Nendick's home address. It was in a suburb ten miles out in

Virginia. It took twenty minutes to get there. He lived on a quiet winding street in a subdivision. The subdivision was old enough for the trees and the foundation plantings to be mature but new enough for the whole place still to look smart and well kept. It was a medium-priced area. There were foreign cars on most of the driveways, but they weren't this year's models. They were clean, but a little tired. Nendick's house was a long low ranch with a khaki roof and a brick chimney. It was dark except for the blue flicker of a television set in one of the windows.

Froelich swung straight onto the driveway and parked in front of the garage. They climbed out into the cold and walked to the front door. Stuyvesant put his thumb on the bell and left it there. Thirty seconds later a light came on in the hallway. It blazed orange in a fan-shaped window above the door. A yellow porch light came on over their heads. The door opened and Nendick just stood in his hallway and said nothing. He was wearing a suit, like he was just home from work. He looked slack with fear, like a new ordeal was about to be piled on top of an old one. Stuyvesant looked at him and paused and then stepped inside. Froelich followed him. Then Reacher. Then Neagley. She closed the door behind her and took up station in front of it like a sentry, feet apart, hands clasped easy in the small of her back.

Nendick still said nothing. Just stood there, slack and staring. Stuyvesant put a hand on his shoulder and turned him round. Pushed him towards the kitchen. He didn't resist. Just stumbled limply towards the back of his house. Stuyvesant followed him and hit a switch and fluorescent tubes sputtered to life above the countertops.

'Sit,' he said, like he was talking to a dog.

Nendick stepped over and sat on a stool at his breakfast bar. Said nothing. Just wrapped his arms around himself like a man chilled by fever.

'Names,' Stuyvesant said.

Nendick said nothing. He *worked* at saying nothing. He stared forward at the far wall. One of the fluorescent lights was faulty. It was struggling to kick in. Its capacitor put an angry buzz into the silence. Nendick's hands started shaking, so he tucked them up under his arms to keep them still and began to rock back and forth on the stool. It creaked gently under his weight. Reacher glanced away and looked around the kitchen. It was a pretty room. There were yellow check drapes at the window. The ceiling was painted to match. There were flowers in vases. They were all dead. There were dishes in the sink. A couple of weeks' worth. Some of them were crusted.

Reacher stepped back to the hallway. Into the living room. The television was a huge thing a couple of years old. It was tuned to a commercial network. The programme seemed to be made up of clips from police traffic surveillance videos several years out of date. The sound was low. Just a constant murmur suggesting extreme and sustained excitement. There was a remote control balanced carefully on the arm of a chair opposite the screen. There was a low mantel above the fireplace with a row of six photographs in brass frames. Nendick and a woman featured in all six of them. She was about his age, maybe just lively enough and attractive enough not to be called plain. The photographs followed the couple from their wedding day through a couple of vacations and some other unspecified events. There were no pictures of children. And this wasn't a house where children lived. There were no toys anywhere. No mess. Everything was frilly and considered and matched and adult.

The remote on the arm of the chair was labelled *Video*, not *TV*. Reacher glanced at the screen and pressed *play*. The cop radio sound died instantly and the video machine clicked and whirred and a second later the picture went black and was replaced by an amateur video of a wedding. Nendick and his wife smiled into the camera from several years in the past. Their heads were close together. They looked happy. She was all in white. He was wearing a suit. They were on a lawn. A blustery day. Her hair was blowing and the soundtrack was dominated by wind noise. She had a nice smile. Bright eyes. She was saying something for posterity, but Reacher couldn't hear the words.

He pressed *stop* and a night-time car chase resumed. He stepped back into the kitchen. Nendick was still shaking and rocking. He still had his hands trapped up under his arms. He still wasn't saying anything. Reacher glanced again at the dirty dishes and the dead flowers.

'We can get her back for you,' he said.

Nendick said nothing.

'Just tell us who, and we'll go get her right now.'

No reply.

'Sooner the better,' Reacher said. 'Thing like this, we don't want to have her wait any longer than she has to, do we?'

Nendick stared at the far wall with total concentration.

'When did they come for her?' Reacher asked. 'Couple of weeks ago?'

Nendick said nothing. Made no sound at all. Neagley came in from the hallway. Drifted away into the half of the kitchen that was set up as a family room. There was a matching set of heavy furniture grouped along one wall, bookcase, credenza, bookcase.

'We can help you,' Reacher said. 'But we need to know where to start.'

Nendick said nothing in reply. Nothing at all. Just stared and shook and rocked and hugged himself tight.

'Reacher,' Neagley called. Soft voice, with some kind of strain in it. He stepped away from Nendick and joined her at the credenza. She handed him something. It was an envelope. There was a Polaroid photograph in it. The photograph showed a woman sitting on a chair. Her face was white and panicked. Her eyes were wide. Her hair was dirty. It was Nendick's wife, looking about a hundred years older than the pictures in the living room. She was holding up a copy of *USA Today*. The masthead was right under her chin. Neagley passed him another envelope. Another Polaroid in it. Same woman. Same pose. Same paper, but a different day.

'Proofs of life,' Reacher said.

Neagley nodded. 'But look at this. What's this proof of?'

She passed him another envelope. A padded brown mailer. Something soft and white in it. Underwear. One pair. Discoloured. Slightly grimy.

'Great,' he said. Then she passed him a fourth envelope. Another padded brown mailer. Smaller. There was a box in it.

It was a tiny neat cardboard thing such as a jeweller might put a pair of earrings in. There was a pad of cotton wool in it. The cotton wool was browned with old blood, because lying on top of it was a fingertip. It had been clipped off at the first knuckle by something hard and sharp. Garden shears, maybe. It was probably from the little finger of the left hand, judging by the size and the curve. There was still paint on the nail. Reacher looked at it for a long moment. Nodded and handed it back to Neagley. Walked round and faced Nendick head on across the breakfast bar. Looked straight into his eyes. Gambled.

'Stuyvesant,' he called. 'And Froelich. Go wait in the hallway.'

They stood still for a second, surprised. He glared hard at them. They shuffled obediently out of the room.

'Neagley,' he called. 'Come over here with me.'

She walked round and stood quiet at his side. He leaned down and put his elbows on the counter. Put his face level with Nendick's. Spoke softly.

'OK, they're gone,' he said. 'It's just us now. And we're not Secret Service. You know that, right? You never saw us before the other day. So you can trust us. We won't screw up like they will. We come from a place where you're not allowed to screw up. And we come from a place where they don't have rules. So we can get her back. We know how to do this. We'll get the bad guys and we'll bring her back. Safe. Without fail, OK? That's a promise. Me to you.'

Nendick leaned his head back and opened his mouth. His lips were dry. They were flecked with sticky foam. Then he closed his mouth. Tight. Clamped his jaw hard. So hard his lips were compressed into a bloodless thin line. He brought one shaking hand out from under his arm and put the thumb and forefinger together like he was holding something small. He drew the small imaginary thing sideways across his lips, slowly, like he was closing a zipper. He put his hand back under his arm. Shook. Stared at the wall. There was crazy fear in his eyes. Some kind of absolute, uncontrolled terror. He started rocking again. Started coughing. He was coughing and choking in his throat. He wouldn't open his mouth. It was clamped tight. He was bucking and shaking on the stool. Clutching his sides. Gulping desperately inside his clamped mouth. His eyes were wild and staring. They were pools of horror. Then they rolled up inside his head and the whites showed and he pitched backward off the stool.

TEN

THEY DID WHAT THEY COULD AT THE SCENE, BUT IT WAS USELESS. Nendick just lay on the kitchen floor, not moving, not really conscious, but not really unconscious either. He was in some kind of fugue state. Like suspended animation. He was pale and damp with perspiration. His breathing was shallow. His pulse was weak. He was responsive to touch and light but nothing else. An hour later he was in a guarded room at the Walter Reed Army Medical Center with a tentative diagnosis of psychosis-induced catatonia.

'Paralysed with fear, in layman's language,' the doctor said. 'It's a genuine medical condition. We see it most often in superstitious populations, like Haiti, or parts of Louisiana. Voodoo country, in other words. The victims get cold sweats, pallor, loss of blood pressure, near-unconsciousness. Not the same thing as adrenalin-induced panic. It's a neurogenic process. The heart slows, the large blood vessels in the abdomen take blood away from the brain, most voluntary function shuts down.'

'What kind of threat could do that to a person?' Froelich asked, quietly.

'One that the person sincerely believes,' the doctor answered.

'That's the key. The victim has to be convinced. My guess is his wife's kidnappers described to him what they would do to her if he talked. Then your arrival triggered a crisis, because he was afraid he *would* talk. Maybe he even wanted to talk, but he knew he couldn't afford to. I wouldn't want to speculate about the exact nature of the threat against his wife.'

'Will he be OK?' Stuyvesant asked.

'Depends on the condition of his heart. If he tends towards heart disease he could be in serious trouble. The cardiac stress is truly enormous.'

'When can we talk to him?'

'No time soon. Depends on him, basically. He needs to come round.'

'It's very important. He's got critical information.'

The doctor shook his head. 'Could be days,' he said. 'Could be never.'

They waited a long fruitless hour during which nothing changed. Nendick just lay there inert, surrounded by beeping machines. He breathed in and out, but that was all. So they gave it up and left him there and drove back to the office in the dark and the silence. Regrouped in the windowless conference room and faced the next big decision.

'Armstrong's got to be told,' Neagley said. 'They've staged their demonstration. No place to go now except stage the real thing.'

Stuyvesant shook his head. 'We never tell them. It's a rigid policy. Has been for a hundred and one years. We're not going to change it now.'

'Then we should limit his exposure,' Froelich said.

'No,' Stuyvesant said. 'That's an admission of defeat in itself, and it's a slippery slope. We pull out once, we'll be pulling out for ever, every single threat we get. And that must not happen. What must happen is that we defend him to the best of our ability. So we start planning, now. What are we defending against? What do we know?'

'That two men are already dead,' Froelich replied.

'Two men and one woman,' Reacher said. 'Look at the statistics. Kidnapped is the same thing as dead, ninety-nine times in a hundred.'

'The photographs were proof of life,' Stuyvesant said.

'Until the poor guy delivered. Which he did almost two weeks ago.'

'He's still delivering. He's not talking. So I'm going to keep on hoping.'

Reacher said nothing.

'Know anything about her?' Neagley asked.

Stuyvesant shook his head. 'Never met her. Don't even know her name. I hardly know Nendick, either. He's just some technical guy I sometimes see around.'

The room went quiet.

'FBI has got to be told as well,' Neagley said. 'This isn't just about Armstrong now. There's a kidnap victim dead or in serious danger. That's the Bureau's jurisdiction, no question. Plus the interstate homicide. That's their bag too.'

The room stayed very quiet. Stuyvesant sighed and looked round at each of the others, slowly and carefully, one at a time.

'Yes,' he said. 'I agree. It's gone too far. They need to know. God knows I don't want to, but I'll tell them. I'll let us take the hit. I'll hand everything over to them.'

There was silence. Nobody spoke. There was nothing to say. It was exactly the right thing to do, in the circumstances. Approval would have seemed sarcastic, and commiseration wasn't appropriate. For the Nendick couple and two unrelated families called Armstrong, maybe, but not for Stuyvesant.

'Meanwhile we'll focus on Armstrong,' he said. 'That's all we can do.'

'Tomorrow is North Dakota again,' Froelich said. 'More open-air fun and games. Same place as before. Not very secure. We leave at ten.'

'And Thursday?'

'Thursday is Thanksgiving Day. He's serving turkey dinners in a homeless shelter here in D.C. He'll be very exposed.'

There was a long moment of silence. Stuyvesant sighed again, heavily, and placed his hands palms down on the long wooden table.

'OK,' he said. 'Be back in here at seven o'clock tomorrow morning. I'm sure the Bureau will be delighted to send over a liaison guy.'

Then he levered himself upright and left the room to head back to his office, where he would make the calls that would put a permanent asterisk next to his career.

'I feel helpless,' Froelich said. 'I want to be more proactive.'

'Don't like playing defence?' he asked.

They were in her bed, in her room. It was larger than the guest room. Prettier. And quieter, because it was at the back of the house. The ceiling was smoother. Although it would take angled sunlight to really test it. Which would happen at sunset instead of in the morning, because the window faced the other way. The bed was warm. The house was warm. It was like a cocoon of warmth in the cold grey city night.

'Defence is OK,' she said. 'But attack *is* defence, isn't it? In a situation like this? But we always let things come to us. Then we just run away from them. We're too operational. We're not investigative enough.'

'You have investigators,' he said. 'Like the guy who watches the movies.'

She nodded against his shoulder. 'The Office of Protection Research. It's a strange role. Kind of academic, rather than specific. Strategic, rather than tactical.'

'So do it yourself. Try a few things.'

'Like what?'

'We're back to the original evidence, with Nendick crapping out. So we have to start over. You should concentrate on the thumbprint.'

'It's not on file.'

'Files have glitches. Files get updated. Prints get added. You should try again, every few days. And you should widen the search. Try other countries. Try Interpol.'

'I doubt if these guys are foreign.'

'But maybe they're Americans who travelled. Maybe they got in trouble in Canada or Europe. Or Mexico or South America.'

'Maybe,' she said.

'And you should check the thumbprint thing as an MO. You know, search the databases to see if anybody ever signed threatening letters with their thumb before. How far back do the archives go?'

'To the dawn of time.'

'So put a twenty-year limit on it. I guess way back at the dawn of time plenty of people signed things with their thumbs.'

She smiled, sleepily. He could feel it against his shoulder.

'Before they learned to write,' he said.

She didn't reply. She was fast asleep, breathing slow, snuggled against his shoulder. He eased his position and felt a shallow dip on his side of the mattress. He wondered if Joe had made it. He lay quiet for a spell and then craned his arm up and switched out the light.

Seemed like about a minute and a half later they were up again and showered and back in the Secret Service conference room eating doughnuts and drinking coffee with an FBI liaison agent named Bannon. Reacher was in his Atlantic City coat and the third of Joe's abandoned Italian suits and the third *Somebody & Somebody* shirt and a plain blue tie. Froelich was in another black trouser suit. Neagley was in the same outfit she had worn on Sunday evening. It was the one that showed off her figure. The one that Nendick had ignored. She was cycling through her wardrobe as fast as the hotel laundry would let her. Stuyvesant was immaculate in his usual Brooks Brothers. Maybe it was fresh on, maybe it wasn't. There was no way to tell. All his suits were the same. He looked very tired. Actually they all looked very tired, and Reacher was a little worried about that. In his experience tiredness impaired operational efficiency as badly as a drink too many.

'We'll sleep on the plane,' Froelich said. 'We'll tell the pilot to fly slow.'

Bannon was a guy of about forty. He was in a tweed sports coat and grey flannels and looked bluff and Irish and was tall and heavy. He had a red complexion that the winter morning hadn't helped. But he was polite and cheerful and he had supplied the doughnuts and the coffee himself. Two different stores, each chosen for its respective quality. He had been well received. Twenty bucks' worth of food and drink had broken a lot of inter-agency ice.

'No secrets either way,' he said. 'That's what we're proposing. And no blame anywhere. But no bullshit, either. I think we got to face the fact that the Nendick woman is dead. We'll look for her like she wasn't, but we shouldn't fool ourselves. So we've got three down already. Some evidence, but not a lot. We're guessing Nendick has met with these guys, and we're assuming they've certainly been to his house, if only to grab up his wife. So that's a crime scene, and we're going over it today, and we'll share what we get. Nendick will help us if he ever wakes up. But assuming he won't anytime soon, we'll go at it from three different directions. First, the message stuff that went down here in D.C. Second, the scene in Minnesota. Third, the scene in Colorado.'

'Are your people in charge out there?' Froelich asked.

'Both places,' Bannon said. 'Our ballistics people figure the Colorado weapon for a Heckler & Koch sub-machine gun called the MP5.'

'We already concluded that,' Neagley said. 'And it was probably silenced, which makes it the MP5SD6.'

Bannon nodded. 'You're one of the ex-military, right? In which case you've seen MP5s before. As I have. They're military and paramilitary weapons. Police and federal SWAT teams use them, people like that.'

Then he went quiet and looked round the assembled faces, like there was more to his point than he had actually articulated.

'What about Minnesota?' Neagley asked.

'We found the bullet,' Bannon said. 'We swept the farmyard with a metal detector. It was buried about nine inches deep in the mud. Consistent with a shot from a small wooded hillside about a hundred and twenty yards away to the north. Maybe eighty feet of elevation.'

'What was the bullet?' Reacher asked.

'NATO 7.62 millimetre,' Bannon said.

Reacher nodded. 'You test it?'

'For what?'

'Burn.'

Bannon nodded. 'Low power, weak charge.'

'Subsonic ammunition,' Reacher said. 'In that calibre it has to be a Vaime Mk2 silenced sniper rifle.'

'Which is also a police and paramilitary weapon,' Bannon

said. 'Often supplied to anti-terrorist units, people like that.'

He looked round the room again, like he was inviting a comment. Nobody made one. So he pitched it himself.

'You know what?' he said.

'What?'

'Put a list of who buys Heckler & Koch MP5s in America side to side with a list of who buys Vaime Mk2s, and you see only one official purchaser on both lists.'

'Who?'

'The United States Secret Service.'

The room went quiet. Nobody spoke. There was a knock at the door. The duty officer. He stood there, framed in the doorway.

'Mail just arrived,' he said. 'Something you need to see.'

They laid it on the conference room table. It was a familiar brown envelope, gummed flap, metal closure. A computer-printed self-adhesive address label. *Brook Armstrong, United States Senate, Washington D.C.* Clear black-on-white Times New Roman lettering. Bannon opened his briefcase and took out a pair of white cotton gloves. Pulled them on, right hand, left hand. Tightened them over his fingers.

'Got these from the lab,' he said. 'Special circumstances. We don't want to use latex. Don't want to confuse the talcum traces.'

The gloves were clumsy. He had to slide the envelope to the edge of the table to pick it up. He held it with one hand and looked for something to open it with. Reacher took his ceramic knife out of his pocket and snapped it open. Offered it handle first. Bannon took it and eased the tip of the blade under the corner of the flap. Moved the envelope backward and the knife forward. The blade cut the paper like cutting air. He handed the knife back to Reacher and pressed on the sides of the envelope so it made a mouth. Glanced inside. Turned the envelope over and tipped something out.

It was a single sheet of letter-size paper. Heavyweight white stock. It landed and skidded an inch on the polished wood and settled flat. It had a question printed over two lines, centred between the margins, a little higher than halfway up the sheet.

Five words, in the familiar severe typeface: *Did you like the demonstration?* The last word was the only word on the second line. That isolation gave it some kind of extra emphasis.

Bannon turned the envelope over and checked the postmark.

'Vegas again,' he said. 'Saturday. They're real confident, aren't they? They're asking if he liked the demonstration three days before they staged it.'

'We have to move out now,' Froelich said. 'Lift-off at ten. I want Reacher and Neagley with me. They've been there before. They know the ground.'

Stuyvesant raised his hand. A vague gesture. Either *OK* or *whatever* or *don't bother me*, Reacher couldn't tell.

'I want twice-daily meetings,' Bannon said. 'In here, seven every morning and maybe ten at night?'

'If we're in town,' Froelich said. She headed for the door. Reacher and Neagley followed her out of the room. Reacher caught her and nudged her elbow and steered her left instead of right, down the corridor towards her office.

'Do the database search,' he whispered.

She glanced at her watch. 'It's way too slow.'

'So start it now and let it compile all day.'

'Won't Bannon do it?'

'Probably. But double-checking never hurt anybody.'

She paused. Then she turned and headed for the interior of the floor. Lit up her office and turned on her computer. The NCIC database had a complex search protocol. She entered her password and clicked the cursor into the box and typed *thumbprint.*

'Be more specific,' Reacher said. 'That's going to give you ten zillion plain-vanilla fingerprint cases.'

She tabbed backward and typed *thumbprint* + *document* + *letter* + *signature.*

'OK?' she said.

He shrugged. 'I was born before these things were invented.'

'It's a start,' Neagley said. 'We can refine it later if we need to.'

So Froelich clicked on *search* and the hard disk chattered and the enquiry box disappeared from the screen.

'Let's go,' she said.

* * *

Moving a threatened vice president-elect from the District of Columbia to the great state of North Dakota was a complicated undertaking. It required eight separate Secret Service vehicles, four police cars, a total of twenty agents, and an aeroplane. Staging the local political rally itself required twelve agents, forty local police officers, four State Police vehicles, and two local canine units. Froelich spent a total of four hours on the radio in order to co-ordinate the whole operation.

She left her own Suburban in the garage and used a stretched Town Car with a driver so she could be free to concentrate on giving orders. Reacher and Neagley sat with her in the back and they drove out to Georgetown and parked near Armstrong's house. Thirty minutes later they were joined by the gun car and two Suburbans. Fifteen minutes after that, an armoured Cadillac stretch showed up and parked with its passenger door tight against the tent. Then two Metro cruisers sealed the street, top and bottom. Their light bars were flashing. All vehicles were using full headlights. The sky was dark grey and a light rain was falling. Everybody kept their engines idling to power their heaters and exhaust fumes were drifting and pooling near the kerbs.

They waited. Froelich talked to the personal detail in the house and the air force ground crew at Andrews. She talked to the cops in their cars. She listened to traffic reports from a radio news helicopter. The city was jammed because of the weather. The Metro traffic division was recommending a long loop right round the Beltway. Andrews reported that the mechanics had signed off on the plane and the pilots were aboard. The personal detail reported that Armstrong had finished his morning coffee.

'Move him,' she said.

The transfer inside the tent was invisible, but she heard it happen in her earpiece. The limo moved away from the kerb and a Suburban jumped ahead of it and formed up behind the lead cop. The gun car came next, then Froelich's stretch, then the second Suburban, then the trail cop. The convoy moved out and straight up Wisconsin Avenue, through Bethesda, travelling directly away from Andrews. But then it turned right and swung onto the Beltway and settled in for a fast clockwise loop. By then Froelich was patched through to Bismarck and was checking the arrival arrangements. Local ETA was one o'clock and she wanted plans in place so she could sleep on the flight.

The convoy used the north gate into Andrews and swept right onto the tarmac. Armstrong's limo stopped with its passenger door twenty feet from the bottom of the steps up to the plane. The plane was a Gulfstream twinjet painted in the air force's ceremonial blue United States of America livery. Its engines were whining loudly and blowing rain across the ground in thin waves. The Suburbans spilled agents and Armstrong slid out of his limo and ran the twenty feet through the drizzle. His personal detail followed, and then Froelich and Neagley and Reacher. A waiting press van contributed two reporters. A second three-man team of agents brought up the rear. Ground crew wheeled the stairs away and a steward closed the plane door.

Inside it was nothing like the Air Force One Reacher had seen in the movies. It was more like the kind of bus a small-time rock band would ride in, a plain little vehicle customized with twelve better-than-stock seats. Eight of them were arranged in two groups of four with tables between each facing pair, and there were four facing ahead in a row straight across the front. The seats were leather and the tables were wood, but they looked out of place in the utilitarian fuselage. There was clearly a pecking order about who sat where. People crowded the aisle until Armstrong chose his place. He went for a backward-facing window seat in the port-side foursome. The two reporters sat down opposite. Maybe they had arranged an interview to kill the downtime. Froelich and the personal detail took the other foursome. The back-up agents and Neagley took the front row. Reacher was left with no choice. The one seat that remained put him directly across the aisle from Froelich, but it also put him right next to Armstrong.

He stuffed his coat into the overhead bin and slid into the seat. Armstrong glanced at him like he was already an old friend. The reporters checked him out. He could feel their enquiring gaze. They were looking at his suit. He could see them thinking: *too upmarket for an agent. So who is this guy? An aide? An appointee?* He buckled his seat belt like sitting next to vice presidents-elect was something he did every four years, regular as clockwork. Armstrong did nothing to disabuse his audience. Just sat there, poised, waiting for the first question.

The engine noise built and the plane moved out to the runway. By the time it took off and levelled out almost everybody except those at Reacher's table was fast asleep. They all just shut down the way professionals do when they're faced with a window between periods of intense activity. Froelich was accustomed to sleeping on planes. That was clear. Her head was tucked down on her shoulder and her arms were folded neatly in her lap. She looked good. The three agents around her sprawled a little less decorously. They were big guys. Wide necks, broad shoulders, thick wrists. One of them had his foot shoved out in the aisle. It looked to be about size fourteen. He assumed Neagley was asleep behind him. She could sleep anywhere. He had once seen her sleep in a tree, on a long stakeout. He found the button and laid his chair back a fraction and got comfortable. But then the reporters started talking. To Armstrong, but about him.

'Can we get a name, sir, for the record?' one of them said.

Armstrong shook his head. 'I'm afraid identities need to remain confidential at this point,' he said.

'But we can assume we're still in the national security arena here?'

Armstrong smiled. Almost winked. 'I can't stop you assuming things,' he said.

The reporters wrote something down. Started a conversation about foreign relations, with heavy emphasis on military resources and spending. Reacher ignored it all and tried to drift off. Came round again when he heard a repeated question and felt eyes on him. One of the reporters was looking in his direction.

'But you *do* still support the doctrine of overwhelming force?' the other guy was asking Armstrong.

Armstrong glanced at Reacher. 'Would you wish to comment on that?'

Reacher yawned. 'Yes, I still support overwhelming force. That's for sure. I support it big time. Always have, believe me.'

The reporters both wrote it down. Armstrong nodded wisely. Reacher laid his chair back a little more and went to sleep.

He woke up on the descent into Bismarck. Everybody around him was already awake. Froelich was talking quietly to her agents, giving them their standard operational instructions. Neagley was listening along with the three guys in her row. He glanced out of Armstrong's window and saw brilliant blue sky and no clouds. The earth was tan and dormant, ten thousand feet below. He could see the Missouri river winding north to south through an endless sequence of bright blue lakes. He could see the narrow ribbon of I-94 running east to west. The brown urban smudge of Bismarck where they met.

'We're leaving the perimeter to the local cops,' Froelich was saying. 'We've got forty of them on duty, maybe more. Plus State troopers in cars. Our job is to stick close together. We'll be in and out quick. We're arriving after the event has started and we're leaving before it finishes.'

'Leave them wanting more,' Armstrong said, to nobody in particular.

'Works in show business,' one of the reporters said. The plane yawed and tilted and settled into a long shallow glide path. Seat backs came upright and belts were ratcheted tight. The reporters stowed their notebooks. They were staying on the plane. No attraction in open-air local politics for important foreign-relations journalists. Froelich glanced across at Reacher and smiled. But there was worry in her eyes.

The plane put down gently and taxied over to a corner of the tarmac where a five-car motorcade waited. There was a State Police cruiser at each end and three identical stretched Town Cars sandwiched between. A small knot of ground crew standing by with a rolling staircase. Armstrong travelled with his detail in the centre limo. The back-up crew took the one behind it. Froelich and Reacher and Neagley took the one in front. The air was freezing, but the sky was bright. The sun was blinding.

'You'll be freelancing,' Froelich said. 'Wherever you feel you need to be.'

There was no traffic. It felt like empty country. There was a short fast trip over smooth concrete roads and suddenly

Reacher saw the familiar church tower in the distance, and the low surrounding huddle of houses. There were cars parked solid along the side of the approach road all the way up to a State Police roadblock a hundred yards from the community centre entrance. The motorcade eased past it and headed for the parking lot. The fences were decorated with bunting and there was a large crowd already assembled, maybe three hundred people. The church tower loomed over all of them, tall and square and solid and blinding white in the winter sun.

'I hope this time they checked every inch of it,' Froelich said.

The five cars swept onto the gravel and crunched to a stop. The back-up agents were out first. They fanned out in front of Armstrong's car, checking the faces in the crowd, waiting until Froelich heard the all-clear from the local police commander on her radio. She got it and instantly relayed it to the back-up leader. He acknowledged immediately and stepped to Armstrong's door and opened it ceremoniously. Reacher was impressed. It was like a ballet. Five seconds, serene, dignified, unhurried, no apparent hesitation at all, but there had already been three-way radio communication and visual confirmation of security. This was a slick operation.

Armstrong stepped out of his car into the cold. He was already smiling a perfect *local-boy-embarrassed-by-all-the-fuss* smile and stretching out his hand to greet his successor at the head of the reception line. He was bareheaded. His personal detail moved in so close they were almost jostling him. The back-up agents got close, too, manoeuvring themselves so they kept the tallest two of the three between Armstrong and the church. Their faces were completely expressionless. Their coats were open and their eyes were always moving.

'That damn church,' Froelich said. 'It's like a shooting gallery.'

'We should go check it again,' Reacher said. 'Ourselves, just to be sure. Have him circulate counterclockwise until we do.'

'That takes him *nearer* the church.'

'He's safer nearer the church. Makes the downward angle too steep. There are wooden louvres up there round the bells. The field of fire starts about forty feet out from the base of the tower. Closer than that, he's in a blind spot.'

Froelich raised her wrist and spoke to her lead agent. Seconds later they saw him ease Armstrong to his right, into a wide counterclockwise loop round the field. The new senator tagged along. The crowd changed direction and moved with them.

'Now find the guy with the church keys,' Reacher said.

Froelich spoke to the local police captain. Listened to his response in her ear.

'The churchwarden will meet us there,' she said. 'Five minutes.'

They got out of the car and walked across the gravel to the church gate. The air was very cold. Armstrong's head was visible among a sea of people. The sun was catching his hair. He was well out in the field, thirty feet from the tower. The new senator was at his side. Six agents close by. The crowd was moving with them, slowly changing its shape like an evolving creature. There were dark overcoats everywhere. Women's hats, mufflers, sunglasses. The grass was brown and dead from night frosts.

Froelich stiffened. Cupped her hand over her ear. Raised the other hand and spoke into her wrist microphone.

'Keep him close to the church,' she said.

Then she dropped her hands and opened her coat. Loosened her gun in its holster.

'State cops on the far perimeter just called in,' she said. 'They're worried about some guy on foot.'

'Where?' Reacher asked.

'In the subdivision.'

'Description?'

'Didn't get one.'

'How many cops on the field?'

'Forty plus, all round the edge.'

'Get them facing outward. Backs to the crowd. All eyes on the near perimeter.'

Froelich spoke to the police captain on the radio and issued the order. Her own eyes were everywhere.

'I got to go,' she said.

Reacher turned to Neagley.

'Check the streets,' he said. 'All the access points we found before.'

Neagley nodded and moved out towards the entrance drive. Long fast strides, halfway between walking and running.

'You found access points?' Froelich asked.

'Like a sieve.'

Froelich raised her wrist. 'Move now, move now. Bring him tight against the tower wall. Cover on all three sides. Stand by with the cars. Now, people.'

She listened to the response. Nodded. Armstrong was coming close to the tower on the other side, maybe a hundred feet away from them, out of their line of sight.

'You go,' Reacher said. 'I'll check the church.'

She raised her wrist.

'Now keep him there,' she said. 'I'm coming by.'

She headed straight back towards the field without another word. Reacher was left alone at the church gate. He stepped through and headed onward towards the building itself. Waited at the door. It was a huge thing, carved oak, maybe four inches thick. It had iron bands and hinges. Big black nail heads. Above it the tower rose seventy feet vertically into the sky. There was a flag and a lightning rod and a weathervane on the top. The weathervane was not moving. The flag was limp. The air was completely still. Cold, dense air, no breeze at all. The sort of air that takes a bullet and wraps around it and holds it lovingly, straight and true.

A minute later there was the noise of shoes on the gravel and he looked back at the gate and saw the churchwarden approaching. He was a small man in a black cassock that reached his feet. He had a cashmere coat over it. A fur hat with earflaps tied under his chin. Thick eyeglasses in gold frames. A huge wire hoop in his hand with a huge iron key hanging off it. It was so big it looked like a prop for a comic movie about medieval jails. He held it out and Reacher took it from him.

'That's the original key,' the warden said. 'From 1870.'

'I'll bring it back to you,' Reacher said. 'Go wait for me on the field.'

'I can wait right here,' the guy said.

'On the field,' Reacher said again. 'Better that way.'

The guy's eyes were wide and magnified behind his glasses.

He turned round and walked back the way he had come. Reacher hefted the big old key in his hand. Stepped to the door and lined it up with the hole. Put it in the lock. Turned it hard. Nothing happened. He tried again. Nothing. He paused. Tried the handle.

The door was not locked.

It swung open six inches with a squeal from the old iron hinges. He remembered the noise. It had sounded much louder when he opened the door at five in the morning. Now it was lost in the low-level hubbub coming from three hundred people on the field.

He pushed the door all the way open. Paused again and then stepped quietly through into the gloom inside. The building was a simple wooden structure with a vaulted roof. The walls were painted a faded parchment white. The pews were worn and polished to a shine. There was stained glass in the windows. At one end there was an altar and a high lectern with steps leading up to it. Some doors to small rooms beyond. Vestries, maybe. He wasn't sure of the terminology.

He closed the door and locked it from the inside. Hid the key inside a wooden chest full of hymnals. Crept the length of the centre aisle and stood still and listened. He could hear nothing. The air smelled of old wood and dusty fabrics and candle wax and cold. He crept on and checked the small rooms behind the altar. There were three of them, all small, all with bare wooden floors. All of them empty except for piles of old books and church garments.

He crept back. Through the door into the base of the tower. There was a square area with three bell ropes hanging down in the centre. The ropes had yard-long faded embroidered sleeves sewn over the raw ends. The sides of the square area were defined by a steep narrow staircase that wound upward into the gloom. He stood at the bottom and listened hard. Heard nothing. Eased himself up. After three consecutive right-angle turns the stairs ended on a ledge. Then there was a wooden ladder bolted to the inside of the tower wall. It ran upward twenty feet to a trapdoor in the ceiling. The ceiling was boarded solid except for three precise nine-inch holes for the bell ropes. If anybody was up there, he could see and hear through the holes. Reacher knew that. He had heard the dogs pattering around below him, five days ago.

He paused at the foot of the ladder. Stood as quiet as possible. Took the ceramic knife out of his coat pocket and shrugged the coat and suit jacket off and left them piled on the ledge. Stepped onto the ladder. It creaked loudly under his weight. He eased upward to the next rung. The ladder creaked again.

He stopped. Took one hand away from the rung it was gripping and stared at the palm. *Pepper. The pepper he had used five days ago was still on the ladder.* It was smeared and smudged on the rungs, maybe by his previous descent five days ago, maybe by some new ascent undertaken today by the cops. *Or by somebody else.* He paused. Eased up another rung. The ladder creaked again.

He paused again. *Assess and evaluate.* He was on a noisy ladder eighteen feet below a trapdoor. Above the trapdoor was an uncertain situation. He was unarmed, except for a knife with a blade three and a half inches long. He took a breath. Opened the knife and held it between his teeth. Reached up and grasped the side rails of the ladder as far above his head as he could stretch. Catapulted himself upward. He made the remaining eighteen feet in three or four seconds. At the top he kept one foot and one hand on the ladder and swung his body out into open space. Stabilized himself with his fingertips spread on the ceiling above. Felt for movement.

There was none. He reached out and poked the trapdoor upward an inch and let it fall closed. Put his fingertips back on the ceiling. No movement up there. No tremor, no vibration. He waited thirty seconds. Still nothing. He swung back onto the ladder and pushed the trapdoor all the way open and swarmed up into the bell chamber.

He saw the bells, hanging mute in their cradles. Three of them, with iron wheels above, driven by the ropes. The bells were small and black and cast from iron. Nothing like the giant bronze masterpieces that grace the ancient cathedrals of Europe. They were just plain rural artefacts from plain rural history. Sunlight came through the louvres and threw bars of cold light across them. The rest of the chamber was empty. There was nothing up there. It looked exactly as he had left it.

Except it didn't.

The dust was disturbed. There were scuffs and unexplained marks on the floor. Heels and toes, knees and elbows. They weren't his from five days ago. He was sure of that. And there was a faint smell in the air, right at the edge of his consciousness. It was the smell of sweat and tension and gun oil and machined steel and new brass cartridge cases. He turned a slow circle and the smell was gone like it had never been there at all. He stood still and put his fingertips against the iron bells, willing them to give up their secret stored vibrations.

Sound came through the louvres, as well as sunlight. He could hear people clustered near the base of the tower seventy feet below. He stepped over and squinted down. The louvres were weathered wooden slats spaced apart and set into a frame at angles of maybe thirty degrees. The fringe of the crowd was visible. The bulk of it was not. He could see cops on the perimeter of the field, thirty yards apart, standing easy and facing the fences. He could see the community centre building. He could see the motorcade waiting patiently in the lot, with the engines running and exhaust vapour clouding white in the cold. He could see the surrounding houses. He could see a lot of things. It was a good firing position. Limited field, but it only takes one shot.

He glanced upward. Saw another trapdoor in the bell chamber ceiling, and another ladder leading up to it. Next to the ladder there were heavy copper grounding straps coming down from the lightning rod. They were green with age. He had ignored the ceiling on his previous visit. He had experienced no desire to climb through and wait eight hours out in the cold. But for somebody looking for an unlimited field of fire on a sunny afternoon the trapdoor would be attractive. It was there for changing the flag, he guessed. The lightning rod and the weathervane might have been there since 1870, but the flag hadn't. It had added a lot of stars since 1870.

He put the knife back between his teeth and started up the new ladder. It was a twelve-foot climb. The wood creaked and gave under his weight. He made it halfway and stopped. His hands were on the side rails. His face was near the upper rungs. They were ancient and dusty. Except for random patches, where they were rubbed perfectly clean. There were two ways to climb a ladder. Either you hold the side rails, or you touch each rung with an overhand grip. He rehearsed in his mind how the grip pattern would go. There would be contact, left and right on alternate rungs. He arched his body outward and looked down. Craned his neck and looked up. He could see clean patches in that exact pattern, to the left and right on alternate rungs. Somebody had climbed the ladder. Recently. Maybe within a day or two. Maybe within an hour or two. Maybe the churchwarden, hanging a laundered flag. Maybe not.

He hung motionless. Chatter from the crowd drifted up to him through the louvres. He was up above the bells. The maker had soldered his initials on top of each of them where the iron narrowed at the neck. *AHB* was written there three times over in shaky lines of melted tin.

He eased upward. Placed his fingertips as before on the wood above his head. But these were thick balks of timber, probably faced with lead on the outside surface. They were as solid as stone. A guy could be dancing a jig up above and he would never feel it. He eased up two more rungs. Hunched his shoulders and stepped up another rung until he was crouched at the top of the ladder with the trapdoor pressing down on his back. He knew it would be heavy. It was probably as thick as the roof itself and weatherproofed with lead. Some kind of a lip arrangement on it to stop rain leaking through. He twisted round to look at the hinges. They were iron. A little rusted. Maybe a little stiff.

He took a long wet breath around the knife handle and snapped his legs straight and exploded up through the trap. It crashed back and he scrambled up and out onto the roof into the blinding daylight. Grabbed the knife from his mouth and rolled away. His face grazed the roof. It was lead, pitted and dulled and greyed by more than a hundred and thirty winters. He snapped upright and spun a full circle on his knees.

There was nobody up there.

It was like a shallow lead-lined box, open to the sky at the top.

The walls were about three feet high. The floor was raised in the centre to anchor the flagpole and the weathervane post and the lightning rod. Up close, they were huge. The lead was applied in sheets, carefully beaten and soldered at the joints. There were shaped funnels in the corners to drain away rain-water and snow melt.

He crawled on his hands and knees to the edge. He didn't want to stand. He guessed the agents below were trained to watch for random movement taking place in high vantage points above them. He eased his head over the parapet. Shivered in the frigid air. He saw Armstrong directly below, seventy feet down. The new senator was standing next to him. The six agents were surrounding them in a perfect circle. Then he saw movement in the corner of his eye. A hundred yards away across the field cops were running. They were gathering at a point near the back corner of the enclosure. They were glancing down at something and spinning away and hunching into their radio microphones. He looked directly down again and saw Froelich forcing her way out through the crowd. She had her index finger pressed onto her earpiece. She was moving fast. Heading towards the cops.

He crawled back again and clambered down through the trapdoor. Slammed it shut above his head and climbed down the ladder. Through the next trapdoor and down the next ladder. He picked up his coat and jacket and ran down the narrow winding stairs. Past the embroidered ends of the bell ropes and through to the main body of the church.

The oak door was standing wide open.

The lid of the hymnal box was up and the key was in the door lock from the inside. He stepped over and stood a yard inside the building. Waited. Listened. Sprinted out into the cold and stopped again six feet down the path. Spun round. There was nobody waiting to ambush him. Nobody there at all. The area was quiet and deserted. He could hear noise far away on the field. He shrugged into his coat and headed towards it. Saw a man running towards him across the gravel, fast and urgent. He was wearing a long brown coat, some kind of heavy twill, halfway between a raincoat and an overcoat. It was flapping open behind him. Tweed jacket and flannel trousers under it.

Stout shoes. He had his hand raised like a greeting. A gold badge palmed in the hand. Some kind of a Bismarck detective. Maybe the police captain himself.

'Is the tower secure?' he shouted from twenty feet away.

'It's empty,' Reacher shouted back. 'What's going on?'

The cop stopped where he was and bent over, panting, his hands on his knees.

'Don't know yet,' he called. 'Some big commotion.'

Then he stared beyond Reacher's shoulder at the church.

'Damn it, you should have locked the door,' he called. 'Can't leave the damn thing open.'

He raced on towards the church. Reacher ran the other way, to the field. Met Neagley running in from the entrance road.

'What?' she shouted.

'It's going down,' he shouted back.

They ran on together. Through the gate and into the field. Froelich was moving fast towards the cars. They changed direction and cut her off.

'Rifle hidden at the base of the fence,' she said.

'Someone's been in the church,' Reacher said. He was out of breath. 'In the tower. Probably right on the roof. Probably still around someplace.'

Froelich looked straight at him and stood completely still for a second. Then she raised her hand and spoke into the microphone on her wrist.

'Stand by to abort,' she said. 'Emergency extraction on my count of three.'

Her voice was very calm.

'Stand by all vehicles. Main car and gun car to target on my count of three.'

She paused a single beat.

'One, two, three, abort now, abort now.'

Two things happened simultaneously. First there was a roar of engines from the motorcade and it split apart like a starburst. The lead cop car jumped forward and the rear cop car slewed backward and the first two stretch limos hauled through a tight turn and accelerated across the gravel and straight out onto the field. At the same time the personal detail jumped all over Armstrong and literally buried him from view. One agent took the lead and the other two took an elbow each and the back-up three piled on and threw their arms up over Armstrong's head from behind and drove him bodily forward through the crowd. It was like a football manoeuvre, full of speed and power. The crowd scattered in panic as the cars bumped across the grass one way and the agents rushed the other way to meet them. The cars skidded to a stop and the personal detail pushed Armstrong straight into the first and the back-up crew piled into the second.

The lead cop had his lights and siren started already and was crawling forward down the exit road. The two loaded limos fishtailed on the grass and turned round on the field and headed back to the blacktop. They rolled up straight behind the cop car and then all three vehicles accelerated hard and headed out while the third stretch headed straight for Froelich.

'We can get these guys,' Reacher said to her. 'They're right here, right now.'

She didn't reply. Just grabbed him and Neagley by the arms and pulled them into the limo with her. It roared after the lead vehicles. The second cop fell in directly behind it and just twenty short seconds after the initial abort command the whole motorcade had formed up in a tight line and was screaming away from the scene at seventy miles an hour with every light flashing and every siren blaring.

Froelich slumped back in her seat.

'See?' she said. 'We're not proactive. Something happens, we run away.'

ELEVEN

FROELICH STOOD IN THE CHILL AND SPOKE TO ARMSTRONG AT THE foot of the plane's steps. It was a short conversation. She told him about the discovery of the concealed rifle and told him it was more than enough to justify the extraction. He didn't argue. Didn't ask any awkward leading questions. He seemed completely unaware of any larger picture. And he seemed completely unconcerned about his own safety. He was more anxious to calculate the public-relations consequences for his successor. He looked away and ran through the pluses and minuses in his head like politicians do and came back with a tentative smile. *No damage done*. Then he ran up the steps to the warmth inside the plane, ready to resume his agenda with the waiting journalists.

Reacher was faster with the seat selection second time round. He took a place in the forward-facing front row, next to Froelich and across the aisle from Neagley. Froelich used the taxi time doing the rounds of her team, quietly congratulating them on their performance. She spoke to each of them in turn, leaning close, talking, listening, finishing with discreet fist-to-fist contact like ballplayers after a vital hit. Reacher watched her. *Good leader*, he thought. She came back to her seat and buckled her belt. Smoothed her hair and pressed her fingertips hard into her temples like she was clearing her mind of past events and preparing to concentrate on the future.

'We should have stayed around,' Reacher said.

'The place is swarming with cops,' Froelich said. 'FBI will join them. That's their job. We focus on Armstrong. And I don't like it any better than you do.'

'What was the rifle? Did you see it?'

She shook her head. 'We'll get a report. They said it was in a bag. Some kind of vinyl carrying case.'

'Hidden in the grass?'

She nodded. 'Where it's long at the base of the fence.'

'When was the church locked?'

'Last thing Sunday. More than sixty hours ago.'

'So I guess our guys picked the lock. It's a crude old mechanism. The keyhole's so big you can practically get your whole hand in there.'

'You sure you didn't see them?'

Reacher shook his head. 'But they saw me. They were in there with me. They saw where I hid the key. They let themselves out.'

'You probably saved Armstrong's life. And my ass. Although I don't understand their plan. They were in the church and their rifle was a hundred yards away?'

'Wait until we know what the rifle was. Then maybe we'll understand.'

The plane turned at the end of the runway and accelerated immediately. Took off and climbed hard. The engine noise throttled back after five minutes and Reacher heard the journalists starting their foreign-relations conversation again. They didn't ask any questions about the early return.

They touched down at Andrews at six thirty local time. The city was quiet. The long Thanksgiving weekend had already started, halfway through the afternoon. The motorcade headed straight in on Branch Avenue and drove through the heart of the capital and out again to Georgetown. Armstrong was shepherded into his house through the white tent. Then the cars turned listlessly and headed back to base. Stuyvesant wasn't around. Reacher and Neagley followed Froelich to her desk and she accessed her NCIC search results. They were hopeless. There was a small proud rubric at the top of the screen that claimed the software had compiled for five hours and twenty-three minutes and come up with no less than 243,791 matches. Anything that ever mentioned any two of a thumbprint or a document or a letter or a signature was neatly listed. The sequence began exactly twenty years ago and averaged more than thirty entries for each of the 7305 days since. Froelich sampled the first dozen reports and then skipped ahead to random interim dates. There was nothing even remotely useful.

'We need to refine the parameters,' Neagley said. She squatted next to Froelich and moved the keyboard closer. Cleared the screen and called up the enquiry box and typed *thumbprint-as-signature*. Reached for the mouse and clicked on *search*. The hard drive chattered and the enquiry box disappeared. The phone rang and Froelich picked it up. Listened for a moment and put it down.

'Stuyvesant's back,' she said. 'He's got the preliminary FBI report on the rifle. He wants us in the conference room.'

'We came close to losing today,' Stuyvesant said.

He was at the head of the table with sheets of faxed paper spread out in front of him. They were covered in dense type, a little blurred from transmission. Reacher could see the cover sheet's heading, upside down. There was a small seal on the left, and *U.S. Department of Justice, Federal Bureau of Investigation* on the right.

'First factor is the unlocked door,' Stuyvesant said. 'The FBI's guess is the lock was picked early this morning. They say a child could have done it with a bent knitting needle. We should have secured it with a temporary lock of our own.'

'Couldn't do it,' Froelich said. 'It's a landmark building. Can't be touched.'

'Then we should have changed the venue.'

'I looked for alternatives first time round. Every other place was worse.'

'You should have had an agent on the roof,' Neagley said.

'No budget,' Stuyvesant said. 'Until after the Inauguration.'

'If you get that far,' Neagley said.

'What was the rifle?' Reacher asked, in the silence.

Stuyvesant squared the paper in front of him. 'Your guess?'

'Something disposable,' Reacher said. 'Something they weren't actually planning on using. In my experience something that gets found that easily is supposed to get found that easily.'

Stuyvesant nodded. 'It was barely a rifle at all. It was an ancient .22 varmint gun. Badly maintained, rusty, probably hadn't been used in a generation. It was not loaded and there was no ammunition with it.'

'Identifying marks?'

'None.'

'Fingerprints?'

'Of course not.'

Reacher nodded. 'Decoy,' he said.

'The unlocked door is persuasive,' Stuyvesant said. 'What did you do when you went in, for instance?'

'I locked it again behind me.'

'Why?'

'I like it that way, for surveillance.'

'But if you were going to be shooting?'

'Then I would have left it open, especially if I didn't have the key.'

'Why?'

'So I could get out fast, afterwards.'

Stuyvesant nodded. 'The unlocked door means they were in there to shoot. My take is they were waiting in there with the HP5 or the Vaime Mk2. Maybe both. They imagined the junk gun would be spotted at the fence, the bulk of the police presence would move somewhat towards it, we would move Armstrong towards the motorcade, whereupon they would have a clear shot at him.'

'Sounds right to me,' Reacher said. 'But I didn't actually see anybody in there.'

'Plenty of places to hide in a country church,' Stuyvesant said. 'Did you check the crypt?'

'No.'

'The loft?'

'No.'

'Plenty of places,' Stuyvesant said again.

'I sensed somebody.'

'Yes,' Stuyvesant said. 'They were in there. That's for sure.'

There was silence.

'Any unexplained attendees?' Froelich asked.

Stuyvesant shook his head. 'It was pure chaos. Cops running everywhere, the crowd scattering. By the time order was restored at least twenty people had left. It's understandable. You're in a crowd on an open field, somebody finds a gun, you run like hell. Why wouldn't you?'

'What about the man on foot in the subdivision?'

'Just a guy in a coat,' Stuyvesant said. 'State cop couldn't really come up with anything more than that. Probably just a civilian out walking. Probably nobody. My guess is our guys were already in the church by that time.'

'Something must have aroused the trooper's suspicions,' Neagley said.

Stuyvesant shrugged. 'You know how it is. How does a North Dakota State trooper react around the Secret Service? He's damned if he does and damned if he doesn't. Somebody looks suspicious, he's got to call it in even if he can't articulate exactly why afterwards. And we can't moan at him for it. I'd rather he erred on the side of caution. Don't want to make him afraid to be vigilant.'

'So we've still got nothing,' Froelich said.

'We've still got Armstrong,' Stuyvesant said. 'And Armstrong's still got a pulse. So go eat dinner and be back here at ten for the FBI meeting.'

First they went back to Froelich's office to check on Neagley's NCIC search. It was done. In fact it had been done before they even stepped away from the desk. The rubric at the top of the screen said the search had lasted nine-hundredths of a second and come up with zero matches. Froelich called up the enquiry box again and typed *thumbprint on letter*. Clicked on *search* and watched the screen. It redrew immediately and came up with no matches in eight-hundredths of a second.

'Getting nowhere even faster now,' she said.

She tried *thumbprint on message*. Same result, no matches in eight-hundredths of a second. She tried *thumbprint on threat*. Identical result, identical eight-hundredths of a second. She sighed with frustration.

'Let me have a go,' Reacher said. She got up and he sat down in her chair and typed *a short letter signed with a big thumbprint*.

'Idiot,' Neagley said.

He clicked the mouse. The screen redrew instantly and reported that within the seven-hundredths of a second it had spent looking the software had detected no matches.

'But it was a new speed record,' Reacher said, and smiled.

Neagley laughed, and the mood of frustration eased a little. He typed *thumbprint and squalene* and hit *search* again. A tenth of a second later the search came back blank.

'Slowing down,' he said.

He tried *squalene* on its own. No match, eight-hundredths of a second.

He typed *squalane* with an *a*. No match, eight-hundredths of a second.

'Forget it,' he said. 'Let's go eat.'

'Wait,' Neagley said. 'Let me try again. This is like an Olympic event.'

She nudged him out of the chair. Typed *single unexplained thumbprint*. Hit *search*. No match, six-hundredths of a second. She smiled.

'*Six* hundredths,' she said. 'Folks, we have a new world record.'

'Way to go,' Reacher said.

She typed *solo unexplained thumbprint*. Hit *search*.

'This is kind of fun,' she said.

No match, six-hundredths of a second.

'Tied for first place,' Froelich said. 'My turn again.'

She took Neagley's place at the keyboard and thought for a long moment.

'OK, here we go,' she said. 'This one either wins me the gold medal, or it'll keep us here all night long.'

She typed a single word: *thumb*. Hit *search*. The enquiry box disappeared and the screen paused for a whole second and came back with a single entry. A single short paragraph. It was a police report from Sacramento in California. An emergency room doctor from a city hospital had notified the local police department five weeks ago that he had treated a man who had severed his thumb in a carpentry accident. But the doctor was convinced by the nature of the wound that it had been deliberate albeit amateur surgery. The cops had followed up and the victim had assured them it had indeed been an accident with a power saw. Case closed, report filed.

'Weird stuff in this system,' Froelich said.

'Let's go eat,' Reacher said again.

'Maybe we should try vegetarian,' Neagley said.

They drove out to Dupont Circle and ate at an Armenian restaurant. Reacher had lamb and Froelich and Neagley stuck to various chickpea concoctions. They had baklava for dessert and three small cups each of strong muddy coffee. They talked a lot, but about nothing. Nobody wanted to talk about Armstrong, or Nendick, or his wife, or men capable of frightening a person to the point of death and then shooting down two innocent civilians who happened to share a name. Froelich didn't want to talk about Joe in front of Reacher, Neagley didn't want to talk about Reacher in front of Froelich. So they talked about politics, like everybody else in the restaurant and probably everybody else in the city. But talking about politics in late November was pretty much impossible without mentioning the new administration, which led back towards Armstrong, so they generalized it away again towards personal views and beliefs. That needed background information, and before long Froelich was asking Neagley about her life and career.

Reacher tuned it out. He knew she wouldn't answer questions about her life. She never did. Never had. He had known her many years, and had discovered absolutely nothing about her background. He assumed there was some unhappiness there. It was pretty common among army people. Some join because they need a job or want to learn a trade, some join because they want to shoot heavy weapons and blow things up. Some, like Reacher himself, join because it's preordained. But most join because they're looking for cohesion and trust and loyalty and camaraderie. They're looking for the brothers and the sisters and the parents they haven't got anywhere else.

So Neagley skipped her early life and ran through her service career for Froelich and Reacher ignored it and looked around the restaurant. It was busy. Lots of couples and families. He guessed people who were cooking big Thanksgiving meals tomorrow didn't want to cook tonight. There were a couple of faces he almost recognized. Maybe they were politicians or television reporters. He tuned the conversation back in again when Neagley started talking about her new career in Chicago. It sounded pretty good. She was partnered with a bunch of people from law enforcement and the military. It was a big firm. They offered a whole range of services from computer security to kidnap protection for travelling executives overseas. If you had to live in one place and go to work every day, that was probably the way to do it. She sounded satisfied with her life.

They were about to order a fourth round of coffee when Froelich's cell phone rang. It was just after nine o'clock. The restaurant had gotten noisy and they missed it at first. Then they became aware of the low insistent trilling inside her purse. Froelich got the phone out and answered the call. Reacher watched her face. Saw puzzlement, and then a little concern.

'OK,' she said, and closed the phone. Looked across at Reacher. 'Stuyvesant wants you back in the office, right now, immediately.'

'Me?' Reacher said. 'Why?'

'He didn't say.'

Stuyvesant was waiting for them behind one end of the reception counter just inside the main door. The duty officer was busy at the other end. Everything looked completely normal except for a telephone directly in front of Stuyvesant. It had been dragged up out of position and was sitting on the front part of the counter, facing outward, trailing its wire behind it. Stuyvesant was staring at it.

'We got a call,' he said.

'Who from?' Froelich asked.

'Didn't get a name. Or a number. Caller ID was blocked. Male voice, no particular accent. He called the switchboard and asked to speak with the big guy. Something in the voice made the duty officer take it seriously, so he patched it through, thinking perhaps the big guy was me, you know, the boss. But it wasn't. The caller didn't want to speak with me. He wanted the big guy he's been seeing around recently.'

'Me?' Reacher said.

'You're the only big guy new on the scene.'

'Why would he want to speak with me?'

'We're about to find out. He's calling back at nine thirty.'

Reacher glanced at his watch. Twenty-two minutes past.

'It's them,' Froelich said. 'They saw you in the church.'

'That's my guess,' Stuyvesant said. 'This is our first real contact. We've got a recorder set up. We'll get a voice print. And we've got a trace on the line. You need to talk for as long as you can.'

Reacher glanced at Neagley. She looked at her watch. Shook her head.

'Not enough time now,' she said.

Reacher nodded. 'Can we get a weather report for Chicago?'

'I could call Andrews,' Froelich said. 'But why?'

'Just do it, OK?'

She stepped away to use another line. The air force meteorological people took four minutes to tell her Chicago was cold but clear and expected to stay that way. Reacher glanced at his watch again. Nine twenty-seven.

'OK,' he said.

'Remember, talk as long as you can,' Stuyvesant said. 'They can't explain you. They don't know who you are. They're worried about that.'

'Is the Thanksgiving thing on the web site?' Reacher asked.

'Yes,' Froelich said.

'Specific location?'

'Yes,' she said again.

Nine twenty-eight.

'What else is upcoming?' Reacher asked.

'Wall Street again in ten days,' Froelich said. 'That's all.'

'What about this weekend?'

'Back to North Dakota with his wife. Late tomorrow afternoon.'

'Is that on the web site?'

Froelich shook her head. 'No, that's completely private,' she said. 'We haven't announced it anywhere.'

Nine twenty-nine.

'OK,' Reacher said again.

Then the phone rang, very loud in the silence.

'A little early,' Reacher said. 'Somebody's anxious.'

'Talk as long as you can,' Stuyvesant said. 'Use their curiosity against them. Keep it going.'

Reacher picked up the phone. 'Hello,' he said.

'You won't get that lucky again,' a voice said.

Reacher ignored it and listened hard to the background sounds.

'Hey,' the voice said. 'I want to talk to you.'

'But I don't want to talk to you, asshole,' Reacher said, and put the phone down.

Stuyvesant and Froelich just stared at him.

'Hell are you doing?' Stuyvesant asked.

'I wasn't feeling very talkative,' Reacher said.

'I told you to talk as long as you could.'

Reacher shrugged. 'You wanted it done different, you should have done it yourself. You could have pretended to be me. Talked to your heart's content.'

'That was deliberate sabotage.'

'No, it wasn't. It was a move in a game.'

'This isn't a damn *game*.'

'That's exactly what it is.'

'We needed information.'

'Get real,' Reacher said. 'You were never going to get information.'

Stuyvesant was silent.

'I want a cup of coffee,' Reacher said. 'You dragged us out of the restaurant before we were finished.'

'We're staying here,' Stuyvesant said. 'They might call back.'

'They won't,' Reacher said.

They waited five minutes at the reception counter and then gave it up and took plastic cups of coffee with them to the conference room. Neagley was keeping herself to herself. Froelich was very quiet. Stuyvesant was very angry.

'Explain,' he said.

Reacher sat down alone at one end of the table. Neagley occupied neutral territory halfway down one side. Froelich and Stuyvesant sat together at the far end.

'These guys use faucet water to seal their envelopes,' Reacher said.

'So?' Stuyvesant said.

'So there's not one chance in a million they're going to make a traceable call to the main office of the United States Secret Service, for God's sake. *They* would have cut the call short. I didn't want to let them have the satisfaction. They need to know if they're tangling with me, then I take the upper hand, not them.'

'You blew it because you think you're in a pissing contest?'

'I didn't blow anything,' Reacher said. 'We got all the information we were ever going to get.'

'We got absolutely nothing.'

'No, you got a voice print. The guy said thirteen words. All the vowel sounds, most of the consonants. You got the sibilant characteristics, and some of the fricatives.'

'We needed to know where they were, you idiot.'

'They were at a pay phone with caller ID blocked. Somewhere in the Midwest. Think about it, Stuyvesant. They were in Bismarck today with heavy weapons. Therefore they're driving. They're on a four-hundred-mile radius by now. They're somewhere in one of about six huge states, in a bar or a country store, using the pay phone. And anybody smart enough to use faucet water to seal an envelope knows exactly how short to keep a phone call to make it untraceable.'

'You don't know they're driving.'

'No,' Reacher said. 'You're quite right. I don't know for sure. There is a slight possibility that they were frustrated about today's outcome. Annoyed, even. And they know from the web site that there's another chance tomorrow, right here. And then nothing much for a spell. So it's possible they ditched their weapons and aimed to fly in tonight. In which case they might be at O'Hare right now, waiting for a connection. It might have been worthwhile putting some cops in place to see who's using the pay phones. But I only had eight minutes. If you had thought about it earlier it might have been practical. You had a whole half-hour. They gave you notice, for God's sake. You could have arranged something easily. In which case I would have talked their damn ears off, to let the cops get a good look around. But you didn't think about it. You didn't arrange it. You didn't arrange anything. So don't talk to *me* about sabotage. Don't be telling me *I*'m the one who blew something here.'

Stuyvesant looked down. Said nothing.

'Now ask him why he wanted the weather report,' Neagley said.

Stuyvesant said nothing.

'Why did you want the weather report?' Froelich asked.

'Because there might still have been time to get something together. If the weather was bad the night before Thanksgiving in Chicago the airport would be so backed up they'd be sitting around there for hours. In which case I would have provoked some kind of a call-back later, for after we got some cops in place. But the weather was OK. Therefore no delays, therefore no time.'

Stuyvesant said nothing.

'Accent?' Froelich asked, quietly. 'Did the thirteen words you granted them give you a chance to pick anything out?'

'You made a recording,' Reacher said. 'But nothing jumped out at me. Not foreign. Not Southern, not East Coast. Probably one of those other places where they don't have much of an accent.'

The room was quiet for a long moment.

'I apologize,' Stuyvesant said. 'You probably did the right thing.'

Reacher shook his head. Breathed out.

'Don't worry about it,' he said. 'We're clutching at straws here. Million to one we were ever going to get a location. It was a snap decision, really. Just a gut thing. If they're puzzled about me, I want to keep them puzzled. Keep them guessing. And I wanted to make them mad at me. I wanted to take some focus off Armstrong. Better that they focus on me for a spell.'

'You want these people coming after you personally?'

'Better than have them coming after Armstrong personally.'

'Are you nuts? He's got the Secret Service around him. You haven't.'

Reacher smiled. 'I'm not too worried about them.'

Froelich moved in her chair.

'So this *is* a pissing contest,' she said. 'God, you're just like Joe, you know that?'

'Except I'm still alive,' Reacher said.

There was a knock at the door. The duty officer put his head into the room.

'Special Agent Bannon is here,' he said. 'Ready for the evening meeting.'

Stuyvesant briefed Bannon privately in his office about the telephone communications. They came back into the conference room together at ten past ten. Bannon still looked more like a city cop than a federal agent. Donegal tweed, grey flannel, stout shoes, red face. Like a wise old high-mileage detective from Chicago or Boston or New York. He was carrying a thin file folder, and he was acting sombre.

'Nendick is still unresponsive,' he said.

Nobody spoke.

'He's no better and no worse,' Bannon said. 'They're still worried about him.'

He sat heavily in the chair opposite Neagley's. Opened his file folder and took out a thin stack of colour photographs. Dealt them like cards around the table. Two each.

'Bruce Armstrong and Brian Armstrong,' he said. 'Late of Minnesota and Colorado, respectively.'

The photographs were large inkjet prints done on glossy paper. Not faxes. The originals must have been borrowed from the families and then scanned and e-mailed. They were snapshots, basically, each blown up and then cropped down to a useful head-and-shoulders format in the local FBI lab, presumably. The results looked artificial. Two bluff open faces, two innocent smiles, two fond gazes directed towards something that should have been there in the shot with them. Their names were neatly written in ballpoint pen in the bottom border. By Bannon himself, maybe. *Bruce Armstrong, Brian Armstrong.*

They weren't really similar to one another. And neither of them looked much like Brook Armstrong. Nobody would have had even a moment's hesitation differentiating between the three of them. Not in the dark, not in a hurry. They were just three American men with fair hair and blue eyes, somewhere in their middle forties, that was all. But therefore, they *were* alike in another way. If you sliced and diced the human population of the world, you'd use up quite a few distinct divisions before you got round to separating the three of them out. Male or female, black or white, Asian or Caucasian or Mongoloid, tall or short, thin or fat or medium, young or old or middle-aged, dark or fair, blue eyes or brown eyes. You would have to make all those separate distinctions before you could say the three Armstrongs looked different from one another.

'What do you think?' Bannon asked.

'Close enough to make the point,' Reacher said.

'We agree,' Bannon said. 'Two widows and five fatherless children between them. This is fun, isn't it?'

Nobody replied to that.

'You got anything else for us?' Stuyvesant asked.

'We're working hard,' Bannon said. 'We're running the thumbprint again. We're trying every database in the known world. But we're not optimistic. We canvassed Nendick's neighbours. They didn't get many visitors to the house. Seems like they socialized as a couple, mostly in a bar about ten miles from their place, out towards Dulles. It's a cop bar. Seems like Nendick trades on his employment status. We're trying to trace anybody he was seen talking to more than the average.'

'What about two weeks ago?' Stuyvesant said. 'When the wife got taken away? Must have been some kind of commotion.'

Bannon shook his head. 'There's a fairly high daytime population in his street. Soccer moms all around. But it's a dry hole. Nobody remembers anything. It could have happened at night, of course.'

'No, I think Nendick delivered her somewhere,' Reacher said. 'I think they made him do it. Like a refinement of the torture. To underline his responsibility. To put an edge on the fear.'

'Possible,' Bannon said. 'He's afraid, that's for damn sure.'

Reacher nodded. 'I think these guys are real good at the cruel psychological nuances. I think that's why some of the messages came here direct. Nothing worse for Armstrong than to hear from the people paid to protect him that he's in big trouble.'

'Except he's not hearing from them,' Neagley said.

Bannon made no comment on that. Stuyvesant paused a second.

'Anything else?' he said.

'We've concluded you won't get any more messages,' Bannon said. 'They'll strike at a time and place of their own choosing, and obviously they won't tip you off as to where and when. Conversely if they try and fail, they won't want you to have known about it ahead of time, otherwise they'd look ineffective.'

'Any feeling about where and when?'

'We'll talk about that tomorrow morning. We're working on a theory right now. I assume you'll all be here tomorrow morning?'

'Why wouldn't we be?'

'It's Thanksgiving Day.'

'Armstrong's working, so we're working.'

'What's he doing?'

'Being a nice guy at a homeless shelter.'

'Is that wise?'

Stuyvesant just shrugged.

'No choice,' Froelich said. 'It's in the Constitution that politicians have to serve turkey dinners on Thanksgiving Day in the worst part of town they can find.'

'Well, wait until we talk tomorrow morning,' Bannon said. 'Maybe you'll want to change his mind. Or amend the Constitution.'

Then he stood up and walked round the table and collected the photographs again, as if they were precious to him.

Froelich dropped Neagley at the hotel and then drove Reacher home with her. She was quiet all the way. Conspicuously and aggressively silent. He stood it until they reached the bridge over the river and then he gave in.

'What?' he asked.

'Nothing,' she said.

'Got to be something,' he said.

She didn't answer. Just drove on and parked as near her place as she could get, which was two streets away. The neighbourhood was quiet. It was late at night before a holiday. People were inside, cosy and relaxed. She shut off the engine, but didn't get out of the car. Just sat there, looking straight ahead through the windshield, saying nothing.

'What?' he asked again.

'I don't think I can stand it,' she said.

'Stand what?'

'You're going to get yourself killed,' she said. 'Just like you got Joe killed.'

'Excuse me?' he said.

'You heard.'

'I didn't get Joe killed.'

'He wasn't cut out for that kind of stuff. But he went ahead and did it anyway. Because he was always comparing himself. He was driven to do it.'

'By me?'

'Who else? He was your brother. He followed your career.'

Reacher said nothing.

'Why do you people have to *be* like this?' she said.

'Us people?' he said back. 'Like what?'

'You men,' she said. 'You military people. Always charging headlong into stupidity.'

'Is that what I'm doing?'

'You know it is.'

'I'm not the one sworn to take a bullet for some worthless politician.'

'Neither am I. That's just a figure of speech. And not all politicians are worthless.'

'So would you take a bullet for him? Or not?'

She shrugged. 'I don't know.'

'And I'm not charging headlong into anything.'

'Yes, you are. You've been *challenged*. And God forbid you should stay cool and just walk away.'

'You *want* me to walk away? Or do you want to get this thing done?'

'You can't do it by butting heads, like you were all rutting deer or something.'

'Why not? Sooner or later it's us or them. That's how it is. That's how it always is. Why pretend any different?'

'Why look for trouble?'

'I'm not looking for trouble. I don't see it as *trouble*.'

'Well, what the hell else is it?'

'I don't know.'

'You don't *know*?'

He paused.

'You know any lawyers?' he asked.

'Any what?'

'You heard,' he said.

'Lawyers? Are you kidding? In this town? It's wall-to-wall lawyers.'

'OK, so picture a lawyer. Twenty years out of law school, lots of hands-on experience. Somebody asks him, can you write this slightly complex will for me? What does he say? What does he do? Does he start trembling with nerves? Does he think he's been challenged? Is it a testosterone thing? No, he just says, sure, I can do that. And then he goes ahead and does it. Because it's his *job*. Pure and simple.'

'This isn't your job, Reacher.'

'Yes, it is, near as makes no difference. Uncle Sam paid me your tax dollars to do exactly this kind of stuff, thirteen straight years. And Uncle Sam sure as hell didn't expect me to run away and get all psychological and conflicted about it.'

She stared forward through the windshield. It was misting fast, from their breath.

'There are hundreds of people on the other side of the Secret Service,' she said. 'In Financial Crimes. Hundreds of them. I don't know how many, exactly. Lots of them. Good people. We're not really investigative, but they are. That's *all* they are. That's what they're *for*. Joe could have picked any ten of them and sent them down to Georgia. He could have picked fifty of them. But he didn't. He had to go himself. He had to go alone. Because he was challenged. He couldn't back off. Because he was always comparing himself.'

'I agree he shouldn't have done it,' Reacher said. 'Like a doctor shouldn't write a will. Like a lawyer shouldn't do surgery.'

'But you made him.'

He shook his head. 'No, I didn't make him,' he said.

She was silent.

'Two points, Froelich,' he said. 'First, people shouldn't have to choose their careers with one eye on what their brother might think. And second, the last time Joe and I had any significant contact I was sixteen years old. He was eighteen. He was leaving for West Point. I was a kid. The *last* thing on his mind was copying me. Are you nuts? And I never really saw him again after that. Funerals only, basically. Because whatever you think about me as a brother, he was no better. He paid no attention to me. Years would go by, I wouldn't hear from him.'

'He followed your career. Your mother sent him stuff. He was comparing himself.'

'Our mother died seven years before he did. I barely had a career back then.'

'You won the Silver Star in Beirut right at the beginning.'

'I was blown up by a bomb,' he said. 'They gave me a medal because they couldn't think what else to do. That's what the army is like. Joe knew that.'

'He was comparing himself,' she said.

Reacher moved in his seat. Watched small swirls of condensation form on the windshield glass.

'Maybe,' he said. 'But not to me.'

'Who then?'

'Our dad, possibly.'

She shrugged. 'He never talked about *him*.'

'Well, there you go,' Reacher said. 'Avoidance. Denial.'

'You think? What was special about your dad?'

Reacher looked away. Closed his eyes.

'He was a Marine,' he said. 'Korea and Vietnam. Very compartmentalized guy. Gentle, shy, sweet, loving man, but a stone-cold killer, too. Harder than a nail. Next to him I look like Liberace.'

'Do *you* compare yourself with him?'

Reacher shook his head. Opened his eyes.

'No point,' he said. 'Next to him I look like Liberace. Always will, no matter what. Which isn't necessarily such a bad thing for the world.'

'Didn't you like him?'
'He was OK. But he was a freak. No room for people like him any more.'
'Joe shouldn't have gone to Georgia,' she said.
Reacher nodded. 'No argument about that,' he said. 'No argument at all. But it was nobody's fault except his own. He should have had more sense.'
'So should you.'
'I've got plenty of sense. Like for instance I joined the Military Police, not the Marine Corps. Like for instance I don't feel compelled to rush around trying to design a new hundred-dollar bill. I stick to what I know.'
'And you think you know how to take out these guys?'
'Like the garbage man knows how to take out the trash. It ain't rocket science.'
'That sounds pretty arrogant.'
He shook his head. 'Listen, I'm sick of justifying myself. It's ridiculous. You know your neighbours? You know the people who live round here?'
'Not really,' she said.
He rubbed mist off the glass and pointed out of his window with his thumb. 'Maybe one of them is an old lady who knits sweaters. Are you going to walk up to her and say, oh my God, what's with *you*? I can't believe you actually have the *temerity* to know how to knit *sweaters*.'
'You're equating armed combat with knitting sweaters?'
'I'm saying we're all good at something. And that's what I'm good at. Maybe it's the only thing I'm good at. I'm not proud of it, and I'm not ashamed of it, either. It's just *there*. I can't help it. I'm genetically programmed to win, is all. Several consecutive generations.'
'Joe had the same genes.'
'No, he had the same parents. There's a difference.'
'I hope your faith in yourself is justified.'
'It is. Especially now, with Neagley here. *She* makes me look like Liberace.'
Froelich looked away. Went quiet.
'What?' he said.
'She's in love with you.'

'Bullshit.'

Froelich looked straight at him. 'How would you know?'

'She's never been interested.'

Froelich just shook her head.

'I just talked to her about it,' he said. 'The other day. She said she's never been interested. She told me that, words of one syllable.'

'And you believed her?'

'Wasn't I supposed to?'

Froelich said nothing. Reacher smiled, slowly.

'What, you think she *is* interested?' he asked.

'You smile just like Joe,' she answered. 'A little shy, a little lopsided. It's the most incredibly beautiful smile I ever saw.'

'You're not exactly over him, are you?' he said. 'At the risk of being the last to know. At the risk of stating the bloody obvious.'

She didn't answer. Just got out of the car and started walking. He followed after her. It was cold and damp on the street. The night air was heavy. He could smell the river, and jet fuel from somewhere. They reached her house. She unlocked the door. They stepped inside.

There was a sheet of paper lying on the hallway floor.

TWELVE

IT WAS THE FAMILIAR HIGH-WHITE LETTER-SIZE SHEET. IT WAS LYING precisely aligned with the oak flooring strips. It was in the geometric centre of the hallway, near the bottom of the stairs, exactly where Reacher had dumped his garbage bag of clothes two nights previously. It had a simple statement printed neatly on it, in the familiar Times New Roman computer script, fourteen point, bold. The statement was five words long, split between two lines in the centre of the page: *It's going to happen soon*. The three words *It's going to* made up the first line on their own. The *happen soon* part was alone on the second line. It looked like a poem or a song lyric. Like it was divided up that way for a dramatic purpose, like there should be a pause between the lines, or a breath, or a drum roll, or a rim shot. *It's going to* . . . bam! . . . *happen soon*. Reacher stared at it. The effect was hypnotic. *Happen soon. Happen soon.*

'Don't touch it,' Froelich said.

'Wasn't going to,' Reacher replied.

He ducked his head back out of the door and checked the street. All the nearby cars were empty. All the nearby windows were closed and draped. No pedestrians. No loiterers in the dark. All was quiet. He came back inside and closed the door slowly and carefully, so as not to disturb the paper with a draught.

'How did they get it in here?' Froelich said.

'Through the door,' Reacher said. 'Probably at the back.'

Froelich pulled the SIG-Sauer from her holster and they walked through the living room together and into the kitchen. The door to the back yard was closed, but it was unlocked. Reacher opened it a foot. Scanned the outside surroundings and saw nothing at all. Eased the door back wide so the inside light fell onto the exterior surface. Leaned close and looked at the scratch plate around the key hole.

'Marks,' he said. 'Very small. They were pretty good.'

'They're here in D.C.,' she said. 'Right now. They're not in some Midwest bar.'

She stared through the kitchen into the living room.

'The phone,' she said.

It was pulled out of position on the table next to the fireside chair.

'They used my phone,' she said.

'To call me, probably,' Reacher said.

'Prints?'

He shook his head. 'Gloves.'

'They've been in my house,' she said.

She moved away from the rear door and stopped at the kitchen counter. Glanced down at something and snatched open a drawer.

'They took my gun,' she said. 'I had a back-up gun in here.'

'I know,' Reacher said. 'An old Beretta.'

She opened the drawer next to it. 'The magazines are gone too,' she said. 'I had ammo in here.'

'I know,' Reacher said again. 'Under an oven glove.'

'How do you know?'

'I checked, Monday night.'

'Why would you?'

'Habit,' he said. 'Don't take it personally.'

She stared at him and then opened the wall cupboard with the money stash in it. He saw her check the earthenware pot. She said nothing, so he assumed the cash was still there. He filed the observation away in the professional corner of his mind, as confirmation of a long-held belief: *people don't like searching above head height.*

Then she stiffened. A new thought.

'They might still be in the house,' she said, quietly.

But she didn't move. It was the first sign of fear he had ever seen from her.

'I'll check,' he said. 'Unless that's an unhealthy response to a challenge.'

She just handed him her pistol. He turned out the kitchen light so he wouldn't be silhouetted on the basement stairs and walked slowly down. Listened hard past the creaks and sighs of the house, and the hum and trickle of the heating system. Stood still in the dark and let his eyes adjust. There was nobody there. Nobody upstairs, either. Nobody hiding and waiting. People hiding and waiting give off human vibrations. Tiny hums and quivers. And he wasn't feeling anything. The house was empty and undisturbed, apart from the displaced telephone and the missing Beretta and the message on the hallway floor. He came back to the kitchen and held out the SIG, butt first.

'Secure,' he said.

'I better make some calls,' she said.

Special Agent Bannon showed up forty minutes later in a Bureau sedan with three members of his task force. Stuyvesant arrived five minutes after them in a department Suburban. They left both vehicles double-parked in the street with their strobes going. The neighbouring houses were spattered with random bursts of light, blue and red and white. Stuyvesant stood still in the open doorway.

'We weren't supposed to get any more messages,' he said.

Bannon was on his knees, looking at the sheet of paper.

'This is generic,' he said. 'We predicted we wouldn't get specificity. And we haven't. The word *soon* is meaningless as to time and place. It's just a taunt. We're supposed to be impressed with how smart they are.'

'I was already impressed with how smart they are,' Stuyvesant said.

Bannon looked up at Froelich. 'How long have you been out?'

'All day,' Froelich said. 'We left at six thirty this morning to meet with you.'

'We?'

'Reacher's staying here,' she said.

'Not any more, he's not,' Bannon said. 'Neither of you is staying here. It's too dangerous. We're putting you in a secure location.'

Froelich said nothing.

'They're in D.C. right now,' Bannon said. 'Probably re-grouping somewhere. Probably got in from North Dakota a couple of hours after you did. They know where you live. And we need to work here. This is a crime scene.'

'This is my house,' Froelich said.

'It's a crime scene,' Bannon said again. 'They've been here. We'll have to rip it up some. Better that you stay away until we put it back together.'

Froelich said nothing.

'Don't argue,' Stuyvesant said. 'I want you protected. We'll put you in a motel. Couple of U.S. Marshals outside the door, until this is over.'

'Neagley, too,' Reacher said.

Froelich glanced at him. Stuyvesant nodded.

'Don't worry,' he said. 'I already sent somebody to pick her up.'

'Neighbours?' Bannon asked.

'Don't really know them,' Froelich answered.

'They might have seen something,' Bannon said. He checked his watch. 'They might still be up. At least I hope so. Dragging witnesses out of bed generally makes them very cranky.'

'So get what you need, people,' Stuyvesant called. 'We're leaving, right now.'

Reacher stood in Froelich's guest room and had a strong feeling he would never come back to it. So he took his things from the bathroom and his garbage bag of Atlantic City clothes and all of Joe's suits and shirts that were still clean. He stuffed clean socks and underwear into the pockets. Carried all the clothes in one hand and Joe's cardboard box under the other arm. He came down the stairs and stepped out into the night air and it hit him that for the first time in more than five years he was leaving a place carrying baggage. He loaded it into the Suburban's trunk and then walked round and climbed into the back seat. Sat still and waited for Froelich. She came out of her house carrying a small valise. Stuyvesant took it from her and stowed it and they climbed into the front together. Took off down the street. Froelich didn't look back.

They drove due north and then turned west all the way through the tourist sites and out again on the other side. They stopped at a Georgetown motel about ten blocks shy of Armstrong's street. There was an old-model Crown Vic parked outside, with a new Town Car next to it. The Town Car had a driver in it. The Crown Vic was empty. The motel itself was a small neat place with dark wood all over it. A discreet sign. It was hemmed in by three embassies with fenced grounds. The embassies belonged to new countries Reacher had never heard of, but their fences were OK. It was a very protected location. Only one way in, and a marshal in the lobby would take care of that. An extra marshal in the corridor would be icing on the cake.

Stuyvesant had booked three rooms. Neagley had already arrived. They found her in the lobby. She was buying soda from a machine and talking to a big guy in a cheap black suit and patrolman's shoes. A U.S. Marshal, without a doubt. The Crown Vic driver. *Their vehicle budget must be smaller than the Secret Service's*, Reacher thought. *As well as their clothing allowance*.

Stuyvesant did the paperwork at the desk and came back with three key cards. Handed them round in an embarrassed little ceremony. Mentioned three room numbers. They were sequential. Then he scrabbled in his pocket and came out with the Suburban's keys. Gave them to Froelich.

'I'll ride back with the guy who brought Neagley over,' he said. 'I'll see you tomorrow, seven o'clock in the office, with Bannon, all of you.'

Then he turned and left. Neagley juggled her key card and her soda and a garment bag and went looking for her room. Froelich and Reacher followed behind her, with a key card each. There was another marshal at the head of the bedroom corridor. He was sitting awkwardly on a plain dining chair. He had it tilted back against the wall for comfort. Reacher squeezed his untidy luggage past him and stopped at his door. Froelich was already two rooms down, not looking in his direction.

He went inside and found a compact version of what he had seen a thousand times before. Just one bed, one chair, a table, a normal telephone, a smaller TV screen. But the rest was generic. Floral drapes, already closed. A floral bedspread, Scotchgarded until it was practically rigid. No-colour bamboo-weave stuff on the walls. A cheap print over the bed, pretending to be a hand-coloured architectural drawing of some part of some ancient Greek temple. He stowed his baggage and arranged his bathroom articles on the shelf above the sink. Checked his watch. Past midnight. Thanksgiving Day, already. He took off Joe's jacket and dropped it on the table. Loosened his tie and yawned. There was a knock at the door. He opened up and found Froelich standing there.

'Come in,' he said.

'Just for a minute,' she said. He walked back and sat on the end of the bed, to let her take the chair. Her hair was a mess, like she had just run her fingers through it. She looked good like that. Younger, and vulnerable, somehow.

'I *am* over him,' she said.

'OK,' he said.

'But I can see how you might think I'm not.'

'OK,' he said again.

'So I think we should be apart tonight. I wouldn't want you to be worried about why I was here. If I *was* here.'

'Whatever you want,' he said.

'It's just that you're so like him. It's impossible not to be reminded. You can see that, can't you? But you were never a substitute. I need you to know that.'

'Still think I got him killed?'

She looked away. 'Something got him killed,' she said. 'Something on his mind, in his background. Something made him think he could beat somebody he couldn't beat. Something made him think he was going to be OK when he wasn't going to be OK. And the same thing could happen to you. You're stupid if you don't see that.'

He nodded. Said nothing. She stood up and walked past him. He caught her perfume as she went by.

'Call me if you need me,' he said.

She didn't reply. He didn't get up.

A half-hour later there was another knock at the door and he opened it up expecting to find Froelich again. But it was Neagley. Still fully dressed, a little tired, but calm.

'You on your own?' she asked.

He nodded.

'Where is she?' Neagley asked.

'She left.'

'Business or lack of pleasure?'

'Confusion,' he said. 'Half the time she wants me to be Joe, the other half she wants to blame me for getting him killed.'

'She's still in love with him.'

'Evidently.'

'Six years after their relationship ended.'

'Is that normal?'

She shrugged. 'You're asking me? I guess some people carry a torch for a long time. He must have been quite a guy.'

'I didn't really know him all that well.'

'Did you get him killed?'

'Of course not. I was a million miles away. Hadn't spoken to him for seven years. I told you that.'

'So what's her angle?'

'She says he was driven to be reckless because he was comparing himself to me.'

'And was he?'

'I doubt it.'

'You said you felt guilty afterwards. You told me that too, when we were watching those surveillance tapes.'

'I think I said I felt angry, not guilty.'

'Angry, guilty, it's all the same thing. Why feel guilty if it wasn't your fault?'

'Now *you*'re saying it was my fault?'

'I'm just asking, what's the guilt about?'

'He grew up under a false impression.'

He went quiet and moved deeper into the room. Neagley

followed him. He lay down on the bed, arms outstretched, hands hanging off the edges. She sat down in the armchair, where Froelich had been.

'Tell me about the false impression,' she said.

'He was big, but he was studious,' Reacher said. 'The schools we went to, being studious was like having *kick my ass* tattooed across your forehead. And he wasn't all that tough, really, although he was big. So he got his ass kicked, regular as clockwork.'

'And?'

'I was two years younger, but I was big *and* tough, and not very studious. So I started to look after him. Loyalty, I guess, and I liked fighting anyway. I was about six. I'd wade in anywhere. I learned a lot of stuff. Learned that style was the big thing. Look like you mean it, and people back off a lot. Sometimes they didn't. I had eight-year-olds all over me the first year. Then I got better at it. I hurt people bad. I was a madman. It got to be a thing. We'd arrive in some new place and pretty quick people would know to lay off Joe, or the psycho would be coming after them.'

'Sounds like you were a lovely little boy.'

'It was the army. Anyplace else they'd have sent me to reform school.'

'You're saying Joe grew to rely on it.'

Reacher nodded. 'It was like that for ten years, basically. It came and went, and it got less as we got older. But more serious when it actually happened. I think he internalized it. Ten years is a significant chunk of time when you're growing up, internalizing things. I think it became part of his mindset to ignore danger because the psycho always had his back. So I think Froelich's right, in a way. He *was* reckless. Not because he was trying to compete, but because deep down he felt he could afford to be. Because I had always looked after him, like his mother had always fed him, like the army had always housed him.'

'How old was he when he died?'

'Thirty-eight.'

'That's twenty years, Reacher. He had twenty years to adjust. We all adjust.'

'Do we? Sometimes I still feel like that same six-year-old. Everybody looking out of the corner of their eye at the psycho.'

'Like who?'

'Like Froelich.'

'She been saying things?'

'I disconcert her, clearly.'

'Secret Service is a civilian organization. Paramilitary at best. Nearly as bad as regular citizens.'

He smiled. Said nothing.

'So, what's the verdict?' Neagley asked. 'You going to be walking around from now on thinking you killed your brother?'

'A little bit, maybe,' he said. 'But I'll get over it.'

She nodded. 'You will. And you should. It wasn't your fault. He was thirty-eight. He wasn't waiting for his little brother to show up.'

'Can I ask you a question?'

'About what?'

'Something else Froelich said.'

'She wonders why we aren't doing it?'

'You're quick,' he said.

'I could sense it,' Neagley said. 'She came across as a little concerned. A little jealous. Cold, even. But then, I'd just kicked her ass with the audit thing.'

'You sure had.'

'We've never even touched, you know that, you and me? We've never had any physical contact of any kind at all. You've never patted me on the back, never even shaken my hand.'

He looked at her, and thought back through fifteen years.

'Haven't I?' he said. 'Is that good or bad?'

'It's good,' she said. 'But don't ask why.'

'OK,' he said.

'Reasons of my own. Don't ask what they are. But I don't like to be touched. And you never touched me. I always figured you could sense it. And I always appreciated that. It's one of the reasons I always liked you so much.'

He said nothing.

'Even if you should have been in reform school,' she said.

'You probably should have been in there with me.'

'We'd have made a good team,' she said. 'We *are* a good team. You should come back to Chicago with me.'

'I'm a wanderer,' he said.

'OK, I won't push,' she said. 'And look on the bright side with Froelich. Cut her some slack. She's probably worth it. She's a nice woman. Have some fun. You're good together.'

'OK,' he said. 'I guess.'

Neagley stood up and yawned.

'You OK?' he asked.

She nodded. 'I'm fine.'

Then she put a kiss on the tips of her fingers and blew it to him from six feet away. Walked out of the room without saying another word.

He was tired, but he was agitated and the room was cold and the bed was lumpy and he couldn't sleep. So he put his pants and shirt back on and walked to the closet and pulled Joe's box out. He didn't expect to find anything of interest in it. It would be abandoned stuff, that was all. Nobody leaves important things in a girlfriend's house when he knows he's going to skip out some day soon.

He put the box on the bed and pulled the flaps open. First thing he saw was a pair of shoes. They were packed heel to toe sideways across one end of the box. They were formal black shoes, good leather, reasonably heavy. They had proper stitched welts and toe caps. Thin laces in five holes. Imported, probably. But not Italian. They were too substantial. British, maybe. Like the air force tie.

He placed them on the bed cover. Put the heels six inches apart and the toes a little farther. The right heel was worn more than the left. The shoes were fairly old, fairly battered. He could see the whole shape of Joe's feet in them. The whole shape of his body, towering above them, like he was standing right there wearing them, invisible. They were like a death mask.

There were three books in the box, packed edge up. One was *Du côté de chez Swann*, which was the first volume of Marcel Proust's *À la recherche du temps perdu*. It was a French paperback with a characteristic severe plain cover. He leafed through. He could manage the language, but the content passed over his head. The second book was a college text about statistical analysis. It was heavy and dense. He leafed through and gave up on both the language and the content. Piled it on top of Proust on the bed.

He picked up the third book. Stared at it. He recognized it. He had bought it for Joe himself, a long time ago, for his thirtieth birthday. It was Dostoevsky's *Crime and Punishment*. It was in English, but he had bought it in Paris at a used-book store. He could even remember exactly what it had cost, which wasn't very much. The Paris bookseller had relegated it to the foreign-language section, and it wasn't a first edition or anything. It was just a nice-looking volume, and a great story.

He opened it to the flyleaf. He had written: *Joe. Avoid both, OK? Happy birthday. Jack.* He had used the bookseller's pen, and the ink had smudged. Now it had faded a little. Then he had written out an address label, because the bookseller had offered to mail it for him. The address was the Pentagon back then, because Joe was still in Military Intelligence when he was thirty. The bookseller had been very impressed. *The Pentagon, Arlington, Virginia, USA.*

He leafed past the title page to the first line: *At the beginning of July, during a spell of exceptionally hot weather, towards evening, a certain young man came down to the street from the room he was renting.* Then he leafed ahead, looking for the axe murder itself, and a folded paper fell out of the book. It was there as a bookmark, he guessed, about halfway through, where Raskolnikov is arguing with Svidrigailov.

He unfolded the paper. It was army issue. He could tell by the colour and the texture. Dull cream, smooth surface. It was the start of a letter, in Joe's familiar neat handwriting. The date was six weeks after his birthday. The text said: *Dear Jack, thanks for the book. It got here eventually. I will treasure it always. I might even read it. But probably not soon, because things are getting pretty busy here. I'm thinking of jumping ship and going to Treasury. Somebody (you'd recognize the name) offered me a job, and*

That was it. It ended abruptly, halfway down the page. He laid it unfolded next to the shoes. Put all three books back in the box. He looked at the shoes and the letter and listened hard inside his head the way a whale listens for another whale across a thousand miles of freezing ocean. But he heard nothing. There was nothing there. Nothing at all. So he crammed the shoes back into the box and folded the letter and tossed it in on top. Closed the flaps again and carried the box across the room and balanced it on top of the trash can. Turned back to the bed and heard another knock at the door.

It was Froelich. She was wearing her suit pants and jacket. No shirt under the jacket. Probably nothing at all under the jacket. He guessed she had dressed quickly because she knew she had to walk near the marshal in the corridor.

'You're still up,' she said.

'Come in,' he said.

She stepped into the room and waited until he closed the door.

'I'm not angry at you,' she said. 'You didn't get Joe killed. I don't really think that. And I'm not angry at Joe for getting killed. That just happened.'

'You're angry at something,' he said.

'I'm angry at him for leaving me,' she said.

He moved back into the room and sat on the end of the bed. This time, she sat right next to him.

'I'm over him,' she said. 'Completely. I promise you. I have been for a long time. But I'm not over how he just walked out on me.'

Reacher said nothing.

'And therefore I'm angry at *myself*,' she said, quietly. 'Because I wished him harm. Inside of me. I so wanted him to crash and burn afterwards. And then he *did*. So I feel terribly guilty. And now I'm worried that you're judging me.'

Reacher paused a beat.

'Nothing to judge,' he said. 'Nothing to feel guilty about, either. Whatever you wished was understandable, and it had no influence on what happened. How could it?'

She was silent.

'He got in over his head,' Reacher said. 'That's all. He took a chance and got unlucky. You didn't cause it. I didn't cause it. It just happened.'

'Things happen for a reason.'

He shook his head. 'No, they don't,' he said. 'They really don't. They just happen. It wasn't your fault. You're not responsible.'

'You think?'

'You're not responsible,' he said again. 'Nobody's responsible. Except the guy who pulled the trigger.'

'I wished him harm,' she said. 'I need you to forgive me.'

'Nothing to forgive.'

'I need you to say the words.'

'I can't,' Reacher said. 'And I won't. You don't need forgiving. It wasn't your fault. Or mine. Or Joe's, even. It just happened. Like things do.'

She was quiet for a long moment. Then she nodded, just slightly, and moved a little closer to him.

'OK,' she said.

'Are you wearing anything under that suit?' he asked.

'You knew I had a gun in the kitchen.'

'Yes, I did.'

'Why did you search my house?'

'Because I've got the gene that Joe didn't have. Things don't happen to me. I don't get unlucky. You carrying a gun now?'

'No, I'm not,' she said.

There was silence.

'And there's nothing under the suit,' she said.

'I need to confirm those things for myself,' he said. 'It's a caution thing. Purely genetic, you understand.'

He undid the first button on her jacket. Then the second. Slipped his hand inside. Her skin was warm and smooth.

They got a wake-up call from the motel desk at six o'clock in the morning. *Stuyvesant must have arranged it last night*, Reacher thought. *I wish he'd forgotten*. Froelich stirred at his side. Then her eyes snapped open and she sat up, wide awake.

'Happy Thanksgiving,' he said.

'I hope it will be,' she said. 'I've got a feeling about today. I think it's the day we win or lose.'

'I like that kind of a day.'

'You do?'

'Sure,' he said. 'Losing is not an option, which means it's the day we win.'

She pushed back the covers. The room heat had gone from too cold to too hot.

'Dress casual,' she said. 'Suits don't look right on a holiday at a soup kitchen. Will you tell Neagley?'

'You tell her. You'll be passing her door. She won't bite.'

'She won't?'

'No,' he said.

She put her suit back on and left. He padded over to the closet and pulled out the bag full of his Atlantic City clothes. He spilled them on the bed and did his best to flatten out the wrinkles. Then he showered without shaving. *She wanted me to look casual*, he thought. He found Neagley in the lobby. She was wearing her jeans and her sweatshirt with a battered leather jacket over it. There was a buffet table with coffee and muffins. The U.S. Marshals had already eaten most of them.

'You two kiss and make up?' Neagley asked.

'A little of each, I guess,' he said.

He took a cup and filled it with coffee. Selected a raisin bran muffin. Then Froelich showed up, newly showered and wearing black denim jeans with a black polo shirt and a black nylon jacket. They ate and drank whatever the marshals had left and then they walked out together to Stuyvesant's Suburban. It was before seven in the morning on Thanksgiving Day and the city looked like it had been evacuated the night before. There was silence everywhere. It was cold, but the air was still and soft. The sun was up and the sky was pale blue. The stone buildings looked golden. The roads were completely empty. It took no time at all to reach the office. Stuyvesant was waiting for them in the conference room. His interpretation of casual was a pair of pressed grey slacks and a pink sweater under a bright blue golf jacket. Reacher guessed all the labels said Brooks Brothers, and he guessed Mrs Stuyvesant had gone to the Baltimore hospital as was usual on a Thursday, Thanksgiving Day or not. Bannon was sitting opposite Stuyvesant. He was in the same tweed and flannel. He would look like a cop whatever day it was. He looked like a guy without too many options in his closet.

'Let's get to it,' Stuyvesant said. 'We've got a big agenda.'

'First item,' Bannon said. 'The FBI formally advises cancellation today. We know the bad guys are in the city and therefore it's reasonable to assume there may be some kind of imminent hostile attempt.'

'Cancellation is out of the question,' Stuyvesant said. 'Free turkey at a homeless shelter might sound trivial, but this is a town that runs on symbols. If Armstrong pulled out the political damage would be catastrophic.'

'OK, then we're going to be there on the ground with you,' Bannon said. 'Not to duplicate your role. We'll stay strictly out of your way on all matters that concern Armstrong's personal security. But if something does go down, the closer we are the luckier we'll get.'

'Any specific information?' Froelich asked.

Bannon shook his head. 'None,' he said. 'Just a feeling. But I would urge you to take it very seriously.'

'I'm taking everything very seriously,' Froelich said. 'In fact, I'm changing the whole plan. I'm moving the event outdoors.'

'*Out*doors?' Bannon said. 'Isn't that worse?'

'No,' Froelich said. 'On balance, it's better. It's a long low room, basically. Kitchen at the back. It's going to get very crowded. We've got no realistic chance of using metal detectors on the doors. It's the end of November, and most of these people are going to be wearing five layers and carrying God knows what kind of metal stuff. We can't search them. It would take for ever and God knows how many diseases my people would catch. We can't wear gloves to do it because that would be seen as insulting. So we have to concede there's a fair chance that the bad guys could mingle in and get close, and we have to concede we've got no real way of stopping them.'

'So how does it help to be outdoors?'

'There's a side yard. We'll put the serving tables in a long line at right angles to the wall of the building. Pass stuff out through the kitchen window. Behind the serving table is the wall of the yard. We'll put Armstrong and his wife and four agents in a line behind the serving table, backs to the wall. We'll have the guests approach from the left, single file through a screen of more agents. They'll get their food and walk on inside to sit down and eat it. The television people will like it better, too. Outside is always better for them. And there'll be orderly movement. Left to right along the table. Turkey from Armstrong, stuffing from Mrs Armstrong. Move along, sit down to eat. Easier to portray, visually.'

'Upside?' Stuyvesant asked.

'Extensive,' Froelich said. 'Much better crowd security. Nobody can pull a weapon before they get near Armstrong, because they're filtering through an agent screen the whole time until they're right across the table from him. Whereupon if they wait to do it at that point, he's got four agents right alongside him.'

'Downside?'

'Limited. We'll be screened on three sides by walls. But the yard is open at the front. There's a block of five-storey buildings directly across the street. Old warehousing. The windows are boarded, which is a huge bonus. But we'll need to put an agent on every roof. So we'll have to forget the budget.'

Stuyvesant nodded. 'We can do that. Good plan.'

'The weather helped us for once,' Froelich said.

'Is this basically a conventional plan?' Bannon asked. 'Like normal Secret Service thinking?'

'I don't really want to comment on that,' Froelich said. 'Secret Service doesn't discuss procedure.'

'Work with me, ma'am,' Bannon said. 'We're all on the same side here.'

'You can tell him,' Stuyvesant said. 'We're already in hip-deep.'

Froelich shrugged. 'OK,' she said. 'I guess it's a conventional plan. Place like that, we're pretty limited for options. Why are you asking?'

'Because we've done a lot of work on this,' Bannon said. 'A lot of thinking.'

'And?' Stuyvesant said.

'We're looking at four specific factors here. First, this all started seventeen days ago, correct?'

Stuyvesant nodded.

'And who's hurting?' Bannon asked. 'That's the first question. Second, think about the demonstration homicides out in Minnesota and Colorado. How were you alerted? That's the second question. Third, what were the weapons used out there? And fourth, how did the last message end up on Ms Froelich's hallway floor?'

'What are you saying?'

'I'm saying all four factors point in one single direction.'

'What direction?'

'What's the purpose behind the messages?'

'They're threats,' Froelich said.

'Who are they threatening?'

'Armstrong, of course.'

'Are they? Some were addressed to you, and some were addressed to him. But has he seen *any* of them? Even the ones addressed directly to him? Does he even know anything about them?'

'We never tell our protectees. That's policy, always has been.'

'So Armstrong's not sweating, is he? Who's sweating?'

'We are.'

'So are the messages *really* aimed at Armstrong, or are they really aimed at the United States Secret Service? In a real-world sense?'

Froelich said nothing.

'OK,' Bannon said. 'Now think about Minnesota and Colorado. Hell of a demonstration. Not easy to stage. Whoever you are, shooting people down takes nerve and skill and care and thought and preparation. Not easy. Not something you undertake lightly. But they undertook it, because they had some kind of point to make. Then what did they do? How did they tip you off? How did they tell you where to look?'

'They didn't.'

'Exactly,' Bannon said. 'They went to all that trouble, took all that risk, and then they sat back and did nothing at all. They just waited. And sure enough, the NCIC reports were filed by the local police departments, and the FBI computers scanned through NCIC like they're programmed to do, and they spotted the word *Armstrong* like they're programmed to do, and we called you with the good news.'

'So?'

'So tell me, how many Joe Publics would know all that would

happen? How many Joe Publics would sit back and take the risk that their little drama would go unconnected for a day or two until you read about it in the newspapers?'

'So what are you saying? Who are they?'

'What weapons did they use?'

'An H&K MP5SD6 and a Vaime Mk2,' Reacher said.

'Fairly esoteric weapons,' Bannon said. 'And not legally available for sale to the public, because they're silenced. Only government agencies can buy them. And only one government agency buys both of them.'

'Us,' Stuyvesant said, quietly.

'Yes, you,' Bannon said. 'And finally, I looked for Ms Froelich's name in the phone book. And you know what? She's not there. She's unlisted. Certainly there was no boxed ad saying, "I'm a Secret Service crew chief and this is where I live." So how did these guys know where to deliver the last message?'

There was a long silence.

'They know me,' Froelich said, quietly.

Bannon nodded. 'I'm sorry, folks, but as of now the FBI is looking for Secret Service people. Not current employees, because current employees would have been aware of the early arrival of the demonstration threat and would have acted a day sooner. So we're focusing on recent ex-employees who still know the ropes. People who knew you wouldn't tell Armstrong himself. People who knew Ms Froelich. People who knew Nendick, too, and where to find him. Maybe people who left under a cloud and are carrying some kind of grudge. Against the Secret Service, not against Brook Armstrong. Because our theory is that Armstrong is a means, not an end. They'll waste a vice president-elect just to get at you, exactly like they wasted the other two Armstrongs.'

The room was silent.

'What would be the motive?' Froelich asked.

Bannon made a face. 'Embittered ex-employees are walking, talking, living, breathing motives. We all know that. We've all suffered from it.'

'What about the thumbprint?' Stuyvesant said. 'All our people are printed. Always have been.'

'Our assumption is that we're talking about two guys. Our assessment is that the thumbprint guy is an unknown associate of somebody who used to work here, who is the latex gloves guy. So we're saying *they* and *them* purely as a convenience. We're not saying they both worked here. We're not suggesting you've got two renegades.'

'Just one renegade.'

'That's our theory,' Bannon said. 'But saying *they* and *them* is useful and instructive, too, because they're a team. We *need* to look at them as a single unit. Because they share information. Therefore what I'm saying is, only one of them worked here, but they both know your secrets.'

'This is a very big department,' Stuyvesant said. 'Big turnover of people. Some quit. Some are fired. Some retire. Some get asked to.'

'We're checking now,' Bannon said. 'We're getting personnel lists direct from Treasury. We're going back five years.'

'You'll get a long list.'

'We've got the manpower.'

Nobody spoke.

'I'm real sorry, people,' Bannon said. 'Nobody likes to hear their problem is close to home. But it's the only conclusion there is. And it's not good news for days like today. These people are here in town right now and they know exactly what you're thinking and exactly what you're doing. So my advice is to cancel. And if you're not going to cancel, then my advice is to take a great deal of care.'

Stuyvesant nodded in the silence. 'We will,' he said. 'You can count on that.'

'My people will be in place two hours in advance,' Bannon said.

'Ours will be in place an hour before that,' Froelich replied.

Bannon smiled a tight little smile and pushed back his chair and stood up. 'See you there,' he said. He left the room and closed the door behind him, firmly, but quietly.

Stuyvesant checked his watch. 'Well?'

They had sat quiet for a moment, and then strolled out to the reception area and got coffee. Then they had regrouped in the conference room, in the same seats, each of them looking at the place Bannon had vacated like he was still there.

'Well?' Stuyvesant said again.

Nobody spoke.

'Inevitable, I guess,' Stuyvesant said. 'They can't pin the thumbprint guy on us, but the other one is *definitely* one of ours. It'll be all smiles over at the Hoover Building. They'll be grinning from ear to ear. Laughing up their sleeves at us.'

'But does that make them wrong?' Neagley asked.

'No,' Froelich said. 'These guys know where I live. So I think Bannon's right.'

Stuyvesant flinched, like the umpire had called *strike one*.

'And you?' he said to Neagley.

'Worrying about DNA on envelopes sounds like insiders,' Neagley said. 'But one thing bothers me. If they're familiar with your procedures, then they didn't interpret the Bismarck situation very well. You said they expected the cops would move towards the decoy rifle and Armstrong would move towards the cars, thereby traversing their field of fire. But that didn't happen. Armstrong waited in the blind spot and the cars came to him.'

Froelich shook her head. 'No, I'm afraid their interpretation was correct,' she said. 'Normally Armstrong would have been well out in the middle of the field, letting people get a good look at him. Right there in the centre of things. We don't usually make them skulk around the edges. It was a last-minute change to keep him near the church. Based on Reacher's input. And normally there's absolutely no way I would allow a rear-wheel-drive limo on the grass. Too easy to bog down and get stuck. That's an article of faith. But I knew the ground was dry and hard. It was practically frozen. So I improvised. That manoeuvre would have struck an insider as completely off the wall. It would have been the very last thing they were expecting. They would have been totally surprised by it.'

Silence.

'Then Bannon's theory is perfectly plausible,' Neagley said. 'I'm very sorry.'

Stuyvesant nodded, slowly. *Strike two*.

'Reacher?' he said.

'Can't argue with a word of it.'

Strike three. Stuyvesant's head dropped, like his last hope was gone.

'But I don't believe it,' Reacher said.

Stuyvesant's head came up again.

'I'm glad they're pursuing it,' Reacher said. 'Because it needs to be pursued, I guess. We need to eliminate all possibilities. And they'll go at it like crazy. If they're right, they'll take care of it for us, that's for sure. So it's one less thing for us to worry about. But I'm pretty sure they're wasting their time.'

'Why?' Froelich asked.

'Because I'm pretty sure neither of these guys ever worked here.'

'So who are they?'

'I think they're both outsiders. I think they're between two and ten years older than Armstrong himself, both of them brought up and educated in remote rural areas where the schools were decent but the taxes were low.'

'What?'

'Think of everything we know. Think of everything we've seen. Then think of the very smallest part of it. The very tiniest component.'

'Tell us,' Froelich said.

Stuyvesant checked his watch again. Shook his head. 'Not now,' he said. 'We need to move. You can tell us later. But you're sure?'

'They're both outsiders,' Reacher said. 'Guaranteed. It's in the Constitution.'

THIRTEEN

EVERY CITY HAS A CUSP, WHERE THE GOOD PART OF TOWN TURNS bad. Washington D.C. was no different. The border between desirable and undesirable ran in a ragged irregular loop, bulging outward here and there to accommodate reclaimed blocks, swooping inward in other areas to claim inroads of its own. It was pierced in some places by gentrified corridors. Elsewhere it worked gradually, shading imperceptibly over hundreds of yards down streets where you could buy thirty different blends of tea at one end and cash cheques at the other for thirty per cent of the proceeds.

The shelter selected for Armstrong's appearance was halfway into the no-man's-land north of Union Station. To the east were train tracks and switching yards. To the west was a highway running underground in a tunnel. All around were decayed buildings. Some of them were warehouses and some of them were apartments. Some of them were abandoned, some of them were not. The shelter itself was exactly what Froelich had described. It was a long low one-storey building made of brick. It had large metal-framed windows evenly spaced in the walls. It had a yard next to it twice its own size. The yard was closed in on three sides by high brick walls. It was impossible to decipher the building's original purpose. Maybe it had been a stable, back when Union Station's freight had been hauled away by horses. Maybe later it was updated with new windows and used as a trucking depot after the horses faded away. Maybe it had served time as an office. It was impossible to tell.

It housed fifty homeless people every night. They were woken early every morning and given breakfast and turned out on the streets. Then the fifty cots were stacked and stored and the floor was washed and the air was misted with disinfectant. Metal tables and chairs were carried in and placed where the beds had been. Lunch was available every day, and dinner, and then the reverse conversion to a dormitory took place at nine every evening.

But this day was different. Thanksgiving Day was always different, and this year it was more different than usual. Wake-up call happened a little earlier and breakfast was served a little faster. The overnighters were shown the door a full half-hour before normal, which was a double blow to them because cities are notoriously quiet on Thanksgiving Day and panhandling receipts are dismal. The floor was washed more thoroughly than usual and more disinfectant was sprayed into the air. The tables were positioned more exactly, the chairs were lined up more precisely, more volunteers were on hand, and all of them were wearing fresh white sweatshirts with the benefactor's name brightly printed in red.

The first Secret Service agents to arrive were the line-of-sight team. They had a large-scale city surveyor's map and a telescopic sight removed from a sniper rifle. One agent walked through every step that Armstrong was scheduled to take. Every separate pace he would stop and turn round and squint through the scope and call out every window and every rooftop he could see. Because if he could see a rooftop or a window, a potential marksman on that rooftop or in that window could see him. The agent with the map would identify the building concerned and check the scale and calculate the range. Anything under seven hundred feet he marked in black.

But it was a good location. The only available sniper nests were on the roofs of the abandoned five-storey warehouses opposite. The guy with the map finished up with a straight line of just five black crosses, nothing more. He wrote *checked with scope, clear daylight, 0845 hrs, all suspect locations recorded* across the bottom of the map and signed his name and added the date. The agent with the scope countersigned and the map was rolled and stored in the back of a department Suburban, awaiting Froelich's arrival.

Next on scene was a convoy of police vans with five separate canine units in them. One unit cleared the shelter. Two more entered the warehouses. The last two were explosives hunters who checked the surrounding streets in all directions on a four-hundred-yard radius. Beyond four hundred yards, the maze of streets meant there were too many potential access routes to check, and therefore too many to bomb with any realistic chance of success. As soon as a building or a street was pronounced safe a D.C. patrolman took up station on foot. The sky was still clear and the sun was still out. It gave an illusion of warmth. It kept grousing to a minimum.

By nine thirty the shelter was the epicentre of a quarter of a square mile of secure territory. D.C. cops held the perimeter on foot and in cars and there were better than fifty more loose in the interior. They made up the majority of the local population. The city was still quiet. Some of the shelter inhabitants were hanging around. There was nowhere productive to go, and they knew from experience that to be early in the lunch line was better than late. Politicians didn't understand portion control, and pickings could be getting slim after the first thirty minutes.

Froelich arrived at ten o'clock exactly, driving a Suburban with Reacher and Neagley riding with her. Stuyvesant was right behind in a second Suburban. Behind him were four more trucks carrying five department sharpshooters and fifteen general-duty agents. Froelich parked on the sidewalk tight against the base of the warehouse wall. Normally she might have just blocked the street beyond the shelter entrance, but she didn't want to reveal the direction of Armstrong's intended approach to onlookers. He was actually scheduled to come in from the south, but that information and ten minutes with a map could predict his route all the way from Georgetown.

She assembled her people in the shelter's yard and sent the sharpshooters to secure the warehouse roofs. They would be up there three hours before the event started, but that was normal. Generally they were the first to arrive and the last to leave. Stuyvesant pulled Reacher aside and asked him to go up there with them.

'Then come find me,' he said. 'I want a first-hand report about how bad it is.'

So Reacher walked across the street with an agent called Crosetti and they ducked past a cop into a damp hallway full of trash and rat droppings. There were stairs winding up through a central shaft. Crosetti was in a Kevlar vest and was carrying a rifle in a hard case. But he was a fit guy. He was half a flight ahead of Reacher at the top.

The stairs came out inside a rooftop hutch. There was a wooden door that opened outward into the sunlight. The roof was flat. It was made of asphalt. There were pigeon corpses here and there, and dirty skylights made of wired glass and small metal turrets on top of ventilation pipes. The roof was lipped with a low wall, set on top with eroded coping stones. Crosetti walked to the left edge, and then the right. Made visual contact with his colleagues either side. Then he walked to the front to check the view. Reacher was already there.

The view was good and bad. Good in the conventional sense because the sun was shining and they were five floors up in a low-built part of town. Bad because the shelter's yard was right there underneath them. It was like looking down into a shoe box from a distance of three feet up and three feet away. The back wall where Armstrong would be standing was dead ahead. It was made out of old brick and looked like the execution wall in some foreign prison. Hitting him would be easier than shooting a fish in a barrel.

'What's the range?' Reacher asked.

'Your guess?' Crosetti said.

Reacher put his knees against the lip of the roof and glanced out and down. 'Ninety yards?' he said.

Crosetti unsnapped a pocket in his vest and took out a range finder. 'Laser,' he said. He switched it on and lined it up. 'Ninety-two to the wall,' he said. 'Ninety-one to his head. That was a pretty good guess.'

'Windage?'

'Slight thermal coming up off the concrete down there,' Crosetti said. 'Nothing else, probably. No big deal.'

'Practically like standing right next to him,' Reacher said.

'Don't worry,' Crosetti said. 'As long as I'm up here nobody else can be. That's the job today. We're sentries, not shooters.'

'Where are you going to be?' Reacher asked.

Crosetti glanced all round his little piece of real estate and pointed. 'Over there, I guess,' he said. 'Tight in the far corner. I'll face parallel with the front wall. Slight turn to my left and I'm covering the yard. Slight turn to my right, I'm covering the head of the stairwell.'

'Good plan,' Reacher said. 'You need anything?'

Crosetti shook his head.

'OK,' Reacher said. 'I'll leave you to it. Try to stay awake, OK?'

Crosetti smiled. 'I usually do.'

'Good,' Reacher said. 'I like that in a sentry.'

He went back down five flights through the darkness and stepped out into the sun. Walked across the street and glanced up. Saw Crosetti nestled comfortably in the angle of the corner. His head and his knees were visible. So was his rifle barrel. It was jutting upward against the bright sky at a relaxed forty-five degrees. He waved. Crosetti waved back. He walked on and found Stuyvesant in the yard. He was hard to miss, given the colour of his sweater and the brightness of the daylight.

'It's OK up there,' Reacher said. 'Hell of a firing platform, but as long as your guys hold it we're safe enough.'

Stuyvesant nodded and turned round and scanned upward. All five warehouse roofs were visible from the yard. All five were occupied by sharpshooters. Five silhouetted heads, five silhouetted rifle barrels.

'Froelich is looking for you,' Stuyvesant said.

Nearer the building staff and agents were hauling long trestle tables into place. The idea was to form a barrier with them. The right-hand end would be hard against the shelter's wall. The left-hand end would be three feet from the yard wall opposite. There would be a pen six feet deep behind the line of tables. Armstrong and his wife would be in the pen with four agents. Directly behind them would be the execution wall. Up close it didn't look so bad. The old bricks looked warmed by the sun. Rustic, even friendly. He turned his back on them and looked up at the warehouse roofs. Crosetti waved again. *I'm still awake,* the wave said.

'Reacher,' Froelich called.

He turned round and found her walking out of the shelter towards him. She was carrying a clipboard thick with paper. She was up on her toes, busy, in charge, in command. She looked magnificent. The black clothes emphasized her litheness and made her eyes blaze with blue. Dozens of agents and scores of cops swirled all around her, every one of them under her personal control.

'We're doing fine here,' she said. 'So I want you to take a stroll. Just check around. Neagley's already out there. You know what to look for.'

'Feels good, doesn't it?' he asked.

'What?'

'Doing something really well,' he said. 'Taking charge.'

'Think I'm doing well?'

'You're the best,' he said. 'This is tremendous. Armstrong's a lucky man.'

'I hope,' she said.

'Believe it,' he said.

She smiled, quickly and shyly, and moved on, leafing through her paperwork. He turned the other way and walked back out to the street. Turned right and planned a route in his head that would keep him on a block-and-a-half radius.

There were cops on the corner and the beginnings of a ragged crowd of people waiting for the free lunch. There were two television trucks setting up fifty yards down the street from the shelter. Hydraulic masts were unfolding themselves and satellite dishes were rotating. Technicians were unrolling cable and shouldering cameras. He saw Bannon with six men and a woman he guessed were the FBI task force. They had just arrived. Bannon had a map unrolled on the hood of his car and his agents were clustered around looking at it. Reacher waved to Bannon and turned left and passed the end of an alley that led down behind the warehouses. He could hear a train on the tracks ahead of him. The mouth of the alley was manned by a

D.C. cop, facing outward, standing easy. There was a police cruiser parked nearby. Another cop in it. Cops everywhere. The overtime bill was going to be something to see.

There were broken-down stores here and there, but they were all closed for the holiday. Some of the storefronts were churches, equally closed. There were auto body shops nearer the railroad tracks, all shuttered and still. There was a pawnbroker with a very old guy outside washing the windows. He was the only thing moving on the street. His store was tall and narrow and had concertina barriers inside the glass. The display space was crammed with junk of every description. There were clocks, coats, musical instruments, alarm radios, hats, record players, car stereos, binoculars, strings of Christmas lights. There was writing on the windows, offering to buy just about any article ever manufactured. If it didn't grow in the ground or move by itself, this guy would give you money for it. He also offered services. He would cash cheques, appraise jewellery, repair watches. There was a tray of watches on view. They were mostly old-fashioned wind-up items, with bulging crystals and big square luminescent figures and sculpted hands. Reacher glanced again at the sign: *Watches Repaired.* Then he glanced again at the old guy. He was up to his elbows in soap suds.

'You fix watches?' he asked.

'What have you got?' the old guy said. He had an accent. Russian, probably.

'A question,' Reacher said.

'I thought you had a watch to fix. That was my business, originally. Before quartz.'

'My watch is fine,' Reacher said. 'Sorry.'

He pulled back his cuff to check the time. Quarter past eleven.

'Let me see that,' the old guy said.

Reacher extended his wrist.

'Bulova,' the old guy said. 'American military issue before the Gulf War. A good watch. You buy it from a soldier?'

'No, I was a soldier.'

The old guy nodded. 'So was I. In the Red Army. What's the question?'

'You ever heard of squalene?'
'It's a lubricant.'
'You use it?'
'Time to time. I don't fix so many watches now. Not since quartz.'
'Where do you get it?'
'Are you kidding?'
'No,' Reacher said. 'I'm asking a question.'
'You want to know where I get my squalene?'
'That's what questions are for. They seek to elicit information.'
The old guy smiled. 'I carry it around with me.'
'Where?'
'You're looking at it.'
'Am I?'
The old guy nodded. 'And I'm looking at yours.'
'My what?'
'Your supply of squalene.'
'I haven't got any squalene,' Reacher said. 'It comes from sharks' livers. Long time since I was next to a shark.'
The old man shook his head. 'You see, the Soviet system was very frequently criticized, and believe me I've always been happy to tell the truth about it. But at least we had education. Especially in the natural sciences.'
'C-thirty-H-fifty,' Reacher said. 'It's an acyclic hydrocarbon. Which when hydrogenated becomes squalane with an *a*.'
'You understand any of that?'
'No,' Reacher said. 'Not really.'
'Squalene is an oil,' the old guy said. 'It occurs naturally in only two places in the known biosphere. One is inside a shark's liver. The other is as a sebaceous product on the skin around the human nose.'
Reacher touched his nose. 'Same stuff? Sharks' livers and people's noses?'
The old guy nodded. 'Identical molecular structure. So if I need squalene to lubricate a watch, I just dab some off on my fingertip. Like this.'
He wiped his wet hand on his trouser leg and extended a finger and rubbed it down where his nose joined his face. Then he held up the fingertip for inspection.

'Put that on the gear wheel and you're OK,' he said.
'I see,' Reacher said.
'You want to sell the Bulova?'
Reacher shook his head. 'Sentimental value,' he said.
'From the army?' the old guy said. 'You're *nekulturniy*.'
He turned back to his task and Reacher walked on.
'Happy Thanksgiving,' he called. There was no reply.
He met Neagley a block from the shelter. She was walking in from the opposite direction. She turned round and walked back with him, keeping her customary distance from his shoulder.
'Beautiful day,' she said. 'Isn't it?'
'I don't know,' he said.
'How would you do it?'
'I wouldn't,' he said. 'Not here. Not in Washington D.C. This is their back yard. I'd wait for a better chance someplace else.'
'Me too,' she said. 'But they missed in Bismarck. Wall Street in ten days is no good to them. Then they're deep into December, and the next thing is more holidays and then the Inauguration. So they're running out of opportunities. And we know they're right here in town.'
Reacher said nothing. They walked past Bannon. He was sitting in his car.

They arrived back at the shelter at noon exactly. Stuyvesant was standing near the entrance. He nodded a cautious greeting. Inside the yard everything was ready. The serving tables were lined up. They were draped with pure white cloths that hung down to the floor. They were loaded with food warmers laid out in a line. There were ladles and long-handled spoons neatly arrayed. The kitchen window opened directly into the pen behind the tables. The shelter hall itself was set up for dining. There were police sawhorses arranged so that the crowd would be funnelled down the left edge of the yard. Then there was a right turn across the face of the serving area. Then another right along the wall of the shelter and in through the door. Froelich was detailing positions for each of the general-duty agents. Four would be at the entrance to the yard. Six would line the approach to the serving area. One would secure each end of the pen, from the outside. Three would patrol the exit line.

'OK, listen up,' Froelich called. 'Remember, it's very easy to look a little like a homeless person, but very hard to look *exactly* like a homeless person. Watch their feet. Are their shoes right? Look at their hands. We want to see gloves, or ingrained dirt. Look at their faces. They need to be lean. Hollow cheeks. We want to see dirty hair. Hair that hasn't been washed for a month or a year. We want to see clothes that are *moulded* to the body. Any questions?'

Nobody spoke.

'Any doubt at all, act first and think later,' Froelich called. 'I'm going to be serving behind the tables with the Armstrongs and the personal detail. We're depending on you not to send us anybody you don't like, OK?'

She checked her watch. 'Five past twelve,' she said. 'Fifty-five minutes to go.'

Reacher squeezed through at the left-hand end of the serving tables and stood in the pen. Behind him was a wall. To his right was a wall. To his left were the shelter windows. Ahead to his right was the approach line. Any individual would pass four agents at the yard entrance and six more as he shuffled along. Ten suspicious pairs of eyes before anybody got face to face with Armstrong himself. Ahead to the left was the exit line. Three agents funnelling people into the hall. He raised his eyes. Dead ahead were the warehouses. Five sentries on five roofs. Crosetti waved. He waved back.

'OK?' Froelich asked.

She was standing across the serving table from him. He smiled.

'Dark or light?' he asked.

'We'll eat later,' she said. 'I want you and Neagley freelance in the yard. Stay near the exit line, so you get a wide view.'

'OK,' he said.

'Still think I'm doing well?'

He pointed left. 'I don't like those windows,' he said. 'Suppose somebody bides his time all the way through the line, keeps his head down, behaves himself, picks up his food, makes it inside, sits down, and then pulls a gun and fires back through the window?'

She nodded. 'Already thought about it,' she said. 'I'm bringing three cops in from the perimeter. Putting one in each window, standing up, facing the room.'

'That should do it,' he said. 'Great job.'

'And we're going to be wearing vests,' she said. 'Everybody in the pen. The Armstrongs, too.'

She checked her watch again. 'Forty-five minutes,' she said. 'Walk with me.'

They walked out of the yard and across the street to where she had parked her Suburban. It was in a deep shadow made by the warehouse wall. She unlocked the tailgate and swung it open. The shadow and the tinted glass made it dark inside. The load bay was neatly packed with equipment. But the back seat was empty.

'We could get in,' Reacher said. 'You know, fool around a little.'

'We could not.'

'You said it was fun, fooling around at work.'

'I meant the office.'

'Is that an invitation?'

She paused. Straightened up. Smiled.

'OK,' she said. 'Why not? I might like that.'

Then she smiled wider.

'OK,' she said again. 'Soon as Armstrong is secure, we'll go do it on Stuyvesant's desk. As a celebration.'

She leaned in and grabbed her vest and stretched up and kissed him on the cheek. Then she ducked away and headed back. He slammed the tailgate and she locked it from forty feet away with the remote.

With thirty minutes to go she put her vest on under her jacket and ran a radio check. She told the police commander he could start marshalling the crowd near the entrance. Told the media they could come into the yard and start the tapes rolling. With fifteen minutes to go she announced that the Armstrongs were on their way.

'Get the food out,' she called.

The kitchen crew swarmed into the pen and the cooks passed pans of food out through the kitchen window. Reacher leaned on the shelter wall at the end of the line of serving tables, on the public side. He put his back flat on the bricks between the kitchen window and the first hall window. He would be looking straight down the food line. A half-turn to his left, he would be looking at the approach line. A half-turn to his right, he would be looking into the pen. People would have to skirt round him with their loaded plates. He wanted a close-up view. Neagley stood six feet away, in the body of the yard, in the angle the sawhorses made. Froelich paced near her, nervous, thinking through the last-minute checks for the hundredth time.

'Arrival imminent,' she said into her wrist microphone. 'Driver says they're two blocks away. You guys on the roof see them yet?'

She listened to her earpiece and then spoke again.

'Two blocks away,' she repeated.

The kitchen crew finished loading the food warmers and disappeared. Reacher couldn't see because of the brick walls but he heard the motorcade. Several powerful engines, wide tyres, approaching fast, slowing hard. A Metro cruiser pulled past the entrance, then a Suburban, then a Cadillac limo that stopped square in the gateway. An agent stepped forward and opened the door. Armstrong stepped out and turned back and offered his hand to his wife. Cameramen pressed forward. The Armstrongs stood up straight together and paused a moment by the limo's door and smiled for the lenses. Mrs Armstrong was a tall blonde woman whose genes had come all the way from Scandinavia a couple of hundred years ago. That was clear. She was wearing pressed jeans and a puffed-up goose-down jacket a size too large to accommodate her vest. Her hair was lacquered back into a frame around her face. She looked a little uncomfortable in the jeans, like she wasn't accustomed to wearing them.

Armstrong was in jeans too, but his were worn like he lived in them. He had a red plaid jacket buttoned tight. It was a little too small to conceal the shape of the vest from an expert eye. He was bareheaded, but his hair was brushed. His personal detail surrounded them and eased them into the yard. Cameras panned as they walked past. The personal agents were dressed like Froelich. Black denim, black nylon jackets zipped over vests. Two of them were wearing sunglasses. One of them was wearing a black ball cap. All of them had earpieces and bulges at their waists where their handguns were.

Froelich led them into the pen behind the serving tables. One agent took each end and stood with arms folded for nothing but crowd surveillance. The third agent and Froelich and the Armstrongs themselves took the middle to do the serving. They milled around for a second and then arranged themselves with the third agent on the left, then Armstrong, then Froelich, then Armstrong's wife on the right. Armstrong picked up a ladle in one hand and a spoon in the other. Checked the cameras were on him and raised the utensils high, like weapons.

'Happy Thanksgiving, everybody,' he called.

The crowd swarmed slowly through the gateway. They were a subdued bunch. They moved lethargically and didn't talk much. No excited chatter, no buzz of sound. Nothing like the hotel lobby at the donor reception. Most of them were swaddled in several heavy layers. Some of them had rope belts. They had hats and fingerless gloves and downcast faces. Each had to pass left and right and left and right through the six screening agents. The first recipient looped past the last agent and took a plastic plate from the first server and was subjected to the full brilliance of Armstrong's smile. Armstrong spooned a turkey leg onto the plate. The guy shuffled along and Froelich gave him vegetables. Armstrong's wife added the stuffing. Then the guy shuffled past Reacher and headed inside for the tables. The food smelled good and the guy smelled bad.

It continued like that for five minutes. Every time a pan of food was emptied it was replaced by a new one passed out through the kitchen window. Armstrong was smiling like he was enjoying himself. The line of homeless people shuffled forward. The cameras rolled. The only sound was the clatter of metal utensils in the serving dishes and the repeated banalities from the servers. *Enjoy! Happy Thanksgiving! Thanks for coming by!*

Reacher glanced at Neagley. She raised her eyebrows. He glanced up at the warehouse roofs. Glanced at Froelich, busy with her long-handled spoon. Looked at the television people. They were clearly bored. They were taping a whole hour and they knew it would be edited to eight seconds maximum with boilerplate commentary laid over it. *Vice President-elect Armstrong served the traditional Thanksgiving turkey today at a homeless shelter here in Washington D.C.* Cut to first-quarter football highlights.

The line was still thirty people long when it happened.

Reacher sensed a dull chalky impact nearby and something stung him on the right cheek. In the corner of his eye he saw a puff of dust around a small cratered chip on the surface of the back wall. No sound. No sound at all. A split second later his brain told him: *bullet. Silencer.* He looked at the line. Nobody moving. He snapped his head to the left and up. *The roof. Crosetti wasn't there. Crosetti was there. He was twenty feet out of position. He was shooting. It wasn't Crosetti.*

Then he tried to defeat time and move faster than the awful slow motion of panic would allow him. He pushed off the wall and filled his lungs with air and turned toward Froelich as slowly as a man running through a swimming pool. His mouth opened and desperate words formed in his throat and he tried to shout them out. But she was already well ahead of him.

She was screaming, '*G-u-u-n!*'

She was spinning in slow motion. Her spoon was loose in the air, arcing up over the table, glittering in the sun, spraying food. She was on Armstrong's left. She was jumping sideways at him. Her left arm was scything up to shield him. She was jumping like a basketball player going for a hook shot. Twisting in mid-air. She got her right hand on his shoulder for a pivot and used the momentum of her left to turn herself around face on to him. She drew her knees up and landed square on his upper chest. Breath punched out of him and his legs buckled and he was going down backward when the second silenced bullet hit her in the neck. There was no sound. No sound at all. Just a bright vivid backward spray of blood in the sunlight, as fine as autumn mist.

It hung there in a long conical cloud, like vapour, pink and iridescent. It stretched to a point as she fell. Her spoon came down through it, tumbling end over end, disturbing its shape. It lengthened in a long graceful curve. She went down and left her blood in the air behind her like a question mark. Reacher turned his head like it was clamped with an enormous weight and saw the slope of a shoulder far away on the roof, moving backward out of sight. He turned infinitely slowly back to the yard and saw the wet pink arrow of Froelich's blood pointing down to a place now out of sight behind the tables.

Then time restarted and a hundred things happened all at once, all at high speed, all with shattering noise. Agents smothered Armstrong's wife and hauled her to the ground. She was screaming loud. Shrieking desperately. Agents pulled their guns and started firing up at the warehouse roof. There was shouting and wailing from the crowd. People were stampeding. Running everywhere under the heavy repeated thumping of powerful handguns. Reacher clawed at the serving tables and hurled them behind him and fought his way through the wreckage to Froelich. Agents were dragging Armstrong out from underneath her. Auto engines were revving. Tyres were squealing. Guns were firing. There was smoke in the air. Sirens were yelping. Armstrong disappeared off the floor and Reacher fell to his knees in a lake of blood next to Froelich and cradled her head in his arms. All her litheness was gone. She was completely limp and still, like her clothes were empty. But her eyes were wide open. They were moving slowly from side to side, searching, like she was curious about something.

'Is he OK?' she whispered.

Her voice was very quiet, but alert.

'Secure,' Reacher said.

He slid a hand under her neck. He could feel her earpiece wire. He could feel blood. She was soaked with it. It was pulsing out. More than pulsing. It was like a warm hard jet, driven by the whole of her blood pressure. It forced and bubbled its way out between his clamped fingers like a strong bathtub faucet being turned high and low, high and low. He raised her head and let it fall back a fraction and saw a ragged exit wound in the right front side of her throat. It was leaking blood. Like a river. Like a flood. It was arterial blood, draining out of her.

'Medics,' he called.

Nobody heard him. His voice didn't carry. There was too

much noise. The agents around him were firing up at the warehouse roof. There was a continuous crashing and booming of guns. Spent shell cases were ejecting and hitting him on the back and bouncing off and hitting the ground with small brassy sounds he could hear quite well.

'Tell me it wasn't one of us,' Froelich whispered.

'It wasn't one of you,' he said.

She dropped her chin to her chest. Welling blood flooded out between the folds of her skin. Poured down and soaked her shirt. Pooled on the ground and ran away between the ridges in the concrete. He flattened his hand hard against the back of her neck. It was slippery. He pressed harder. The flow of blood loosened his grip, like it was hosing his hand away. His hand was slipping and floating on the tide.

'Medics,' he called again, louder.

But he knew it was useless. She probably weighed about one-twenty, which meant she had eight or nine pints of blood in her. Most of them were already gone. He was kneeling in them. Her heart was doing its job, thumping away valiantly, pumping her precious blood straight out onto the concrete around his legs.

'Medics,' he screamed.

Nobody came.

She looked straight up at his face. 'Remember?' she whispered.

He bent closer.

'How we met?' she whispered.

'I remember,' he said.

She smiled weakly, like his answer satisfied her completely. She was very pale now. There was blood everywhere on the ground. It was a vast spreading pool. It was warm and slick. Now it was frothing and foaming at her neck. Her arteries were empty and filling with air. Her eyes moved in her head and then settled on his face. Her lips were stark white. Turning blue. They fluttered soundlessly, rehearsing her last words.

'I love you, Joe,' she whispered.

Then she smiled, peacefully.

'I love you too,' he said.

He held her for long moments more until she bled out and

died in his arms about the same time Stuyvesant gave the cease-firing order. There was sudden total silence. The strong coppery smell of hot blood and the cold acid stink of gunsmoke hung in the air. Reacher looked up and back and saw a cameraman shouldering his way towards him with his lens tilting down like a cannon. Saw Neagley stepping into his path. Saw the cameraman pushing her. She didn't seem to move a muscle but suddenly the cameraman was falling. He saw Neagley catch the camera and heave it straight over the execution wall. He heard it crash to the ground. He heard an ambulance siren starting up far in the distance. Then another. He heard cop cars. Feet running. He saw Stuyvesant's pressed grey pants next to his face. He was standing in Froelich's blood.

Stuyvesant did nothing at all. Just stood there for what felt like a very long time, until they all heard the ambulance in the yard. Then he bent down and tried to pull Reacher away. Reacher waited until the paramedics got very close. Then he laid Froelich's head gently on the concrete. Stood up, sick and cramped and unsteady. Stuyvesant caught his elbow and walked him away.

'I didn't even know her name,' Reacher said.

'It was Mary Ellen,' Stuyvesant told him.

The paramedics fussed around for a moment. Then they went quiet and gave it up and covered her with a sheet. Left her there for the medical examiners and the crime scene investigators. Reacher stumbled and sat down again, with his back to the wall, his hands on his knees, his head in his hands. His clothes were soaked with blood. Neagley sat down next to him, an inch away. Stuyvesant squatted in front of them both.

'What's happening?' Reacher asked.

'They're locking the city down,' Stuyvesant said. 'Roads, bridges, the airports. Bannon's in charge of it. He's got all his people out, and Metro cops, U.S. Marshals, cops from Virginia, State troopers. Plus some of our people. We'll get them.'

'They'll use the railroad,' Reacher said. 'We're right next to Union Station.'

Stuyvesant nodded. 'They're searching every train,' he said. 'We'll get them.'

'Was Armstrong OK?'

'Completely unharmed. Froelich did her duty.'

There was a long silence. Reacher looked up.

'What happened on the roof?' he asked. 'Where was Crosetti?'

Stuyvesant looked away.

'Crosetti was decoyed somehow,' he said. 'He's in the stairwell. He's dead too. Shot in the head. With the same silenced rifle, probably.'

Another long silence.

'Where was Crosetti from?' Reacher asked.

'New York, I think,' Stuyvesant said. 'Maybe Jersey. Somewhere up there.'

'That's no good. Where was Froelich from?'

'She was a Wyoming girl.'

Reacher nodded. 'That'll do,' he said. 'Where's Armstrong now?'

'Can't tell you that,' Stuyvesant said. 'Procedure.'

Reacher raised his hand and looked at his palm. It was rimed with blood. All the lines and scars were outlined in red.

'Tell me,' he said. 'Or I'll break your neck.'

Stuyvesant said nothing.

'Where is he?' Reacher repeated.

'The White House,' Stuyvesant said. 'In a secure room. It's procedure.'

'I need to go talk to him.'

'Now?'

'Right now.'

'You can't.'

Reacher looked away, beyond the fallen tables. 'I can.'

'I can't let you do that.'

'So try to stop me.'

Stuyvesant was quiet for a long moment.

'Let me call him first,' he said.

He stood up awkwardly and walked away.

'You OK?' Neagley asked.

'It's like Joe all over again,' Reacher said. 'Like Molly Beth Gordon.'

'Nothing you could have done.'

'Did you see it?'

Neagley nodded.

'She took a bullet for him,' Reacher said. 'She told me that was just a figure of speech.'

'Instinct,' Neagley said. 'And she was unlucky. Must have missed her vest by half an inch. Subsonic bullet, it would have bounced right off.'

'Did you see the shooter?'

Neagley shook her head. 'I was facing front. Did you?'

'A glimpse,' Reacher said. 'One man.'

'Hell of a thing,' Neagley said.

Reacher nodded and wiped his palms on his pants, front and back. Then he ran his hands through his hair. 'If I wrote insurance I wouldn't touch any of Joe's old friends. I'd tell them to commit suicide and save the bad guys the trouble.'

'So what now?'

He shrugged. 'You should go home to Chicago.'

'You?'

'I'm going to stick around.'

'Why?'

'You know why.'

'The FBI will get them.'

'Not if I get them first,' Reacher said.

'You made up your mind?'

'I held her while she bled to death. I'm not going to just walk away.'

'Then I'll stick around, too.'

'I'll be OK on my own.'

'I know you will,' Neagley said. 'But you'll be better with me.'

Reacher nodded.

'What did she say to you?' Neagley asked.

'She said nothing to me. She thought I was Joe.'

He saw Stuyvesant picking his way back through the yard. Hauled himself upright with both hands against the wall.

'Armstrong will see us,' Stuyvesant said. 'You want to change first?'

Reacher looked down at his clothes. They were soaked with Froelich's blood in big irregular patches. It was cooling and drying and blackening.

'No,' he said. 'I don't want to change first.'

* * *

They used the Suburban that Stuyvesant had arrived in. It was still Thanksgiving Day and D.C. was still quiet. They saw almost no civilian activity. Almost everything out and moving was law enforcement. There was a double ring of hasty police roadblocks on every thoroughfare around the White House. Stuyvesant kept his strobes going and was waved through all of them. He showed his ID at the White House vehicle gate and parked outside the West Wing. A Marine sentry passed them to a Secret Service escort who led them inside. They went down two flights of stairs to a vaulted basement built from brick. There were plant rooms down there. Other rooms with steel doors. The escort stopped in front of one of them and knocked hard.

The door was opened from the inside by one of Armstrong's personal detail. He was still wearing his Kevlar vest. Still wearing his sunglasses, although the room had no windows. Just bright fluorescent tubes on the ceiling. Armstrong and his wife were sitting together on chairs at a table in the centre of the room. The other two agents were leaning against the walls. The room was silent. Armstrong's wife had been crying. That was clear. Armstrong himself had a smudge of Froelich's blood on the side of his face. He looked deflated. Like this whole White House thing was no longer fun.

'What's the situation?' he asked.

'Two casualties,' Stuyvesant said quietly. 'The sentry on the warehouse roof, and M.E. herself. They both died at the scene.'

Armstrong's wife turned away like she had been slapped.

'Did you get the people who did it?' Armstrong asked.

'The FBI is leading the hunt,' Stuyvesant said. 'Just a matter of time.'

'I want to help,' Armstrong said.

'You're going to help,' Reacher said.

Armstrong nodded. 'What can I do?'

'You can issue a formal statement,' Reacher said. 'Immediately. In time for the networks to get it on the evening news.'

'Saying what?'

'Saying you're cancelling your holiday weekend in North

Dakota out of respect for the two dead agents. Saying you're holing up in your Georgetown house and going absolutely nowhere at all before you attend a memorial service for your lead agent in her home town in Wyoming on Sunday morning. Find out the name of the town and mention it loud and clear.'

Armstrong nodded again. 'OK,' he said. 'I could do that, I guess. But why?'

'Because they won't try again here in D.C. Not against the security you're going to have at your house. So they'll go home and wait. Which gives me until Sunday to find out where they live.'

'You? Won't the FBI find them today?'

'If they do, that's great. I can move on.'

'And if they don't?'

'Then I'll find them myself.'

'And if *you* fail?'

'I don't plan to fail. But if I do, then they'll show up in Wyoming to try again. At Froelich's service. Whereupon I'll be waiting for them.'

'No,' Stuyvesant said. 'I can't allow it. Are you crazy? We can't secure a situation out west on seventy-two hours' notice. And I can't use a protectee as *bait*.'

'He doesn't have to actually go,' Reacher said. 'There probably won't even *be* a service. He just has to say it.'

Armstrong shook his head. 'I can't say it if there isn't going to be a service. And if there is a service, I can't say it and not show up.'

'If you want to help, that's what you've got to do.'

Armstrong said nothing.

They left the Armstrongs in the West Wing basement and were escorted back to the Suburban. The sun was still shining and the sky was still blue. The buildings were still white and golden. It was still a glorious day.

'Take us back to the motel,' Reacher said. 'I want to get a shower. Then I want to meet with Bannon.'

'Why?' Stuyvesant asked.

'Because I'm a witness,' Reacher said. 'I saw the shooter. On the roof. Just a glimpse of his back as he moved away from the edge.'

'You got a description?'

'Not really,' Reacher said. 'It was only a glimpse. I couldn't describe him. But there was something about the way he moved. I've seen him before.'

FOURTEEN

HE PEELED OFF HIS CLOTHES. THEY WERE STIFF AND COLD AND clammy with blood. He dropped them on the closet floor and stepped into the bathroom. Set the shower going. The tray under his feet ran red and then pink and then clear. He washed his hair twice and shaved carefully. Dressed in another of Joe's shirts and another of his suits and chose the regimental tie that Froelich had bought, as a tribute. Then he went back out to the lobby.

Neagley was waiting for him there. She had changed, too. She was wearing a black suit. It was the old army way. *If in doubt, go formal.* She had a cup of coffee ready for him. She was talking to the U.S. Marshals. They were a new crew. The day shift, he guessed.

'Stuyvesant's coming back,' she told him. 'Then we go meet with Bannon.'

He nodded. The marshals were quiet around him. Almost respectful. Towards him or because of Froelich, he didn't know.

'Tough break,' one of them said.

Reacher looked away. 'I guess it was,' he replied. Then he looked back. 'But hey, shit happens,' he said.

Neagley smiled, briefly. It was the old army way. *If in doubt, be flippant.*

Stuyvesant showed up an hour later and drove them to the Hoover Building. The balance of power had changed. Killing federal agents was a federal crime, so now the FBI was firmly in charge. Now it was a straightforward manhunt. Bannon met them in the main lobby and took them up in an elevator to their conference room. It was better than Treasury's. It was panelled in wood and had windows. There was a long table with clusters of glasses and bottles of mineral water. Bannon was conspicuously democratic and avoided the head of the table. He just dumped himself down in one of the side chairs. Neagley put herself on the same side, two places away. Reacher sat down opposite her. Stuyvesant chose a place three away from Reacher and poured himself a glass of water.

'Quite a day,' Bannon said in the silence. 'My agency extends its deepest sympathies to your agency.'

'You haven't found them,' Stuyvesant said.

'We got a heads up from the medical examiner,' Bannon said. 'Crosetti was shot through the head with a NATO 7.62 round. Died instantly. Froelich was shot through the throat from behind, same gun, probably. The bullet clipped her carotid artery. But I guess you already know that.'

'You haven't found them,' Stuyvesant said again.

Bannon shook his head. 'Thanksgiving Day,' he said. 'Pluses and minuses. Main minus was that we were short of personnel because of the holiday, and so were you, and so were the Metro cops, and so was everybody else. Main plus was that the city itself was very quiet. On balance it was quieter than we were shorthanded. The way it turned out we were the majority population all over town five minutes after it happened.'

'But you didn't find them.'

Bannon shook his head again. 'No,' he said. 'We didn't find them. We're still looking, of course, but being realistic we would have to say they're out of the District by now.'

'Outstanding,' Stuyvesant said.

Bannon made a face. 'We're not turning cartwheels. But there's nothing to be gained by yelling at us. Because we could yell right back. Somebody got through the screen *you* deployed. Somebody decoyed *your* guy off the roof.' He looked directly at Stuyvesant as he said it.

'We paid for it,' Stuyvesant said. 'Big time.'

'How did it happen?' Neagley asked. 'How did they get up there at all?'

'Not through the front,' Bannon said. 'There was a shitload of cops watching the front. They saw nothing, and they can't all have fallen asleep at the critical time. Not down the back alley either. There was a cop on foot and a cop in a car watching, both ends. Those four all say they saw nobody either, and we believe all four of them. So we think the bad guys got into a building a block over. Walked through the building and out a rear door into the alley halfway down. Then they skipped ten feet across the alley and got in the back of the warehouse and walked up the stairs. No doubt they exited the same way. But they were probably running, on the way out.'

'How did they decoy Crosetti?' Stuyvesant said. 'He was a good agent.'

'Yes, he was,' Reacher said. 'I liked him.'

Bannon shrugged again. 'There's always a way, isn't there?'

Then he looked around the room, the way he did when he wanted people to understand more than he was saying. Nobody responded.

'Did you check the trains?' Reacher asked.

Bannon nodded. 'Very carefully. It was fairly busy. People heading out for family dinners. But we were thorough.'

'Did you find the rifle?'

Bannon just shook his head. Reacher stared at him.

'They got away *carrying a rifle*?' he said.

Nobody spoke. Bannon looked back at Reacher.

'You saw the shooter,' he said.

Reacher nodded. 'Just a glimpse, for a quarter-second, maybe. In silhouette, as he moved away.'

'And you figure you've seen him before.'

'But I don't know where.'

'Outstanding,' Bannon said.

'There was something about the way he moved, that's all. The shape of his body. His clothing, maybe. It's just out of reach. Like the next line of an old song.'

'Was he the guy from the garage video?'

'No,' Reacher said.

Bannon nodded. 'Whatever, it doesn't mean much. Stands to reason you've seen him before. You've been in the same place at the same time, in Bismarck for sure, and maybe elsewhere. We already know they've seen *you*. Because of the phone call. But it would be nice to have a name and face, I guess.'

'I'll let you know,' Reacher said.

'Your theory still standing?' Stuyvesant asked.

'Yes,' Bannon said. 'We're still looking at your ex-employees. Now more than ever. Because we think that's why Crosetti left his post. We think he saw somebody he knew and trusted.'

They drove the half-mile west on Pennsylvania Avenue and parked in the garage and rode up to the Secret Service's own conference room. Every inch of the short journey was bitter without Froelich.

'Hell of a thing,' Stuyvesant said. 'I never lost an agent before. Twenty-five years. And now I've lost two in a day. I *want* these guys, so bad.'

'They're dead men walking,' Reacher said.

'All the evidence is against us,' Stuyvesant said.

'So what are you saying? You don't want them if they're yours?'

'I don't want them to *be* ours.'

'I don't think they *are* yours,' Reacher said. 'But either way, they're going down. Let's be real straight about that. They've crossed so many lines I've given up counting.'

'I don't want them to be ours,' Stuyvesant said again. 'But I'm afraid Bannon might be right.'

'It's either, or,' Reacher said. 'That's all. Either he's right or he's wrong. If he's right, we'll know soon enough because he'll bust his balls to show us. Thing is, he'll never look at the possibility that he's wrong. He wants to be right too much.'

'Tell me he's wrong.'

'I think he *is* wrong. And the upside is, if I'm wrong that he's wrong, it doesn't matter worth a damn. Because he's going to leave no stone unturned. We can absolutely rely on him. He doesn't need our input. Our responsibility is to look at what he's *not* looking at. Which I think is the right place to look anyway.'

'Just tell me he's wrong.'

'His thing is like a big pyramid balancing on its point. Very impressive, until it falls over. He's betting everything on the fact that Armstrong hasn't been told. But there's no logic in that. Maybe these guys *are* targeting Armstrong personally. Maybe they just didn't know you wouldn't tell him.'

Stuyvesant nodded.

'I might buy that,' he said. 'God knows I want to. But there's the NCIC thing. Bannon was right about that. If they were outside our community, they'd have pointed us towards Minnesota and Colorado personally. We have to face that.'

'The weapons are persuasive too,' Neagley said. 'And Froelich's address.'

Reacher nodded. 'So is the thumbprint, actually. If we really want to depress ourselves we should consider if maybe they *knew* the print wouldn't come back. Maybe they ran a test from this end.'

'Great,' Stuyvesant said.

'But I still don't believe it,' Reacher said.

'Why not?'

'Get the messages and take a real close look.'

Stuyvesant waited a beat and then stood up slowly and left the room. Came back three minutes later with a file folder. He opened it up and laid the six official FBI photographs in a neat line down the centre of the table. He was still wearing his pink sweater. The bright colour was reflected in the glossy surfaces of the eight-by-tens as he leaned over them. Neagley moved round the table and all three of them sat side by side so they could read the messages the right way up.

'OK,' Reacher said. 'Examine them. Everything about them. And remember why you're doing it. You're doing it for Froelich.'

The line of photographs was four feet long, and they had to stand up and shuffle left to right along the table to inspect them all.

You are going to die.

Vice-President-elect Armstrong is going to die.
The day upon which Armstrong will die is fast approaching.
A demonstration of your vulnerability will be staged today.
Did you like the demonstration?
It's going to happen soon.

'So?' Stuyvesant asked.

'Look at the fourth message,' Reacher said. '*Vulnerability* is correctly spelled.'

'So?'

'That's a big word. And look at the last message. The apostrophe in *it's* is correct. Lots of people get that wrong, you know, *it's* and *its*. There are periods at the ends, except for the question mark.'

'So?'

'The messages are reasonably literate.'

'OK.'

'Now look at the third message.'

'What about it?'

'Neagley?' Reacher asked.

'It's a little fancy,' she said. 'A little awkward and old-fashioned. The *upon which* thing. And the *fast approaching*.'

'Exactly,' Reacher said. 'A little archaic.'

'But what does all this prove?' Stuyvesant asked.

'Nothing, really,' Reacher said. 'But it suggests something. Have you ever read the Constitution?'

'Of what? The United States?'

'Sure.'

'I guess I've read it,' Stuyvesant said. 'A long time ago, probably.'

'Me too,' Reacher said. 'Some school I was at gave us a copy each. It was a thin little book, thick cardboard covers. Very narrow when it was shut. The edges were hard. We used to karate-chop each other with it. Hurt like hell.'

'So?'

'It's a legal document, basically. Historical, too, of course, but it's fundamentally legal. So when somebody prints it up as a book, they can't mess with it. They have to reproduce it exactly word for word, otherwise it wouldn't be valid. They can't modernize the language, they can't clean it up.'

'Obviously not.'

'The early parts are from 1787. The last amendment in my copy was the twenty-sixth, from 1971, lowering the voting age to eighteen. A span of a hundred and eighty-four years. With everything reproduced exactly like it was written down at the particular time.'

'So?'

'One thing I remember is that in the first part, *Vice President* is written without a hyphen between the two words. Same in the latest part. No hyphen. But in the stuff that was written in the middle period, there *is* a hyphen. It's *Vice-President* with a hyphen between the words. So clearly from about the 1860s up to maybe the 1930s it was considered correct usage to have a hyphen there.'

'These guys use a hyphen,' Stuyvesant said.

'They sure do,' Reacher said. 'Right there in the second message.'

'So what does that mean?'

'Two things,' Reacher said. 'We know they paid attention in class, because they're reasonably literate. So the first thing it means is that they went to school someplace where they used old textbooks and old style manuals that were way out of date. Which explains the third message's archaic feel, maybe. And which is why I figured they might be from a poor rural area with low school taxes. Second thing it means is they never worked for the Secret Service. Because you guys are buried in paperwork. I've never seen anything like it, even in the army. Anybody who worked here would have written *Vice President* a million times over in their career. All with the modern usage without the hyphen. They would have gotten totally used to it that way.'

There was quiet for a moment.

'Maybe the other guy wrote it,' Stuyvesant said. 'The one who didn't work here. The one with the thumbprint.'

'Makes no difference,' Reacher said. 'Like Bannon figured, they're a unit. They're collaborators. And perfectionists. If one guy had written it wrong, the other guy would have corrected it. But it wasn't corrected, therefore neither of them knew it was wrong. Therefore neither of them worked here.'

Stuyvesant was silent for a long moment.

'I want to believe it,' he said. 'But you're basing everything on a hyphen.'

'Don't dismiss it,' Reacher said.

'I'm not dismissing it,' Stuyvesant said. 'I'm thinking.'

'About whether I'm crazy?'

'About whether I can afford to back this kind of hunch.'

'That's the beauty of it,' Reacher said. 'It doesn't matter if I'm completely wrong. Because the FBI is taking care of the alternative scenario.'

'It could be deliberate,' Neagley said. 'They might be misleading us. Trying to disguise their background or their education level. Throwing us off.'

Reacher shook his head.

'I don't think so,' he said. 'This is too subtle. They'd do all the usual things. Gross misspellings, bad punctuation. A hyphen between *Vice* and *President* is something you don't know from right or wrong. It's something you just do.'

'What are the exact implications?' Stuyvesant asked.

'Age is critical,' Reacher said. 'They can't be older than early fifties, to be running around doing all this stuff. Up ladders, down stairs. They can't be younger than mid-forties, because you read the Constitution in junior high, and surely by 1970 every school in America had new books. I think they were in junior high at or towards the end of the period when isolated rural schools were still way behind the times. You know, maybe one-room schoolhouses, fifty-year-old textbooks, out-of-date maps on the wall, you're sitting there with all your cousins listening to some grey-haired old lady.'

'It's very speculative,' Stuyvesant said. 'It's a pyramid too, balancing on its point. Looks good until it falls over.'

Silence in the room.

'Well, I'm going to pursue it,' Reacher said. 'With Armstrong, or without him. With you, or without you. By myself, if necessary. For Froelich's sake. She deserves it.'

Stuyvesant nodded. 'If neither of them worked for us, how would they know to rely on an FBI scan of the NCIC reports?'

'I don't know,' Reacher said.

'How did they decoy Crosetti?'

'I don't know.'

'How would they get our weapons?'

'I don't know.'

'How did they know where M. E. lived?'

'Nendick told them.'

Stuyvesant nodded. 'OK. But what would be their motive?'

'Animosity against Armstrong personally, I guess. A politician must make plenty of enemies.'

Silence again.

'Maybe it's half and half,' Neagley said. 'Maybe they're outsiders with animosity against the Secret Service. Maybe guys who got rejected for a job. Guys who really wanted to work here. Maybe they're some kind of nerdy law-enforcement buffs. They might know about NCIC. They might know what weapons you buy.'

'That's possible,' Stuyvesant said. 'We turn down a lot of people. Some of them get very upset about it. You could be right.'

'No,' Reacher said. 'She's wrong. Why would they wait? I'm sticking by my age estimate. And nobody applies for a Secret Service job at the age of fifty. If they ever got turned down, it was twenty-five years ago. Why wait until now to retaliate?'

'That's a good point too,' Stuyvesant said.

'This is about Armstrong personally,' Reacher said. 'It has to be. Think about the time line here. Think about cause and effect. Armstrong became the running mate during the summer. Before that nobody had ever heard of him. Froelich told me that herself. Now we're getting threats against him. Why now? Because of something he did during the campaign, that's why.'

Stuyvesant stared down at the table. Placed his hands flat on it. Moved them in small neat circles like there was a wrinkled tablecloth under them that needed flattening. Then he leaned over and butted the first message under the second. Then both of them under the third. He kept at it until he had all six stacked neatly. He scooped his file folder under the pile and closed it.

'OK, this is what we're going to do,' he said. 'We're going to give Neagley's theory to Bannon. Somebody we refused to hire is more or less in the same category as somebody we eventually fired. The bitterness component would be about the same. The FBI can deal with all of that as a whole. We've got the paperwork. They've got the manpower. And the balance of probability is that they're correct. But we'd be derelict if we didn't also consider the alternative. That they might not be correct. So we're going to spend our time looking at Reacher's theory. Because we've got to do *something*, for Froelich's sake, apart from anything else. So where do we start?'

'With Armstrong,' Reacher said. 'We figure out who hates him and why.'

Stuyvesant called a guy from the Office of Protection Research and ordered him into the office immediately. The guy pleaded he was eating Thanksgiving dinner with his family. Stuyvesant relented and gave him two hours to finish up. Then he headed back to the Hoover Building to meet with Bannon again. Reacher and Neagley waited in reception. There was a television in there and Reacher wanted to see if Armstrong delivered on the early news. It was a half-hour away.

'You OK?' Neagley asked.

'I feel weird,' Reacher said. 'Like I'm two people. She thought it was Joe with her at the end.'

'What would Joe have done about it?'

'Same as I'm going to do about it, probably.'

'So go ahead and do it,' Neagley said. 'You always were Joe as far as she was concerned. You may as well square the circle for her.'

He said nothing.

'Close your eyes,' Neagley said. 'Clear your mind. You need to concentrate on the shooter.'

Reacher shook his head. 'I won't get it if I concentrate.'

'So think about something else. Use peripheral vision. Pretend you're looking somewhere else. The next roof along, maybe.'

He closed his eyes. Saw the edge of the roof, harsh against the sun. Saw the sky, bright and pale all at the same time. A winter sky. Just a trace of uniform misty haze all over it. He gazed at the sky. Recalled the sounds he had been hearing.

Nothing much from the crowd. Just the clatter of serving spoons, and Froelich saying *thanks for stopping by.* Mrs Armstrong saying *enjoy*, nervously, like she wasn't quite sure what she had gotten herself into. Then he heard the soft *chunk* of the first silenced bullet hitting the wall. It had been a poor shot. It had missed Armstrong by four feet. Probably a rushed shot. The guy comes up the stairs, stands in the rooftop doorway, calls softly to Crosetti. *And Crosetti responds.* The guy waits for Crosetti to come to him. Maybe backs away into the stairwell. Crosetti comes on. Crosetti gets shot. The rooftop hutch muffles the sound from the silencer. The guy steps over the body and runs crouched straight to the lip of the roof. Kneels and fires hastily, too soon, before he's really settled, and he misses by four feet. The miss craters the brick and a small chip flies off and hits Reacher in the cheek. The guy racks the bolt and aims more carefully for the second shot.

He opened his eyes.

'I want you to work on *how*,' he said.

'How what, exactly?' Neagley said.

'How they lured Crosetti away from his post. I want to know how they did that.'

Neagley was quiet for a moment.

'I'm afraid Bannon's theory fits best,' she said. 'Crosetti looked up and saw somebody he recognized.'

'Assume he didn't,' Reacher said. 'How else?'

'I'll work on it. You work on the shooter.'

He closed his eyes again and looked at the next roof along. Back down at the serving tables. Froelich, in the last minute of her life. He recalled the spray of blood and his immediate instinctive reaction. *Incoming lethal fire. Point of origin?* He had glanced up and seen . . . what? The curve of a back or a shoulder. It was moving. The shape and the movement were somehow one and the same thing.

'His coat,' he said. 'The shape of his coat over his body, and the way it draped when he moved.'

'Seen the coat before?'

'Yes.'

'Colour?'

'I don't know. Not sure it really *had* a colour.'

'Texture?'

'Texture is important. Not thick, not thin.'

'Herringbone?'

Reacher shook his head. 'Not the coat we saw on the garage video. Not the guy, either. This guy was taller and leaner. Some length in his upper body. It gave the coat its drape. I think it was a long coat.'

'You only saw his shoulder.'

'It *flowed* like a long coat.'

'How did it flow?'

'Energetically. Like the guy was moving fast.'

'He would be. Far as he knew he'd just shot Armstrong.'

'No, like he was always energetic. A rangy guy, decisive in his movements.'

'Age?'

'Older than us.'

'Build?'

'Moderate.'

'Hair?'

'Don't remember.'

He kept his eyes closed and searched his memory for coats. *A long coat, not thick, not thin.* He let his mind drift, but it always came back to the Atlantic City coat store. Standing there in front of a rainbow of choice, five whole minutes after taking a stupid random decision that had led him away from the peace and quiet of a lonely motel room in La Jolla, California.

He gave up on it twenty minutes later and gestured for the duty officer to turn the television sound up for the news. The story led the bulletin, obviously. The coverage opened with a studio portrait of Armstrong in a box behind the anchorman's shoulder. Then it cut to video of Armstrong handing his wife out of the limo. They stood up together and smiled. Started to walk past the camera. Then the tape cut to Armstrong holding up his ladle and his spoon. A smile on his face. The voice-over paused long enough for the live sound to come up: *Happy Thanksgiving, everybody!* Then there were seven or eight seconds taken from a little later on when the food line was really moving.

Then it happened.

Because of the silencer there was no gunshot, and because there was no gunshot the cameraman didn't duck or startle in the usual way. The picture held steady. And because there was no gunshot it seemed completely inexplicable why Froelich was suddenly jumping at Armstrong. It looked a little different, seen from the front. She just took off from her left foot and twisted up and sideways. She looked desperate, but graceful. They ran it once at normal speed, and then again in slow motion. She got her right hand on his left shoulder and pushed him down and herself up. Her momentum carried her all the way round and she drew her knees up and simply knocked him over with them. He fell and she followed him down. She was a foot below her maximum height when the second bullet came in and hit her.

'Shit,' Reacher said.

Neagley nodded, slowly. 'She was too quick. A quarter-second slower she'd still have been high enough in the air to take it in the vest.'

'She was too good.'

They ran it again, normal speed. It was all over in a second. Then they let the tape run on. The cameraman seemed rooted to the spot. Reacher saw himself barging through the tables. Saw the other agents firing. Froelich was out of sight, on the floor. The camera ducked because of the firing, but then came up level again and started moving in. The picture wobbled as the guy stumbled over something. There were long moments of total confusion. Then the cameraman started forward again, hungry for a shot of the downed agent. Neagley's face appeared, and the picture went black. Coverage switched back to the anchorman. The anchorman looked straight at the camera and announced that Armstrong's reaction had been immediate and emphatic.

The picture cut to tape of an outdoors location Reacher recognized as the West Wing's parking lot. Armstrong was standing there with his wife. They were both still in their casual clothes, but they had taken their Kevlar vests off. Somebody had cleaned Froelich's blood from Armstrong's face. His hair was combed. He looked resolute. He spoke in low, controlled tones, like a plain man wrestling with strong emotions. He talked about his extreme sadness that two agents had died. He extolled their qualities as individuals. He offered sincere sympathy to their families. He went on to say he hoped it would be seen that they had died protecting democracy itself, not just himself in person. He hoped their families might take some small measure of comfort from that, as well as a great deal of justified pride. He promised swift and certain retribution against the perpetrators of the outrage. He assured America that no amount of violence or intimidation could deter the workings of government, and that the transition would continue unaffected. But he finished by saying that as a mark of his absolute respect, he was remaining in Washington and cancelling all engagements until he had attended a memorial service for his personal friend and protection team leader. He said the service would be held on Sunday morning, in a small country church in a small Wyoming town called Grace, where no finer metaphor for America's enduring greatness could be found.

'Guy's full of shit,' the duty officer said.

'No, he's OK,' Reacher said.

The bulletin cut to first-quarter football highlights. The duty officer muted the sound and turned away. Reacher closed his eyes. Thought of Joe, and then of Froelich. Thought of them together. Then he rehearsed his upward glance once again. The curved spray of Froelich's blood, the curve of the shooter's shoulder, retreating, swinging away, *swooping* away. The coat flowing with him. *The coat.* He ran it all again, like the TV station had rerun its tape. He froze on the coat. *He knew.* He opened his eyes wide.

'Figured how yet?' he asked.

'Can't get past Bannon's take,' Neagley answered.

'Say it.'

'Crosetti saw somebody he knew and trusted.'

'Man or woman?'

'Man, according to you.'

'OK, say it again.'

Neagley shrugged. 'Crosetti saw some man he knew and trusted.'

Reacher shook his head. 'Two words short. Crosetti saw some *type of* man he knew and trusted.'

'Who?' she asked.

'Who can get in and out of anywhere without suspicion?'

Neagley looked at him. 'Law enforcement?'

Reacher nodded. 'The coat was long, kind of reddish-brown, faint pattern to it. Too thin for an overcoat, too thick for a raincoat, flapping open. It swung as he ran.'

'As who ran?'

'That Bismarck cop. The lieutenant or whatever he was. He ran over to me after I came out of the church. It was him on the warehouse roof.'

'It was a *cop*?'

'That's a very serious allegation,' Bannon said. 'Based on a quarter-second of observation from ninety yards during extreme mayhem.'

They were back in the FBI's conference room. Stuyvesant had never left it. He was still in his pink sweater. The room was still impressive.

'It was him,' Reacher said. 'No doubt about it.'

'Cops are all fingerprinted,' Bannon said. 'Condition of employment.'

'So his partner isn't a cop,' Reacher said. 'The guy on the garage video.'

Nobody spoke.

'It was him,' Reacher said again.

'How long did you see him for in Bismarck?' Bannon asked.

'Ten seconds, maybe,' Reacher said. 'He was heading for the church. Maybe he'd seen me inside, ducked out, saw me leave, turned round, got ready to go back in.'

'Ten and a quarter seconds total,' Bannon said. 'Both times in panic situations. Defence counsel would eat you up.'

'It makes sense,' Stuyvesant said. 'Bismarck is Armstrong's home town. Home towns are the places to look for feuds.'

Bannon made a face. 'Description?'

'Tall,' Reacher said. 'Sandy hair going grey. Lean face, lean body. Long coat, some kind of a heavy twill, reddish-brown, open. Tweed jacket, white shirt, tie, grey flannel pants. Big old shoes.'

'Age?'

'Middle or late forties.'

'Rank?'

'He showed me a gold badge, but he stayed twenty feet away. I couldn't read it. He struck me as a senior guy. Maybe a detective lieutenant, maybe even a captain.'

'Did he speak?'

'He shouted from twenty feet away. Couple of dozen words, maybe.'

'Was he the guy on the phone?'

'No.'

'So now we know both of them,' Stuyvesant said. 'A shorter squat guy in a herringbone overcoat from the garage video and a tall lean cop from Bismarck. The squat guy spoke on the phone, and it's his thumbprint. And he was in Colorado with the machine gun because the cop is the marksman with the rifle. That's why he was heading for the church tower. He was going to shoot.'

Bannon opened a file. Pulled a sheet of paper. Studied it carefully.

'Our Bismarck field office listed all attending personnel,' he said. 'There were forty-two local cops on the field. Nobody above the rank of sergeant except for two, firstly the senior officer present, who was a captain, and his second-in-command, who was a lieutenant.'

'Might have been either one of them,' Reacher said.

Bannon sighed. 'This puts us in a difficult spot.'

Stuyvesant stared at him. 'Now you're worried about upsetting the Bismarck PD? You didn't worry too much about upsetting us.'

'I'm not worried about upsetting anybody,' Bannon said. 'I'm thinking tactically, is all. If it had been a patrolman out there I could call the captain or the lieutenant and ask him to investigate. Can't do that the other way around. And alibis are going to be all over the place. Senior ranks will be off-duty today for the holiday.'

'Call now,' Neagley said. 'Find out who's not in town. They

can't be home yet. You're watching the airports.'

Bannon shook his head. 'People aren't home today for lots of reasons. They're visiting family, stuff like that. And this guy *could* be home already. He could have gotten through the airports easy as anything. That's the whole point, isn't it? Mayhem like we had today, multiple agencies out and looking, nobody knows each other, all he's got to do is hustle along holding his badge up and he walks straight through anywhere. That's obviously how they got into the immediate area. And out again. What's more natural in the circumstances than a cop running full speed with his badge held up?'

The room went quiet.

'Personnel files,' Stuyvesant said. 'We should get Bismarck PD to send us their files and let Reacher look at the photographs.'

'That would take days,' Bannon said. 'And who would I ask? I might be speaking directly to the bad guy.'

'So speak to your Bismarck field office,' Neagley said. 'Wouldn't surprise me if the local FBI had illicit summaries on the whole police department, with photographs.'

Bannon smiled. 'You're not supposed to know about things like that.'

Then he stood up slowly and went out to his office to make the necessary call.

'So Armstrong made the statement,' Stuyvesant said. 'Did you see it? But it's going to cost him politically, because I can't let him go.'

'I need a decoy, is all,' Reacher said. 'Better for me if he doesn't really show up. And the last thing I care about right now is politics.'

Stuyvesant didn't answer. Nobody spoke again. Bannon came back into the room after fifteen minutes. He had a completely neutral look on his face.

'Good news and bad news,' he said. 'Good news is that Bismarck isn't the largest city on earth. Police department employs a hundred and thirty-eight people, of which thirty-two are civilian workers, leaving a hundred and six badged officers. Twelve of those are women, so we're down to ninety-four already. And thanks to the miracles of illicit intelligence and modern technology we'll have scanned and e-mailed mug shots of all ninety-four of them within ten minutes.'

'What's the bad news?' Stuyvesant asked.

'Later,' Bannon said. 'After Reacher has wasted a little more of our time.'

He looked around the room. Wouldn't say anything more. In the end the wait was a little less than ten minutes. An agent in a suit hurried in with a sheaf of paper. He stacked it in front of Bannon. Bannon pushed the pile across to Reacher. Reacher picked it up and flicked through. Sixteen sheets, some of them still a little wet from the printer. Fifteen sheets had six photographs each and the sixteenth had just four. Ninety-four faces in total. He started with the last sheet. None of the four faces was even close.

He picked up the fifteenth sheet. Glanced across the next six faces and put the paper down again. Picked up the fourteenth sheet. Scanned all six pictures. He worked fast. He didn't need to study carefully. He had the guy's features fixed firmly in his mind. But the guy wasn't on the fourteenth sheet. Or the thirteenth.

'How sure are you?' Stuyvesant asked.

Nothing on the twelfth sheet.

'I'm sure,' Reacher said. 'That was the guy, and the guy was a cop. He had a badge and he looked like a cop. He looked as much like a cop as Bannon.'

Nothing on the eleventh sheet. Or the tenth.

'I don't look like a cop,' Bannon said.

Nothing on the ninth sheet.

'You look exactly like a cop,' Reacher said. 'You've got a cop coat, cop pants, cop shoes. You've got a cop face.'

Nothing on the eighth sheet.

'He acted like a cop,' Reacher said.

Nothing on the seventh sheet.

'He smelled like a cop,' Reacher said.

Nothing on the sixth sheet. Nothing on the fifth sheet.

'What did he say to you?' Stuyvesant asked.

Nothing on the fourth sheet.

'He asked me if the church was secure,' Reacher said. 'I

asked him what was going on. He said some kind of big commotion. Then he yelled at me for leaving the church door open. Just like a cop would talk.'

Nothing on the third sheet. Or the second. He picked up the first sheet and knew instantly that the guy wasn't on it. He dropped the paper and shook his head.

'OK, now for the bad news,' Bannon said. 'Bismarck PD had nobody there in plain clothes. Nobody at all. It was considered a ceremonial occasion. They were all in full uniform. All forty-two of them. Especially the brass. The captain and the lieutenant were in full *dress* uniform. White gloves and all.'

'The guy was a Bismarck cop,' Reacher said.

'No,' Bannon said. 'The guy was not a Bismarck cop. At best he was a guy impersonating a Bismarck cop.'

Reacher said nothing.

'But he was obviously making a pretty good stab at it,' Bannon said. 'He convinced you, for instance. Clearly he had the look, and the mannerisms.'

Nobody spoke.

'So nothing's changed, I'm afraid,' Bannon said. 'We're still looking at recent Secret Service ex-employees. Because who better to impersonate a provincial cop than some other law-enforcement veteran who just worked his whole career alongside provincial cops at events exactly like that one?'

FIFTEEN

THE STAFFER FROM THE OFFICE OF PROTECTION RESEARCH WAS waiting when Reacher and Neagley and Stuyvesant got back to the Treasury Building. He was standing in the reception area wearing a knitted sweater and blue pants, like he had run straight in from the family dinner table. He was about Reacher's age and looked like a university professor except for his eyes. They were wise and wary, like he had seen a few things, and heard about plenty more. His name was Swain. Stuyvesant introduced him all round and disappeared. Swain led Reacher and Neagley through corridors they hadn't used before to an area that clearly doubled as a library and a lecture room. It had a dozen chairs set facing a podium and was lined on three walls with bookshelves. The fourth wall had a row of hutches with computers on desks. A printer next to each computer.

'I heard what the FBI is saying,' Swain said.

'You believe it?' Reacher asked.

Swain just shrugged.

'Yes or no?' Reacher asked.

'I guess it's not impossible,' Swain said. 'But there's no reason to believe it's likely. Just as likely that it's ex-FBI agents. Or *current* FBI agents. As an agency we're better than they are. Maybe they're trying to bring us down.'

'Think we should look in that direction?'

'You're Joe Reacher's brother, aren't you?'

Reacher nodded.

'I worked with him,' Swain said. 'Way back.'

'And?'

'He used to encourage random observations.'

'So do I,' Reacher said. 'You got any?'

'My job is strictly academic,' Swain said. 'You understand? I'm purely a researcher. A scholar, really. I'm here to analyse.'

'And?'

'This situation feels different from anything else I've seen. The hatred is very visible. Assassinations fall into two groups, ideological or functional. A functional assassination is where you need to get rid of a guy for some specific political or economic reason. An ideological assassination is where you murder a guy because you hate him, basically. There have been plenty of attempts along those lines, over the years. I can't tell you about any of them except to say that most don't get very far. And that there's certainly always plenty of hatred involved. But usually it's well hidden, down at the conspirator level. They whisper among themselves. All we ever see is the result. But this time the hatred is right there in our face. They've gone to a lot of trouble and taken a lot of risks to make sure we know all about it.'

'So what's your conclusion?'

'I just think the early phase was extraordinary. The messages? Think about the risks. Think about the energy required to minimize those risks. They put unbelievable resources into the early phase. So I have to assume they felt it was worthwhile.'

'But it wasn't,' Neagley said. 'Armstrong has never even seen any of the messages. They were wasting their time.'

'Simple ignorance,' Swain said. 'Were *you* aware we absolutely won't discuss threats with a protectee?'

'No,' Neagley said. 'I was surprised.'

'Nobody's aware,' Swain said. 'Everybody's surprised. These guys thought they were getting right to him. So I'm convinced it's personal. Aimed at him, not us.'

'So are we,' Reacher said. 'You got a specific reason?'

'You'll think I'm naive,' Swain said. 'But I don't believe anybody who works or has worked for us would have killed the other two Armstrongs. Not just like that.'

Reacher shrugged. 'Maybe you're naive. Maybe you aren't. But it doesn't matter. We're convinced anyway.'

'What's your reason?'

'The hyphen in the second message.'

'The hyphen?' Swain said. Then he paused. 'Yes, I see. Plausible, but a little circumstantial, wouldn't you say?'

'Whatever, we're working with the assumption it was personal.'

'OK, but why? Only possible answer is they absolutely hate him. They wanted to taunt him, scare him, make him suffer first. Just shooting him isn't enough for them.'

'So who are they? Who hates him that bad?'

Swain made a gesture with his hand, like he was pushing that question aside.

'Something else,' he said. 'This is a little off the wall, but I think we're miscounting. How many messages have there been?'

'Six,' Reacher said.

'No,' Swain said. 'I think there have been seven.'

'Where's the seventh?'

'Nendick,' Swain said. 'I think Nendick delivered the second message, and *was* the third message. You see, you got here and forty-eight hours later you got to Nendick, which was pretty quick. But with respect, we'd have gotten there anyway, sooner or later. It was inevitable. If it wasn't the cleaners, it had to be the tapes. So we'd have gotten there. And what was waiting for us? Nendick wasn't just a delivery system. He was a message *in himself.* He showed what these people are capable of. Assuming Armstrong was in the loop, he'd have been getting pretty shaky by that point.'

'Then there are nine messages,' Neagley said. 'On that basis, we should add in the Minnesota and the Colorado situations.'

'Absolutely,' Swain said. 'You see what I mean? Everything has fear as its purpose. Every single thing. Suppose Armstrong *was* in the loop all along. He gets the first message, he's worried. *We* get the second message, he's more worried. We trace its source, and he starts to feel better, but no, it gets even worse, because we find Nendick paralysed with fear. Then we get the demonstration threat, he's worried some more. Then the demonstration happens, and he's devastated by how ruthless it was.'

Reacher said nothing. Just stared at the floor.

'You think I'm over-analytical,' Swain said.

Reacher shook his head, still looking at the floor. 'No, I think I'm under-analytical. Maybe. Possibly. Because what are the thumbprints about?'

'They're a taunt of a different sort,' Swain said. 'They're a boast. A puzzle. A tease. *Can't catch me* sort of thing.'

'How long did you work with my brother?'

'Five years. I worked *for* him, really. I say *with him* as a vain attempt at status.'

'Was he a good boss?'

'He was a great boss,' Swain said. 'Great guy all round.'

'And he ran random-observation sessions?'

Swain nodded. 'They were fun. Anybody could say anything.'

'Did he join in?'

'He was very lateral.'

Reacher looked up. 'You just said everything has fear as its purpose, every single thing. Then you said the thumbprints are a taunt of a different sort. So not everything is the same, right? Something's different.'

Swain shrugged. 'I could stretch it. The thumbprints induce the fear that these guys are too clever to be caught. Different sort of fear, but it's still *fear*.'

Reacher looked away. Went quiet. Thirty seconds, a whole minute.

'I'm going to cave in,' he said. 'Finally. I'm going to be like Joe. I'm wearing his suit. I was sleeping with his girlfriend. I keep meeting his old colleagues. So now I'm going to make a lateral random off-the-wall observation, just like he did, apparently.'

'What is it?' Neagley said.

'I think we missed something,' Reacher said. 'Just skated right on by it.'

'What?'

'I've got all these weird images going round in my head. Like for instance, Stuyvesant's secretary doing things at her desk.'

'What things?'

'I think we've got the thumbprint exactly ass-backward. All along we've assumed they knew it was untraceable. But I think we're completely wrong. I think it's just the opposite. I think they expected it *would* be traceable.'

'Why?'

'Because I think the thumbprint thing is exactly the same as the Nendick thing. I met a watchmaker today. He told me where squalene comes from.'

'Sharks' livers,' Neagley said.

'And people's noses,' Reacher said. 'Same stuff. That gunk you wake up with in the morning is squalene. Same chemical exactly.'

'So?'

'So I think our guys gambled and got unlucky. Suppose you picked a random male person aged about sixty or seventy. What are the chances he'd have been fingerprinted at least once in his lifetime?'

'Pretty good, I guess,' Neagley said. 'All immigrants are printed. American born, he'd have been drafted for Korea or Vietnam and printed even if he didn't go. He'd have been printed if he'd ever been arrested or worked for the government.'

'Or for some private corporations,' Swain said. 'Plenty of them require prints. Banks, retailers, people like that.'

'OK,' Reacher said. 'So here's the thing. I don't think the thumbprint comes from one of the guys themselves. I think it comes from somebody else entirely. From some innocent bystander. From somebody they picked out at random. And it was supposed to lead us directly *to* that somebody.'

The room went quiet. Neagley stared at Reacher.

'What for?' she said.

'So we could find another Nendick,' he said. 'The thumbprint was *on* every message, and the guy it came from *was* a message, just like Swain says Nendick was. We were supposed to trace the print and find the guy and find an exact replica of the Nendick situation. Some terrified victim, too scared to open his mouth and tell us anything. A message in himself. But by pure accident our guys hit on somebody who had never been printed, so we didn't find him.'

'But there were six paper messages,' Swain said. 'Probably twenty days between the first one going in the mail and the last one being delivered to Froelich's house. So what does that mean? All the messages were prepared in advance? That's way too much planning ahead, surely.'

'It's possible,' Neagley said. 'They could have printed dozens of variations, one for every eventuality.'

'No,' Reacher said. 'I think they printed them up as they went along. I think they kept the thumbprint available to them at all times.'

'How?' Swain asked. 'They abducted some guy and took him hostage? They've stashed him somewhere? They're taking him everywhere with them?'

'Couldn't work,' Neagley said. 'Can't expect us to find him if he's not home.'

'He's home,' Reacher said. 'But his thumb isn't.'

Nobody spoke.

'Fire up a computer,' Reacher said. 'Search NCIC for the word *thumb*.'

'We've got a big field office in Sacramento,' Bannon said. 'Three agents are already mobile. A doctor, too. We'll know in an hour.'

This time Bannon had come to them. They were in the Secret Service conference room, Stuyvesant at the head of the table, Reacher and Neagley and Swain together on one side, Bannon alone on the other.

'It's a bizarre idea,' Bannon said. 'What would they do? Keep it in the freezer?'

'Probably,' Reacher said. 'Thaw it a bit, rub it down their nose, print it on the paper. Just like Stuyvesant's secretary with her rubber stamp. It's probably drying out a bit with age, which is why the squalene percentage keeps getting higher.'

'What are the implications?' Stuyvesant said. 'Assuming you're right?'

Reacher made a face. 'We can change one major assumption. Now I would guess they've both got prints on file, and they've both been wearing the latex gloves.'

'Two renegades,' Bannon said.

'Not necessarily ours,' Stuyvesant said.

'So explain the other factors,' Bannon said.

Stuyvesant was silent. Bannon shrugged.

'Come on,' he said. 'We've got an hour. And I don't want to be looking in the wrong place. So convince me. Show me these are private citizens gunning for Armstrong personally.'

Stuyvesant glanced at Swain, but Swain said nothing.

'Time is ticking by,' Bannon said.

'This isn't an ideal context,' Swain said.

Bannon smiled. 'What, you only preach to the choir?'

Nobody spoke.

'You've got no case,' Bannon said. 'I mean, who cares about a vice president? They're nobodies. What was it, a bucket of warm spit?'

'It was a pitcher,' Swain said. 'John Nance Garner said the vice presidency isn't worth a pitcher of warm spit. He also called it a spare tyre on the automobile of government. He was FDR's first running mate. John Adams called it the most insignificant office man had ever invented, and he was the first vice president of all.'

'So who cares enough to shoot a spare tyre or an insignificant pitcher of spit?'

'Let me start from the beginning,' Swain said. 'What does a vice president do?'

'He sits around,' Bannon says. 'Hopes the big guy dies.'

Swain nodded. 'Somebody else said the Vice President's job is merely about waiting. In case the President dies, sure, but more often for the nomination in his own right eight years down the track. But in the short term, what is the Vice President *for*?'

'Beats the hell out of me,' Bannon said.

'He's there to be a candidate,' Swain said. 'That's the bottom line. His design life lasts from when he's tapped in the summer until election day. He's useful for four or five months, tops. He starts out as a pick-me-up for the campaign. Everybody's bored to death with the presidential nominees by midsummer, so the

VP picks put a jolt into the campaigns. Suddenly we've all got something else to talk about. Somebody else to analyse. We look at their qualities and their records. We figure out how well they balance the tickets. That's their initial function. Balance and contrast. Whatever the presidential nominee isn't, the VP nominee *is*, and vice versa. Young, old, racy, dull, northern, southern, dumb, smart, hard, soft, rich, poor.'

'We get the picture,' Bannon said.

'So he's there for what he *is*,' Swain said. 'Initially he's just a photograph and a biography. He's a *concept*. Then his duties start. He's got to have campaigning skills, obviously. Because he's there to be the attack dog. He's got to be able to say the stuff the presidential candidate isn't allowed to say himself. If the campaign scripts an attack or a put-down, it's the VP candidate they get to deliver it. Meanwhile the presidential candidate stands around somewhere else looking all statesman-like. Then the election happens and the presidential candidate goes to the White House and the VP gets put away in a closet. His usefulness is over, first Tuesday in November.'

'Was Armstrong good at that kind of stuff?'

'He was excellent. The truth is he was a very negative campaigner, but the polls didn't really show it because he kept that nice smile on his face the whole time. Truth is he was deadly.'

'And you think he trod on enough toes to get himself assassinated for it?'

Swain nodded. 'That's what I'm working on now. I'm analysing every speech and comment, matching up his attacks against the profile of the people he was attacking.'

'The timing is persuasive,' Stuyvesant said. 'Nobody can argue with that. He was in the House for six years and the Senate for another six and barely got a nasty letter. This whole thing was triggered by something recent.'

'And his recent history is the campaign,' Swain said.

'Nothing way in his background?' Bannon asked.

Swain shook his head. 'We're covered four ways,' he said. 'First and most recent was your own FBI check when he was nominated. We've got a copy and it shows nothing. Then we've got opposition research from the other campaign from this time around and from both of his congressional races. Those guys dig up way more stuff than you do. And he's clean.'

'North Dakota sources?'

'Nothing,' Swain said. 'We talked to all the papers up there, matter of course. Local journalists know everything, and there's nothing wrong with the guy.'

'So it was the campaign,' Stuyvesant said. 'He pissed somebody off.'

'Somebody who owns Secret Service weapons,' Bannon said. 'Somebody who knows about the interface between the Secret Service and the FBI. Somebody who knows you can't mail something to the Vice President without it going through the Secret Service office first. Somebody who knew where Froelich lived. You ever heard of the duck test? If it looks like a duck, sounds like a duck, walks like a duck?'

Stuyvesant said nothing. Bannon checked his watch. Took his cell phone out of his pocket and laid it on the table in front of him. It sat there, silent.

'I'm sticking with the theory,' he said. 'Except now I'm listing both of the bad guys as yours. If this phone rings and Reacher turns out to be right, that is.'

The phone rang right then. He had the ringer set to a squeaky little rendition of some famous classical overture. It sounded ludicrous in the sombre stillness of the room. He picked it up and clicked it on. The fatuous tune died. Somebody must have said *chief*? because he said *yeah* and then just listened, not more than eight or nine seconds. Then he clicked the phone off and dropped it back in his jacket pocket.

'Sacramento?' Stuyvesant asked.

'No,' Bannon said. 'Local. They found the rifle.'

They left Swain behind and headed over to the FBI labs inside the Hoover Building. An expert staff was assembling. They all looked a lot like Swain himself, academic and scientific types dragged in from home. They were dressed like family men who had expected to remain inert in front of the football game for the rest of the day. A couple of them had already enjoyed a couple of beers. That was clear. Neagley knew one of them, vaguely, from her training stint in the labs many years before.

'Was it a Vaime Mk2?' Bannon asked.

'Without a doubt,' one of the techs said.

'Serial number on it?'

The guy shook his head. 'Removed with acid.'

'Anything you can do?'

The guy shook his head again. 'No,' he said. 'If it was a stamped number, we could go down under it and find enough distressed crystals in the metal to recover the number, but Vaime uses engraving instead of stamping. Nothing we can do.'

'So where is it now?'

'We're fuming it for prints,' the guy said. 'But it's hopeless. We got nothing on the fluoroscope. Nothing on the laser. It's been wiped.'

'Where was it found?'

'In the warehouse. Behind the door of one of the third-floor rooms.'

'I guess they waited in there,' Bannon said. 'Maybe five minutes, slipped out at the height of the mayhem. Cool heads.'

'Shell cases?' Neagley asked.

'None,' the tech said. 'They must have collected their brass. But we've got all four bullets. The three from today are wrecked from impact on hard surfaces. But the Minnesota sample is intact. The mud preserved it.'

He walked to a lab bench where the bullets were laid out on a sheet of clean white butcher paper. Three of them were crushed to distorted blobs by impact. One of the three was clean. That was the one that had missed Armstrong and hit the wall. The other two were smeared with black residue from Crosetti's brains and Froelich's blood respectively. The remains of the human tissue had printed on the copper jackets and burned on the hot surface in characteristic lacy patterns. Then the patterns had collapsed after the bullets had flown on and impacted whatever came next. The back wall, in Froelich's case. The interior hallway wall, presumably, in Crosetti's. The Minnesota bullet looked new. Its passage through the farmyard mud had scoured it clean.

'Get the rifle,' Bannon said.

It came out of the laboratory still smelling of the hot super-glue fumes that had been blown all over it in the hope of finding latent fingerprints. It was a dull, boxy, undramatic weapon. It was painted all over in factory-finish black epoxy paint. It had a short stubby bolt and a relatively short barrel made much longer by the fat suppressor. It had a powerful scope fixed to the sight mounts.

'That's the wrong scope,' Reacher said. 'That's a Hensoldt. Vaime uses Bushnell scopes.'

'Yeah, it's been modified,' one of the techs said. 'We already logged that.'

'By the factory?'

The guy shook his head. 'I don't think so,' he said. 'High standard, but it's not factory workmanship.'

'So what does that mean?' Bannon asked.

'I'm not sure,' Reacher said.

'Is a Hensoldt better than a Bushnell?'

'Not really. They're both fine scopes. Like BMW and Mercedes. Like Canon and Nikon.'

'So a person might have a preference?'

'Not a government person,' Reacher said. 'Like, what would you say if one of your crime scene photographers came to you and said, I want a Canon instead of this Nikon you gave me?'

'I'd probably tell him to get lost.'

'Exactly. He works with what he's got. So I don't see somebody going to their department armourer and asking him to junk a thousand-dollar Bushnell just because he prefers the feel of a thousand-dollar Hensoldt.'

'So why the switch?'

'I'm not sure,' Reacher said again. 'Damage, maybe. If you drop a rifle you can damage a sniper scope pretty easily. But a government repairer would use another Bushnell. They don't just buy the rifles. They buy crateloads of spare parts along with them.'

'Suppose they were short? Suppose the scopes got damaged a lot?'

'Then they might use a Hensoldt, I guess. Hensoldts usually come with SIG rifles. You need to look at your lists again. Find out if there's anybody who buys Vaimes *and* SIGs for their snipers.'

'Is the SIG silenced too?'

'No,' Reacher said.

'So there you go,' Bannon said. 'Some agency needs two types of sniper rifles, it buys Vaimes as the silenced option and SIGs as the unsilenced option. Two types of scope in the spare-parts bins. They run out of Bushnells, they start in on the Hensoldts.'

'Possible,' Reacher said. 'You should make the enquiries. You should ask specifically if anybody has fitted a Hensoldt scope to a Vaime rifle. And if they haven't, you should start asking commercial gunsmiths. Start with the expensive ones. These are rare pieces. This could be important.'

Stuyvesant was staring into the distance. Worry in the slope of his shoulders.

'What?' Reacher asked.

Stuyvesant focused, and shook his head. A defeated little gesture.

'I'm afraid we bought SIGs,' he said, quietly. 'We had a batch of SG550s about five years ago. Unsilenced semi-automatics, as an alternative option. But we don't use them much because the automatic mechanism makes them a little inaccurate for close crowd situations. They're mostly stored. We use the Vaimes everywhere now. So I'm sure the SIG parts bins are still full.'

The room was quiet for a moment. Then Bannon's phone rang again. The insane little overture trilled into the silence. He clicked it on and put it to his ear and said *yeah* and listened.

'I see,' he said. Listened some more.

'The doctor agree?' he asked. Listened some more.

'I see,' he said, and listened.

'I guess,' he said, and listened.

'Two?' he asked, and listened.

'OK,' he said, and clicked the phone off.

'Upstairs,' he said. He was pale.

Stuyvesant and Reacher and Neagley followed him out to the elevator and rode with him up to the conference room. He sat at the head of the table and the others stayed together towards the other end, like they didn't want to get too close to the news. The sky was full dark outside the windows. Thanksgiving Day was grinding to a close.

'His name is Andretti,' Bannon said. 'Age seventy-three,

retired carpenter, retired volunteer firefighter. He's got granddaughters. That's where the pressure came from.'

'Is he talking?' Neagley asked.

'Some,' Bannon said. 'Sounds like he's made of slightly sterner stuff than Nendick.'

'So how did it go down?'

'He frequents a cop bar outside of Sacramento, from his firefighting days. He met two guys in there.'

'Were they cops?' Reacher asked.

'Cop-like,' Bannon said. 'That was his description. They got to talking, they got to showing each other pictures of the family. They got to talking about what a rotten world it is, and what they would do to protect their families from it. It was gradual, he said.'

'And?'

'He clammed up on us for a spell, but then our doctor took a look at his hand. The left thumb has been surgically removed. Well, not really *surgically*. Somewhere between severed and hacked off, our guy said. But there was an attempt at neatness. Andretti stuck to his carpentry story. Our doctor said, no way was that a saw. Like, no *way*. Andretti seemed pleased to be contradicted, and he talked some more.'

'And?'

'He lives alone. Widower. The two cop-like guys had wormed an invitation home with him. They were asking him, what would you do to protect your family? Like, what would you *do*? How far would you go? It was all rhetorical at first, and then it got practical fast. They told him he would have to give up his thumb or his granddaughters. His choice. They held him down and did it. They took his photographs and his address book. Told him now they knew what his granddaughters looked like and where they lived. Told him they'd take out their ovaries the same way they'd taken off his thumb. And he was ready to believe them, obviously. He would be, right? They'd just done it to *him*. They stole a cooler from the kitchen and some ice from the refrigerator to transport the thumb. They left and he made it to the hospital.'

Silence in the room.

'Descriptions?' Stuyvesant asked.

Bannon shook his head. 'Too scared,' he said. 'My guys talked about Witness Protection for the whole family, but he's not going to bite. My guess is we've got all we're going to get.'

'Forensics in the house?'

'Andretti cleaned it thoroughly. They made him. They watched him do it.'

'What about the bar? Anybody see them talking?'

'We'll ask. But this was nearly six weeks ago. Don't hold your breath.'

Nobody spoke for a long time.

'Reacher?' Neagley said.

'What?'

'What are you thinking?'

He shrugged.

'I'm thinking about Dostoevsky,' he said. 'I just found a copy of *Crime and Punishment* that I sent Joe for a birthday present. I remember I almost sent him *The Brothers Karamazov* instead, but I decided against it. You ever read that book?'

Neagley shook her head.

'Part of it is about what the Turks did in Bulgaria,' he said. 'There was all kinds of rape and pillage going on. They hanged prisoners in the mornings after making them spend their last night nailed to a fence by their ears. They threw babies in the air and caught them on bayonets. They said the best part was doing it in front of the mothers. Ivan Karamazov was seriously disillusioned by it all. He said *no animal could ever be so cruel as a man, so artfully, so artistically cruel*. Then I was thinking about these guys making Andretti clean his house while they watched. I guess he had to do it one-handed. He probably struggled with it. Dostoevsky put his feelings in a book. I don't have his talent. So now I'm thinking I'm going to find these guys and impress on them the error of their ways in whatever manner my own talent allows.'

'You didn't strike me as a reader,' Bannon said.

'I get by,' Reacher said.

'And I would caution you against vigilantism.'

'That's a big word for a special agent.'

'Whatever, I don't want independent action.'

Reacher nodded. 'Noted,' he said.

Bannon smiled. 'You done the puzzle yet?'

'What puzzle?'

'We're assuming that Vaime rifle was in Minnesota on Tuesday and North Dakota yesterday. Now it's here in D.C. today. They didn't fly it in, that's for damn sure, because putting long guns on a commercial flight leaves a paper trail a mile long. And it's too far to drive in the time they had. So either one guy was on his own with the Heckler & Koch in Bismarck while the other guy was driving all the way from Minnesota to here with the Vaime. Or if both guys were in Bismarck then they must own two Vaimes, one there, one stashed here. And if both guys were in Bismarck but they own only one Vaime, then somebody else drove it in from Minnesota for them, in which case we're dealing with three guys, not two.'

Nobody spoke.

'I'm going back to see Swain,' Reacher said. 'I'll walk. It'll do me good.'

'I'll come with you,' Neagley said.

It was a fast half-mile west on Pennsylvania Avenue. The sky was still cloudless, which made the night air cold. There were some stars visible through the faint city smog and the orange glow of street lighting. There was a small moon, far away. No traffic. They walked past the Federal Triangle and the bulk of the Treasury Building came closer. The White House road-blocks had gone. The city was back to normal. It was like nothing had ever happened.

'You OK?' Neagley asked.

'Facing reality,' Reacher said. 'I'm getting old. Slowing up, mentally. I was pretty pleased about getting to Nendick as fast as I did, but I was supposed to get there right away. So in fact I was terrible. Same with the thumbprint. We spent hours boxing around that damn print. Days and days. We twisted and turned to accommodate it. Never saw the actual intention.'

'But we got there in the end.'

'And I'm feeling guilty, as usual.'

'Why?'

'I told Froelich she was doing well,' Reacher said. 'But I should have told her to double the sentries on the roof.

One guy on the edge, one in the stairwell. Might have saved her.'

Neagley was silent. Six strides, seven.

'It was her job, not yours,' she said. 'Don't feel guilty. You're not responsible for everybody in the world.'

Reacher said nothing. Just walked.

'And they were masquerading as cops,' Neagley said. 'They'd have walked through two sentries just the same as one. They'd have walked through a *dozen* sentries. Fact is, they *did* walk through a dozen sentries. More than that. They must have. The whole area was crawling with agents. There's nothing anybody could have done different. Shit happens.'

Reacher said nothing.

'Two sentries, they'd *both* have gotten killed,' Neagley said. 'Another casualty wouldn't have helped anybody.'

'You think Bannon looks like a cop?' Reacher asked.

'You think there are three guys?' Neagley asked back.

'No. Not a chance. This is a two-guy thing. Bannon's missing something very obvious. Occupational hazard with a mind like his.'

'What's he missing?'

'You think he looks like a cop?'

Neagley smiled, briefly. 'Exactly like a cop,' she said. 'He probably was a cop before he joined the Bureau.'

'What makes him look like a cop?'

'Everything. Every single thing. It's in his pores.'

Reacher went quiet. Walked on.

'Something in Froelich's pep talk,' he said. 'Just before Armstrong showed up. She was warning her people. She said it's very easy to look a little like a homeless person, but very difficult to look exactly like a homeless person. I think it's the same with cops. If I put a tweed sports coat on and grey flannels and plain shoes and held up a gold badge, would I look like a cop?'

'A little. But not exactly.'

'But these guys *do* look exactly like cops. I saw one of them and never thought twice. And they're in and out of everywhere without a single question.'

'It would explain a lot of things,' Neagley said. 'They were right at home in the cop bar with Nendick. And with Andretti.'

'Like Bannon's duck test,' Reacher said. 'They look like cops, they walk like cops, they talk like cops.'

'And it would explain how they knew about DNA on envelopes, and the NCIC computer thing. Cops would know that the FBI networks all that information.'

'And the weapons. They might filter through to second-tier SWAT teams or State Police specialists. Especially refurbished items with non-standard scopes.'

'But we know they aren't cops. You went through ninety-four mug shots.'

'We know they aren't Bismarck cops,' Reacher said. 'Maybe they're cops from somewhere else.'

Swain was still waiting for them. He looked unhappy. Not necessarily with the waiting. He looked like a man with bad news to hear, and bad news to give. He looked a question at Reacher, and Reacher nodded, once.

'His name was Andretti,' he said. 'Same situation as Nendick, basically. He's holding up better, but he's not going to talk, either.'

Swain said nothing.

'Your score,' Reacher said. 'You made the connection. And the rifle was a Vaime with a Hensoldt scope where a Bushnell should be.'

'I don't specialize in firearms,' Swain said.

'You need to tell us what you know about the campaign. Who got mad at Armstrong?'

There was a short silence. Then Swain looked away.

'Nobody,' he said. 'What I said in there wasn't true. Thing is, I finished the analysis days ago. He upset people, for sure. But nobody very significant. Nothing out of the ordinary.'

'So why say it?'

'I wanted to get the FBI off their track, was all. I don't think it was one of us. I don't like to see our agency getting abused that way.'

Reacher said nothing.

'It was for Froelich and Crosetti,' Swain said. 'They deserve better than that.'

'So you've got a feeling and we've got a hyphen,' Reacher

said. 'Most cases I ever dealt with had stronger foundations than that.'

'What do we do now?'

'We look somewhere else,' Neagley said. 'If it's not political it must be personal.'

'I'm not sure if I can show you that stuff,' Swain said. 'It's supposed to be confidential.'

'Is there anything bad in it?'

'No, or you'd have heard about it during the campaign.'

'So what's the problem?'

'Is he faithful to his wife?' Reacher asked.

'Yes,' Swain said.

'Is she faithful to him?'

'Yes.'

'Is he kosher financially?'

'Yes.'

'So everything else is deep background. How can it hurt to let us take a look?'

'I guess it can't.'

'So let's go.'

They headed through the back corridors towards the library, but when they got there the phone was ringing. Swain picked it up and then handed it to Reacher.

'Stuyvesant, for you,' he said.

Reacher listened for a minute and then put the phone down.

'Armstrong's coming in,' he said. 'He's upset and restless and wants to talk to everybody he can find who was there today.'

They left Swain in the library and walked back to the conference room. Stuyvesant came in a minute later. He was still in his golf clothes. He still had Froelich's blood on his shoes. It was splashed up on the welts, black and dry. He looked close to exhaustion. And mentally shattered. Reacher had seen it before. A guy goes twenty-five years, and it all falls apart in one terrible day. A suicide bombing will do it, or a helicopter crash or a secrets leak or a furlough rampage. Then the retributive machinery clanks into action and a flawless career spent garnering nothing but praise is trashed at the stroke of a pen, because it all has to be somebody's *fault*. Shit happens, but never in an official inquiry commission's final report.

'We're going to be thin on the ground,' Stuyvesant said. 'I gave most people twenty-four hours and I'm not dragging them back in just because the protectee can't sleep.'

Two more guys came in five minutes later. Reacher recognized one of them as a rooftop sharpshooter and the other as one of the agent screen around the food line. They nodded tired greetings and turned round and went and got coffee. Came back in with a plastic cup for everybody.

Armstrong's security preceded him like the edge of an invisible bubble. There was radio communication with the building while he was still a mile away. There was a second call when he reached the garage. His progress into the elevator was reported. One of his personal detail entered the reception area and announced an all-clear. The other two brought Armstrong inside. The procedure was repeated at the conference room door. The first agent came in, glanced around, spoke into his cuff, and Armstrong leapfrogged past him into the room.

He had changed into casual clothes that didn't suit him. He was in corduroy pants and a patterned sweater and a suede jacket. All the colours matched and all the fabrics were stiff and new. It was the first false note Reacher had seen from him. It was like he had asked himself *what would a vice president wear?* instead of just grabbing whatever was at the front of his closet. He nodded sombre greetings all round and moved towards the table. Didn't speak to anybody. He seemed awkward. The silence grew. It reached the point where it was embarrassing.

'How's your wife, sir?' the sharpshooter asked.

It was the perfect political question, Reacher thought. It was an invitation to talk about somebody else's feelings, which was always easier than talking about your own. It was collegial, in that it said *we all are on the inside here, so let's talk about somebody who isn't*. And it said *here's your chance to thank us for saving her ass, and yours*.

'She's very shaken,' Armstrong said. 'It was a terrible thing. She wants you to know how sorry she is. She's been giving me a hard time, actually. She says it's wrong of me to be putting you people at risk.'

It was the perfect political answer, Reacher thought. It invited only one reply: *just doing our job, sir*.

'It's our job, sir,' Stuyvesant said. 'If it wasn't you, it would be somebody else.'

'Thank you,' Armstrong said. 'For being so gracious. And thank you for performing so superbly well today. From both of us. From the bottom of our hearts. I'm not a superstitious guy, but I kind of feel I owe you now. Like I won't be free of an obligation until I've done something for you. So don't hesitate to ask me. Anything at all, formal or informal, collective or individual. I'm your friend for life.'

Nobody spoke.

'Tell me about Crosetti,' Armstrong said. 'Did he have family?'

The sharpshooter nodded. 'A wife and a son,' he said. 'The boy is eight, I think.'

Armstrong looked away. 'I'm so sorry,' he said.

Silence in the room.

'Is there anything I can do for them?' Armstrong asked.

'They'll be looked after,' Stuyvesant said.

'Froelich had parents in Wyoming,' Armstrong said. 'That's all. She wasn't married. No brothers or sisters. I spoke with her folks earlier today. After I saw you at the White House. I felt I ought to offer my condolences personally. And I felt I should clear my statement with them, you know, before I spoke to the television people. I felt I couldn't misrepresent the situation without their permission, just for the sake of a decoy scheme. But they liked the idea of a memorial service on Sunday. So much so that they're going to go ahead with it, in fact. So there will be a service, after all.'

Nobody spoke. Armstrong picked a spot on the wall, and looked hard at it.

'I want to attend it,' he said. 'In fact, I'm *going* to attend it.'

'I can't permit that,' Stuyvesant said.

Armstrong said nothing.

'I mean, I advise against it,' Stuyvesant said.

'She was killed because of me. I want to attend her service.

It's the least I can do. I want to speak there, actually. I guess I should talk to her folks again.'

'I'm sure they'd be honoured, but there are security issues.'

'I respect your judgement, of course,' Armstrong said. 'But it isn't negotiable. I'll go on my own, if I have to. I might prefer to go on my own.'

'That isn't possible,' Stuyvesant said.

Armstrong nodded. 'So find three agents who want to be there with me. And only three. We can't turn it into a circus. We'll get in and out fast, unannounced.'

'You announced it on national television.'

'It isn't negotiable,' Armstrong said again. 'They won't want to turn the whole thing into a circus. That wouldn't be fair. So, no media and no television. Just us.'

Stuyvesant said nothing.

'I'm going to her service,' Armstrong said. 'She was killed because of me.'

'She knew the risks,' Stuyvesant said. 'We all know the risks. We're here because we want to be.'

Armstrong nodded. 'I spoke with the director of the FBI. He told me the suspects got away.'

'It's just a matter of time,' Stuyvesant said.

'My daughter is in the Antarctic,' Armstrong said. 'It's coming up to midsummer down there. The temperature is up to twenty below zero. It'll peak at maybe eighteen below in a week or two. We just spoke on the satellite phone. She says it feels unbelievably warm. We've had the same conversation for the last two years straight. I used to take it as a kind of metaphor. You know, everything's relative, nothing's *that* bad, you can get used to anything. But now I don't know any more. I don't think I'll ever get over today. I'm alive only because another person is dead.'

Silence in the room.

'She knew what she was doing,' Stuyvesant said. 'We're all volunteers.'

'She was terrific, wasn't she?'

'Let me know when you want to meet with her replacement.'

'Not yet,' Armstrong said. 'Tomorrow, maybe. And ask around about Sunday. Three volunteers. Friends of hers who would want to be there anyway.'

Stuyvesant was silent. Then he shrugged.

'OK,' he said.

Armstrong nodded. 'Thank you for that. And thank you for today. Thank you all. From both of us. That's really all I came here to say.'

His personal detail picked up the cue and moved him to the door. The invisible security bubble rolled out with him, probing forward, checking sideways, checking backward. Three minutes later a radio call came in from his car. He was secure and mobile north and west towards Georgetown.

'Shit,' Stuyvesant said. 'Now Sunday is going to be a damn nightmare on top of everything else.'

Nobody looked at Reacher, except Neagley. They walked out alone and found Swain in the reception area. He had his coat on.

'I'm going home,' he said.

'In an hour,' Reacher said. 'First you're going to show us your files.'

SIXTEEN

THE FILES WERE BIOGRAPHICAL. THERE WERE TWELVE IN total. Eleven were bundles of raw data like newspaper cuttings and interviews and depositions and other first-generation paperwork. The twelfth was a comprehensive summary of the first eleven. It was as thick as a medieval Bible and it read like a book. It narrated the whole story of Brook Armstrong's life, and every substantive fact had a number following it in parentheses. The number indicated on a scale of one to ten how solidly the fact had been authenticated. Most of the numbers were tens.

The story started on page one with his parents. His mother had grown up in Oregon, moved to Washington State for college, returned to Oregon to start work as a pharmacist. Her own parents and siblings were sketched in, and the whole of her education was listed from kindergarten to postgraduate school. Her early employers were listed in sequence, and the start-up of her own pharmacy business had three pages all to itself. She still owned it and still took income from it, but she was now retired and sick with something that was feared to be terminal.

His father's education was listed. His military service had a start date and a medical discharge date, but there were no details beyond that. He was an Oregon native who married the pharmacist on his return to civilian life. They moved to an isolated village in the south-west corner of the state and he used family money to buy himself a lumber business. The newlyweds had a daughter soon afterwards and Brook Armstrong himself was born two years later. The family business prospered and grew to a decent size. Its progress and development took up several pages. It provided a pleasant provincial lifestyle.

The sister's biography was a half-inch thick so Reacher skipped over it and started in on Brook's education. It began like everybody else's in kindergarten. There were endless details. Too many to pay close attention to, so he leafed ahead and skimmed. Armstrong went all the way through the local school system. He was good at sports. He got excellent grades. The father had a stroke and died just after Armstrong left home for college. The lumber business was sold. The pharmacy continued to prosper. Armstrong himself spent seven years in two different universities, first Cornell in upstate New York and then Stanford in California. He had long hair but no proven drug use. He met a Bismarck girl at Stanford. They were both political science postgraduates. They got married. They made their home in North Dakota and he started his political career with a campaign for a seat in the State legislature.

'I need to get home,' Swain said. 'It's Thanksgiving and I've got kids and my wife is going to kill me.'

Reacher looked ahead at the rest of the file. Armstrong was just starting in on his first minor election and there were six more inches of paperwork to go. He fanned through it with his thumb.

'Nothing here to worry us?' he asked.

'Nothing anywhere,' Swain said.

'Does this level of detail continue throughout?'

'It gets worse.'

'Am I going to find anything if I read all night?'

'No.'

'Was all of it used in this summer's campaign?'

Swain nodded. 'Sure. It's a great bio. That's why he was

picked in the first place. Actually we got a lot of the detail *from* the campaign.'

'And you're sure nobody in particular was upset *by* the campaign?'

'I'm sure.'

'So where exactly does your feeling come from? Who hates Armstrong that bad and why?'

'I don't know exactly,' Swain said. 'It's just a feeling.'

Reacher nodded. 'OK,' he said. 'Go home.'

Swain picked up his coat and left in a hurry and Reacher sampled his way through the remaining years. Neagley leafed through the endless source material. They both gave it up after an hour.

'Conclusions?' Neagley asked.

'Swain has got a very boring job,' Reacher said.

She smiled. 'Agreed,' she said.

'But something kind of jumps out at me. Something that's not here, rather than something that *is* here. Campaigns are cynical, right? These people will use any old thing that puts them in a good light. So for instance, we've got his mother. We've got endless detail about her college degrees and her pharmacy thing. Why?'

'To appeal to independent women and small business people.'

'OK, and then we've got stuff about her getting sick. Why?'

'So Armstrong looks like a caring son. Very dutiful and full of family values. It humanizes him. And it authenticates his issues about health care.'

'And we've got plenty of stuff about his dad's lumber company.'

'For the business lobby again. And it touches on environmental concerns. You know, trees and logging and all that kind of thing. Armstrong can say he's got practical knowledge. He's walked the walk, at one remove.'

'Exactly,' Reacher said. 'Whatever the issue, whatever the constituency, they find a bone to throw.'

'So?'

'They took a pass on military service. And usually they love all that stuff, in a campaign. Normally if your dad was in the army, you'd shout it from the rooftops to wrap up another whole bunch of issues. But there's no detail at all. He joined, he got discharged. That's all we know. See what I mean? We're drowning in detail everywhere else, but not there. It stands out.'

'The father died ages ago.'

'Doesn't matter. They'd have been all over it if there was something to be gained. And what was the medical discharge for? If it had been a wound they'd have made something out of it, for sure. Even a training accident. The guy would have been a big hero. And you know what? I don't like to see unexplained medical discharges. You know how it was. It makes you wonder, doesn't it?'

'I guess it does. But it can't be connected. It happened before Armstrong was even born. Then the guy died nearly thirty years ago. And you said it yourself, this all was triggered by something Armstrong did in the campaign.'

Reacher nodded. 'But I'd still like to know more about it. We could ask Armstrong direct, I guess.'

'Don't need to,' Neagley said. 'I can find out, if you really need me to. I can make some calls. We've got plenty of contacts. People who figure on getting a job with us when they quit are generally interested in making a good impression beforehand.'

Reacher yawned. 'OK, do it. First thing tomorrow.'

'I'll do it tonight. The military still works twenty-four hours a day. Hasn't changed any since we quit.'

'You should sleep. It can wait.'

'I never sleep any more.'

Reacher yawned again. 'Well, I'm going to.'

'Bad day,' Neagley said.

Reacher nodded. 'As bad as they get. So make the calls if you want to, but don't wake me up to tell me about them. Tell me about them tomorrow.'

The night duty officer fixed them a ride back to the Georgetown motel and Reacher went straight to his room. It was quiet and still and empty. It had been cleaned and tidied. The bed was made. Joe's box had gone. He sat in the chair for a moment and wondered if Stuyvesant had thought to cancel Froelich's booking. Then the night-time silence pressed in on him and he was overcome by a sense of something *not there*. A sense of absence. Things that should be there and weren't. *What exactly?* Froelich, of course. He had an ache for her. She should be there, and she wasn't. She had been there the last time he was in the room. Early that morning. *Today's the day we win or lose*, she had said. *Losing is not an option*, he had replied.

Something *not there*. Maybe Joe himself. Maybe lots of things. There were lots of things missing from his life. Things not done, things not said. *What exactly?* Maybe it was just Armstrong's father's service career on his mind. *But maybe it was more than that. Was something else missing?* He closed his eyes and chased it hard but all he saw was the pink spray of Froelich's blood arcing backward into the sunlight. So he opened his eyes again and stripped off his clothes and showered for the third time that day. He found himself staring down at the tray like he was still expecting to see it run red. But it stayed clear and white.

The bed was cold and hard and the new sheets were stiff with starch. He slipped in alone and stared at the ceiling for an hour and thought hard. Then he switched off abruptly and made himself sleep. He dreamed of his brother strolling hand in hand with Froelich all the way round the Tidal Basin in summer. The light was soft and golden and the blood streaming from her neck hung in the still warm air like a shimmering red ribbon five feet above the ground. It hung there undisturbed by the passing crowds and it made a full mile-wide circle when she and Joe arrived back where they had started. Then she changed into Swain and Joe changed into the Bismarck cop. The cop's coat flapped open as he walked and Swain said *I think we miscounted* to everybody he met. Then Swain changed into Armstrong. Armstrong smiled his brilliant politician's smile and said *I'm so sorry* and the cop turned and threaded a long gun out from under his flapping coat and slowly racked the bolt and shot Armstrong in the head. There was no sound, because the gun was silenced. No sound, even as Armstrong hit the water and floated away.

There was an alarm call from the desk at six o'clock and a minute later there was a knock at the door. Reacher rolled out of bed and wrapped a towel round his waist and checked the spy hole. It was Neagley, with coffee for him. She was all dressed and ready to go. He let her in and sat on the bed and started the coffee and she paced the narrow alley that led to the window. She was wired. Looked like she'd been drinking coffee all night.

'OK, Armstrong's father?' she said, like she was asking the question for him. 'He was drafted right at the end of Korea. Never saw active service. But he went through officer training and came out a second lieutenant and was assigned to an infantry company. They were stationed in Alabama, some place that's long gone. They were ordered to achieve battle readiness for a fight everybody knew was already over. And you know how that stuff went, right?'

Reacher nodded sleepily. Sipped his coffee.

'Some idiot captain running endless competitions,' he said. 'Points for this, points for that, deductions all over the place, at the end of the month Company B gets to keep a flag in its barracks for kicking Company A's ass.'

'And Armstrong senior usually won,' Neagley said. 'He ran a tight unit. But he had a temper problem. It was unpredictable. If somebody screwed up and lost points he could fly into a rage. Happened a couple of times. Not just the usual officer bullshit. It's described in the records as serious uncontrolled temper tantrums. He went way too far, like he couldn't stop himself.'

'And?'

'They let him get away with it twice. It wasn't constant. It was purely episodic. But the third time, there was some real serious physical abuse and they kicked him out for it. And they covered it up, basically. They gave him a psychological discharge, wrote it up as generic battle stress, even though he'd never been a combat officer.'

Reacher made a face. 'He must have had friends. And so must you, to get that deep into the records.'

'I've been on the phone all night. Stuyvesant's going to have a coronary when he sees the motel bill.'

'How many individual victims?'

'My first thought, but we can forget them. There were three, one for each incident. One was KIA in Vietnam, one died ten years ago in Palm Springs and the third is more than seventy years old, lives in Florida.'

'Dry hole,' Reacher said.

'But it explains why they left it out of the campaign.'

Reacher nodded. Sipped his coffee. 'Any chance Armstrong himself inherited the temper? Froelich said she'd seen him angry.'

'That was my second thought,' Neagley said. 'It's conceivable. There was something there below the surface when he was insisting on going to her service, wasn't there? But I assume the broader picture would have come out already, long ago. The guy's been running for office at one level or another his whole life. And this all started with the campaign this summer. We already agreed on that.'

Reacher nodded, vaguely. 'The campaign,' he repeated. He sat still with the coffee cup in his hand. Stared straight ahead at the wall, one full minute, then two.

'What?' Neagley asked.

He didn't reply. Just got up and walked to the window. Pulled back the shades and looked out at slices and slivers of D.C. under the grey dawn sky.

'What did Armstrong *do* in the campaign?' he asked.

'Lots of things.'

'How many representatives does New Mexico have?'

'I don't know,' Neagley said.

'I think it's three. Can you name them?'

'No.'

'Would you recognize any of them on the street?'

'No.'

'Oklahoma?'

'Don't know. Five?'

'Six, I think. Can you name them?'

'One of them is an asshole, I know that. Can't remember his name.'

'Senators from Tennessee?'

'What's your point?'

Reacher stared out of the window.

'We've got Beltway disease,' he said. 'We're all caught up in it. We're not looking at this thing like real people. To almost everybody else out there in the country all these politicians are absolute nobodies. You said it yourself. You said you're interested in politics but you couldn't name all hundred senators. And most people are a thousand times less interested than you. Most people wouldn't recognize another state's junior senator if he ran up and bit them in the ass. Or she, as Froelich would have said. She actually admitted nobody had ever heard of Armstrong before.'

'So?'

'So Armstrong did one absolutely basic, fundamental, elemental thing in the campaign. He put himself in the public eye, nationally. For the very first time in his life ordinary people outside of his home state and outside of his circle of friends saw his face. Heard his name. For the first time ever. I think this all could be as basic as that.'

'In what way?'

'Suppose his face came back at somebody from way in the past. Completely out of the blue. Like a sudden shock.'

'Like who?'

'Like you're some guy somewhere and long ago some young man lost his temper and smacked you around. Some situation like that. Maybe in a bar, maybe over a girl. Maybe he humiliated you by doing so. You never see the guy again, but the incident festers in your mind. Years pass, and suddenly there's the guy all over the papers and the TV. He's a politician, running for vice president. You never heard of him in the years before, because you don't watch C-SPAN or CNN. But now, there he is, everywhere, in your face. So what do you do? If you're politically aware you might call the opposing campaign and dish the dirt. But you're not politically aware, because this is the first time you've ever seen him since the fight in the bar a lifetime ago. So what do you do? The sight of him brings it all back. It's been festering.'

'You think about some kind of revenge.'

Reacher nodded. 'Which would explain Swain's thing about wanting him to suffer. But maybe Swain's been looking in the wrong place. Maybe we all have. Because maybe this isn't personal to Armstrong the politician. Maybe it's personal to Armstrong the man. Maybe it's *really* personal.'

Neagley stopped pacing and sat down in the chair. 'It's very tenuous,' she said. 'People get over things, don't they?'

'Do they?'

'Mostly.'

Reacher glanced down at her. 'You haven't gotten over whatever makes it that you don't like people to touch you.'

The room went quiet.

'OK,' she said. '*Normal* people get over things.'

'Normal people don't kidnap women and cut thumbs off and kill innocent bystanders.'

She nodded. 'OK,' she said again. 'It's a theory. But where can we go with it?'

'Armstrong himself, maybe,' Reacher said. 'But that would be a difficult conversation to have with a vice president-elect. And would he even remember? If he inherited the kind of temper that gets a guy thrown out of the army he could have had dozens of fights long ago. He's a big guy. Could have spread mayhem far and wide before he got a handle on it.'

'His wife? They've been together a long time.'

Reacher said nothing.

'Time to get going,' Neagley said. 'We meet with Bannon at seven. Are we going to tell him?'

'No,' Reacher said. 'He wouldn't listen.'

'Go shower,' Neagley said.

Reacher nodded. 'Something else first. It kept me awake last night for an hour. It nagged at me. Something that's not here, or something that hasn't been done.'

Neagley shrugged. 'OK,' she said. 'I'll think about it. Now get your ass in gear.'

He dressed in the last of Joe's suits. It was charcoal grey and as fine as silk. He used the last of the clean shirts. It was stiff with starch and as white as new snow. The last tie was dark blue with a tiny repeated pattern. When you looked very closely you saw that each element of the pattern was a diagram of a pitcher's hand, gripping a baseball, preparing to throw a knuckleball.

He met Neagley out in the lobby and ate a muffin from the buffet and took a cup of coffee with him in the Secret Service

Town Car. They were late into the conference room. Bannon and Stuyvesant were already there. Bannon was still dressed like a city cop. Stuyvesant was back in a Brooks Brothers suit. Reacher and Neagley left one seat unoccupied between themselves and Stuyvesant. Bannon stared at the empty place, as if maybe it was supposed to symbolize Froelich's absence.

'The FBI is not going to have agents in Grace, Wyoming,' he said. 'Special request from Armstrong, via the Director. He doesn't want a circus out there.'

'Suits me,' Reacher said.

'You're wasting your time,' Bannon said. 'We're complying only because we're happy to. The bad guys know how this stuff works. They were in the business. They'll have understood his statement was a trap. So they won't show up.'

Reacher nodded. 'Won't be the first trip I ever wasted.'

'I'm warning you against independent action.'

'There won't *be* any action, according to you.'

Bannon nodded. 'Ballistics tests are in,' he said. 'The rifle we found in the warehouse is definitely the same gun that fired the Minnesota bullet.'

'So how did it get here?' Stuyvesant asked.

'We burned more than a hundred man-hours last night,' Bannon said. 'All I can tell you for sure is how it *didn't* get here. It didn't fly in. We checked all commercial arrivals into eight airports and there were no firearms manifests at all. Then we traced all private planes into the same eight airports. Nothing even remotely suspicious.'

'So they drove it in?' Reacher said.

Bannon nodded. 'But Bismarck to D.C. is more than thirteen hundred miles. That's more than twenty hours absolute minimum, even driving like a lunatic. Impossible, in the time frame. So the rifle was never in Bismarck. It came in direct from Minnesota, which was a little more than eleven hundred miles in forty-eight hours. Your grandmother could do that.'

'My grandmother couldn't drive,' Reacher said. 'Still figuring on three guys?'

Bannon shook his head. 'No, on reflection we're sticking at two. The whole thing profiles better that way. We figure the team was split one and one between Minnesota and Colorado on Tuesday and it stayed split afterwards. The guy pretending to be the Bismarck cop was acting solo at the church. We figure he had the sub-machine gun only. Which makes sense, because he knew Armstrong was going to be buried in agents as soon as the decoy rifle was discovered. And a sub-machine gun is better than a rifle against a cluster of people. Especially an H&K MP5. Our people say it's as accurate as a rifle at a hundred yards and a lot more powerful. Thirty-round magazines, he would have chewed through six agents and gotten to Armstrong easy enough.'

'So why was the other guy bothering to drive here at the time?' Stuyvesant asked.

'Because these are your people,' Bannon said. 'They're realistic professionals. They knew the odds. They knew they couldn't guarantee a hit in any one particular place. So they went through Armstrong's schedule and planned to leapfrog ahead of each other to cover all the bases.'

Stuyvesant said nothing.

'But they were together yesterday,' Reacher said. 'You're saying the first guy drove the Vaime here and I saw the guy from Bismarck on the warehouse roof.'

Bannon nodded. 'No more leapfrogging, because yesterday was the last good opportunity for a spell. The Bismarck guy must have flown in, commercial, not long after the air force brought you back.'

'So where's the H&K? He must have abandoned it in Bismarck somewhere between the church and the airport. You find it?'

'No,' Bannon said. 'But we're still looking.'

'And who was the guy the State trooper saw in the sub-division?'

'We're discounting him. Almost certainly just a civilian.'

Reacher shook his head. 'So this solo guy hid the decoy rifle and legged it back to the church with the H&K all by himself?'

'I don't see why not.'

'Have you ever hidden out and lined up to shoot a man?'

'No,' Bannon said.

'I have,' Reacher said. 'And it's not a lot of fun. You need to be comfortable, and relaxed, and alert. It's a muscle thing. You get there well ahead of time, you settle in, you adjust your position, you figure out your range, you check the wind, you assess the angle of elevation or depression, you calculate the bullet drop. Then you lie there, staring through the sight. You get your breathing slow, you let your heart rate drop. And you know what you want at that point, more than anything else in the whole world?'

'What?'

'You want somebody you trust watching your back. All of your concentration is out there in front of you, and you start to feel an itch in your spine. If these guys are realistic professionals like you say they are, then no way would one of them work that church tower alone.'

Bannon was silent.

'He's right,' Neagley said. 'Best guess is the guy in the subdivision was the back-watcher, on his way from hiding the decoy. He was looping round, well away from the fence. The shooter was hiding out in the church, waiting for him to get back.'

'Which begs a question,' Reacher said. 'Like, who was it on the road from Minnesota at the time?'

Bannon shrugged. 'OK,' he said. 'So there *are* three of them.'

'All ours?' Stuyvesant asked, neutrally.

'I don't see why not,' Bannon said.

Reacher shook his head. 'You're obsessed. Why don't you just arrest everybody who ever worked for the Secret Service? There are probably some hundred-year-olds left over from FDR's first term.'

'We're sticking with our theory,' Bannon said.

'Fine,' Reacher said. 'Keeps you out of my hair.'

'I warned you against vigilantism, twice.'

'And I heard you twice.'

The room went silent. Then Bannon's face softened. He glanced across at Froelich's empty chair.

'Even though I would completely understand your motive,' he said.

Reacher stared down at the table. 'It's two guys, not three,' he said. 'I agree with you, it profiles better. A thing like this, the best choice would be one guy on his own, but that's never practical, so it's got to be two. But not three. A third guy multiplies the risk by a hundred.'

'So what happened with the rifle?'

'They messengered it, obviously,' Reacher said. 'FedEx or UPS or somebody. Maybe the USPS itself. They probably packaged it up with a bunch of saws and hammers and called it a delivery of tool samples. Some bullshit story like that. Addressed to a motel here, awaiting their arrival. That's what I would have done, anyway.'

Bannon looked embarrassed. Said nothing. Just stood up and left. The door clicked shut behind him. The room went quiet. Stuyvesant stayed in his seat, a little awkward.

'We need to talk,' he said.

'You're firing us,' Neagley said.

He nodded. Put his hand in his inside jacket pocket and came out with two slim white envelopes.

'This isn't internal any more,' he said. 'You know that. It's gotten way too big.'

'But you know Bannon is looking in the wrong place.'

'I hope he'll come to realize that,' Stuyvesant said. 'Then maybe he'll start looking in the right place. Meanwhile we'll defend Armstrong. Starting with this craziness in Wyoming. That's what we do. That's all we *can* do. We're reactive. We're defensive. We've got no legal basis to employ outsiders in a proactive role.'

He slid the first envelope along the shiny tabletop. Gave it enough force that it carried exactly six feet and spun to a stop in front of Reacher. Then the second, with a gentler motion, so it stopped in front of Neagley.

'Later,' Reacher said. 'Fire us later. Give us the rest of the day.'

'Why?'

'We need to talk to Armstrong. Just me and Neagley.'

'About what?'

'About something important,' Reacher said. Then he went quiet again.

'The thing we talked about this morning?' Neagley asked him.

'No, the thing that was on my mind last night.'

'Something not there, something not done?'
He shook his head. 'It was something not *said*.'
'What wasn't said?'
He didn't answer. Just gathered up both envelopes and slid them back along the tabletop. Stuyvesant stopped them dead with the flat of his hand. Picked them up and held them, uncertain.
'I can't let you talk to Armstrong without me,' he said.
'You'll have to,' Reacher said. 'It's the only way he'll talk at all.'
Stuyvesant said nothing. Reacher glanced at him. 'Tell me about the mail system. How long have you been checking Armstrong's mail?'
'From the start,' Stuyvesant said. 'Since he was picked as the candidate. That's absolutely standard procedure.'
'How does it work?'
Stuyvesant shrugged. 'It's easy enough. At first the agents at his house opened everything delivered there and we had a guy at the Senate Offices opening the stuff that went there and a guy in Bismarck looking after the local items. But after the first couple of messages we centralized everything right here for convenience.'
'But everything always got passed on to him except for the threats?'
'Obviously.'
'You know Swain?'
'The researcher? I know him a little.'
'You should promote him. Or give him a bonus. Or a big kiss on the forehead. Because he's the only person around here with an original idea in his head. Us included.'
'What's his idea?'
'We need to see Armstrong. As soon as possible. Me and Neagley, alone. Then we'll consider ourselves fired and you'll never see us again. And you'll never see Bannon again, either. Because your problem will be over a couple of days later.'
Stuyvesant put both envelopes back in his jacket.

It was the day after Thanksgiving and Armstrong was in self-imposed exile from public affairs, but arranging a meeting with him was intensely problematic. Straight after the morning meeting Stuyvesant promoted one of Froelich's original six male rivals to replace her, and the guy was full of all kinds of macho *now-we-can-do-this-properly* bullshit. He kept it firmly under control in front of Stuyvesant because of sensitivity issues, but he threw up every kind of obstacle he could find. The main stumbling block was a decades-old rule that no protectee can be alone with visitors without at least one protection agent present. Reacher saw the logic in that. Even if they were strip-searched for weapons he and Neagley could have completely dismembered Armstrong in about a second and a half. But they had to meet alone. That was vital. Stuyvesant was reluctant to overrule the new team leader on his first day, but eventually he quoted the Pentagon security clearances and decreed that the presence of two agents immediately outside the door would be sufficient. Then he called Armstrong at home to clear it with him personally. He got off the phone and said that Armstrong sounded a little concerned about something and would call right back.

They waited and Armstrong called back after twenty minutes and told Stuyvesant three things: first, his mother's health had taken a sudden turn for the worse, therefore second, he wanted to be flown out to Oregon that afternoon, therefore third, the meeting with Reacher and Neagley would have to be short and it would have to be delayed two hours while he packed.

So Reacher and Neagley went to Froelich's office to wait some more, but it had already been taken over by the new guy. The little plant was gone. Furniture had been moved. Things had been changed around. All that remained of Froelich was a faint trace of her perfume in the air. So they went back to the reception area and sprawled in the leather chairs. Watched the muted television. It was tuned to a news channel, and they saw Froelich die all over again, silently and in slow motion. They saw part of Armstrong's subsequent statement. They saw Bannon interviewed outside the Hoover Building. They didn't ask for the sound to be turned up. They knew what he would be saying. They watched football highlights from the Thanksgiving Day games. Then Stuyvesant called them back to his office.

His secretary wasn't there. She was clearly enjoying a long

weekend at home. They walked through the empty area and sat down in front of Stuyvesant's immaculate desk while he ran through the rules of engagement.

'No physical contact,' he said.

Reacher smiled. 'Not even a handshake?'

'I guess a handshake is OK,' Stuyvesant said. 'But nothing else. And you are not to reveal anything about the current situation. He doesn't know, and I don't want him to find out from you. Is that understood?'

Reacher nodded.

'Understood,' Neagley said.

'Don't upset him and don't harass him. Remember who he is. And remember he's preoccupied with his mother.'

'OK,' Reacher said.

Stuyvesant looked away. 'I've decided I don't want to know why you want to see him. And I don't want to know what happens afterwards, if anything. But I do want to say thanks for everything you've already done. Your audit will help us, and I think you probably saved us in Bismarck, and your hearts have been in the right place throughout, and I'm very grateful for all of that.'

Nobody spoke.

'I'm going to retire,' Stuyvesant said. 'I'd have to fight to save my career now, and the truth is I don't like my career enough to fight for it.'

'These guys were never your agents,' Reacher said.

'I know that,' Stuyvesant said. 'But I lost two people. Therefore my career is over. But that's my decision and my problem. All I mean to say to you is I'm glad I got the chance to meet Joe's brother, and it was a real pleasure working with you both.'

Nobody spoke.

'And I'm glad you were there at the end for M. E.'

Reacher looked away. Stuyvesant took the envelopes out of his pocket again.

'I don't know whether to hope you're right or wrong,' he said. 'About Wyoming, I mean. We'll have three agents and some local cops. That's not a lot of cover, if things turn out bad.'

He passed the envelopes across the desk.

'There's a car waiting downstairs,' he said. 'You get a one-way ride to Georgetown, and then you're on your own.'

They went down in the elevator and Reacher detoured into the main hall. It was vast and dark and grey and deserted, and the cold marble echoed with his footsteps. He stopped underneath the carved panel and glanced up at his brother's name. Glanced at the empty space where Froelich's would soon be added. Then he glanced away and walked back and joined Neagley. They pushed through the small door with the wired glass porthole and found their car.

The white tent was still in place across the sidewalk in front of Armstrong's house. The driver pulled up with the rear door tight against the contour and spoke into his wrist microphone. A second later Armstrong's front door opened and three agents stepped out. One walked forward through the canvas tunnel and opened the car door. Reacher got out and Neagley slid out beside him. The agent closed the door again and stood impassive on the kerb and the car drove away. The second agent held his arms out in a brief mime that they should stand still and be searched. They waited in the whitened canvas gloom. Neagley tensed while strange hands patted her down. But it was superficial. They barely touched her. And they missed Reacher's ceramic knife. It was hidden in his sock.

The agents led them inside to Armstrong's hallway and closed the door. The house was larger than it appeared from the outside. It was a big substantial place that looked like it had been standing for a hundred years and was good for maybe a hundred more. The hallway had dark antiques and striped paper on the walls and a clutter of framed pictures everywhere. There were rugs on the floors laid over thick wall-to-wall carpeting. There was a battered garment bag resting in a corner, presumably ready for the emergency trip to Oregon.

'This way,' one of the agents said.

He led them deep into the house and through a dog-leg in the hallway to a huge eat-in kitchen that would have looked at home in a log cabin. It was all pine, with a big table at one end and all the cooking equipment at the other. There was a strong smell of coffee. Armstrong and his wife were sitting at the table with heavy china mugs and four different newspapers. Mrs Armstrong was wearing a jogging suit and a sheen of sweat, like there might be a home gym in the basement. It looked like she wasn't going to Oregon with her husband. She had no make-up on. She looked a little tired and dispirited, like the events of Thanksgiving Day had altered her feelings in a fundamental way. Armstrong himself looked composed. He was wearing a clean shirt under a jacket with the sleeves pulled up over his forearms. No tie. He was reading the editorials from the *New York Times* and the *Washington Post* side by side.

'Coffee?' Mrs Armstrong asked.

Reacher nodded and she stood up and walked into the kitchen area and pulled two more mugs off hooks and filled them. Walked back with one in each hand. Reacher couldn't decide if she was short or tall. She was one of those women who look short in flat shoes and tall in heels. She handed the mugs over without much expression. Armstrong looked up from his papers.

'I'm sorry to hear about your mother,' Neagley said.

Armstrong nodded. 'Mr Stuyvesant told me you want a private conversation,' he said.

'Private would be good,' Reacher said.

'Should my wife join us?'

'That depends on your definition of privacy.'

Mrs Armstrong glanced at her husband. 'You can tell me afterwards,' she said. 'Before you leave. If you need to.'

Armstrong nodded again and made a show of folding his newspapers. Then he stood up and detoured to the coffee machine and refilled his mug.

'Let's go,' he said.

He led them back to the dog-legged hallway and into a side room. Two agents followed and stood one each side of the door on the outside. Armstrong glanced out at them as if in apology and shut the door on them. Walked round and stood behind a desk. The room was set up like a study, but it was more recreational than for real. There was no computer. The desk was a big old item made from dark wood. There were leather chairs and books chosen for the look of their spines. There was panelling and an old Persian rug. There was an air freshener somewhere putting fragrance into the hush. There was a framed photograph on the wall, showing a person of indeterminate gender standing on an ice floe. He or she was wearing an enormous padded down coat with a hood and thick mittens that reached the elbow. The hood had a big fur ruff that framed the face tight. The face itself was entirely hidden by a ski mask and smoked yellow snow goggles. One of the elbow-high mittens was raised in greeting.

'Our daughter,' Armstrong said. 'We asked her for a photo, because we miss her. That's what she sent. She has a sense of humour.'

He sat down behind the desk. Reacher and Neagley took a chair each.

'This all feels very confidential,' Armstrong said.

Reacher nodded. 'And in the end I think we'll all agree it should be kept confidential.'

'What's on your mind?'

'Mr Stuyvesant gave us some ground rules,' Reacher said. 'I'm going to start breaking them right now. The Secret Service intercepted six threatening messages against you. The first came in the mail eighteen days ago. Two more came in the mail subsequently and three were hand-delivered.'

Armstrong said nothing.

'You don't seem surprised,' Reacher said.

Armstrong shrugged. 'Politics is a surprising business,' he said.

'I guess it is,' Reacher said. 'All six messages were signed with a thumbprint. We traced the print to an old guy in California. His thumb had been amputated and stolen and used like a rubber stamp.'

Armstrong said nothing.

'The second message showed up in Stuyvesant's own office. Eventually it was proved that a surveillance technician named Nendick had placed it there. Nendick's wife had been kidnapped in order to coerce his actions. He was so frightened of the danger to her posed by his inevitable interrogation that he went into some kind of a coma. But we're guessing she was already dead by then anyway.'

Armstrong was silent.

'There's a researcher in the office called Swain who made an important mental connection. He felt we were miscounting. He realized that Nendick was supposed to be a message in himself, thereby making seven messages, not six. Then we added the guy in California who'd had his thumb removed and made it eight messages. Plus there were two homicides on Tuesday which made the ninth and tenth messages. One in Minnesota, and one in Colorado. Two unrelated strangers named Armstrong were killed as a kind of demonstration against you.'

'Oh no,' Armstrong said.

'So, ten messages,' Reacher said. 'All of them designed to torment you, except you hadn't been told about any of them. But then I started wondering whether we're *still* miscounting. And you know what? I'm pretty sure we are. I think there were at least eleven messages.'

Silence in the small room.

'What would be the eleventh?' Armstrong asked.

'Something that slipped through,' Reacher said. 'Something that came in the mail, addressed to you, something that the Secret Service didn't see as a threat. Something that meant nothing at all to them, but something that meant a lot to *you*.'

Armstrong said nothing.

'I think it came first,' Reacher said. 'Right at the very beginning, maybe, before the Secret Service even caught on. I think it was like an *announcement*, that only you would understand. So I think you've known about all this all along. I think you know who's doing it, and I think you know *why*.'

'People have died,' Armstrong said. 'That's a hell of an accusation.'

'Do you deny it?'

Armstrong said nothing.

Reacher leaned forward. 'Some crucial words were never spoken,' he said. 'Thing is, if I was standing there serving turkey and then somebody started shooting and somebody else was suddenly bleeding to death on top of me, sooner or later I'd be asking, who the hell *were* they? What the hell did they *want*? Why the hell were they *doing* that? Those are fairly basic questions. I'd be asking them loud and clear, believe me. But you didn't ask them. We saw you twice, afterwards. In the White House basement, and then later at the office. You said all kinds of things. You asked, had they been captured yet? That was your big concern. You never asked who they might be or what their possible motive was. And why didn't you ask? Only one possible explanation. You already *knew*.'

Armstrong said nothing.

'I think your wife knows, too,' Reacher said. 'You conveyed her anger at you for putting people at risk. I don't think she was generalizing. I think she knows you know, and she thinks you should have told somebody.'

Armstrong was silent.

'So I think you're feeling a little guilty now,' Reacher said. 'I think that's why you agreed to make the television statement for me and that's why you suddenly want to go to the service itself. Some kind of a conscience thing. Because you *knew*, and you didn't tell anybody.'

'I'm a politician,' Armstrong said. 'We have hundreds of enemies. There was no point in speculating.'

'Bullshit,' Reacher said. 'This isn't political. This is personal. Your kind of political enemy is some North Dakota soybean grower you made ten cents a week poorer by altering a subsidy. Or some pompous old senator you declined to vote with. The soybean grower might make a half-hearted effort against you at election time and the senator might bide his time and screw you on some big floor issue but neither one of them is going to do what these guys are doing.'

Armstrong said nothing.

'I'm not a fool,' Reacher said. 'I'm an angry man who watched a woman I was fond of bleed to death.'

'I'm not a fool either,' Armstrong said.

'I think you are. Something's coming back at you from the past and you think you can just ignore it and hope for the best? Didn't you realize it would happen? You people have no perspective. You thought you were world famous already just because you were in the House and the Senate? Well, you weren't. Real people never heard of you until the campaign this summer. You thought all your little secrets were already out? Well, they weren't, either.'

Armstrong said nothing.

'Who are they?' Reacher asked.

Armstrong shrugged. 'Your guess?'

Reacher paused.

'I think you've got a temper problem,' he said. 'Same as your dad. I think way back before you learned to control it you made people suffer, and some of them forgot about it, but some of them didn't. I think it's a part of some particular person's life that somebody once did something bad to them. Maybe hurt them, or hurt their self-esteem, or screwed them up in some other kind of a big way. I think that particular person repressed it deep down inside until they turned on the TV one day and saw your face for the first time in thirty years.'

Armstrong sat still for a long moment.

'How far along is the FBI with this?' he asked.

'They're nowhere. They're out beating the bushes for people that don't exist. We're way ahead of them.'

'And what are your intentions?'

'I'm going to help you,' Reacher said. 'Not that you deserve it in any way at all. It'll be a purely accidental by-product of me standing up for Nendick and his wife, and an old guy called Andretti, and two people called Armstrong, and Crosetti, and especially for Froelich, who was my brother's friend.'

There was silence.

'Will this stay confidential?' Armstrong asked.

Reacher nodded. 'It'll have to. Purely for my sake.'

'Sounds like you're contemplating a very serious course of action.'

'People play with fire, they get burned.'

'That's the law of the jungle.'

'Where the hell else do you think you live?'

Armstrong was quiet, another long moment.

'So then you'll know my secret and I'll know yours,' he said.

Reacher nodded. 'And we'll all live happily ever after.'

There was another long silence. It lasted a whole minute. Reacher saw Armstrong the politician fade away, and Armstrong the man replace him.

'You're wrong in most ways,' he said. 'But not all of them.'

He leaned down and opened a drawer. Took out a padded

mailer and tossed it on the desk. It skidded on the shiny wood and came to rest an inch from the edge.

'I guess this counts as the first message,' he said. 'It arrived on election day. I suppose the Secret Service must have been a little puzzled, but they didn't see anything really wrong with it. So they passed it right along.'

The mailer was a standard commercial stationery product. It was addressed to *Brook Armstrong, United States Senate, Washington D.C.* The address was printed on a familiar self-adhesive label in the familiar computer font, Times New Roman, fourteen point, bold. It had been mailed somewhere in the state of Utah on 28 October. The flap had been opened a couple of times and resealed. Reacher eased it back and looked inside. Held it so Neagley could see.

There was nothing in the envelope except a miniature baseball bat. It was the kind of thing sold as a souvenir or given away as a token. It was plain lacquered softwood the colour of honey. It was about an inch wide around the barrel and would have been about fifteen inches long except that it was broken near the end of the handle. It had been broken deliberately. It had been partially sawn through and then snapped where it was weak. The raw end had been scratched and scraped to make it look accidental.

'I don't have a temper problem,' Armstrong said. 'But you're right, my father did. We lived in a small town in Oregon, kind of lonely and isolated. It was a lumber town, basically. It was a mixed sort of place. The mill owners had big houses, the crew chiefs had smaller houses, the crews lived in shanties or rooming houses. There was a school. My mother owned the pharmacy. Down the road was the rest of the state, up the road was virgin forest. It felt like the frontier. It was a little lawless, but it wasn't too bad. There were occasional whores and a lot of drinking, but overall it was just trying to be an American town.'

He went quiet for a moment. Placed his hands palm down on the desk and stared at them.

'I was eighteen,' he said. 'Finished with high school, ready for college, spending my last few weeks at home. My sister was away travelling somewhere. We had a mailbox at the gate. My father had made it himself, in the shape of a miniature lumber mill. It was a nice thing, made out of tiny strips of cedar. At Hallowe'en in the previous year it had been smashed up, you know, the traditional Hallowe'en thing where the tough kids go out cruising with a baseball bat, bashing mailboxes. My father heard it happening and he chased them, but he didn't really see them. We were a little upset, because it was a nice mailbox and destroying it seemed kind of senseless. But he rebuilt it stronger and became kind of obsessed about protecting it. Some nights he hid out and guarded it.'

'And the kids came back,' Neagley said.

Armstrong nodded. 'Late that summer,' he said. 'Two kids, in a truck, with a bat. They were big guys. I didn't really know them, but I'd seen them around before, here and there. They were brothers, I think. Real hard kids, you know, delinquents, bullies from out of town, the sort of kids you always stayed well away from. They took a swing at the box and my dad jumped out at them and there was an argument. They were sneering at him, threatening him, saying bad things about my mother. They said, bring her on out and we'll show her a good time with this bat, better than you can show her. You can imagine the gestures that went with it. So then there was a fight, and my dad got lucky. It was just one of those things, two lucky punches and he won. Or maybe it was his military training. The bat had bust in half, maybe against the box. I thought that would be the end of it, but he dragged the kids into the yard and got some logging chain and some padlocks and got them chained up to a tree. They were kneeling down, facing each other around the trunk. My dad's mind was gone. His temper had kicked in. He was hitting them with the broken bat. I was trying to stop him, but it was impossible. Then he said he was going to show *them* a good time with the bat, with the broken end, unless they begged him not to. So they begged. They begged long and loud.'

He went quiet again.

'I was there all the time,' he said. 'I was trying to calm my father down, that's all. But these guys were looking at me like I was *participating*. There was this *thing* in their eyes, like I was a witness to their worst moment. Like I was seeing them being totally humiliated, which I guess is the worst thing you can do to a bully. There was absolute hatred in their eyes. Against *me*. Like they were saying, you've seen this, so now you have to die. It was literally as bad as that.'

'What happened?' Neagley asked.

'My father kept them there. He said he was going to leave them there all night and start up again in the morning. We went inside and he went to bed and I snuck out again an hour later. I was going to let them go. But they were already gone. They'd gotten out of the chains somehow. Escaped. They never came back. I never saw them again. I went off to college, never really came home again except for visits.'

'And your father died.'

Armstrong nodded. 'He had blood pressure problems, which was understandable, I guess, given his personality. I kind of forgot about the two kids. It was just an episode that had happened in the past. But I didn't *really* forget about them. I always remembered the look in their eyes. I can see it right now. It was stone-cold hatred. It was like two cocky thugs who couldn't stand to be seen any other way than how they chose to be seen. Like I was committing a mortal sin just for happening to see them losing. Like I was *doing* something to them. Like I was their enemy. They stared at me. I gave up trying to understand it. I'm no kind of a psychologist. But I never forgot that look. When that package came I wasn't puzzled for a second who had sent it, even though it's been nearly thirty years.'

'Did you know their names?' Reacher asked.

Armstrong shook his head. 'I didn't know much about them, except I guess they lived in some nearby town. What are you going to do?'

'I know what I'd *like* to do.'

'What's that?'

'I like to break both your arms and never see you again as long as I live. Because if you'd spoken up on election day Froelich would still be alive.'

'Why the hell didn't you?' Neagley asked.

Armstrong shook his head. There were tears in his eyes.

'Because I had no idea it was serious,' he said. 'I really didn't, I promise you, on my daughter's life. Don't you see? I just thought it was supposed to remind me or unsettle me. I wondered whether maybe in their minds they still thought I was in the wrong back then, and it was supposed to be a threat of political embarrassment or exposure or something. Obviously I wasn't worried about that because I wasn't in the wrong back then. Everybody would understand that. And I couldn't see any other logical reason for sending it. I was thirty years older, so were they. I'm a rational adult, I assumed they were. So I thought it was maybe just an unpleasant joke. I didn't conceive of any *danger* in it. I absolutely promise you that. I mean, why would I? So it unsettled me for an hour, and then I dropped it. Maybe I half expected some kind of lame follow-up, but I figured I'd deal with that when it happened. But there *was* no follow-up. It didn't happen. Not as far as I knew. *Because nobody told me.* Until now. Until *you* told me. And according to Stuyvesant you shouldn't be telling me even now. And people have suffered and *died*. Christ, why did he keep me out of the loop? I could have given him the whole story if he'd just *asked*.'

Nobody spoke.

'So you're right and you're wrong,' he said. 'I knew who and why, but I didn't know all along. I didn't know the middle. I knew the beginning, and I knew the end. I knew as soon as the shooting started, believe me. I mean, I just *knew*. It was an unbelievable shock, out of the blue. Like, *this* is the follow-up? It was an insane development. It was like half expecting a rotten tomato to be thrown at me one day and getting a nuclear missile instead. I thought the world had gone mad. You want to blame me for not speaking out, OK, go ahead and blame me, but how could I have known? How could I have predicted this kind of insanity?'

Silence for a beat.

'So that's my guilty secret,' Armstrong said. 'Not that I did anything wrong thirty years ago. But that I didn't have the right kind of imagination to see the implications of the package three weeks ago.'

Nobody spoke.

'Should I tell Stuyvesant now?' Armstrong asked.

'Your choice,' Reacher said.

There was a long pause. Armstrong the man faded away again, and Armstrong the politician came back to replace him.

'I don't want to tell him,' he said. 'Bad for him, bad for me. People have suffered and died. It'll be seen as a serious misjudgement on both our parts. He should have asked, I should have told.'

Reacher nodded. 'So leave it to us. You'll know our secret and we'll know yours.'

'And we'll all live happily ever after.'

'Well, we'll all live,' Reacher said.

'Descriptions?' Neagley asked.

'Just kids,' Armstrong said. 'Maybe my age. I only remember their eyes.'

'What's the name of the town?'

'Underwood, Oregon,' Armstrong said. 'Where my mother still lives. Where I'm going in an hour.'

'And these kids were from the area?'

Armstrong glanced at Reacher. 'And you predicted they'll go home to wait.'

'Yes,' Reacher said. 'I did.'

'And I'm heading right there.'

'Don't worry about it,' Reacher said. 'That theory is way out of date now. I assume they expected you'd remember them, and I assume they didn't anticipate the communication breakdown between yourself and the Secret Service. And they wouldn't want you to be able to lead *them* right to their door. Therefore their door has changed. They don't live in Oregon any more. That's one thing we can be absolutely sure of.'

'So how are you going to find them?'

Reacher shook his head. 'We can't find them. Not now. Not in time. They'll have to find us. In Wyoming. At the memorial service.'

'I'm going there too. With minimal cover.'

'So just hope it's all over before you arrive.'

'Should I tell Stuyvesant?' Armstrong asked again.

'Your choice,' Reacher said again.

'I can't cancel the appearance. That wouldn't be right.'

'No,' Reacher said. 'I guess it wouldn't.'

'I can't tell Stuyvesant now.'

'No,' Reacher said. 'I guess you can't.'

Armstrong said nothing. Reacher stood up to leave, and Neagley did the same.

'One last thing,' Reacher said. 'We think these guys grew up to be cops.'

Armstrong sat still. He started to shake his head, but then he stopped and looked down at the desk. His face clouded, like he was hearing a faint thirty-year-old echo.

'Something during the beating,' he said. 'I only half heard it, and I'm sure I discounted it at the time. But I think at one point they claimed their dad was a cop. They said he could get us in big trouble.'

Reacher said nothing.

The protection agents showed them out. They walked the length of the canvas tent and stepped off the kerb into the street. Turned east and got back on the sidewalk and settled in for the trek to the subway. It was late morning and the air was clear and cold. The neighbourhood was deserted. Nobody was out walking. Neagley opened the envelope Stuyvesant had given her. It contained a cheque for five thousand dollars. The memo line was written up as *professional consultation*. Reacher's envelope contained two cheques. One was for the same five grand fee and the other was for his audit expenses, repaid to the exact penny.

'We should go shopping,' Neagley said. 'We can't go hunting in Wyoming dressed like this.'

'I don't want you to come with me,' Reacher said.

SEVENTEEN

THEY HAD THE ARGUMENT RIGHT THERE ON THE STREET AS THEY walked through Georgetown.

'Worried about my safety?' Neagley asked. 'Because you shouldn't be. Nothing's going to happen to me. I can look after myself. And I can make my own decisions.'

'I'm not worried about your safety,' Reacher said.

'What then? My performance? I'm way better than you.'

'I know you are.'

'So what's your problem?'

'Your licence. You've got something to lose.'

Neagley said nothing.

'You've got a licence, right?' Reacher said. 'To be in the business you're in? And you've got an office and a job and a home and a fixed location. I'm going to disappear after this. You can't do that.'

'Think we're going to get caught?'

'I can afford to take the risk. You can't.'

'There's no risk if we don't get caught.'

Now Reacher said nothing.

'It's like you told Bannon,' she said. 'I'm lying there lined up on these guys, I'm going to get an itch in my spine. I need you to watch my back.'

'This isn't your fight.'

'Why is it yours? Because some woman your brother once dumped got herself killed doing her job? That's tenuous.'

Reacher said nothing.

'OK, it's your fight,' Neagley said. 'I know that. But whatever thing you've got in your head that *makes* it your fight makes it *my* fight too. Because I've got the same thing in *my* head. And even if we didn't think the same, if I had a problem, wouldn't you help me out?'

'I would if you asked.'

'So we're even.'

'Except I'm not asking.'

'Not right now. But you will be. You're two thousand miles from Wyoming and you don't have a credit card to buy a plane ticket with, and I do. You're armed with a folding knife with a three-inch blade and I know a guy in Denver who will give us any weapons we want, no questions asked, and you don't. I can rent a car in Denver to get us the rest of the way, and you can't.'

They walked on, twenty yards, thirty.

'OK,' Reacher said. 'I'm asking.'

'We'll get the clothes in Denver,' she said. 'I know some good places.'

They made it to Denver before three in the afternoon mountain time. The high plains lay all around them, tan and dormant. The air was thin and bitter cold. There was no snow yet, but it was coming. The runway ploughs were lined up and ready. The snowdrift fences were prepared. The car rental companies had shipped their sedans south and brought in plenty of new four-wheel-drives. Neagley signed for a GMC Yukon at the Avis counter. They shuttled to the lot and picked it up. It was black and shiny and looked a lot like Froelich's Suburban except it was two feet shorter.

They drove it into the city. It was a long, long way. Space seemed infinitely available even after D.C., which wasn't the most crowded place in the east. They parked in a downtown garage and walked three blocks and Neagley found the store she was looking for. It was an all-purpose outdoor equipment place. It had everything from boots and compasses to zinc stuff designed to stop you getting sunburn on your nose. They bought a birdwatcher's spotting scope and a hiker's large-scale map of central Wyoming and then they moved to the clothing racks. They were full of the kind of stuff you could use halfway up the Rockies and then wear around town without looking like a complete idiot. Neagley went for a walker's heavy-duty outfit in greens and browns. Reacher duplicated his Atlantic City purchases at twice the price and twice the quality. This time he added a hat, and a pair of gloves. He dressed in the changing cubicle. Left Joe's last surviving suit stuffed in the garbage can.

Neagley found a pay phone on the street and stopped in the cold long enough to make a short call. Then they went back to the truck and she drove it out of the garage and through the city centre towards the dubious part of town. There was a strong smell of dog food in the air.

'There's a factory here,' she said.

Reacher nodded. 'No kidding.'

She came off a narrow street into some kind of industrial park and nosed through a tangle of low-built metal structures. There were linoleum dealers and brake shops and places where you could get four snow tyres for ninety-nine bucks and other places where you could get your steering realigned for twenty. On one corner there was a long low workshop standing on its own in the centre of a quarter-acre of cracked blacktop. The building had a closed roll-up door and a hand-painted sign that read: *Eddie Brown Engineering.*

'This is your guy?' Reacher asked.

Neagley nodded. 'What do we want?'

Reacher shrugged. 'No point planning it to death. Something short and something long, one of each, plus some ammunition, I guess. That should do it.'

She stopped in front of the roll-up door and hit the horn. A guy came out of a personnel entrance and got halfway to the car before he saw who it was. He was tall and heavy through the neck and shoulders. He had short fair hair and an open amiable face, but he had big hands and thick wrists and wasn't the sort of guy you'd mess with on a whim. He sketched a wave and ducked back inside and a moment later the big door starting rolling up. Neagley drove in under it and it came back down behind them.

On the inside the building was about half the size it should have been, but apart from that it looked convincing. The floor was grease-stained concrete and there were metalworkers' lathes here and there, and drilling machines and stacks of raw sheet metal and bundles of steel rods. But the back wall was ten feet closer on the inside than the exterior proportions dictated. Clearly there was a handsome-sized room concealed behind it.

'This is Eddie Brown,' Neagley said.

'Not my real name,' the big guy said.

He accessed the concealed room by pulling on a big pile of scrap metal. It was all welded together and welded in turn to a steel panel hidden behind it. The whole thing swung open on silent oiled hinges like a giant three-dimensional door. The guy calling himself Eddie Brown led them through it into a whole different situation.

The concealed room was as clean as a hospital. It was painted white and lined on all four sides by shelves and racks. On three walls the shelves held handguns, some of them boxed, some of them loose. The racks were full of long guns, rifles and carbines and shotguns and machine guns, yards of them, all of them neat and parallel. The air was full of the stink of gun oil. The fourth wall was lined like a library with boxes of ammunition. Reacher could smell the new brass and the crisp cardboard and faint traces of powder.

'I'm impressed,' he said.

'Take what you need,' Eddie said.

'Where do the serial numbers lead to?'

'The Austrian Army,' Eddie said. 'They kind of fizzle out after that.'

Ten minutes later they were back on the road, with Reacher's new jacket carefully spread out in the Yukon's load space over two nine-millimetre Steyr GBs, a Heckler & Koch MP5 unsilenced machine gun, an M16 rifle, and boxes full of two hundred rounds for each weapon.

* * *

They entered Wyoming after dark, driving north on I-25. They turned left at Cheyenne and picked up I-80. They rolled west to Laramie and then headed north. The town called Grace was still five hours away, well beyond Casper. The map showed it nestled in the middle of nowhere between towering mountains on one side and infinite grasslands on the other.

'We'll stop in Medicine Bow,' Reacher said. 'Sounds like a cool place. We'll aim to get to Grace at dawn tomorrow.'

Medicine Bow didn't look like much of a cool place in the dark, but it had a motel about two miles out with rooms available. Neagley paid for them. Then they found a steakhouse a mile in the other direction and ate twelve-ounce sirloins that cost less than a drink in D.C. The place closed up around them so they took the hint and headed back to their rooms. Reacher left his coat in the truck, to hide the firepower from curious eyes. They said goodnight in the lot. Reacher went straight to bed. He heard Neagley in the shower. She was singing to herself. He could hear it, through the wall.

He woke up at four in the morning, Saturday. Neagley was showering again, and still singing. He thought: *when the hell does she sleep?* He rolled out of bed and headed for the bathroom. Turned his shower on hot, which must have made hers run cold, because he heard a muffled scream through the wall. So he turned it off again and waited until he heard her finish. Then he showered and dressed and met her out by the car. It was still pitch dark. Still very cold. There were flakes of snow blowing in from the west. They were drifting slowly through the parking lot lights.

'Can't find any coffee,' Neagley said.

They found some an hour north. A roadside diner was opening for breakfast. They saw its lights a mile away. It was next to the mouth of a dirt road leading down through the darkness to the Medicine Bow National Forest. The diner looked like a barn, long and low, made out of red boards. Cold outside, warm inside. They sat at a table by a curtained window and ate eggs and bacon and toast and drank strong bitter coffee.

'OK, we'll call them one and two,' Neagley said. 'One is the

Bismarck guy. You'll recognize him. Two is the guy from the garage video. We might recognize him from his build. But we don't really know what he looks like.'

Reacher nodded. 'So we'll look for the Bismarck guy hanging out with some other guy. No point planning it to death.'

'You don't sound very enthusiastic.'

'You should go home.'

'Now that I've gotten you here?'

'I've got a bad feeling about this.'

'You're uptight that Froelich was killed. That's all. Doesn't mean anything's going to happen to me.'

He said nothing.

'We're two against two,' Neagley said. 'You and me against two bozos, and you're worried about it?'

'Not very,' he said.

'Maybe they won't even show. Bannon figured they'd know it was a trap.'

'They'll show,' Reacher said. 'They've been challenged. It's a testosterone thing. And they've got more than enough screws loose to jump right on it.'

'Nothing's going to happen to me, if they do.'

'I'd feel bad if it did.'

'It's not going to,' she said.

'Tell me I'm not making you do this.'

'My own free will,' she said.

He nodded. 'So let's go.'

They got back on the road. Snowflakes hung in the headlight beams. They drifted in weightlessly from the west and shone bright in the light and then whipped backward as they drove. They were big flakes, dry and powdery, not many of them. The road was narrow. It wandered left and right. The surface was lumpy. All around it in the darkness was a vastness so large it sucked the noise of the car away into nothing. They were driving in a bright tunnel of silence, leaping ahead from one lonely snowflake to the next.

'I guess Casper will have a police department,' Reacher said.

Neagley nodded at the wheel. 'Could be a hundred strong. Casper is nearly as big as Cheyenne. Nearly as big as Bismarck, actually.'

'And they'll be responsible for Grace,' Reacher said.

'Alongside the State troopers, I guess.'

'So any other cops we find there are our guys.'

'You're still certain they're cops?'

He nodded. 'It's the only way everything makes sense. The initial contact with Nendick and Andretti in the cop bars, the familiarity with the NCIC, the access to the government weapons. Plus the way they slip in and out everywhere. Crowds, confusion, a gold shield gets you anywhere. And if Armstrong's right and their dad was a cop, that's a pretty good predictor. It's a family trade, like the military.'

'My dad wasn't in the military.'

'But mine was, so there's fifty per cent right away. Better than most other professions. And you know what the clincher is?'

'What?'

'Something we should have figured long ago. But we just skated right on by. We missed it, totally. *The two dead Armstrongs.* How the hell do you just *find* two white guys with fair hair and blue eyes and the right dates of birth and the right faces and above all the right first and last names? That's a very tall order. But these guys did it. And there's only one practical way of doing it, which is the national DMV database. Driving licence information, names, addresses, dates of birth, photographs. It's all right there, everything you need. And nobody can get into it, except cops, who can dial it right up.'

Neagley was silent for a moment.

'OK, they *are* cops,' she said.

'They sure are. And we're brain dead for not spotting it on Tuesday.'

'But cops would have heard of Armstrong long ago, wouldn't they?'

'Why would they? Cops know about their own little world, that's all, same as anybody else. If you worked in some rural police department in Maine or Florida or outside San Diego you might know the New York Giants' quarterback or the Chicago White Sox centre fielder but there's no reason why you would have heard of North Dakota's junior senator. Unless you were a politics junkie, and most people aren't.'

Neagley drove on. Way to the right, far to the east, a narrow band of sky was a fraction lighter than it had been. It had turned the colour of dark charcoal against the blackness beyond it. The snow was no heavier, no lighter. The big lazy flakes drifted in from the mountains, floating level, sometimes rising.

'So which is it?' she asked. 'Maine or Florida or San Diego? We need to know, because if they're flying in they won't be armed with anything they can't pick up here.'

'California is a possibility,' Reacher said. 'Oregon isn't. They wouldn't have revealed their specific identity to Armstrong if they still lived in Oregon. Nevada is a possibility. Or Utah or Idaho. Anywhere else is too far.'

'For what?'

'To be on a reasonable radius from Sacramento. How long does a stolen cooler of ice last?'

Neagley said nothing.

'Nevada or Utah or Idaho,' Reacher said. 'That's my guess. Not California. I think they wanted a state line between them and the place they went for the thumb. Feels better, psychologically. I think they're a long day's drive from Sacramento. Which means they're probably a long day's drive from here, too, in the other direction. So I think they'll be coming in by road, armed to the teeth.'

'When?'

'Today, if they've got any sense.'

'The bat was mailed in Utah,' Neagley said.

Reacher nodded. 'OK, so scratch Utah. I don't think they wanted to mail anything in their home state.'

'So Idaho or Nevada,' Neagley said. 'We better watch for licence plates.'

'This is a tourist destination. There are going to be plenty of out-of-state plates. Like we've got Colorado plates.'

'How will they aim to do it?'

'Edward Fox,' Reacher said. 'They want to survive, and they're reasonable with a rifle. Hundred and twenty yards in Minnesota, ninety in D.C. They'll aim to get him in the church doorway, somewhere like that. Maybe out in the graveyard. Drop him right next to somebody else's headstone.'

Neagley slowed and turned right onto Route 220. It was a

better road, wider, newer blacktop. It ran with a river wandering next to it. The sky was lighter in the east. Up ahead was a faint glow from the city of Casper, twenty miles north. The snow was still blowing in from the west, slow and lazy.

'So what's our plan?' Neagley asked.

'We need to see the terrain,' Reacher said.

He looked sideways out of the window. He had seen nothing but darkness since leaving Denver.

They stopped on the outer edge of Casper for gas and more coffee and a bathroom. Then Reacher took a turn at the wheel. He picked up Route 87 north out of town and drove fast for thirty miles because Route 87 was also I-25 again and was wide and straight. And he drove fast because they were late. Dawn was in full swing to the east and they were still well short of Grace. The sky was pink and beautiful and the light came in brilliant horizontal shafts and lit the mountainsides in the west. They were meandering through the foothills. On their right, to the east, the world was basically flat all the way to Chicago and beyond. On their left, distant in the west, the Rocky Mountains reared two miles high. The lower slopes were dotted with stands of pine and the peaks were white with snow and streaked with grey crags. For miles either side of the ribbon of road was high desert, with sagebrush and tan grasses blazing purple in the early sun.

'Been here before?' Neagley asked.

'No,' he said.

'We need to turn,' she said. 'Soon, east towards Thunder Basin.'

He repeated the name in his head, because he liked the sound of the words. *Thunder Basin. Thunder Basin.*

He made a shallow right off the highway onto a narrow county road. It was signposted up to Midwest and Edgerton. The land fell away to the east. Pines a hundred feet tall threw morning shadows a hundred yards long. There was endless ragged grassland interrupted here and there by the remains of old industrial enterprises. There were square stone foundations a foot high and tangles of old iron.

'Oil,' Neagley said. 'And coal mining. All closed down eighty years ago.'

'The land looks awful flat,' Reacher said.

But he knew the flatness was deceptive. The low sun showed him creases and crevices and small escarpments that were nothing compared to the mountains on his left but were a long way from being *flat*. They were in a transition area, where the mountains shaded randomly into the high plains. The geological tumult of a million years ago rippled outward all the way to Nebraska, frozen in time, leaving enough cover to hide a walking man in a million different places.

'We need it to be totally flat,' Neagley said.

Reacher nodded at the wheel. 'Except for one little hill a hundred yards from where Armstrong's going to be. And another little hill a hundred yards back from it, where we can watch from.'

'It isn't going to be that easy.'

'It never is,' Reacher said.

They drove on, another whole hour. They were heading north and east into emptiness. The sun rose well clear of the horizon. The sky was banded pink and purple. Behind them the Rockies blazed with reflected light. Ahead and to the right the grasslands ran into the distance like a stormy ocean. There was no more snow in the air. The big lazy flakes had disappeared.

'Turn here,' Neagley said.

'Here?' He slowed to a stop and looked at the turn. It was just a dirt road, leading south to the middle of nowhere.

'There's a town down there?' he asked.

'According to the map,' Neagley said.

He backed up and made the turn. The dirt road ran a mile through pines and then broke out with a view of absolutely nothing.

'Keep going,' Neagley said.

They drove on, twenty miles, thirty. The road rose and fell. Then it peaked and the land fell away in front of them into a fifty-mile-wide bowl of grass and sage. The road ran ahead through it straight south like a faint pencil line and crossed a river in the base of the bowl. Two more roads ran in to the bridge from nowhere. There were tiny buildings scattered randomly. The whole thing looked like a capital letter K, lightly peppered with habitation where the strokes of the letter met at the bridge.

'That's Grace, Wyoming,' Neagley said. 'Where this road crosses the south fork of the Cheyenne river.'

Reacher eased the Yukon to a stop. Put it in park and crossed his arms on the top of the wheel. Leaned forward with his chin on his hands and stared ahead through the windshield.

'We should be on horses,' he said.

'Wearing white hats,' Neagley said. 'With Colt .45s.'

'I'll stick with the Steyrs,' Reacher said. 'How many ways in?'

Neagley traced her finger over the map. 'North or south,' she said. 'On this road. The other two roads don't go anywhere. They peter out in the brush. Maybe they head out to old cattle ranches.'

'Which way will the bad guys come?'

'Nevada, they'll come in from the south. Idaho, from the north.'

'So we can't stay right here and block the road.'

'They might be down there already.'

One of the buildings was a tiny pinprick of white in a square of green. *Froelich's church*, he thought. He opened his door and got out of the car. Walked around to the tailgate and came back with the birdwatcher's spotting scope. It was like half of a huge pair of binoculars. He steadied it against the open door and put it to his eye.

The optics compressed the view into a flat grainy picture that danced and quivered with his heartbeat. He focused until it was like looking down at the town from a half-mile away. The river was a narrow cut. The bridge was a stone structure. The roads were all dirt. There were more buildings than he had first thought. The church stood alone in a tended acre inside the south angle of the K. It had a stone foundation and the rest of it was clapboard painted white. It would have looked right at home in Massachusetts. Its grounds widened out to the south and were mowed grass studded with headstones.

South of the graveyard was a fence, and behind the fence was a cluster of two-storey buildings made of weathered cedar. They were set at random angles to each other. North of the church were more of the same. Houses, stores, barns. Along the short legs of the K were more buildings. Some of them were painted white. They were close together near the centre of town, farther apart as the distance increased. The river ran blue and clear, east and north into the sea of grass. There were cars and pick-ups parked here and there. Some pedestrian activity. It looked like the population might reach a couple of hundred.

'It was a cattle town, I guess,' Neagley said. 'They brought the railroad in as far as Casper, through Douglas. They must have driven the herds sixty, seventy miles south and picked it up there.'

'So what do they do now?' Reacher asked.

The town wobbled in the scope as he spoke.

'No idea,' she said. 'Maybe they all invest on-line.'

He passed her the scope and she refocused and stared down through it. He watched the lens move fractionally up and down and side to side as she covered the whole area.

'They'll set up to the south,' she said. 'All the pre-service activity will happen south of the church. They've got a couple of old barns a hundred yards out, and some natural cover.'

'How will they aim to get away?'

The scope moved an eighth of an inch, to the right.

'They'll expect roadblocks north and south,' she said. 'Local cops. That's a no-brainer. Their badges might get them through, but I wouldn't be counting on it. This is a whole different situation. There might be confusion, but there won't be crowds.'

'So how?'

'I know how I'd do it,' she said. 'I'd ignore the roads altogether. I'd take off across the grass, due west. Forty miles of open country in some big four-wheel-drive, and you hit the highway. I doubt the Casper PD has got a helicopter. Or the Highway Patrol. There are only two highways in the whole state.'

'Armstrong will come in a helicopter,' Reacher said. 'Probably from some air force base in Nebraska.'

'But they won't use his helicopter to chase the bad guys.

They'll be exfiltrating him or taking him to a hospital. I'm sure that's some kind of standard protocol.'

'Highway Patrol would set up north and south on the highway. They'll have nearly an hour's warning.'

Neagley lowered the scope and nodded. 'I'd anticipate that. So I'd drive straight *across* the highway and get back off-road. West of the highway is ten thousand square miles of nothing between Casper and the Wind River Reservation, with only one major road through it. They'd be long gone before somebody whistled up a helicopter and started the search.'

'That's a bold plan.'

'I'd go for it,' Neagley said.

Reacher smiled. 'I know *you* would. Question is, will these guys? I'm wondering if they'll take one look and turn round and forget about it.'

'Doesn't matter. We'll take them down while they're looking. We don't need to catch them in the act.'

Reacher climbed back into the driver's seat.

'Let's go to work,' he said.

The bowl was very shallow. They lost maybe a hundred feet of elevation in the twenty miles they drove before they reached the town. The road was hard-packed dirt, smooth as glass, beautifully scraped and contoured. An annual art, Reacher guessed, performed anew every year when the winter snows melted and the spring rains finished. It was the kind of road Model T Fords rolled down in documentary films. It curved as it approached the town so that the bridge could cross the river at an exact right angle.

The bridge seemed to represent the geographic centre of town. There was a general store that offered postal service and a breakfast counter. There was a forge set back behind it that had probably fixed ranch machinery way back in history. There was a feed supplier's office and a hardware store. There was a one-pump gas station with a sign that read: *Springs Repaired.* There were sidewalks made of wood fronting the buildings. They ran like boat docks, floating on the earth. There was a quiet leathery man loading groceries into a pick-up bed.

'They won't come here,' Reacher said. 'This is the most exposed place I've ever seen.'

Neagley shook her head. 'They won't know that until they've seen it for themselves. They might be in and out in ten minutes, but ten minutes is all we need.'

'Where are we going to stay?'

She pointed. 'Over there.'

It was a plain-fronted red cedar building with numerous small windows and a sign that read: *Clean Rooms.*

'Terrific,' Reacher said.

'Drive around,' Neagley said. 'Let's get a feel for the place.'

A letter K has only four options for exploration, and they had already covered the northern leg on the way in. Reacher backed up to the bridge and struck out north and east, following the river. That road led past eight houses, four on each side, and then narrowed after another half-mile to a poor stony track. There was a barbed-wire fence lost in the grass on the left, and another on the right.

'Ranch land,' Neagley said.

The ranches themselves were clearly miles away. Fragments of the road were visible as it rose and fell over gentle contours into the distance. Reacher turned the truck round and headed back and turned down the short south-east leg. It had more houses and they were closer together, but it was otherwise similar. It narrowed after the same distance and ran on towards nothing visible. There was more barbed wire and an inexplicable wooden shed with no door. Inside the shed was a rusting pick-up truck with pale weedy grass growing up all round it. It looked like it had been parked there back when Richard Nixon was vice president.

'OK, go south,' Neagley said. 'Let's see the church.'

The south leg led seventy miles to Douglas, and they drove the first three miles of it. The town's power and telephone lines came in from that direction, strung on tarred poles, looping on into the distance, following the road. The road passed the church and the graveyard, then the cluster of cedar buildings, then a couple of abandoned cattle barns, then maybe twenty or thirty small houses, and then the town finished and there was just infinite grassland ahead. But it wasn't flat. There were crevices and crevasses worn smooth by ten thousand years of winds and weather. They undulated calmly, up and down to maximum depths of ten or twelve feet, like slow ocean swells. They were all connected in a network. The grass itself was a yard high, brown and dead and brittle. It swayed in waves under the perpetual breeze.

'You could hide an infantry company in there,' Neagley said.

Reacher turned the car and headed back towards the church. Pulled over and parked level with the graveyard. The church itself was very similar to the one outside Bismarck. It had the same steep roof over the nave and the same blocky square tower. It had a clock on the tower and a weathervane and a flag, and a lightning rod. It was white, but not as bright. Reacher glanced west to the horizon and saw grey clouds massing over the distant mountains.

'It's going to snow,' he said.

'We can't see anything from here,' Neagley said.

She was right. The church was built right in the river valley bottom. Its foundation was probably the lowest structure in town. The road to the north was visible for maybe a hundred yards. Same in the south. It ran in both directions and rose over gentle humps and disappeared from sight.

'They could be right on top of us before we know it,' Neagley said. 'We need to be able to see them coming.'

Reacher nodded. Opened his door and climbed out of the car. Neagley joined him and they walked towards the church. The air was cold and dry. The graveyard lawn was dead under their feet. It felt like the beginning of winter. There was a new grave site marked out with cotton tape. It lay to the west of the church, in virgin grass on the end of a row of weathered headstones. Reacher detoured to take a look. There were four Froelich graves in a line. Soon to be a fifth, on some sad day in the near future. He looked at the rectangle of tape and imagined the hole dug deep and crisp and square.

Then he stepped away and looked around. There was flat empty land opposite the church on the east side of the road. It was a big enough space to land a helicopter. He stood and imagined it coming in, rotors thumping, turning in the air to face the passenger door towards the church, setting down. He imagined Armstrong climbing out. Crossing the road. Approaching the church. The vicar would probably greet him near the door. He stepped sideways and stood where Armstrong might stand and raised his eyes. Scanned the land to the south and west. *Bad news*. There was some elevation there, and about a hundred and fifty yards out there were waves and shadows in the moving grass that must mean dips and crevices in the earth beneath it. There were more beyond that distance, all the way out to infinity.

'How good do you think they are?' he asked.

Neagley shrugged. 'They're always either better or worse than you expect. They've shown some proficiency so far. Shooting downhill, thin air, through grass, I'd be worried out to about five hundred yards.'

'And if they miss Armstrong they'll hit somebody else by mistake.'

'Stuyvesant needs to bring a surveillance helicopter too. This angle is hopeless, but you could see everything from the air.'

'Armstrong won't let him,' Reacher said. 'But we've got the air. We've got the church tower.'

He turned and walked back towards it.

'Forget the rooming house,' he said. 'This is where we're going to stay. We'll see them coming, north or south, night or day. It'll all be over before Stuyvesant or Armstrong even get here.'

They were ten feet from the church door when it opened and a clergyman stepped out, closely followed by an old couple. The clergyman was middle-aged and looked very earnest. The old couple were both maybe sixty years old. The man was tall and stooped, and a little underweight. The woman was still good-looking, a little above average height, trim and nicely dressed. She had short fair hair turning grey the way fair hair does. Reacher knew exactly who she was, immediately. And she knew who he was, or thought she did. She stopped talking and stopped walking and just stared at him the same way her daughter had. She looked at his face, confused, like she was comparing similarities and differences against a mental image.

'You?' she said. 'Or is it?'

Her face was strained and tired. She was wearing no make-up. Her eyes were dry, but they hadn't been for the last two days. That was clear. They were rimmed with red and lined and swollen.

'I'm his brother,' Reacher said. 'I'm very sorry for your loss.'

'You should be,' she said. 'Because this is entirely Joe's fault.'

'Is it?'

'He made her change jobs, didn't he? He wouldn't date a co-worker, so *she* had to change. *He* wouldn't change. She went over to the dangerous side, while he stayed exactly where he was, safe and sound. And now look what's come of it.'

Reacher paused.

'I think she was happy where she was,' he said. 'She could have changed back, you know, afterwards, if she wasn't. But she didn't. So I think that means she wanted to stay there. She was a fine agent, doing important work.'

'How could she change back? Was she supposed to see him every day like nothing had happened?'

'I meant she could have waited the year, and then changed back.'

'What difference does a year make? He broke her heart. How could she *ever* work for him again?'

Reacher said nothing.

'Is he coming here?' she asked.

'No,' Reacher said. 'He's not.'

'Good,' she said. 'Because he wouldn't be welcome.'

'No, I guess he wouldn't,' Reacher said.

'I suppose he's too *busy*,' she said.

She walked off, towards the dirt road. The clergyman followed her, and so did Froelich's father. But then he hesitated and turned back.

'She knows it's not really Joe's fault,' he said. 'We both know Mary Ellen was doing what she wanted.'

Reacher nodded. 'She was terrific at it.'

'Was she?'

'Best they ever had.'

The old man nodded, like he was satisfied.

'How is Joe?' he asked. 'I met him a couple of times.'

'He died,' Reacher said. 'Five years ago. In the line of duty.'

There was quiet for a moment.

'I'm very sorry,' the old man said.

'But don't tell Mrs Froelich,' Reacher said. 'If it helps her not to know.'

The old man nodded again and turned away and set off after his wife with a strange loping stride.

'See?' Neagley said quietly. 'Not everything is your fault.'

There was a notice board planted in the ground near the church door. It was like a very slim cabinet mounted on sturdy wooden legs. It had glass doors. Behind the doors was a square yard of green felt with slim cotton tapes thumbtacked diagonally all over it. Notices typed on a manual typewriter were slipped behind the tapes. At the top was a permanent list of regular Sunday services. The first was held every week at eight o'clock in the morning. This was clearly a denomination that demanded a high degree of commitment from its parishioners. Next to the permanent list was a hastily typed announcement that this Sunday's eight o'clock service would be dedicated to the memory of Mary Ellen Froelich. Reacher checked his watch and shivered in the cold.

'Twenty-two hours,' he said. 'Time to lock and load.'

They brought the Yukon nearer to the church and opened the tailgate. Bent over together and loaded all four weapons. They took a Steyr each. Neagley took the H&K and Reacher took the M16. They distributed the spare rounds between them, as appropriate. Then they locked the car and left it.

'Is it OK to bring guns into a church?' Neagley asked.

'It's OK in Texas,' Reacher said. 'Probably compulsory here.'

They hauled the oak door open and stepped inside. It was very similar to the Bismarck building. Reacher wondered briefly whether rural communities had bought their churches by mail order, the same as everything else. It had the same parchment-white paint, the same shiny pews, the same pulpit. The same three bell ropes hanging down inside the tower. The same staircase. They went all the way up to the high ledge and found a ladder bolted to the wall, with a trapdoor above it.

'Home sweet home,' Reacher said.

He led the way up the ladder and through the trapdoor and into the bell chamber. The bell chamber was not the same as the one in Bismarck. It had a clock added into it. There was a four-foot cube of brass machinery mounted centrally on iron girders just above the bells. The clock had two faces, both driven simultaneously by the same gears inside the cube. Long iron shafts ran straight out from the cube, through the walls, through the backs of the faces, all the way to the external hands. The faces were mounted in the openings where the louvres had been, to the east and the west. The machinery was ticking loudly. Gear wheels and ratchets were clicking. They were setting up tiny sympathetic resonances in the bells themselves.

'We've got no view east or west,' Reacher said.

Neagley shrugged. 'North and south is all we need,' she said. 'That's where the road runs.'

'I guess,' he said. 'You take the south.'

He ducked under the girders and the iron shafts and crawled over to the louvre facing north. Knelt up and looked out. Got a perfect view. He could see the bridge and the river. He could see the whole town. He could see the dirt road leading north. Maybe ten straight miles of it. It was completely empty.

'You OK?' he called.

'Excellent,' Neagley called back. 'I can almost see Colorado.'

'Shout when you spot something.'

'You too.'

The clock ticked *thunk, thunk, thunk*, once a second. The sound was loud and precise and tireless. He glanced back at the mechanism and wondered whether it would drive him crazy before it sent him to sleep. He heard expensive alloy touching wood ten feet behind him as Neagley put her sub-machine gun down. He laid his M16 on the boards next to his knees. Squirmed around until he was as comfortable as he was going to get. Then he settled in to watch and wait.

EIGHTEEN

THE AIR WAS COLD AND SEVENTY FEET ABOVE GROUND THE BREEZE was a wind. It came in through the louvres and scoured his eyes and made them water. They had been there two hours, and nothing had happened. They had seen nothing and heard nothing except for the clock. They had learned its sound. Each *thunk* was made up of a bundle of separate metallic frequencies, starting low down with the muted bass ring of the bigger gears, ranging upward to the tiny treble click of the escapement lever, and finishing with a faint time-delayed *ding* resonating off the smallest bell. It was the sound of madness.

'I got something,' Neagley called. 'SUV, I think, coming in from the south.'

He took a quick look north and got up off his knees. He was stiff and cold and very uncomfortable. He picked up the bird-watcher's scope.

'Catch,' he called.

He tossed it in an upward loop over the clock shaft. Neagley twisted and caught it one-handed and turned back to the louvre panel. Put the scope to her eye.

'Might be a new model Chevy Tahoe,' she called. 'Light gold metallic. Sun is on the windshield. No ID on the occupants.'

Reacher looked north again. The road was still empty. He could see ten miles. It would take ten minutes to cover ten miles even at a fast cruise. He stood up straight and stretched. Ducked under the clock shafts and crawled over next to Neagley. She moved to her right and he wiped his eyes and stared out south. There was a tiny gold speck on the road, all alone, maybe five miles away.

'Not exactly busy,' she said. 'Is it?'

She passed him the scope. He refocused it and propped its weight on a louvre and squinted through it. The telephoto compression held the truck motionless. It looked like it was bouncing and swaying on the road but making absolutely no forward progress at all. It looked dirty and travel-stained. It had a big chrome front fender all smeared with mud and salt. The windshield was streaked. The sun's reflection made it impossible to see who was riding in it.

'Why is it still sunny?' he said. 'I thought it was going to snow.'

'Look to the west,' Neagley said.

He put the scope down and turned and put the left side of his face tight against the louvres. Closed his right eye and looked out sideways with his left. The sky was split in two. In the west it was almost black with clouds. In the east it was pale blue and hazy. Giant multiple shafts of sunlight blazed down through mist where the two weather systems met.

'Unbelievable,' he said.

'Some kind of inversion,' Neagley said. 'I hope it stays where it is or we'll freeze our asses off up here.'

'It's about fifty miles away.'

'And the wind generally blows in from the west.'

'Great.'

He picked up the scope again and checked on the golden truck. It was maybe a mile closer, bucking and swaying on the dirt. It must have been doing about sixty.

'What do you think?' Neagley said.

'Nice vehicle,' he said. 'Awful colour.'

He watched it come on another mile and then handed back the scope.

'I should check north,' he said.

He crawled under the clock shaft and made it back to his own louvre. There was nothing happening in the north. The road was still empty. He reversed his previous manoeuvre and put his right cheek against the wood and closed his left eye with his hand and checked west again. The snow clouds were clamped down on the mountains. It was like night and day, with an abrupt transition where the foothills started.

'It's a Chevy Tahoe for sure,' Neagley called. 'It's slowing down.'

'See the plate?'

'Not yet. It's about a mile out now, slowing.'

'See who's in it?'

'I've got sun and tinted glass. No ID. Half a mile out now.'

Reacher glanced north. No traffic.

'Nevada plates, I think,' Neagley called. 'Can't read them. They're all covered in mud. It's right on the edge of town. It's going real slow now. Looks like a reconnaissance cruise. It's not stopping. Still no ID on the occupants. It's getting real close now. I'm looking right down at the roof. Dark tint on the rear side glass. I'm going to lose them any second. It's right underneath us now.'

Reacher stood up tight against the wall and peered down at the best angle he could get. The way the louvres were set in the frame gave him a blind spot maybe forty feet deep.

'Where is it now?' he called.

'Don't know.'

He heard the sound of an engine over the moan of the wind. A big V-8, turning slowly. He stared down and a metallic gold hood slid into view. Then a roof. Then a rear window. The truck passed all the way underneath him and rolled through the town and crossed the bridge at maybe twenty miles an hour. It stayed slow for a hundred more yards. Then it accelerated. It picked up speed fast.

'Scope,' he called.

Neagley tossed it back to him and he rested it on a louvre and watched the truck drive away to the north. The rear window was tinted black and there was an arc where the wiper had cleared the salt spray. The rear bumper was chrome. He could see raised lettering that read *Chevrolet Tahoe*. The rear plate was indecipherable. It was caked with road salt. He could see hand marks where the tailgate had been raised and lowered. It looked like a truck that had done some serious mileage in the last day or two.

'It's heading out,' he called.

He watched it in the scope all the way. It bounced and swayed and grew smaller and smaller. It took ten whole minutes to drive all the way out of his field of vision. It rose up over the last hump in the road and then disappeared with a last flash of sun on gold paint.

'Anything more?' he called.

'Clear to the south,' Neagley called back.

'I'm going down for the map. You can watch both directions while I'm gone. Do some limbo dancing under this damn clock thing.'

He crawled to the trapdoor and got his feet on the ladder. Went down, stiff and sore and cold. He made it to the ledge and down the winding staircase. Out of the tower and out of the church into the weak midday sun. He limped across the graveyard towards the car. Saw Froelich's father standing right next to it, looking at it like it might answer a question. The old guy saw his approach reflected in the window glass and spun round to face him.

'Mr Stuyvesant is on the phone for you,' he said. 'From the Secret Service office in Washington D.C.'

'Now?'

'He's been holding twenty minutes. I've been trying to find you.'

'Where's the phone?'

'At the house.'

The Froelich house was one of the white buildings on the short south-eastern leg of the K. The old guy led the way with his long loping stride. Reacher had to hurry to keep up with him. The house had a front garden with a white picket fence. It was full of herbs and cottage plants that had died back from the cold. Inside it was dim and fragrant. There were wide dark boards on the floors. Rag rugs here and there. The old guy led the way into a front parlour. There was an antique table under the window with a telephone and a photograph on it. The telephone was an old model with a heavy receiver and a plaited cord insulated with brown fabric. The photograph was of Froelich herself, aged about eighteen. Her hair was a little longer than she had kept it, and a little lighter. Her face was open and innocent, and her smile was sweet. Her eyes were dark blue, alive with hopes for the future.

There was no chair next to the table. Clearly the Froelichs came from a generation that preferred to stand up while talking on the telephone. Reacher unravelled the cord and held the phone to his ear.

'Stuyvesant?' he said.

'Reacher? You got any good news for me?'

'Not yet.'

'What's the situation?'

'The service is scheduled for eight o'clock,' Reacher said. 'But I guess you know that already.'

'What else do I need to know?'

'You coming in by chopper?'

'That's the plan. He's still in Oregon right now. We're going to fly him to an air base in South Dakota and then take a short hop in an air force helicopter. We'll have eight people altogether, including me.'

'He only wanted three.'

'He can't object. We're all her friends.'

'Can't you have a mechanical problem? Just stay in South Dakota?'

'He'd know. And the air force wouldn't play anyway. They wouldn't want to go down in history as the reason why he couldn't make it.'

Reacher stood and looked out of the window. 'OK, so you'll see the church easy enough. You'll land across the street to the east. There's a good place right there. Then he's got about fifty yards to the church door. I can absolutely guarantee the immediate surroundings. We're going to be in the church all night. But you're going to hate what you see farther out. There's about a hundred-fifty-degree field of fire to the south and west. It's completely open. And there's plenty of concealment.'

Silence in D.C.

'I can't do it,' Stuyvesant said. 'I can't bring him into that. Or any of my people. I'm not going to lose anybody else.'

'So just hope for the best,' Reacher said.

'Not my way. You're going to have to deliver.'

'We will if we can.'

'How will I know? You don't have radios. Cell phones won't work out there. And it's too cumbersome to keep on using this land line.'

Reacher paused for a second.

'We've got a black Yukon,' he said. 'Right now it's parked on the road, right next to the church, to the east. If it's still there when you show up, then pull out and go home. Armstrong will just have to swallow it. But if it's gone, then we're gone, and we won't be gone unless we've delivered, you follow?'

'OK, understood,' Stuyvesant said. 'A black Yukon east of the church, we abort. No Yukon, we land. Have you searched the town?'

'We can't do a house-to-house. But it's a very small place. Strangers are going to stand out, believe me.'

'Nendick came round. He's talking a little. He says the same as Andretti. He was approached by the two of them and took them to be cops.'

'They are cops. We're definite about that. Did you get descriptions?'

'No. He's still thinking about his wife. Didn't seem right to tell him he probably didn't need to.'

'Poor guy.'

'I'd like to get some closure for him. At least find her body, maybe.'

'I'm not planning an arrest here.'

Silence in D.C.

'OK,' Stuyvesant said. 'I guess we won't be seeing you either way. So, good luck.'

'You too,' Reacher said.

He put the receiver back in the cradle and tidied the cord into a neat curl on the table. Looked out at the view. The window faced north and east across an empty ocean of waist-high grass. Then he turned away from it and saw Mr Froelich watching him from the parlour doorway.

'They're coming here, aren't they?' the old man said. 'The people who killed my daughter? Because Armstrong is coming here.'

'They might be here already,' Reacher said.

Mr Froelich shook his head. 'Everybody would be talking about it.'

'Did you see that gold truck come through?'

The old man nodded. 'It passed me, going real slow.'

'Who was in it?'

'I didn't see. The windows were dark. I didn't like to stare.'

'OK,' Reacher said. 'If you hear about anybody new in town, come and tell me.'

The old man nodded again. 'You'll know as soon as I do. And I'll know as soon as anybody new arrives. Word travels fast here.'

'We'll be in the church tower,' Reacher said.

'Are you here on behalf of Armstrong?'

Reacher said nothing.

'No,' Mr Froelich said. 'You're here to take an eye for an eye, aren't you?'

Reacher nodded. 'And a tooth for a tooth.'

'A life for a life.'

'Two for five, to be accurate,' Reacher said. 'They get the fat end of the deal.'

'Are you comfortable with that?'

'Are you?'

The old guy's watery eyes flicked all round the sunless room and came to rest on his daughter's eighteen-year-old face.

'Do you have a child?' he asked.

'No,' Reacher said. 'I don't.'

'Neither do I,' the old man said. 'Not any more. So I'm comfortable with it.'

Reacher walked back to the Yukon and took the hiker's map off the back seat. Then he climbed the church tower and found Neagley shuttling back and forth between the north and south side.

'All clear,' she said, over the tick of the clock.

'Stuyvesant called,' he said. 'To the Froelichs' house. He's panicking. And Nendick woke up. Same approach as Andretti.'

He unfolded the map and spread it out flat on the bell chamber floor. Put his finger on Grace. It was in the centre of a rough square made by four roads. The square was maybe eighty miles high and eighty wide. The right-hand perimeter was made by Route 59, which ran up from Douglas in the south through a town called Bill to a town called Wright in the north. The top edge of the square was Route 387, which ran west from Wright to Edgerton. Both roads were shown on the map as secondaries. They had driven part of 387 already and knew it to be a pretty decent strip of blacktop. The left-hand edge of the square was I-25 which came down from Montana in the north and ran straight past Edgerton and all the way down to Casper. The bottom of the square was also I-25, where it came out of Casper and dog-legged east to Douglas before turning south again and heading for Cheyenne. The whole eighty-mile square was split into two more or less equal vertical rectangles by the dirt road that ran north to south through Grace. That road showed up on the map as a thin dotted grey line. The key in the margin called it an unpaved minor track.

'What do you think?' Neagley asked.

Reacher traced the square with his finger. Widened his radius and traced a hundred miles east, and north, and west, and south. 'I think that in the whole history of the western United States no person has ever just *passed through* Grace, Wyoming. It's inconceivable. Why would anybody? Any coherent journey south to north or east to west would miss it altogether. Casper to Wright, say. Bottom left to top right. You'd use I-25 east to Douglas and Route 59 north out of Douglas to Wright. Coming through Grace makes no sense at all. It saves no miles. It just slows you down, because it's a dirt track. And would you even notice the track? Remember what it looked like at the north end? I thought it was going nowhere.'

'And we've got a hiker's map,' Neagley said. 'Maybe it's not even on a regular road map.'

'So that truck passed through for a reason,' Reacher said. 'Not by accident, not for the fun of it.'

'Those were the guys,' Neagley said.

Reacher nodded. 'They were on their reconnaissance run.'

'I agree,' Neagley said. 'But did they like what they saw?'

Reacher closed his eyes. *What did they see?* They saw a tiny town with no safe hiding places. A helicopter landing site just fifty yards from the church. And a black SUV that looked a little like an official Secret Service vehicle already parked on the road, big and obvious. With Colorado plates, and Denver was probably the nearest Secret Service field office.

'I don't think they were turning cartwheels,' he said.

'So will they abort? Or will they come back?'

'Only one way to find out,' Reacher said. 'We wait and see.'

They waited. The sun fell away into afternoon and the temperature dropped like a stone. The clock ticked 3600 times every hour. Neagley went out for a walk and came back with a bag from the grocery store. They ate an improvised lunch. Then they developed a new look-out pattern based on the fact that no vehicle could get all the way through either field of view in less than about eight minutes. So they sat comfortably and every five minutes by Neagley's watch they knelt up and shuffled over to their louvres and scanned the length of the road. Each time there was a small thrill of anticipation, and each time it was disappointed. But the regular physical movement helped against the cold. They started stretching in place, to keep loose. They did press-ups, to keep warm. The spare rounds in their pockets jingled loudly. *Battle rattle*, Neagley called it. From time to time Reacher pressed his face against the louvres and stared out at the snowfall in the west. The clouds were still low and black, held back by an invisible wall about fifty miles away.

'They won't come back,' Neagley said. 'They'd have to be insane to try anything here.'

'I think they are insane,' Reacher said.

He watched and waited, and listened to the clock. He had had enough just before four o'clock. He used the blade of his knife to cut through the accumulation of old white paint and lifted one of the louvres out of the frame. It was a simple length of wood, maybe three feet long, maybe four inches wide, maybe an inch thick. He held it out in front of him like a spear and crawled over and pushed it into the clock mechanism. The gear wheels jammed on it and the clock stopped. He pulled the wood out again and crawled away and slotted it back in the frame. The silence was suddenly deafening.

They watched and waited. It got colder, to the point where they both started shivering. But the silence helped. Suddenly, it helped a lot. Reacher crawled over and checked his partial view to the west again and then crawled back and picked up the map. Stared at it hard, lost in thought. He used his finger and thumb like a compass and measured distances. *Forty, eighty, a hundred and twenty, a hundred and sixty miles. Slow, faster, fast, slow. Overall average speed maybe forty. That's four hours.*

'Sun sets in the west,' he said. 'Rises in the east.'

'On this planet,' Neagley said.

Then they heard the staircase creak below them. They heard feet on the ladder. The trapdoor lifted an inch and fell back and then crashed all the way open and the vicar put his head up into the bell chamber and stared at the sub-machine gun pointing at him from one side and the M16 rifle from the other.

'I need to talk to you about those things,' he said. 'You can't expect me to happy about having weapons in my church.'

He stood there on the ladder, looking like a severed head. Reacher laid the M16 back on the floor. The vicar stepped up another rung.

'I understand the need for security,' he said. 'And we're honoured to host the Vice President-elect, but I really can't permit engines of destruction in a hallowed building. I would have expected somebody to discuss it with me.'

'Engines of destruction?' Neagley repeated.

'What time does the sun set?' Reacher asked.

The vicar looked a little surprised by the change of subject. But he answered very politely.

'Soon,' he said. 'It falls behind the mountains quite early here. But you won't see it happen today. There are clouds. There's a snowstorm coming in from the west.'

'And when does it rise?'

'This time of year? A little before seven o'clock, I suppose.'

'You heard a weather report for tomorrow?'

'They say much the same as today.'

'OK,' Reacher said. 'Thanks.'

'Did you stop the clock?'

'It was driving me nuts.'

'That's why I came up. Do you mind if I set it going again?'

Reacher shrugged. 'It's your clock.'

'I know the noise must be bothersome.'

'Doesn't matter,' Reacher said. 'We'll be out of here as soon as the sun sets. Weapons and all.'

The vicar hauled himself all the way up into the chamber and leaned over the iron girders and fiddled with the mechanism. There was a setting device linked to a separate miniature clock that Reacher hadn't noticed before. It was buried within the gear wheels. It had an adjustment lever attached to it. The vicar checked his wristwatch and used the lever to force the exterior hands round to the correct time. The miniature clock hands moved with them. Then he simply turned a gear wheel with his hand until the mechanism picked up the momentum for itself and started again on its own. The heavy *thunk, thunk, thunk* came back. The smallest bell rang in sympathy, one tiny resonance for every second that passed.

'Thank you,' the vicar said.

'An hour at most,' Reacher said. 'Then we'll be gone.'

The vicar nodded like his point was made and threaded himself down through the trapdoor. Pulled it closed after him.

'We can't leave here,' Neagley said. 'Are you crazy? They could come in at night easy as anything. Maybe that's exactly what they're waiting for. They could drive back in without headlights.'

Reacher glanced at his watch.

'They're already here,' he said. 'Or almost here.'

'Where?'

'I'll show you.'

He pulled the louvre out of the frame again and handed it to her. Crawled under the clock shaft to the bottom of the next ladder that led up through the roof to the outside. Climbed up it and eased the roof trapdoor open.

'Stay low,' he called.

He swam out, keeping his stomach flat on the roof. The

construction was just about identical to the Bismarck roof. There was soldered lead sheathing built up into a shallow box. Drains in the corners. A substantial anchor for the flagpole and the weathervane and the lightning rod. And a three-foot wall all round the edge. He turned a circle on his stomach and leaned down and took the louvre from Neagley. Then he got out of her way and let her crawl up next to him. The wind was strong and the air was bitterly cold.

'Now we kind of kneel low,' he said. 'Close together, facing west.'

They knelt together, shoulder to shoulder, hunched down. He was on the left, she was on the right. He could still hear the clock. He could feel it, through the lead and the heavy wooden boards.

'OK, like this,' he said. He held the louvre in front of his face, with his left hand holding the left end. She took the right end in her right hand. They shuffled forward on their knees until they were tight against the low wall. He eased his end of the louvre level with the top of the wall. She did the same.

'More,' he said. 'Until we've got a slit to see through.'

They raised it higher in concert until it was horizontal with an inch of space between its lower edge and the top of the wall. They gazed out through the gap. They would be visible if somebody was watching the tower very carefully, but overall it was a pretty unobtrusive tactic. As good as he could improvise, anyway.

'Look west,' he said. 'Maybe a little bit south of west.'

They squinted into the setting sun. They could see forty miles of waving grass. It was like an ocean, bright and golden in the evening backlight. Beyond it was the darkening snowstorm. The area between was misty and sheets of late sunlight speared backward through it right at them. There were shifting curtains of sun and shadow and colour and rainbows that started nowhere and ended nowhere.

'Watch the grassland,' he said.

'What am I looking for?'

'You'll see it.'

They knelt there for minutes. The sun inched lower. The last rays tilted flatter into their eyes. Then they saw it. They saw it together. About a mile out into the sea of grass the dying sun flashed gold once on the roof of the Tahoe. It was crawling east through the grassland, very slowly, coming directly towards them, bouncing gently over the rough terrain, lurching up and down through the dips and the hollows at walking speed.

'They were smart,' Reacher said. 'They read the map and had the same idea you did, to exit across open country to the west. But then they looked at the town and knew they had to come in that way too.'

The sun slid into the low clouds fifty miles west and the resulting shadow raced east across the grassland and the golden light died. Twilight came down like a circuit breaker had popped open and then there was nothing more to be seen. They lowered the louvre screen and ducked away flat to the roof. Crawled across the lead and back down into the bell chamber. Neagley threaded her way under the clock shaft and picked up the Heckler & Koch.

'Not yet,' Reacher said.

'So when?'

'What will *they* do now?'

'I guess they'll get as close as they dare. Then they'll set up and wait.'

Reacher nodded. 'They'll turn the truck round and park it facing west in the best hollow they can find about a hundred, two hundred yards out. They'll check their sightlines to the east and make sure they can see but can't be seen. Then they'll sit tight and wait for Armstrong to show.'

'That's fourteen hours.'

'Exactly,' Reacher said. 'We're going to leave them out there all night. We'll let them get cold and stiff and tired. Then the sun will rise right in their eyes. We'll be coming at them out of the sun. They won't even see us.'

They hid the long guns under the pew nearest the church door and left the Yukon parked where it was. Walked up towards the bridge and took two rooms in the boarding house. Then they headed for the grocery store to get dinner ingredients. The sun was gone and the temperature was below freezing. There was snow in the air again. Big feathery flakes were drifting around, reluctant to settle. They swirled and hung in the air and rose back up like tiny birds.

The breakfast counter was all closed down, but the woman in the store offered to microwave something from the freezer cabinet. She seemed to assume Reacher and Neagley were a Secret Service advance detail. Everybody seemed to know Armstrong was expected at the service. She heated up some meat pies and some slushy vegetables. They ate them at the darkened counter. They tasted as good as field rations. The woman wouldn't take money for them.

The rooms in the boarding house were clean, as advertised. They had walls panelled with pine boards. Rag rugs on the floors. One single bed in each, with flowery counterpanes washed so many times they were nearly transparent. There was a bathroom at the far end of the corridor. Reacher let Neagley take the room nearer to it. Then she joined him in his room for a spell, because she was restless and wanted to talk. They sat side by side on the bed, because there was no other furniture.

'We'll be going up against a prepared position,' she said.

'The two of us against two bozos,' Reacher replied. 'You worried now?'

'It's gotten harder.'

'Tell me again,' he said. 'I'm not making you do this, am I?'

'You can't do it alone.'

He shook his head. 'I could do it alone one-handed with my head in a bag.'

'We know nothing about them.'

'But we can make some kind of an assessment. The tall guy in Bismarck is the shooter, and the other guy watches his back and drives. Big brother, little brother. There'll be a lot of loyalty. It's a brother thing. This whole deal is a brother thing. Explaining the motivation to somebody who wasn't close would be hard. You can't just walk up to a stranger and say hey, I want to shoot a guy because his dad threatened to put a stick up my ass and I had to beg him not to.'

Neagley said nothing.

'I'm not asking you to participate,' Reacher said.

Neagley smiled. 'You're an idiot. I'm worried about you, not me.'

'Nothing's going to happen to me,' Reacher said. 'I'm going to die an old man in some lonely motel bed.'

'This all is a brother thing for you too, isn't it?'

He nodded. 'Has to be. I don't really give a damn about Armstrong. I liked Froelich, but I would never have known her except for Joe.'

'*Are* you lonely?'

'Sometimes. Not usually.'

She moved her hand, very slowly. It started an inch from his hand. She made the inch last like a million miles. Her fingers moved imperceptibly over the washed-out counterpane until they were a fraction from his. Then they lifted and moved more, until they were directly over his and just a fraction above. It was like there was a layer of air between their hands, compressed so hard it was warm and liquid. She floated her hand on the air and kept it motionless. Then she pressed harder and brought it down and her fingers touched the backs of his fingers, very lightly. She turned her elbow so her hand lay precisely aligned. Then she pushed down harder. Her palm felt warm. Her fingers were long and cool. Their tips lay on his knuckles. They moved and traced the lines and scars and tendons. They raked down between his. He turned his hand over. She pressed her palm into his. Laced her fingers through his fingers and squeezed. He squeezed back.

He held her hand for five long minutes. Then she slowly pulled it away. Stood up and stepped to the door. Smiled.

'See you in the morning,' she said.

He slept badly and woke up at five, worried about the endgame. Complications crowded in on him. He threw back the covers and slipped out of bed. Dressed in the dark and walked down the stairs and out into the night. It was bitter cold and the snowflakes were blowing in faster. They looked wet and heavy. The weather was moving east. Which was good, he guessed.

There was no light. All the town's windows were dark, there were no streetlights, there was no moon, there were no stars. The church tower loomed up in the middle distance, faint and grey and ghostly. He walked in the middle of the dirt road and crossed the graveyard. Found the church door and went inside. Crept up the tower stairs by feel. Found the ladder in the dark and climbed up into the bell chamber. The clock ticked loudly. Louder than in the daytime. It sounded like a mad blacksmith beating his iron hammer against his anvil once a second.

He ducked under the clock shaft and found the next ladder. Climbed up out of the darkness onto the roof. Crawled over to the west wall and raised his head. The landscape was infinitely dark and silent. The distant looming mountains were invisible. He could see nothing. He could hear nothing. The air was freezing. He waited.

He waited thirty minutes in the cold. It set his eyes watering and his nose running. He started shivering violently. *If I'm cold, they're nearly dead*, he thought. And sure enough after thirty long minutes he heard the sound he had been listening for. The Tahoe's engine started. It was far away, but it sounded deafening in the night silence. It was somewhere out there to the west, maybe a couple of hundred yards distant. It idled for ten whole minutes, running the heater. He couldn't fix an exact location by sound alone. But then they made a fatal mistake. They flicked the dome light on and off for a second. He saw a brief yellow glow deep down in the grass. The truck was down in a dip. Absolutely concealed, its roof well below the average grade level. A little south of west, but not by much. Maybe a hundred and fifty yards out. It was a fine location. They would probably use the truck itself as the shooting platform. Lie prone on the roof, aim, fire, jump down, jump in, drive away.

He put both arms flat along the wall and faced due west and fixed the memory of the brief yellow flash in his mind against the location of the tower. A hundred and fifty yards out, maybe thirty yards south of perpendicular. He crawled back into the bell tower, past the hammering clock, down to the nave. He retrieved the long guns from under the pew and left them on the cold ground underneath the Yukon. He didn't want to put them inside. Didn't want to answer their flash of light with one of his own.

Then he walked back to the boarding house and found Neagley coming out of her room. It was nearly six o'clock. She was showered and dressed. They went into his room to talk.

'Couldn't sleep?' he asked.

'I never sleep,' she said. 'They still there?'

He nodded. 'But there's a problem. We can't take them down where they are. We need to move them first.'

'Why?'

'Too close to home. We can't start World War Three out there an hour before Armstrong gets here. And we can't leave two corpses lying around a hundred and fifty yards from the town. People here have seen us. There'll be early cops up from Casper. Maybe State troopers. You've got your licence to think about. We need to drive them off and take them down somewhere deserted. West, where it's snowing, maybe. This snow will be around until April. That's what I want. I want to do it far away and I want it to be April before anybody knows that anything happened here.'

'OK, how?'

'They're Edward Fox. They're not John Malkovich. They want to live to fight another day. We can make them run if we do it right.'

They were back at the Yukon before six thirty. The snowflakes were still drifting in the air. But the sky was beginning to lighten in the east. There was a band of dark purple on the horizon, and then a band of charcoal, and then the blackness of night. They checked their weapons. Laced their shoes, zipped their coats, swung their shoulders to check freedom of action. Reacher put his hat on, and his left glove. Neagley put her Steyr in her inside pocket and slung the Heckler & Koch over her back.

'See you later,' she whispered.

She walked west into the graveyard. He saw her step over the low fence and turn a little south and then she disappeared in the darkness. He walked to the base of the tower and stood flat against the middle of the west wall and recalculated the Tahoe's position. Pointed his arm out straight towards it and walked back, moving his arm to compensate for his changes of position, keeping the target locked in. He laid the M16 on the ground with the muzzle pointing a little south of west. He stepped behind the Yukon and leaned on the tailgate and waited for the dawn.

It came slowly and gradually and magnificently. The purple colour grew lighter and reddened at its base and spread upward and outward until half the sky was streaked with light. Then an orange halo appeared two hundred miles away in South Dakota and the earth tumbled towards it and the first slim arc of the sun burst up over the horizon. The sky blazed pink. Long high clouds burned red. Reacher watched the sun and waited until it climbed high enough to hurt his eyes and then he unlocked the Yukon and started the engine. He blipped it loud and turned the radio on full blast. He ran the tuning arrows up and down until he found some rock and roll and left the driver's door open so the music beat against the dawn silence. Then he picked up the M16 and knocked the safety off and put it to his shoulder and fired a single burst of three, aiming a little south of west directly over the hidden Tahoe. He heard Neagley answer immediately with a triple of her own. The MP5 had a faster cyclic rate and a distinctive chattering sound. She was triangulated in the grass a hundred yards due south of the Tahoe, firing directly north over it. He fired again, three more from the east. She fired again, three more from the south. The four bursts of fire crashed and rolled and echoed over the landscape. They said: *we . . . know . . . you're . . . there.*

He waited thirty seconds, as planned. There was no response from the Tahoe's position. No lights, no movement, no return fire. He raised the rifle again. Aimed high. Squeezed the trigger. *We.* The Heckler & Koch chattered far away to his left. *Know.* He fired again. *You're.* She fired again. *There.*

No response. He wondered for a second whether they'd already slipped away in the last hour. Or gotten really smart and moved through the town to the east. They were dumb to attack into the sun. He spun round and saw nothing behind him except lights snapping on in windows. Heard nothing anywhere except the ringing in his ears and the deafening rock and roll music from the car. He turned back ready to fire again and saw the Tahoe burst up out of the grass a hundred and fifty yards in front of him. The dawn sun flashed gold and chrome against its tailgate. It bucked over a rise with all four wheels off the ground and crashed back to earth and accelerated away from him into the west.

He threw the rifle into the Yukon's back seat and slammed the door and killed the radio and accelerated straight across the graveyard. Smashed through the wooden fence and plunged into the grassland. Hung a fast curve south. The terrain was murderous. The car was crashing and bouncing over ruts and pitching wildly over long swells. He steered one-handed and clipped his belt with the other. Pulled it tight against the locking mechanism to keep him clamped to the seat. He saw Neagley racing towards him through the grass on his left. He jammed on the brakes and she wrenched the nearside rear door open and threw herself inside behind him. He took off again and she slammed the door and fought her way over into the front passenger seat. She belted herself in and jammed the Heckler & Koch down between her knees and braced herself with both hands on the dash like she was fighting a roller coaster ride.

'Perfect,' she said. She was panting hard. He raced on. Curved back to the north until he found the swath the Tahoe had blasted through the grass. He got himself centred in it and hit the gas. The ride was worse than any roller coaster. It was a continuous violent battering. The car was leaping and shuddering and going alternately weightless and then crashing back to earth and taking off again. The engine was screaming. The wheel was writhing in his hands and kicking back hard enough to break his thumbs. He kept his fingers sticking straight out and steered with his palms only. He was afraid they were going to shatter an axle.

'See them yet?' he shouted.

'Not yet,' she shouted back. 'They could be three hundred yards ahead.'

'I'm afraid the car will break.'

He hit the gas harder. He was doing nearly fifty miles an hour. Then sixty. The faster he went, the better it rode. It spent less actual time on the ground.

'I see them,' Neagley called.

They were two hundred yards ahead, intermittently visible as they bucked up and down through the sea of grass like a manic gold dolphin riding the waves. Reacher pressed on and pulled a little closer. He had the advantage. They were clearing a path for him. He crept up to about a hundred yards back and held steady. The engine roared and the suspension bucked and crashed and banged.

'They can run,' he screamed.

'But they can't hide,' Neagley screamed back.

Ten minutes later they were ten miles west of Grace and felt like they had been badly beaten in a fistfight. Reacher's head was hitting the roof over every bump and his arms were aching. His shoulders were wrenched. The engine was still screaming. The only way he could keep his foot on the gas pedal was to mash it all the way down to the carpet. Neagley was bouncing around at his side and flailing back and forth. She had given up bracing herself with her arms in case she broke her elbows.

Over the next ten murderous miles the terrain shaded into something new. They were literally in the middle of nowhere. The town of Grace was twenty miles behind them and the highway was twenty miles ahead. The grade was rising. The land was breaking up into sharper ravines. There was more rock. There was still grass growing, and it was still tall, but it was thinner because the roots were shallower. And there was snow on the ground. The grass stalks were rigid with ice and they came up out of a six-inch white blanket. Both cars slowed, a hundred yards apart. Within another mile the chase had slowed to a ludicrous twenty-mile-an-hour procession. They were inching down forty-five-degree faces, plunging hood-deep through accumulated snow in the bottoms, clawing up the rises with their transmissions locked in four-wheel-drive. The crevasses ran maybe ten or fifteen feet deep. The endless wind from the west had packed the snow into them with the lee faces bare and the windward faces smooth and sheer. There were flakes in the air, whipping horizontally towards them.

'We're going to get stuck,' Neagley said.

'They got in this way,' Reacher said. 'Got to be able to get out.'

They lost sight of the Tahoe ahead of them every time it

dropped away into a ravine. They glimpsed it only when they laboured up a peak and caught sight of it up on a peak of its own three or four dips in front. There was no rhythm. No co-ordination. Both trucks were diving and then clawing randomly upward. They had slowed to walking pace. Reacher had the transmission locked in low-range and the truck was slipping and sliding. Far to the west the snowstorm was wild. The weather was blowing in fast.

'It's time,' Reacher said. 'Any one of these ravines, the snow will hide them all winter.'

'OK, let's go for it,' Neagley said.

She buzzed her window down and a flurry of snow blew in on a gale of freezing air. She picked up the Heckler & Koch and clicked it to full auto. Reacher accelerated hard and plunged through the next two dips as fast as the truck could take it. Then he jammed on the brakes at the top of the third peak and flicked the wheel left. The truck slewed sideways and slid to a stop with the passenger window facing forward and Neagley leaned all the way out and waited. The gold Tahoe reared up a hundred yards ahead and she loosed a long raking burst of fire aimed low at the rear tyres and the fuel tank. The Tahoe paused fractionally and then rocked over the peak of its rise and disappeared again.

Reacher spun the wheel and hit the gas and crawled after it. The stop had cost them maybe another hundred yards. He ploughed through three consecutive ravines and stopped again on the fourth peak. They waited. Ten seconds, fifteen. The Tahoe did not reappear. They waited twenty seconds. Thirty.

'Hell is it?' Reacher muttered.

He slid the truck down the windward face, through the snow, up the other side. Straight over the top into the next dip. Up the rise, over the top, down into the snow. No sign of the Tahoe. He powered on. The tyres spun and the engine screamed. He made it up the next rise. Stopped dead at the top. The land fell away twenty feet into a broad gulch. It was thick with snow and the icy stalks of grass showed less than a foot above it. The Tahoe's incoming tracks from the day before were visible straight ahead, almost obscured by wind and fresh snowfall. But its outgoing tracks were deep and new. They turned sharply right and ran away to the north, through a tight curve in the ravine, and then out of sight behind a snow-covered outcrop. There was silence all around. Snow was driving straight at them. It was coming *upward* at them, off the bottom of the dip.

Time and space, Reacher thought. Four dimensions. A classic tactical problem. The Tahoe might have U-turned and might be aiming to arrive back at the crucial place at the crucial time. It could retrace its path and be back near the church just before Armstrong touched down. But to chase it blind would be suicide. Because it might not be doubling back at all. It might be waiting in ambush round the next corner. But to spend too long thinking about it would be suicide too. Because it might not be doubling back *or* waiting in ambush. It might be circling right round and aiming to come up behind them. A classic problem. Reacher glanced at his watch. *Almost the point of no return*. They had been gone nearly thirty minutes. Therefore it would take nearly thirty to get back. And Armstrong had been due in an hour and five.

'Feel like getting cold?' he said.

'No alternative,' Neagley said back. She opened her door and slid out into the snow. Ran clumsily to her right, fighting through the drifts, over the rocks, aiming to connect the legs of the U. He took his foot off the brake and nudged the wheel and eased down the slope. Turned hard right in the ravine bottom and followed the Tahoe's tracks. It was the best solution he could improvise. If the Tahoe *was* doubling back, he couldn't wait for ever. No point in driving cautiously back to the church and arriving there after Armstrong was already dead. And if he *was* driving straight into an ambush, he was happy enough to do it with Neagley standing behind his opponents with a sub-machine gun in her hands. He figured that would pretty much guarantee his survival.

But there was no ambush. He came round the rocks and turned back east and saw nothing at all except empty wheel tracks in the snow and Neagley standing fifty yards farther on with the sun on her back and her gun raised over her head. The *all clear* signal. He hit the gas and raced up towards her. The truck slipped and slid and skidded in the Tahoe's impacted ruts. He bounced over hidden rocks. He touched the brake. The truck lurched and drifted sideways and stopped with the front wheels down in a snow-filled trench. Neagley fought her way through the drifts and pulled the door. Icy air followed her inside.

'Hit it,' she said. She was panting again. 'They must be at least five minutes ahead of us by now.'

He touched the gas. All four wheels spun uselessly. The truck stayed motionless and all four tyres whined in the snow and the front end dug in deeper.

'Shit,' he said.

He tried again. Same result. The truck shuddered and rocked and didn't go anywhere. He switched the transmission out of locked-low-range and tried again. Same result. He let the engine idle and put the transmission in reverse, then drive, then reverse, then drive. The truck rocked urgently back and forth, back and forth, six inches, a foot. But it didn't climb out of the trench.

Neagley glanced at her watch. 'They're out there ahead of us. They could get back there in time.'

Reacher nodded and touched the gas and kept on banging the transmission lever into reverse, into drive, into reverse. The truck bucked and bounced. But it didn't climb out of the trench. The tyre treads howled on the glassy snow. The front end dodged left and right with the engine torque and the rear end squirmed with it.

'Armstrong's in the air now,' Neagley said. 'And our car isn't parked next to the church any more. So he's going to go ahead and land.'

Reacher looked at his own watch. Fought his rising panic.

'You do it,' he said. 'Keep it rocking back and forward.'

He twisted round and grabbed his gloves. Unclipped his belt and opened his door and slid out into the snow.

'And if it goes, don't stop for anything,' he said.

He floundered round to the rear of the truck. Stamped and kicked at the snow until he got his feet braced against rock. Neagley slid across into the driver's seat. She built up a rhythm, drive and reverse, drive and reverse, little taps on the gas as the gears slid home. The truck rocked on its springs and began to roll back and forth along a foot and a half of impacted ice.

Reacher put his back against the tailgate and hooked his hands under the rear bumper. Moved with the truck as it pushed back at him. Straightened his legs and heaved as it moved away. The tyre treads were full of snow. They flung little white hieroglyphs into the air as they spun. The exhaust fumes burbled out near his knees and hung in the air. He stumbled forward and pushed backward, again, and again. Now the truck was moving two feet at a time. He clamped his hands harder. Snow was blowing straight out of the west into his face. He started counting. *One, two . . . three. One, two . . . three.* He started walking the truck backward and heaving it forward. Now it was moving three feet with each change of direction. He stamped a chain of footholds. *One, two . . . three.* On the last *three* he shoved with all his strength. He felt the truck climb up out of the trench. Felt it fall back in again. The tailgate butted him hard in the back. He stumbled forward and floundered for grip. Rebuilt his rhythm. He was sweating in the cold. He was out of breath. *One, two . . . three.* He heaved again and the truck disappeared out from behind him and he fell backward into the snow.

He rolled up through the stink of gasoline exhaust. The truck was twenty yards ahead. Neagley was driving it as slow as she dared. He slipped and slid and chased after it. He swerved right to get in its wheel track. The ground rose. Neagley gunned it to maintain her momentum. He was running hard but she was driving away from him. He sprinted. He smashed the toes of his boots into the snow to keep from slipping. She slowed at the top of the rise. The truck went up and over. He saw the whole underside. The fuel tank, the differential. She braked gently and he caught the door handle and flung the door open and floundered downhill alongside the truck until he had built enough speed to fling himself inside. He hauled himself into the seat and slammed the door and she stamped hard on the gas and the violent battering roller coaster ride came back.

'Time?' she screamed.

He fought to keep his wrist still and stared at his watch. He was breathing too hard to speak. He just shook his head. They were at least ten minutes behind. And it was a crucial ten minutes. The Tahoe would arrive back at its starting point about two minutes into it and Armstrong would touch down after another five. Neagley drove on. She hurtled up the rises and took off and plunged hood-deep into the drifts and battered her way through and did it all over again. Without the wheel to hold on to Reacher was thrown all over the place. He fought the alternate weightlessness and physical pounding and caught blurred glimpses of the time on his watch. He stared through the windshield at the sky in the east. The sun was in his eyes. He dropped his gaze to the terrain. Nothing there. No Tahoe. It was long gone. All that remained were its tracks through the snow, deep twinned ruts that narrowed in the far distance ahead. They pointed resolutely towards the town of Grace like arrows. They were full of ice crystals that burned red and yellow against the early dawn light.

Then they changed. They swooped a tight ninety-degree left and disappeared into a north–south ravine.

'What?' Neagley shouted.

'Follow,' Reacher gasped.

The ravine was narrow, like a trench. It ran steeply downhill. The Tahoe's tracks were clearly visible for fifty yards and then they swerved out of sight again, a sharp right behind a rock outcrop the size of a house. Neagley braked hard as the grade fell away. She stopped. She paused a beat and Reacher's mind screamed *an ambush now?* a split second after her foot hit the gas again and her hands turned the wheel. The Yukon locked into the Tahoe's ruts and its two-ton weight slid it helplessly down the icy slope. The Tahoe burst out of hiding, backward, directly in front of them. It jammed to a skidding stop right across their path. Neagley was out of her door before the Yukon stopped moving. She rolled in the snow and floundered away to the north. The Yukon slewed violently and stalled in a snowdrift. Reacher's door was jammed shut by the depth of the snow. He used all his strength and forced it half open and scraped out through the gap. Saw the driver spilling from the Tahoe, slipping and falling in the snow. Reacher rolled away and pulled his Steyr from his pocket. Thrashed round to the back of the Yukon and crawled forward through the snow along its other side. The Tahoe driver was holding a rifle, rowing himself through the snow with its muzzle, slipping and sliding. He was heading for cover in the rock. He was the guy from

Bismarck. No doubt about that. Lean face, long body. He even had the same coat on. He was bulling through the snowdrift with the coat flapping open and small snowstorms kicking outward from his knees at every step. Reacher raised the Steyr and steadied it against the Yukon's fender and tracked the guy's head. Tightened his finger on the trigger. Then he heard a voice, loud and urgent, right behind him.

'Hold your fire,' the voice called.

He turned and saw a second guy ten yards north and west. Neagley was stumbling through the snow directly ahead of him. He had her Heckler & Koch held low in his left hand. A handgun in his right, jammed in her back. He was the guy from the garage video. No doubt about that, either. Tweed overcoat, short, wide in the shoulders, a little squat. No hat this time. He had the same face as the Bismarck guy, a little fatter. The same greying sandy hair, a little thicker. *Brothers.*

'Throw the weapon down, sir,' he called.

It was a perfect cop line and he had a perfect cop voice. Neagley mouthed *I'm sorry.* Reacher reversed the Steyr in his hand. Held it by the barrel.

'Throw down the weapon, sir,' the squat guy called again.

His brother from Bismarck changed direction and ploughed forward through the snow and moved in closer. He raised the rifle. It was a Steyr too, a long handsome gun. It was all covered with snow. It was pointing straight at Reacher's head. The low morning sun made the shadow of the barrel ten feet long. Reacher thought: *what happened to that lonely motel bed?* Snowflakes swirled and the air was bitter cold. He pulled his arm back and tossed his pistol high in the air. It arced lazily thirty feet through the falling snow and landed and buried itself in a drift. The guy from Bismarck fumbled in his pocket with his left hand and pulled out his badge. Held it high in his palm. The badge was gold. It was backed by a worn leather slip. The leather was brown. The rifle wavered. The guy fumbled the badge away again and brought the rifle to his shoulder and held it level and steady.

'We're police officers,' he said.

'I know you are,' Reacher said back. He glanced around. The snow was falling hard. It was whipping and swirling. The crevasse they were in was like a cave with no roof. It was probably the loneliest place on the planet. The guy from the garage video pushed Neagley nearer. She stumbled and he caught up with her and pushed her off to one side and kept his handgun hard in her back.

'But who are you?' the Bismarck guy asked.

Reacher didn't answer. Just checked the geometry. It wasn't attractive. He was triangulated twelve feet from either guy, and the snow underfoot was slick and slow.

The Bismarck guy smiled. 'You here to make the world safe for democracy?'

'I'm here because you're a lousy shot,' Reacher said. 'You got the wrong person on Thursday.' Then he moved very cautiously and pulled his cuff and checked his watch. And smiled. 'And you lose again. It's too late now. You're going to miss him.'

The Bismarck guy just shook his head. 'Police scanner. In our truck. We're listening to Casper PD. Armstrong is delayed twenty minutes. There was a weather problem in South Dakota. So we decided to hang out and let you catch us up.'

Reacher said nothing.

'Because we don't like you,' the Bismarck guy said. He spoke along the rifle stock. His lips moved against it. 'You're poking around where you're not welcome. In a purely private matter. In something that doesn't concern you at all. So consider yourselves under arrest. You want to plead guilty?'

Reacher said nothing.

'Or you just want to plead?'

'Like you did?' Reacher said. 'When that ball bat was getting close?'

The guy went quiet for a second.

'Your attitude isn't helping your cause,' he said.

He paused again, five long seconds.

'The jury is back,' he said.

'What jury?'

'Me and my brother. That's all the jury you've got. We're your whole world right now.'

'Whatever happened, it was thirty years ago.'

'A guy does something like that, he should pay.'

'The guy died.'

The Bismarck cop shrugged. The rifle barrel moved. 'You should read your Bible, my friend. The sins of the fathers, you ever heard of that?'

'What sins? You lost a fight, is all.'

'We never lose. Sooner or later, we always win. And Armstrong *watched.* Snot-nosed rich kid, all smiling and grinning. A man doesn't forget a thing like that.'

Reacher said nothing. The silence was total. Each snowflake felt separately audible as it hissed and whirled through the air. *Keep him talking,* Reacher thought. *Keep him moving.* But he looked into the crazed eyes and couldn't think of a thing to say.

'The woman goes in the truck,' the guy said. 'We'll have a little fun with her, after we deal with Armstrong. But I'm going to shoot you right now.'

'Not with that rifle,' Reacher said. *Keep him talking. Keep him moving.* 'The muzzle is full of slush. It'll blow up in your hands.'

There was a long silence. The guy calculated the distance between himself and Reacher, just a glance. Then he lowered the rifle. Reversed it in his hands, in and out fast, long enough to check. The muzzle was packed with icy snow. *The M16 is on the Yukon's back seat,* Reacher thought. *But the door is blocked shut by the drift.*

'You want to bet your life on a little slush?' the Bismarck guy asked.

'Do you?' Reacher said. 'The breech will blow, take your ugly face off. Then I'll take the barrel and shove it up your ass. I'll pretend it was a baseball bat.'

The guy's face darkened. But he didn't pull the trigger.

'Step away from the car,' he said, like the cop he was. Reacher took a long pace away from the Yukon, up and down in the snow, like wading.

'And another.'

Reacher moved again. He was six feet from the car. Six feet from his M16. Thirty feet from his nine-millimetre, far away in the snow. He glanced around. The Bismarck brother held the rifle in his left hand and put his right under his coat and came out with a handgun. It was a Glock. Black and square and ugly. *Probably police department issue.* He released the safety and levelled it one-handed at Reacher's face.

'Not that one either,' Reacher said.

Keep him talking. Keep him moving.

'Why not?'

'That's your work gun. Chances are you've used it before. So there are records. They find my body, the ballistics will come right back at you.'

The guy stood still for a long moment. Didn't speak. Nothing in his face. But he put the Glock away again. Raised the rifle. Shuffled backward through the snow towards the Tahoe. The rifle traversed and stayed level with Reacher's chest. Reacher thought: *just pull the damn trigger. Let's all have a laugh.* The guy fumbled behind him and opened the Tahoe's rear door, driver's side. Dropped the rifle in the snow and came out with a handgun, all in one move. It was an old M9 Beretta, scratched and stained with dried oil. The guy tracked forward again through the drift. Stopped six feet away from Reacher. Raised his arm. Unlatched the safety with his thumb and levelled the weapon straight at the centre of Reacher's face.

'Throw-down gun,' he said. 'No records on this one.'

Reacher said nothing.

'Say goodnight now,' the guy whispered.

Nobody moved.

'On the click,' Reacher said.

He stared straight ahead at the gun. Saw Neagley's face in the corner of his eye. Saw that she didn't understand what he meant, but saw her nod anyway. It was just a fractional movement of her eyelids. Like half a blink. The Bismarck guy smiled. Tightened his finger. His knuckle shone white. He squeezed the trigger.

There was a dull click.

Reacher came out with his ceramic knife already open and brushed it sideways across the guy's forehead. Then he caught the Beretta's barrel in his left hand and jerked it up and jerked it down full force across his knee and shattered the guy's forearm. Pushed him away and spun round. Neagley had hardly moved. But the guy from the garage video was inert in the snow by her feet. He was bleeding from both ears. She was holding her Heckler & Koch in one hand and the guy's handgun in the other.

'Yes?' she said.

He nodded. She stepped a pace away so her clothes wouldn't get splashed and pointed the handgun at the ground and shot the garage guy three times. *Bang bang . . . bang.* A double-tap to the head, and then an insurance round in the chest. The sound of the shots clapped and rolled like thunder. They both turned away. The Bismarck guy was stumbling around in the snow, completely blind. His forehead was sliced to the bone and blood was pouring out of the wound in sheets and running down into his eyes. It was in his nose and in his mouth. His panting breath was bubbling out through it. He was cradling his broken arm. Staggering about, left and right, turning circles, raising his left forearm to his face, trying to wipe the blood out of his eyes so he could see.

Reacher watched him for a moment, nothing in his face. Then he took the Heckler & Koch from Neagley and set it to fire a single round and waited until the guy had pirouetted round backward and shot him through the throat from the rear. He tried to put the bullet exactly where Froelich had taken hers. The spent brass expelled and hit the Tahoe twenty feet away with a loud *clang* and the guy pitched forward on his face and lay still and the snow turned bright red all around him. The crash of the shot rolled away and absolute silence rolled back to replace it. Reacher and Neagley stood still and held their breath and listened hard. Heard nothing except the sound of the snow falling.

'How did you know?' Neagley asked, quietly.

'It was Froelich's gun,' he said. 'They stole it from her kitchen. I recognized the scratches and the oil marks. She'd kept the clips loaded in a drawer for about five years.'

'It still might have fired,' Neagley said.

'The whole of life is a gamble,' Reacher said. 'From the very beginning to the very end. Wouldn't you say?'

The silence closed in tighter. And the cold. They were alone in a thousand square miles of freezing emptiness, breathing hard, shivering, a little sick with adrenalin.

'How long will the church thing last?' he asked.

'I don't know,' Neagley said. 'Forty minutes? An hour?'

'So we don't need to rush.'

He waded over and retrieved his Steyr from where it had fallen. The snow was already starting to cover the two bodies. He took wallets and badges from the pockets. Wiped his knife clean on the Bismarck guy's twill coat. Opened all four of the Tahoe's doors so the snow would drift inside and bury it quicker. Neagley wiped the garage guy's pistol on her coat and dropped it. Then they floundered back to the Yukon and climbed inside. Took a last look back. The scene was already rimed with new snow, whitening fast. It would be gone within forty-eight hours. The icy wind would freeze the whole tableau inside a long smooth east–west drift until the spring sunshine released it again.

Neagley drove, slowly. Reacher piled the wallets on his knees and started with the badges. The truck was lurching gently and it took effort just to hold them still in front of his eyes long enough to look at them.

'County cops from Idaho,' he said. 'Some rural place south of Boise, I think.'

He put both badges into his pocket. Opened the Bismarck guy's wallet. It was a brown leather trifold, dry and cracked and moulded around the contents. There was a milky plastic window on the inside with a police ID behind it. The guy's lean face stared out from the photograph.

'His name was Richard Wilson,' he said. 'Basic grade detective.'

There were two credit cards and an Idaho driving licence in the wallet. And scraps of paper, and almost three hundred dollars in cash. He spilled the paper on his knees and put the cash in his pocket. Opened the garage guy's wallet. It was phony alligator, black, and it had an ID from the same police department.

'Peter Wilson,' he said. He checked the driving licence. 'A year younger.'

Peter had three credit cards and nearly two hundred dollars. Reacher put the cash in his pocket and glanced ahead. The snow clouds were behind them and the sky was clear in the east. The sun was out and in their eyes. There was a small black dot in the air. The church tower was barely visible, almost twenty miles away. The Yukon bounced its way towards it, relentlessly. The black dot grew larger. There was a grey blur of rotors above it. It looked motionless in the air. Reacher steadied himself against the dash and looked up through the windshield. There was a tinted band across the top of the glass. The helicopter eased down through it. He could make out its shape. It was fat and bulbous at the front. Probably a Night Hawk. It picked up a visual on the church and turned towards it. It drifted in like a fat insect. The Yukon bounced gently over washboard depressions. The wallets slid off Reacher's knees and the paper scraps scattered. The helicopter was hovering. Then it was swinging in the air, turning its main door towards the church.

'Golf clubs,' Reacher said. 'Not tool samples.'

'What?'

He held up a scrap of paper. 'A UPS receipt. Next-day air. From Minneapolis. Addressed to Richard Wilson, arriving guest, at a D.C. motel. A carton, a foot square, forty-eight inches long. Contents, one bag of golf clubs.'

Then he went quiet. Stared at another scrap of paper.

'Something else,' he said. 'For Stuyvesant, maybe.'

They watched the distant helicopter land and stopped right there in the middle of the empty grassland. Got out into the freezing cold sunshine and walked aimless circles and stretched and yawned. The Yukon ticked loudly as it cooled. Reacher piled the badges with the police IDs and the driving licences on the passenger seat and then hurled the empty wallets far into the landscape.

'We need to sanitize,' he said. They wiped their prints off all four weapons and threw them into the grass, north and south and east and west. Emptied the spare rounds from their pockets and hurled them away in looping brassy swirls through the sunlight. Followed them with the birdwatcher's scope. Reacher kept his hat and gloves. And the ceramic knife. He had grown fond of it.

Then they drove the rest of the way to Grace slow and easy and bumped up out of the grassland and through the wrecked fence and across the graveyard. Parked near the waiting helicopter and got out. They could hear the groan of the organ and the sound of people singing inside the church. No crowds. No media. It was a dignified scene. There was a Casper PD cruiser parked at a discreet distance. There was an air force crewman in a flight suit standing next to the helicopter. He was alert and vigilant. Probably not an air force crewman at all. Probably one of Stuyvesant's guys in a borrowed outfit. Probably had a rifle hidden just inside the cabin door. Probably a Vaime Mk2.

'You OK?' Neagley asked.

'I'm always OK,' Reacher said. 'You?'

'I'm fine.'

They stood there for fifteen minutes, not really sure if they were hot or cold. There was a loud mournful piece from the distant organ, and then quiet, and then the muffled sound of feet moving on dusty boards. The big oak door opened and a small crowd filtered out into the sunshine. The vicar stood outside the door with Froelich's parents and spoke to everybody as they left.

Armstrong came out after a couple of minutes with Stuyvesant at his side. They were both in dark overcoats. They were surrounded by seven agents. Armstrong spoke to the vicar and shook hands with the Froelichs and spoke some more. Then his detail brought him away towards the helicopter. He saw Reacher and Neagley and detoured near them, a question in his face.

'We all live happily ever after,' Reacher said.

Armstrong nodded once. 'Thank you,' he said.

'You're welcome,' Reacher said.

Armstrong hesitated a second longer and then turned away without shaking hands and walked on towards the chopper. Stuyvesant came next, on his own.

'Happily?' he repeated.

Reacher gathered the badges and the IDs and the licences from his pockets. Stuyvesant cupped his hands to take them all.

'Maybe more happily than we thought,' Reacher said. 'They weren't yours, that's for sure. They were cops, from Idaho, near Boise. You've got the addresses there. I'm sure you'll find what you need. The computer, the paper and the printer, Andretti's thumb in the freezer. Something else, maybe.'

He took a scrap of paper from his pocket.

'I found this too,' he said. 'It was in one of the wallets. It's a register receipt. They went to the grocery store late on Friday and bought six TV dinners and six big bottles of water.'

'So?' Stuyvesant said.

Reacher smiled. 'My guess is they weren't doing their regular weekly marketing, not in the middle of everything else they were doing. I think maybe they were making sure Mrs Nendick could eat while they came out here. I think she's still alive.'

Stuyvesant snatched the receipt and ran for the helicopter.

Reacher and Neagley said their goodbyes at the Denver airport late the next morning, Monday. Reacher signed over his fee cheque to her and she bought him a first-class ticket on United to New York La Guardia. He walked her to the gate for her Chicago flight. People were already boarding. She didn't say anything. Just placed her bag on the floor and stood still directly in front of him. Then she stretched up and hugged him, fast, like she didn't really know how to do it. She let go after a second and picked up her bag and walked down the jetway. Didn't look back.

He made it into La Guardia late in the evening. Took a bus and a subway to Times Square and walked Forty-second Street until he found B.B. King's new club. A four-piece guitar band was just finishing its first set. They were pretty good. He listened until the set ended and then walked back to the ticket taker.

'Was there an old woman here last week?' he asked. 'Sounded a little like Dawn Penn? With an old guy on keyboards?'

The ticket taker shook his head. 'Nobody like that,' the guy said. 'Not here.'

Reacher nodded once and stepped out into the shiny darkness. It was cold on the street. He headed west for the Port Authority and a bus out of town.